TOLTEC

PROLOGUE

Toltec City of Chichen Itza, Mexico
1096 A.D.

Standing atop the giant pyramid temple, overlooking the great city of Chichen Itza, King Ce Acatl Topiltzin knew the end was near. The divine ruler of the vast and once powerful Toltec empire was facing a serious dilemma. He knew that many towns and villages along the borders had been sacked and burned, its inhabitants slaughtered by warring tribes from the south and northwest. Nomadic Chitimecs and Mayas were determined to absorb the rich Toltec culture into their own in order to acquire the empire's great treasures and vast lands. Even the emerging Aztecs were slowly hacking off pieces of territories to the west. The great king had recently moved his residence and capital from the once powerful cultural center of Tula, now under control of the dreaded Aztecs.

The Toltecs, a warlike people themselves, had inherited most of their land from the early Maya civilization and other lesser-known tribes. They were superb builders and artisans, deriving many of their skills and much of their culture from the earlier Mayans. The Toltecs conquered large areas throughout the Yucatan Peninsula and their empire had flourished, but years of relative peace and inactivity caused the populace and ruling class to become complacent. The once strong legions of Toltec warriors had diminished in size and power and now were no match for the invading hoards.

As Topiltzin gazed at the panoramic beauty and magnitude of his capital city with its magnificent stone buildings and expansive plazas, he looked somewhat bewildered. He had appealed to the great-feathered serpent deity Quetzalcoatl to intervene and repel the attackers away from the borders. He did not understand why the great Quetzalcoatl was so angry. The chief had taken the extreme steps of offering human sacrifices to the sun god Tonatiuh, but even this great deity had not intervened.

Topiltzin's brave warriors fought long and hard, but he did not have enough active soldiers to protect the vast borders, so the raids continued. He had even replaced some of his generals, but nothing could stop the Chichimec and Maya warriors from overrunning his borders. Topiltzin felt powerless to prevent the inevitable conquest of his nation. In a matter of weeks, Chichen Itza and other cultural centers would fall. Topiltzin knew what he must do. He summoned his three top generals and head priests and instructed them to send runners to the four corners of his land to gather the empire's wealth and arrange for its transportation to the City of Coba. There, a suitable site would be prepared to hide and protect the Toltec treasure. He then dispatched a runner to his eastern empire with an urgent message for his Governor, King Tialoc, ordering him to come immediately to Chichen Itza for an important summit.

Tialoc was preparing to visit his beautiful mistress Xepocotec when the messenger arrived with the summons. The old king was notably annoyed, but did not show it as he told the runner that he would hastily depart for the meeting. Tialoc had heard stories about the Mayan raiding parties, but had not yet encountered any of these nuisances on his western borders. He gathered his two high priests and a small contingency of officers and royal guards and headed off for Chichen Itza. The city was about sixty miles from Coba so he knew the journey would take two and one-half cycles of the moon, or two and a half days.

His visit to his beloved Xepocotec would have to wait until his return. Tialoc had built a city in her honor, using his best builders, stonecutters, architects, slave masters and thousands of workers. The city took ten years to build and boasted some of the finest structures within the empire, especially the beautiful high temple resting atop the dominating pyramid there. The pyramid was a marvel, containing secret passages and special chambers protected by a series of locks and other ingenious devices to safeguard the tombs and their contents. Any unwanted guest would find many unpleasant surprises should they be so foolish as to force their way into these inner sanctums.

To ensure utmost security, he had built the city in a remote and inaccessible location protected by heavy jungle growth full of the most unpleasant creatures. Moreover, it was situated in a bowl shaped valley in the cone of an ancient volcano. The only access from Coba was by river about a mile from the city. To allow easy access between both cities, two man-made canals connected Coba to the river and Xepocotec to an adjoining lake that provided fish and other aquatic food for the inhabitants. To ensure greater protection from unwanted intruders, Tialoc had vats of the dreaded devilfish, or red piranha, brought up from the great Amazon River to the south and deposited into the lake.

King Tialoc's journey to Chichen Itza was a familiar one. When he arrived at the capital city, Topiltzin immediately called for his subordinate ruler to join him in the royal palace atop the great pyramid. King Topiltzin wore a fine woven purple robe adorned with white egret feathers and trimmed with blue-gray feathers from the great blue heron. He was a striking figure, portraying the very essence of royalty. Topiltzin greeted Tialoc warmly and offered him a mug of the local distilled brew called pulque. Tialoc found the smooth tasting liquid cool and refreshing after his tedious journey.

"How are you, old friend?" Topiltzin asked warmly. "Thank you for coming on such short notice, there are most urgent matters that we must discuss."

"My thanks to you, great one," Tialoc replied with genuine appreciation of his beloved king. "I am fine and the journey was nothing compared to the pleasure of seeing you again in your great city."

Also attending the meeting were several of Topiltzin's highest-ranking military officers and several high priests. Topiltzin explained, "I called each of you together to address a most grave and urgent matter. Large numbers of Chitimec and Maya warriors are attacking our borders to the south and west. As you know, Aztec tribes have already occupied Tula. Many of our villages have been burned and our people massacred. My informants tell me that invaders are currently massing at our southern borders near Chiapas and western borders near Palenque. They are well equipped and outnumber our weakened legions by four to one. Our warriors have become soft and our army has dwindled. I am afraid, if the invaders attack in force, we will be unable to defend this city or protect the balance of our empire for very long. I have dispatched messengers throughout the land and notified our military and civilian nobles to gather the empire's wealth and transfer it to our eastern city of Coba. I instructed them to do this quickly as we are running out of time."

"What do you consider as wealth, my noble one?" asked a general named Solcheten.

Topiltzin replied, "We must gather all of our yellow metal bars and precious objects that we have received from our sun God Tonatiuh, and all of the many colored shiny stones that fill our sacred urns. The stones are gifts from our gods and must be protected as well. When all of the treasure is delivered to Coba, you, Tialoc, must find a suitable place to hide it. I am sure there is such a place in your vast jungle, is there not?"

Tialoc thought for a few moments as he walked over to the window and looked out over the city. "Yes, great Topiltzin, there is such a place to hide our empire's wealth. I will transfer it to our remote city of Xepocotec and store it in hidden chambers within the temple pyramid there. We will transport the treasure by barges since the only way to get there is by the river. It is doubtful the invaders would be able to find the city, much less the treasures hidden within the pyramid. It will be safe there, oh great one."

Topiltzin nodded. "This is good. Return now to Coba, collect the treasures of our empire, and transfer them to your jungle city."

"What about you my king?" Tialoc asked. Where will you go? You are welcome to join me in Coba."

"No my friend," Topiltzin answered with a finality in his voice. "I will stay here and fight and die with my soldiers."

Tialoc left for Coba early the next morning, driving his party as fast as possible. Topiltzin's departing words stuck with him, adding greater urgency to his mission. Upon his arrival, he called his generals, high priests and chief builders together. He explained the situation and immediately called for the construction of two sturdy wooden barges. The barges would be loaded with the empire's treasures and towed by his two royal boats from Coba to the docks of Xepocotec. He also sent his chief architect and trusted builders to Xepocotec to prepare a storage chamber deep within the temple pyramid. "I want you to construct a site that will be very difficult to find and one that will stop unwanted intruders."

Within the next few days, gold, precious gems, and artifacts arrived from throughout the Toltec realm. Some of the treasure came by donkey-driven carts and some on the backs of slaves. Trunks full of small solid gold ingots and assorted golden ornaments and vessels were received, along with numerous leather bags and hand carved wooden boxes filled with diamonds, rubies, emeralds and sapphires of various sizes. Other boxes arrived containing the realm's finest sculptures and other magnificent artifacts.

The boat builders and slaves worked day and night constructing the barges to carry the treasure to Xepocotec. They were shallow-keel vessels twenty paces across and forty paces long with an open deck to facilitate the loading and unloading process. The barges would attach to the royal boats and be towed from the canal of Coba through the river passage to the guarded lake and then up the canal to the dock of Xepocotec. Tialoc himself would personally escort and supervise the transport and final storage of the treasure into the hidden vaults.

It took twelve days to complete construction on the barges before Tialoc was summoned to the docks for final inspection. Sturdy beams of oak comprised the framing and the deck and hull planking was constructed from cypress. Huge bamboo stalks formed large out-riggers firmly positioned to stabilize the heavy weight. Tialoc was pleased and said to his head boat builder, Textumzal, "You have honored yourself and your fine helpers with the construction of these barges. You have earned ten fingers of gold as a reward."

He then turned to his highest ranking general and priest, "I want all of the treasure of our empire brought from the gathering places to these barges and promptly loaded and secured to await my orders for sailing. I expect this to be done by the end of three full cycles of the sun."

It took three days, nights, and two hundred men to load the barges with the empire's wealth. The flotilla was ready to depart by the fourth morning. They were careful to distribute the heavy weight to ensure the barges would float evenly. Tialoc went to the docks where the crew awaited his command to depart. Upon his gesture, the high priest raised his arms to the heavens and asked Quetzalcoatl to protect them and provide them safe passage to Xepocotec. The mooring lines were cast and the two royal boats, with their sixty oarsmen, pushed away from the wharf and into the canal with the treasure barges in tow.

Once through the canal, they floated into the gentle current of the river, moving downstream toward the lake and jungle city. Tialoc felt the heavy responsibility on his shoulders but pleased with the mission thus far. He was especially excited about finally spending time with his sensual mistress Xepocotec. The old chief sent word of his progress and knew she would be waiting on the dock to greet him. Just the thought of her caresses sent shivers of anticipation and excitement through his loins, although tempered by the critical task of first securing the vast treasure hoard entrusted to his care. There would be plenty of time for Xepocotec and her tantalizing pleasures. She always made his aging bones feel young again.

The trip down river was uneventful as the boats entered the lake. They spotted the familiar stone tower and began the wide turn into the entrance of the canal. One of the workers was rearranging a heavy crate of gold ingots when the box slipped and dropped on his sandaled foot, mashing it into a bloody pulp. The pain was unbearable as he reeled backward and tumbled over the narrow sideboard into the lake. Immediately, a spreading cloud of bloodstained water surrounded him, and deep within the recesses of the lake, the acute senses of the red piranha detected the scent of blood. Instantly, hundreds of small silvery fish darted to the spot where the injured man was thrashing frantically. The piranhas propelled their flashing mass into a turbulent feeding frenzy and attacked the hapless worker from all sides. His frantic, piercing screams filled the air as his body transformed into a red churning and boiling mass of shredded flesh and muscle. It was over quickly and the bones picked clean, leaving only a bare human skeleton that slowly sank to the bottom. The men who witnessed this terrible scene from the boats and barges could only stare in horror.

Despite the gruesome incident, the boats continued across the lake, turned into the canal and slowly moved toward the docks. A small crowd assembled along the canal and at the docks to welcome them. Tialoc saw Xepocotec standing among the priests. She waved as soon as she saw him. They pulled into the small lagoon and the heavy-laden barges were disengaged and tightly secured to the dock. The advance party awaited their arrival with specially designed carts and a series of block and tackle rigs assembled to haul the treasure-laden carts up the steep incline to the top of the hill. While workers began transferring treasure crates to the carts, hundreds of workers waited at the crest to move the carts to the pyramid.

Another pulley rig, attached to large woven baskets, moved the treasure up the pyramid incline and onto a platform where it was moved into the temple. Additional carts within the temple were waiting to transport the treasure down steep passages into a large specially prepared chamber deep within the pyramid—it was an ingenious system requiring precise coordination. Hundreds of workers finished unloading the treasure from the barges and carted it to the temple where it was finally stored deep within the pyramid. Except for a few broken bones and many cuts and bruises, the overall progress went well. It took six days to complete the monumental task.

The chamber sealing ceremony was an elaborate ceremony performed by the high priest and the head architect who had devised a series of intricate steps to regulate the weights and balances needed to begin the process of sealing the passages and rooms far below. Tialoc smiled when he heard the soft rumble deep within the heavy walls as a huge slab of granite slowly fell into place, sealing the passageway leading to the treasure chamber.

As a final step for concealment, stonemasons cemented a large granite carving of Quetzalcoatl to the upper face of the slab and erected a large stone altar abutting the massive panel. Six of the finest preselected artists began to adorn the surrounding walls with painted murals depicting everyday life within the Toltec culture. The paintings would function as cultural art icons for future generations, but most importantly, served to disguise the treasure entrance. Tialoc declared a celebration to honor the gods and hail the successful completion of the job.

Large crowds assembled in the city courtyard and the festivities began. Clay urns filled with pulque lined the square and servants passed through the throngs carrying baskets of food. The relentless pounding of drums led the excited crowd into a ritual of chants and dances around the fire pits. The night ended in a naked carnal frenzy for those who had the prowess and ability to stay awake. Early in the festivities, Tialoc made his way to the chambers of his mistress who teased him, tantalized him and brought him to new heights of sexual ecstasy. The home brewed ale did its part in promoting the process. Xepocotec provided welcome solace to the old man and he repaid her favors by adorning her in the finest robes and lavishing her with the best of worldly comforts.

When the ceremonies ended five days later, Tialoc and his large entourage said their farewells and boarded the boats for the trip back to Coba. He sent a messenger to Chichen Itza with a sealed dispatch to Topiltzin. The message was short… *All the wealth of the empire is secured in a very safe and remote place and now protected by the gods for all times.*

The Toltec empire was eventually absorbed into the Mayan tribes they had formerly conquered, and the Mayas built great pyramids, temples, and cities over many former Toltec structures. By the mid-12th century, what was left of the scattered Toltecs and Mayas was conquered and absorbed by the warring Aztecs. They dominated Mexico for several centuries, until 1521 when the Aztec empire was overwhelmed by the guns, cold steel and killing diseases of Cortez and the Spanish Conquistadors.

The Toltec people of Coba, The Great Builders, and those of the City of Xepocotec mysteriously vanished into history.

1.

Western Tennessee, Early October, 1864

The sniper spotted the small troop of men emerging from the woods far across the field. He was certain they would follow the narrow track along the stream. He pulled the large butternut colored coat from his saddlebag and pulled it tightly over his Union blue woolen jacket. He had lifted it from of a dead rebel soldier at Vicksburg with the thought it might come in handy for better concealment. The pants he wore were a faded nut-brown flannel, closely blending with the early fall's foliage. His rifle-musket was an Austrian-made model 1863, often called a Lorenz, and was fitted with a mounted scope. Rather than have the rifle re-bored to the standard .58 calibre U. S. Army Springfield issue, he kept the bore sized at .54 calibre as provided by the manufacturer. It was deadly accurate. He picked a small grove of hardwood trees about a hundred fifty paces from the stream, then found a decent sized oak with low branches. The position wasn't comfortable, but he was able to steady his legs in the crook of a heavy branch and rest the rifle barrel in the V of a smaller off-shooting branch. From his location, he had a clear field of fire from the tree to the stream bank. Now all he could do was wait.

A frigid wind was blowing that wet October day as the band of Confederate cavalry trotted along the small creek. The young troopers pulled their coats tightly around their necks in a vain attempt to ward off the penetrating wind. Many of these battle weary troopers had survived over three years of war and all wished this accursed conflict would come to an end. The early adventures and chivalry of war had long since passed, leaving each man with an intimate knowledge of the reality of war with its constant hunger, disease, cruel weather conditions, and death. They were simply sick of war and yearned to go home.

By the fall of 1864, the Civil War was nearly settled, with the southern armies on the defensive throughout the eastern and western theaters. The Confederacy had passed its high water mark with the victory at Chancellorsville in 1863 and with General Robert E. Lee's invasion of Maryland in July of that year. His resounding defeat at Gettysburg was the turning point in the east and the loss of Vicksburg gave control of the Mississippi River to Union forces in the west.

In the preceeding month, General Ulysses S. Grant had been placed in command of all the Union forces with the objective of directing Sherman and his western armies toward Atlanta, and Meade, with the Army of the Potomac, against Lee's army of Northern Virginia. Some of the bloodiest battles were yet to be fought in the east, but much of the action in the western campaigns was now relegated to smaller engagements by opposing cavalry units in Tennessee, Missouri, and Mississippi. Such was the case of an unusual skirmish in western Tennessee that occurred mid-

October, 1864, in a very unlikely and obscure place called Cockelberry Creek.

The diminishing Confederate high command, under General Nathan Bedford Forrest, had received word of a secret shipment of Union gold to be transported from Frankfort, Kentucky to Nashville. Forrest immediately dispached a Confederate cavalry unit from Memphis to intercept the Union detachment and confiscate the gold. The approaching Confederates were commanded by Captain Elijah Walker and consisted of twenty cavalry troopers. Captain Walker led his small band along Cedar Creek, a small stream that wound its way through the west Tennessee rolling hills, and fed into the larger stream a few miles ahead. With another three miles to go, Walker deployed his men to intercept the Union detachment moving in their direction.

The small detachment of Union troops, under the command of Captain Simon Murphy, carried a substantial shipment of fifty thousand dollars in gold coins obtained from a federal vault in Frankfort, Kentucky. It was destined for the Union Army Headquarters in Nashville. What Murphy did not know was that the Confederate detachment had also learned of the gold shipment and was prepared to intercept it along the trail. Cockelberry Creek was a good location for an ambush because the dense woods would provide excellent cover for the troops.

The explosion of a single rifle shot shattered the stillness of the late morning. The heavy .54 caliber slug sped through the air and embedded into the bank on the far side of the creek, missing Sergeant Sam Dixon's head by inches. Dixon felt the strong pressure wave of the bullet as it passed by his ear. He and the other troopers leaped from their horses and found cover in the tall weeds along the bank. "Damned Yankee sniper," he mumbled. "That bastard nearly blew my head off. Shot sounded like it came from that clump of trees over yonder."

"What trees?" one of the troopers asked.

"That small clump to the right. About a hundred yards or so."

"I think I see him, Sarge!" shouted Private Mann as he pointed in the general direction.

"Where?"

"I can barely see his feet in that big oak tree over there. The top of him blends in with the leaves." Dixon looked around frantically.

Captain Walker crawled along the bank and made his way over to the sergeant. "Got him spotted yet, Sam?" he asked in a low voice.

"Yes, sir. He's sitting up in that big oak," he answered, pointing to the spot.

"You and Mann work your way around to the right and I'll get Kincade and Smith to flank him to the left. You're a good shot, so maybe you can get a bead on him while we create a little diversion. We'll see if we can draw another shot and spot his smoke."

Sergeant Dixon and Private Mann moved out to the right, staying well below the top of the creek bank, while Captain Walker whispered instructions to Corporal Kincade and Private Smith. Both men nodded and moved out through the tall weeds on their left. For the next few minutes, there was nothing but the sound of the wind blowing through the rustling weeds.

Another shot came from the direction of the oak tree, the Union sniper having spotted the two men moving around to his left. His shot was low and kicked up a splash of dirt in front of Kincade's feet.

"I see him now, Sarge," Mann whispered, bringing his captured Sharps breechloader up to draw a bead. He held the lightweight carbine steady, took careful aim, then squeezed the trigger. The slug found its mark and a rifle dropped to the ground from the branches above. The troopers could see the tree limbs moving, followed by a large, limp body falling through the branches to the ground. Sergeant Dixon and Private Mann rushed over to the base of the tree. "Yep, one less Yankee sniper we have to worry about," the sergeant quipped. "He's even wearing one of our uniforms over his blues."

Captain Walker and several other troopers made their way over to the tree. "Damned good shot, Sergeant. The slug caught him in the chest."

"It was Mann here that made that shot, Captain."

"Good job, Mann. You caught him square. Okay boys, let's get mounted. One of you boys grab that Yankee's rifle. Probably a lot newer than anything we got."

"Do you reckon this sniper is part of the detachment we're suppose to ambush?" Dixon asked.

"I doubt it," Walker replied. "He's too far away from the spot where the Yankee unit should be about now. He's probably a loner out trying to be a hero."

"Reckon they heard the shot?" Mann asked.

"Unlikely. We're still about two or three miles from the contact point. Besides, the wind is blowing toward us, so they'd have to have some mighty fine ears to hear the gunshot from this distance. Okay Sarge, let's move the men out. We've got some ground to cover."

As the Federals advanced through the woods, a Confederate scout reported their approach to Captain Walker, who moved his detachment closer to the creek. Moments before, Captain Murphy's lead scout had also seen the Confederates from a concealed vantage point in the woods and rode back to report the pending ambush. Murphy quickly deployed his troopers across the creek on to a small wooded hill and opened fire on the approaching Confederates as they moved into position. Surprised by this reverse ambush, Captain Walker dispersed his Confederates to the fallen logs on the opposite side of the creek. Both units began to fire and bullets whistled through the air like swarms of angry bees. By some miraculous act of fate, none of the soldiers were killed or wounded. The fallen logs and dense cover stopped most of the musket slugs. Both commanders could see the stalemate developing.

A Union corporal, peering through foliage, saw the Confederate officer move toward the logs and debris piled along the bank. He took careful aim with his Sharps carbine and slowly squeezed the trigger. The hammer struck the percussion cap, exploding the black powder charge and propelled the .54 caliber conical ball forward. The spinning projectile sped across the creek. There was no way it could miss. Captain Walker was crouched behind a fallen log when the projectile slammed into the tree limb inches above his head. The heavy slug severed the branch and scattered chips and splinters over his hat and shoulders. "My God!" he moaned, "damned slug almost took the top of my head off. What the hell have we got ourselves into anyway? We could keep each other pinned down here for days. Wonder what the Yanks will do if I try talking some sense into them?"

Walker shouted at the top of his lungs, "If you Yanks surrender and give us the gold shipment, we'll let you go unharmed!"

Although the unexpected voice with the distinct southern drawl took him off guard, Murphy yelled back, "What the hell makes you think you're in a position to demand our surrender, Reb? We have as many guns as you do. Besides, we don't have any gold shipment!"

"We know you're carrying a gold shipment and delivering it to your headquarters in Nashville," Walker shouted.

"What makes you Rebs think you know so damn much?" cried Murphy.

"Don't make any difference, just turn the gold shipment over and nobody gets hurt."

Murphy thought for a few moments before answering. "Hey, Reb, it's getting dark. Let's call a truce and have a meeting over a campfire and cup of coffee. No point in yelling back and forth all night and wasting bullets in the dark."

The response took the young southerner totally off guard. *Wonder what kind of Yankee trick this is,* he thought. The silence that followed was deafening. Maybe he's serious and wants to talk. He hesitated for a moment then shouted back. "Okay, Yank, sounds reasonable to me."

Murphy was surprised at his own actions. "Can't believe I just called a truce with that band of rebels," he muttered. "Maybe this damn war is getting to me and maybe I'm just tired of all the killing."

Murphy and Walker ordered their men to stop firing and make camp for the night. An overnight truce was now in effect. Truces were a sacrament of honor during the Civil War and the troopers from both sides felt relatively secure to move about freely with the knowledge that no one would start firing and violate the truce. With a little nervous tension on both sides, they kept a watchful eye on each other.

Campfires were lit and the boys in blue began brewing coffee made from real roasted beans. Coffee was a luxury the Confederates had not tasted for a very long time and the smell of fresh brew drifting across the creek was intoxicating.

"How about you Yanks passing over some of that coffee," a young boy from Arkansas called out. "That smell is driving us nuts over here."

A shout echoed back over the creek. "We might give you a few cups if you'll send over some of your tobacco. We mean the real stuff."

Back and forth they bantered, and, in an unprecended act, actually agreed to cross lines and exchange coffee and tobacco. Both sides stacked arms and the Confederates crossed the creek to make the exchanges.

"Hey, boys," shouted one of the Confederates, "we've got two jugs of real Tennessee corn whiskey in our baggage. What say we get that liquor out and have us a few snorts?"

The Federals responded by letting out a loud cheer. So it was that young soldiers from both sides now sat around the campfires together, smoking tobacco, drinking coffee, sipping corn whiskey, and swapping stories. One of the men said, "Just imagine, two hours ago we were trying to kill each other." There were raucous snorts and laughter in response.

Walker and Murphy cautiously stood, staring at one another. Finally, after a few moments of silence, each man introduced himself and warily shook hands. Murphy was the first to make the surprising observation. "Captain, damned if you and I don't look like we may be related. Where were your ancestors from?"

Walker took a sip of coffee. "Well, based on what my father told me, my family came from Ireland back in the early 1700s and landed somewhere in Massachusetts then later drifted into Pennsylvania. My parents left Pennsylvania and moved down to Kentucky around 1840."

"That's interesting," Murphy observed. My great-grandfather was John O'Reilly Murphy, also from Pennsylvania." "I recon he was a farmer most of his life."

"That's funny," Walker remarked, "because my great-grandfather's name was also John O'Reilly Murphy. My grandmother was a Murphy who married my grandfather, James Walker."

Murphy shook his head in astonishment. "Sounds to me that my grandfather and your grandmother could have been brother and sister. If that's true, I'm guessing that would make us blood cousins. As far as I'm concerned, this changes a few things. We just can't go about shooting at each other and killing our own kin."

"You're right about that. Sure would hate to kill a cousin and have it on my conscience, even if he is a Yankee!" Walker declared.

Simon Murphy had been born and raised in rural Calhoun County, Michigan. His father tried his hand at farming before opening a small hardware store in Battle Creek. Simon worked alongside his father at the hardware store but found the routine extremely boring. His three years at the University of Michigan did not satisfy his desire for adventure, so he dropped out and went back home to ponder his future. When President Lincoln called for volunteers to join the army to put down the Southern Rebellion, young Murphy found a chance to escape his dull existence and find adventure and excitement.

He was a confident and capable officer, possessing a cool and calculating ability to make good decisions under fire. However, like many of his comrades, as the war wound down, he became wary of many dangerous decisions and orders handed down from incompetent superiors. He was no longer willing to take unnecessary risks that might get him killed so near the end.

With a sly grin, Walker asked his new found cousin, "By the way, how much gold you got in those leather bags?"

Murphy hesitated then whispered. "About fifty thousand dollars, U.S. gold eagles. How in the world did you know we were carrying gold?"

"Let's just say we have a beautiful lady in the right place, who knows how to use her southern charms."

Elijah Walker, born on a Kentucky farm, spent most of his youth helping his father with farm duties, a chore he found most unfullfilling. While visiting a cousin in Alabama in 1861, young Elijah was caught up in the popular fervor of secession during a recruiting campaign to organize a company of Confederate cavalry. Much like Murphy's experience, Elijah Walker enlisted and fought in several western campaigns. At Shiloh, he received his baptism of fire in the deadly confrontation at the dense oak thicket called the Hornet's Nest. His heroic actions were reported to General Beauregard and Elijah received a battlefield commission in June, 1862. He quickly rose through the ranks to captain and was well suited for the hardships of battle and living outdoors. Elijah possessed a passionate and cheerful temperament, but the horrors of the past three and a half years had hardened him far beyond his years. His humor and optimism had sustained him through those horrors, however, like his Confederate comrades, he was sick of this useless war and saw the old South fast diminishing. Also, like many others at the end, he was fighting an inner conflict—whether to stay with a losing cause or turn his horse toward the western frontier.

Elijah looked at his new cousin and wondered if he would be receptive to an idea he was hatching. The thought of splitting fifty thousand in gold made the idea more tempting. *Oh what the hell,* he thought. *Sure won't hurt in asking, especially if he really is my cousin.*

"If you're interested, I have a crazy but pretty sensible idea."

Simon nodded to confirm his curiosity. "Well, I'm listening..."

"I think we can both agree this damn war is about over."

"Yep, guess you can say that. You'll admit we won the war, won't you?"

"Well…yes," replied Elijah. "Our side has about run out of everything to fight with, including soldiers. Lot of 'em have headed out to Texas and even to Mexico and California, and God only knows where else. Been kicking the idea around myself."

His new northern cousin agreed. "I've seen enough killing in the past three years to last a lifetime. It's about time this damn war stops so we can all get back to some normal living."

"Yeah, at least you got some place to go home to," Elijah said wearily. "Most of the places I've seen around here have burned to the ground."

"What was this crazy idea you mentioned?" Simon asked curiously.

Elijah hesitated for a moment to collect his thoughts. "Why don't you and I send our men home on furlough and take the gold and quit this senseless war? I would sure hate to be one of the last killed before peace is called."

Simon took a few moments before responding. "You're asking me to be a deserter?"

"Hell no," Elijah answered, "I'm just suggesting that you and I drop out of sight until the war ends, then when tempers cool and things get back to normal, we'll come back."

Simon could not believe what he was hearing. *I'm actually sitting here listening to an enemy officer ask me if I would like to steal a United States army gold shipment and desert? And only two hours ago we were trying to kill each other. What kind of a lunatic does he think I am?*

The young northerner was already having his own inner struggle about many of the inexperienced and untrained Union officers Washington had been deploying. Simon had received several ill-conceived orders from incompetent officers that were killing men needlessly. He did not want to be another name on the casualty rolls, but to desert his post in the middle of a war was unthinkable; after all, he was a commissioned officer in the Army of the United States.

The temperature had dropped to freezing and light snow began to fall. Simon pulled his heavy wool greatcoat up tighter around his neck and stared into the flickering red coals of the campfire. *If Walker is really a blood cousin, I guess it makes it a family matter now, but the chances of pulling this off are pretty slim. And what if we get caught with the gold? We would be branded as spies and hanged or shot by a firing squad.*

Besides, where the hell would we go with all that gold? His mind was reeling with questions.

2.

There was something about the Confederate officer Simon liked, aside from perhaps being a distant cousin. He turned away from the fire and walked over to the creek, staring at the flowing clear water. The southerner seemed confident and sincere, he thought, walking back to Elijah and the warmth of the fire. "Hate to admit it, cousin, but I've been thinking the same thing ever since they turned this gold shipment over to me. I'm fed up with being shot at all the time. Besides, this damn war is about over anyway," he paused, thinking. "We would need to locate in a secure spot far away from the country if we decide to leave and sit out the rest of the war. We might try for Canada, but unfortunately, it's a long way through a lot of Union territory and army checkpoints." He shook his head, "Doubt if we'd ever make it up there."

"I've got a better idea," Elijah offered. "How about a tropical island down in the Caribbean? With fifty thousand dollars in gold, we could disappear anywhere for several years. We'd probably be listed as missing in action, then soon be forgotten, like thousands of other guys. We'd never be missed."

"You really think we can get away with it?" Simon asked. The thought of sitting out the rest of the war on a lush tropical island was intriguing.

Elijah, seeing his cousin warm to the idea, pressed on. "Don't see why not. Our little skirmish will soon be forgotten anyway."

"This skirmish might be forgotten," Simon countered, "but I don't think the government will quickly forget the sudden disappearance of fifty thousand dollars in gold coins."

"We can always say Confederate guerillas stole it…"

Simon stared at his cousin. He was still having difficulty overcoming his guilty conscience. Then again he thought of an island in the Caribbean—with real girls. Not a bad place to sit out the rest of this lousy war, that is, if they didn't get shot getting there.

Grinning, he looked at Elijah for a moment, then said, "Okay, let's do it! My God! I must be crazy as a loon."

The two officers returned to their units and gathered the blue and grey clad troopers into a single group. By then most of the men were deep into the whiskey jugs and having a pretty good time of it.

Murphy shouted, "Okay boys, gather around! It turns out that the good rebel captain here happens to be my blood relative, so it doesn't seem right that we should be trying to kill each other. We both agree the war's about over anyhow. Why don't all of you take a two week leave and skeedaddle on home to your families."

The men looked at one another in stunned disbelief, then erupted into cheering and clapping. Sergeant Dixon drew Elijah aside. "Sir, are you really serious about our going home?"

"Yep, I am. And I'd sure hate to see you or any of the boys get killed so near the end. Y'all need to be home with your families to be ready for spring planting. Why don't you just get 'em home safe and I'll catch up in a few days."

"Lots of Yankees between here and Huntsville."

"Yeah, I know. We're slightly northwest of Nashville so, if you travel on a straight line south, you'll bypass Nashville and most checkpoints. Be sure and skirt around the small towns and stay in the trees as much as possible."

With a wide grin, Sergeant Sam Dixon gave Elijah a stiff salute. "Yes, sir, I'll get 'em home in one piece, you can count on that."

The Confederate and Union troopers were elated and asked no further questions as they gathered their belongings, mounted their horses, and took off in different directions before the generous captains could change their mind. With Sergeant Dixon leading the small band, it was relatively easy for the Southerners to find their way home to Alabama. The Union troopers were only a few miles from the Kentucky state line and only a day's ride to the Ohio River and safely into Indiana. Two of the Federals did actually make it home to Michigan while the rest of the confused Union soldiers rode back to their command headquarters in Paducah and reported for duty rather than take the chance of being mistaken for deserters. Most of the Union troopers had sobered up on the ride back and sensed something was not quite right about the whole affair.

Captains Murphy and Walker slung the bags of gold coins onto their saddles, mounted their horses, and headed south for the Texas border. They avoided several towns and villages east of Memphis and made their way into Mississippi. The civilian clothes they borrowed from a clothesline passed them off as locals and, for most of the journey, they simply stayed clear of towns and any contact with people. They were well aware it would be impossible to explain the large amount of gold in their saddlebags should they be confronted by the authorities.

Passing a Catholic church on the outskirts of Greenwood, they stole priest's robes and other vestments from another clothesline and were now dressed as traveling clerics. Along the way they passed a Confederate patrol whose young officer asked that they stop and give hasty confessionals and brief prayers to three of the Catholic troopers. "By the way," the young lieutenant asked, "would you say a prayer for all of us while you're at it? We could all use a little outside help these days. This war ain't going too good."

The charade was easier for Simon who was raised a Catholic, but Elijah, a baptized Presbyterian, did not have a clue about church ritual, so he wisely stayed in the background, making signs of the cross as Simon spoke a few words he remembered from the liturgy of his youth. The irony was that no one else, including the young troopers, knew much more about the Catholic order of service than they did, so Simon and Elijah were accepted as two wandering priests and dismissed to go their way and save more lost souls.

After a harrowing trip of several days, avoiding a few more Confederate and Union patrols, they decided to stop for a rest near the town of Alexandria, Louisiana.

Simon could sense Elijah had something on his mind. "What the hell is bothering you?"

"Well, I figure we need to bury most of this gold and come back for it when the war is over. If we're caught, we'll have a tough time explaining how two wandering priests happen to be traveling with a fortune in gold."

"Yeah, I guess you're right, but we're out in the middle of nowhere."

Looking around, Elijah pointed to a distant hill with a large oak tree sitting on the top. "Up near that large oak tree would be fine. It looks like an easy place to remember when we return."

They approached the tree and looked around for some distinct features. The white oak was situated on a grassy knoll overlooking a wildflower meadow bordered by a small creek. "What'll we call this hill?" Elijah asked.

"Well, since we met over at that creek in Tennessee, let's just name it after the creek and call it Cockelberry Hill."

"Cockelberry Hill," Elijah repeated. "I like it."

They chose the west side of the large oak, walked off ten paces and dug a hole about three feet deep. After separating the coins and retaining about ten thousand dollars for themselves, they dropped the rest into the cache and neatly covered it up. They found a large rock, placed it over the hole, then raked more dirt and leaves over the stone. Taking a few moments to view the landscape around them, they committed their surroundings to memory.

Leaving Cockelberry Hill, they headed southwest toward the Texas border. The two had decided the Cayman Islands would be their initial destination, and eventually Mexico. The plan was to travel south to the Port of Galveston where they would purchase a one-way passage to Georgetown. Still adorned in the borrowed Catholic vestments, the gently rolling wooded hills offered them relatively good concealment through the scenic Louisiana countryside. On the outskirts of the little town of DeRidder, they were detained at a crossroad checkpoint by Union pickets and held until a small cavalry detachment arrived to relieve the sentries.

"What do we do now?" Elijah whispered.

"I guess all we can do is wait and try to save more souls from the devil's work," Simon said with a grin.

By mid-afternoon, the cavalry detachment rode up and confronted the two priests calmly sitting on a log beside the road. A young second lieutenant approached Simon. "Father, I'm Lieutenant William Macon. May I ask what you and your associate are doing riding out here in the countryside without escort?"

"Hello, Lieutenant," Simon responded in a gentle priestly tone. "We have been reassigned to a new mission in Corpus Christi and are en route there now."

"Don't you know there are bands of rebel guerillas scouring the countryside?"

"Thank you for your concern, Lieutenant, but the Lord will see to our safety," Simon said with confidence.

The lieutenant nodded at Simon. "Father, while you are here, we're in need of your services at our evening Mass."

"I'm sorry, Lieutenant, Father Elijah and I are in a great hurry to get to our destination, so I must regretfully decline."

"Nonsense, Father, you are the only two priests within a hundred miles and our good Irish boys would really appreciate a real Mass. Anyway, it might do all of us some good. We'll escort both of you into town."

Elijah gave his cousin an anxious look, which Simon hoped no one else noticed.

The town of DeRidder consisted of a few farmhouses, a church, and a country store. Scores of Union soldiers were lounging around and going about their various chores, with sleeping high on the list. The service would start promptly at six p.m. in the church. Elijah nudged Simon and spoke with a desperate-sounding whisper, "We can't conduct a whole service with these men. Hell, I grew up a Presbyterian anyway."

"Well, don't count on me to conduct a complete Catholic Mass," Simon confessed. Reckon if I even did try, they'll know the whole thing is a fake. We gotta figure a way out of here."

Elijah glanced at the general store across the street. "Seems to me like we could use a little diversion. I saw an ammunition storage tent behind the store. Give me fifteen minutes, then meet me behind the church with the horses."

"What are you planning to do?"

"Just watch and listen and get the horses ready to haul it out of here."

Elijah casually walked down the dirt road to the country store, smiling at the passing faces and giving the sign of the cross, just like it came naturally to him. He slipped behind the little store and into the supply tent. It only took him moments to find what he was looking for. One keg of black blasting powder and twenty feet of slow-burning fuse was just the ticket for their escape. He placed the keg between two other kegs, removed the lid, and inserted one end of the fuse into the powder. He cut the cord to what he estimated to be a fifteen-minute fuse, placed the lid loosely back on the keg and touched a match to the end. Easing out of the tent, he casually walked back up the road to the church and then strolled around to the rear where his cousin was nervously waiting with their horses.

"What now?" Simon asked.

"We just wait…"

It only took six minutes. The powder keg exploded and ignited several other nearby kegs. The massive explosion leveled the general store and collapsed the east half of the church. While the town was enveloped in a cloud of thick black smoke, Elijah jumped on his horse and shouted, "Let's get the hell out of here."

"Praise the Lord!" Simon shouted as they both galloped into the cotton field behind the church and into the woods beyond. "When you said a little diversion, I didn't expect you to blow up the whole bloody town!"

"Must have been a few more hidden powder kegs there than I figured."

They rode at a full gallop toward the Texas border. Luckily, they had not been spotted.

"What happens when the lieutenant finds us missing?" Simon wondered aloud.

"As well as I can figure it, he'll think we're either buried under the church rubble or we bolted out of there. If he thinks we had anything to do with the explosion, which he'll probably figure out soon enough, then the whole damn Union army will be looking for us. If we're caught, they sure won't treat us like priests. We'll either be strung up on the highest tree or shot by a firing squad. I suggest we get to the Texas coast—fast."

The Sabine River appeared before them. They turned to the south, keeping the river constantly in sight. By late afternoon, Simon and Elijah came upon an old weathered ferry. The bearded operator, who introduced himself as Ben, looked the two strangers over. "Y'all men of the cloth?"

"Yes, we're priests headed for our new mission in Texas," Simon answered with clerical politeness.

"Have to have at least four passengers to cross over. You only got two."

"Well, Ben, if you'll count our horses as passengers, that'll give four," Simon persisted.

"Them horses ain't people. Don't count. Need at least four people to move this barge. That's the rules."

"We'll give you two five-dollar gold half eagles to take us over," Elijah said. That's ten dollars in gold."

"Well, in that case, I'll do it. Ain't supposed to, but I'll make an exception since y'all are preachers."

"We're Catholic priests," Simon reminded Ben.

"Whatever. All the same to me," Ben said with a shrug, and then ferried them across the Sabine River into Texas.

"Preachers my eye," Elijah laughed. "It was those half eagles that did it. You see Simon, the shine of gold works every time!"

The ride south to the Gulf of Mexico was uneventful. Simon and Elijah traveled around the outskirts of Port Arthur and made their way to the Bolivar Peninsula, following the coast all the way to Galveston. It took four days to get there from the little town they had blown off the map. Ten gold eagles booked them passage on a two-masted schooner bound for the port of Georgetown. The cousins sold their horses to a stable keeper for twenty dollars, left the priests' vestments in a back pew at the nearby Calvary Baptist Church, and, to ease their conscience, dropped a few gold coins in the donation box. From the local general store, they stocked up on a few essentials before boarding the schooner. It was a clear and calm Saturday morning.

3.

The schooner was old, and despite its appearance, remarkably seaworthy. Sleeping two nights in narrow hammocks were back-breakers. However, after sleeping on cold, wet ground for the past three years, the hammocks felt like feather-stuffed mattresses. There were no complaints from either of the two veterans. Luckily, the sea was calm, thanks to excellent weather, and provided both Elijah and Simon sufficient time to unwind from the nerve-wracking events of the last few days. The staple of fish and shrimp stew and rice was edible and filling – it sure beat hard tack, fatback and beans.

"Reckon we've been missed by now?" Elijah asked as he and Simon stood by the railing looking out over the gentle rolling waves.

"I don't know about your side, but I imagine we have a whole division scouring the countryside looking for that gold shipment."

"You having any second thoughts about what we did?"

"Don't know," Simon mused, "but I do know one thing for sure. It's too damned late to worry about that now."

They arrived in Georgetown two days later, and the first order of business was to find a place to live. A two room weather-beaten shack on an isolated plot facing the ocean became their home. The shack had survived a couple of hurricanes, but despite the dreadful condition, it beat sleeping on the beach—the rental for ten American dollars per month suited them just fine. It took several days and boxes of nails to make it habitable, but for two veterans of many rugged campaigns, camping in tents and sleeping on the ground in horrible weather, the old shanty was at least dry and the tropical breezes flowing through the open windows kept it quite comfortable. A big plus was the back porch that gave them a great view of the beach and ocean. To them, the whole setup was a Caribbean paradise.

The days and weeks passed quickly. Simon and Elijah spent their time exploring the endless stretches of beaches and quickly found there was little to do in the Caymans except fish, swim, and sleep. One of their favorite pastimes was the pursuit of local senoritas in old Georgetown, who, on a rare occasion, would allow themselves to be persuaded, usually after overindulging in spirited beverages. This was certainly better than the horrors of war, although the thought of being branded as deserters was not very comforting to either of them. The local authorities left them alone and did not seem to care who they were as long as they behaved themselves. Communications between most Caribbean islands and the United States mainland were so bad that it was probable no one locally would ever find out they were deserters with a fortune in gold coins. Even though most of the coins were cached in Louisiana, there were enough left to raise some suspicion. However, none of this mattered to the authorities as long as the two Americans were spending money on the island.

Elijah and Simon soon became restless and discussed the possibility of traveling over to the Mexican mainland. They were fascinated by the local stories of lost treasures and ancient hidden cities long forgotten in the jungles of the Yucatan and Quintana Roo. Simon wanted to explore the ruins of the ancient tribes while Elijah had visions of gold and precious gemstones hidden in secret underground vaults.

In a sudden rush of guilt, they even considered the possibility of going back to the United States and rejoining the war. Realizing they would probably be treated as thieves, traitors, and fugitives, they quickly put this option aside. However, both men knew they would eventually have to return to the states when the war officially ended. After all, they had a large cache of gold coins waiting for them. They would bide their time and make plans when they knew all the battles were over.

Time in the Caymans continued to pass slowly and, one late summer day when Elijah and Simon were sitting on the beach sipping a local mixture of rum, coconut milk, orange juice and a bit of lime, Simon suddenly sat up and turned to Elijah. "Dammit, Cousin, we need some excitement. Let's jump a skiff, sail over to the mainland, and check out some of the ancient ruins in the Yucatan that we keep hearing about."

"Yeah, and how do we manage to find all these ruins when we get there?"

"We'll hire a guide. The barkeeper over at Hangman's Reef grew up in Mexico. He remembers visiting old ruins when he was a kid – said the area is full of old ruins."

Elijah took a sip of his drink and wiggled his toes into the warm sand. "So, what else did he say? Did he mention lost treasure or anything important like that?"

"Naw! He mostly talked about the old buildings and the pyramids."

"How exciting," Elijah said sarcastically, as he took another big swallow of the potent rum drink.

"Well, it could be—you never know. We might even stumble on lost Indian treasure buried in a cave or pyramid. I've heard the pyramids and temples are full of hidden passages and chambers."

Elijah sat in silence for a few moments, considering the idea. "Well, I have to admit I'm getting bored with this place. I'm also tired of chasing giggling senoritas who don't want to be caught. Hell, the last one was old enough to be my mama, and if that wasn't bad enough, she was cactus ugly!"

"Doubt if you'll find too many tropical beauties hanging around the Mexican jungle," Simon said. "But I heard there were some interesting ruins in Coba and Chichen Itza. Just yesterday, in Hangman's Reef, some local was talking to the barkeeper about a legend of a huge sapphire called The Star of the Sun. Said the sapphire is hidden somewhere in a temple called Cobazen. It's supposed to be at least seventy-five carats and worth a fortune. Maybe we should go look for it. That sapphire and our buried gold would fix us for life."

"I hope you don't believe all the crap you hear in that whiskey dump of a cantina," Elijah retorted.

"Not really," Simon admitted. "Well, whatta ya say? Shall we go?"

"We'll need a boat to take us over to the mainland."

"We have some gold coins left," Simon reminded him with a smile.

They awoke to a sunrise exploding with yellow and orange streaks across the endless horizon. Both felt a strong sense of excitement and anticipation as they walked down to the harbor. A weathered old ship, moored alongside a dilapidated pier, caught their eye. Nearby, an old man sat on a wooden bucket carving what appeared to be a hammerhead shark from a piece of driftwood. Simon went up to him. "Hola, mi amigo! Nice fish you're carving there."

The old man sat in silence as if he were stone deaf.

"How would you like to rent your boat for a few days to a couple of Americanos?"

The old man looked at them with an uncomprehending shrug.

Elijah jumped in. "We would like to rent your boat to take us over to the mainland and we will pay our passage in gold coins."

As if by a miracle, the old Mexican replied in broken English, "Si, Americanos! Amigos! Buenos Dias! I use this old scow for hauling people and cargo over to the mainland, and sometimes even for fishing. She is a two-mast brigantine built for the shallow coastal waters. My ship may be old, but she's seaworthy enough."

Elijah and Simon nodded.

The old man continued. "You mentioned gold. How much gold?"

"How much will you charge for two passengers?" Elijah asked.

The old man was much friendlier and attentive now as he introduced himself as Ramirez Don Sanchez Lopez. "I am descended from a noble Aztec king named Tezhechilizen who ruled the Yucatan in the Fourth Dynasty. His spirit still guards the ruins and he and his followers still live in caves deep below the Temple of Coba."

"So will you give us passage to the mainland, Señor Lopez?" Simon asked.

"Si, I will take you but it will cost you ten American gold pieces for the both of you. We will sail tomorrow morning from this mooring."

"Agreed, Señor Lopez."

The two Americans walked back to their beach bungalow, packed their meager belongings, and made especially sure they had an ample supply of ammunition for their Navy Colt revolvers. A quick stop to the local cantina was necessary to pick up some bottles of tequila and rum to round out their essential supplies.

The next morning they awoke to another blazing bright dawn. "It has to be a good omen," Elijah said.

Elijah remembered what the old man had said about his ancestors. "Do you really believe our captain thinks the ghosts of his ancestors are still living in the ruins of the old cities?"

"Who knows?" Simon said. "Just a superstitious old man trying to scare us."

Elijah agreed. "Yeah, but he probably believes it."

They arrived at the pier to find Ramirez Lopez waiting for them at the gangway. "My gold coins, amigos, then we cast off."

Simon placed ten shiny American Eagles in his hand. The old man looked around, and then quickly shoved them into his pockets.

It was high tide. With the mooring lines released, the brigantine departed Georgetown harbor. Simon and Elijah stood by the railing and watched as the old man turned the wheel to catch the wind. From the aft bridge, Ramirez shouted down to his young passengers, "Hey amigos, I could use a little help. You can help prepare the rigging since you two are the only crew I have today."

"What the hell is he talking about?" Elijah shouted.

"He wants us to become sailors and help sail this bucket," Simon yelled back.

After a few shouts, curses, and plenty of coaxing, the two Americans finally got the picture. The old sailor was glad to provide plenty of instruction, and soon Simon and Elijah were able to perform some of the simpler chores necessary for sailing a brigantine. The hardest part was climbing the two masts and unfurling the sails while balancing themselves on flimsy rigging and holding tightly to the shrouds and halyards. In spite of all their fumbling, the young Americans finally released the sails in time to catch an easterly breeze that pushed the ship westward toward the Mexican coast.

By the end of the day, the strenuous work left the new sailors exhausted from all the tugging, pulling, and climbing.

"I didn't know we were hired on as members of the crew," Elijah grumbled, "especially since we paid that old geezer all that gold to get passage."

"Quit griping, Elijah, maybe we learned something that might prove useful."

The ship was riding well from favorable winds, but late in the afternoon, Lopez saw a boiling sheet of dark black clouds fast approaching from the southwest. The old man shouted, "Amigos, we are in for a big storm. Fasten down everything that's loose and get the sails furled quickly!"

"What does that mean?"

"That means we climb back up the masts and tie the sails back to the yard arms."

"Oh shit!"

The old man shouted again. "After you finish, get to the leeward side of the ship and secure yourselves with a line around your waist."

"What's leeward mean," asked Elijah.

"Away from the wind," Simon mumbled.

"Are you sure you weren't in the Navy?"

No sooner had they secured the ship than the storm hit the small vessel with a fury. Lightning bolts flashed across the sky and the wind slammed them with the vengeance of the gods. The constant rolling thunderclaps reminded them of a cannon barrage at the Battle of Vicksburg. The rain came down in solid sheets and pelted them unmercifully as the sudden fury of the storm pitched and tossed the ship in every direction. The old man and the two young American passengers held on for dear life. To wash overboard in this storm meant certain death. The brigantine, though old and weathered, tossed and tumbled over the waves like a bobbing cork, but in spite of all the pounding, her builders had constructed her well and the little ship managed to hold together. The sickening effects from the constant violent motion took its toll and the young Americans turned away from the wind and lost everything they had eaten. "I'd give up my entire share of our gold coins to be off this damned wooden bucket and back on dry land," Elijah mumbled.

"Don't let the old man hear you or he may just run this thing into the nearest island!" Simon yelled back.

The storm unleashed its fury for over two hours, then slowly calmed. On the western horizon, the fading sun appeared between the distant broken clouds. For over an hour, all Elijah and Simon could do was lie on deck in agony until their stomachs quieted, color slowly returned and they began to feel normal again. "No more ships for me," gasped Elijah.

Daybreak came with a clear sky and calm seas. Elijah was pouring his first cup of coffee when he heard the old man shout, "Land ho! That island you see over there to the southeast is Cozumel. The Yucatan coast is not very far to the northeast. I will anchor at the small fishing village, Puerto Muerta, and there you can hire my nephew, Santos Lopez, who will guide you to the ruins you seek—for some of your gold, of course."

It was mid-afternoon when the ship dropped anchor near a beautiful white sand beach bordering a tiny ramshackle fishing village. Waving goodbye to Ramirez, Simon and Elijah walked to the main street and stopped at a small hotel called Posada Del Mar. The place looked like it had weathered one too many hurricanes.

"Ah, Señora," Elijah said in broken Spanish to the rather portly woman behind the desk, "do you have rooms for two weary American travelers?"

"Si, I have two rooms for one dollar Americano per night."

Several months in the Caymans had allowed both men to learn enough Spanish to converse fairly well with the locals.

"Si usted por favor, Señora, do you know where we can find Santos Lopez?"

"Oh, si, Señor, Santos lives with his sister in the little house at the end of the street, the one with yellow shutters."

The Americans secured their belongings in the rooms, concealed their revolvers in their belts and left the hotel. The small house where Santos lived was easy to find. Simon knocked and was surprised when a beautiful, dark haired young woman opened the door. "Hola," she said. "You are Americanos, si?"

"Si, Señorita, we are Americans and we are looking for Santos Lopez," Simon said politely.

"That would be my brother."

"Your Uncle Ramirez told us we could hire Santos to guide us into the interior and the ancient ruins."

"You know our Uncle Ramirez?"

"Si, Señorita. He brought us over from Georgetown in his boat."

"My brother knows most of the ruins well, but is afraid to go there because of things that have happened in the past. The ruins are full of very bad spirits from our ancient ancestors."

"We're not afraid of spirits and we will pay him well for his services," Simon said reassuringly.

"He might consider taking you for enough payment. You can find him in the cantina across from the hotel."

"Gracias, Señorita."

"My name is Rosita."

Politely bowing he replied, "Thank you, Rosita. My name is Simon, and this is Elijah."

"Pleased to meet you, Miss," Elijah said with a sly smile.

Rosita frowned. "You must be very careful in the cantina, amigos. The place is full of thieves who will cut your throat if they think you have any money."

"Thank you for the warning. We'll be watchful," Elijah said.

The Loco Lobo was a dark, dingy-looking place. Several unsavory characters sat at tables, drinking an unpleasant looking liquid that resembled bad beer. The bartender was a greasy slob with long, stringy black hair and a huge belly. Simon and Elijah eased up to the bar and ordered two margaritas. The bar keeper roared with laughter and poured straight shots of tequila into two dirty shot glasses. "You gringos must think you are in Mexico City ordering sissy drinks like that." He slid the glasses toward them and bellowed, "Two American dollars."

Simon tossed a five-dollar gold piece across the bar. The sight of the shiny coin created a murmur among the curious and observant crowd. "Keep the change, amigo."

He turned to face the rough looking patrons and quietly announced, "Amigos, we are looking for Santos Lopez and not looking for trouble."

A dark, rough hulk of a man shouted, "Ah, gringos, if you have more gold, it might loosen our thick tongues." A splattering of laughter rippled around the room.

A young man in his early twenties stood up. "I am Santos Lopez. How can I help you?"

"Let's go outside and talk," Elijah replied softly. "We come to you on the recommendation of your Uncle Ramirez."

Ignoring the hard stares that followed them through the door, the three left the bar and made their way across the street. Santos looked the strangers over. "You should not flash gold coins in there. Most of those men will not hesitate to slit your throats for ten centavos. Now what is it that you want, amigos?"

Simon answered the young Mexican. "Your uncle said you could guide us to some of the old Mayan ruins where there might be hidden treasures."

"Yes," Santos replied, "I am familiar with many of the old ruins, but those places are haunted by the ancient ones. I think it unwise to go there."

"We will pay you twenty-five American gold eagles. That is a small fortune in your town."

Santos thought for a few moments. "Si, amigos, I could use the money. My sister and I run a small fishing business, but the fishing has not been good lately. I agree to take you, but you must understand the trip into the jungle is very dangerous. I cannot guarantee your safety."

"We can handle ourselves," Simon said. "We spent three years fighting in the American war and nothing could be worse than that."

"Then we must depart Puerto Muerta quickly to avoid those banditos. I am certain they are making plans at this moment to kill and rob you in the middle of the night. Gather your belongings now and we will camp on the trail in a safe place I know. Are you staying at the hotel?" he asked.

"Yes," Simon replied.

"When you gather your things, leave by the back door. You can meet me in a few minutes at my house."

Twenty minutes later, Simon and Elijah slipped from their rooms and made their way to Santos's house. He was waiting with three worn out and scraggy-looking burros. "We will be traveling west and must make the mountains before dark.

These burros will help us make better time, but the banditos have horses and may catch up with us tomorrow. I have a secure place we can hide in the mountains, but we must hurry… now."

Within the hour, Simon and Elijah could feel the burro's spine wearing into their buttocks. "My God," moaned Elijah, "I feel like I'm riding a moving fence rail. I'd be better off walking than busting my ass on this bony monster."

Santos had ridden many burros and knew the torture the Americans were experiencing. "We must hurry to my hidden cave. We have about five more miles to go and should arrive before sundown."

"If the banditos don't kill us, these damned jackasses will," Elijah grumbled. In spite of the pain and discomfort, they continued westward, bucking and bumping on the backs of the wretched animals. As the sun was setting, Santos announced, "Our hiding place is just up ahead."

They approached a steep bend in the road and Santos stopped and pointed to a spot higher up the slope. The two Americans gazed up the incline, but could see nothing except rocks and scrubs.

"The path is well hidden," Santos said. "We'll have to walk the burros up the mountain and to the cave. They can't carry our weight up the steep path."

"Thank God," Elijah mumbled in gratitude.

Neither Elijah nor Simon could see signs of a path branching off the main trail. "Follow me," Santos ordered as he disappeared through some thick underbrush.

The climb was steep and tiring, but they trudged upward, with the burros in tow. The path wound through boulders and brush and was hardly visible. As they approached the summit, they came to a grouping of large boulders and Santos led them through a concealed opening to another path that wound behind the boulders, then ended at a narrow opening. The entrance was barely large enough to allow the burros to enter. Entering a small cavern, Santos reached for a kerosene lantern hidden on a small ledge and lit it with a match. The lantern blazed bright and revealed a spacious cavern beyond the opening. The walls were stacked with wooden boxes and barrels. On one side was a small enclosure made of tree limbs that served as a temporary holding corral. In one corner were three bales of hay and a bucket of water for the animals. A small clear spring trickled at the far end of the cavern, and then flowed for about twenty feet before finding its way back into the rocks.

Even Simon was duly impressed with Santos's cozy hideaway. He turned to the young Mexican and said, "You speak very good English, my friend, for one who lives in a small Mexican fishing village."

Santos chuckled. "I was educated at a Catholic university in America – in your city of New Orleans. I studied English, American history, geology, anthropology, and early Indian cultures. I had a special interest in learning more about the history of my ancestors. I spent three and a half years there until my father died. My mother and Rosita needed me back in Puerto Muerta to help run our family fishing business. We have three boats and manage to survive. When you asked me to take you to the ruins, I thought it would be a good way to help me get enough money to move us to the west coast of Mexico for a better life."

Santos' response cleared some of Simon's questions as he turned and motioned toward the far wall. "What's in the boxes and barrels?" he asked.

"I have enough food and supplies here to last us a month and, if you will open the top crate, you will find some new American rifles that were stolen by Apache Indians from your army in New Mexico. Some of our banditos stole them from the Indians and I have friends that took them away one night when they were all drunk. This cave is a good place to hide them. I think we'll need these new repeating guns where we're going."

Elijah opened the box and pulled out a new .52 caliber repeating carbine rifle. The name on the barrel identified the manufacturer as the Spencer Repeating Rifle Company of Boston, Massachusetts. Elijah looked at Simon as he held the rifle in the air. "These are some mighty fine looking rifles. It's a shame we didn't have them at Vicksburg."

Simon examined the Spencer, moving the cocking lever back and forth. "I've never seen repeater guns quite like these before. They must be something new our army is supplying the cavalry units in the southwest territories. I reckon it's just a matter of time before they get to our Union army units fighting in the south."

"All I know is we'll be glad to have them if the banditos find us," Santos said.

4.

Early the next morning, Elijah awoke, sensing something was terribly wrong. He quickly shook Simon and Santos and whispered to them. Before turning in, both Elijah and Simon had examined the rifles and found they held seven rounds of .52-caliber cartridges and operated by cocking the lever down and back. They loaded three of the rifles and placed extra ammo in leather pouches that could attach to their belts.

As Elijah eased out of the entrance of the cave, he heard the faint sound of movement farther down the mountain. It was becoming lighter and Elijah reached a vantage point through an opening in the boulders, providing a panoramic view of the slopes below. Gathered on the path they had ascended yesterday was a collection of men and horses. Elijah counted ten men and one woman. One particularly ugly brute turned toward him and shoved the woman to the front, holding a long knife to her throat. "Santos, we know you're up there," he shouted. "Throw down the Americans' gold and we will spare you and the gringos. No one needs to get hurt. We have your sister with us. We persuaded her to tell us the location of your secret hiding place. We do not want to harm her or you and your gringo friends. We'll let her go if you toss all the gringo's gold down to us."

Elijah heard the words and whispered, "Yeah, you mangy bastards, you'll see us dead whether we give you the coins or not. Looks like we'll be using these new Spencers sooner than I thought!"

"All we want are the Americans' gold coins," the voice boomed out. "We know they have more gold or they would not have tossed the five-dollar piece to the barkeeper. Do it now or your sister is as good as dead. I know you can hear me. You have five minutes to make up your mind. After that, Rosita goes over the cliff and your bodies will soon follow. The buzzards and wolves will have your carcass for dinner!"

Simon and Santos crept over to the boulders where Elijah knelt. When Santos saw his sister restrained below, he gritted his teeth and balled his fists.

"I have an idea," Elijah offered. "I'll work my way down the mountain and get behind them. You two spread out and find a good vantage point, then wait for my signal. When they lift their heads, pick off as many as you can."

"But how will we know your signal?" Santos asked.

"You'll know..."

Elijah grabbed his new rifle and used the concealment of the rocks and scrub to make his way down the mountain. Simon and Santos separated and found two well-concealed openings with a good view of the area below. Elijah had worked his way around to the left and crouched between two large boulders. He could see the Mexicans kneeling behind a rock outcropping awaiting orders from an ugly and mean looking character who appeared to be the leader. *This tactic worked at turkey shoots up in Kentucky so I don't know why it wouldn't work here with these buzzards.*

He cupped his hands and let out a loud shrill screech that was supposed to imitate a turkey's mating call. The curious Mexicans raised their heads, trying to see what was making this god-awful noise. Santos and Simon picked their targets and fired at the same time. Two of the bandits tumbled over backward and a second volley brought down another two. "God bless new Spencer repeaters," Simon mumbled.

Elijah moved further down the hill, hoping to get a better vantage point. Guarded by a lone sentry, Rosita was sitting on the ground a few yards behind the others. She saw Elijah and did not make a sound. He put his finger to his mouth, indicating for her to be silent, then shrieked another turkey call. As the startled guard raised his musket, Elijah shot him between the eyes, throwing him backwards into the rocks. His companions reacted to the strange noise and again rose from their cover. Elijah shot another in the chest and shots rang out from above, dropping three more. Two more bandits arose and bolted for the path in an attempt to escape from the deadly fire. Elijah brought down one with a shot through his neck and the other man dropped with more shots from above. The leader had enough and threw his rifle to the ground. "Americano, I give up, do not shoot!"

Before Elijah could react, the man grabbed Rosita around her throat, drew a long knife and held the blade to her neck. "Gringo," he cried, "I am backing down the path with the girl and if you make one move to stop me, she dies!"

Slowly he moved toward the path with Rosita shielding him. With his eyes fixed on Elijah, the bandit did not notice Rosita's movement as she bit down on his hand as hard as she could. The Mexican screamed and relaxed his grip long enough for Rosita to turn and bring her knee up sharply into his groin. He doubled over in pain, dropping the knife onto the rocks. She gave him a sudden shove to his shoulder causing him to lose his balance and stumble toward the ledge. He slipped on loose gravel and slipped over the edge. With outstretched arms, he made a feeble attempt to grab a rock protrusion, but only came up with hands filled with loose gravel and sand. With a look of shock on his face, arms and legs flailing, he sailed out into the ravine to the boulders waiting below.

"Ah, Rosita," Elijah exclaimed, "you seem to know how to take care of yourself. "

She just smiled back. "When you live around these animals you learn how to defend yourself. There were just too many of them. The swine came to my house and threatened to kill me if I didn't lead them to the cave. I knew Santos and you Americans would think of something."

Simon and Santos climbed down the path where the bodies of the dead Mexicans lay sprawled among the rocks. Looking at the carnage surrounding them, Santos said, "We can't bury these devils because the ground is too rocky. We can throw them over the cliff into the ravine where the vultures and wolves will finish their remains in a few days. Besides, we don't want any of their friends to find out what happened here."

One by one, the bodies tumbled over the cliff into the ravine below, where they would eventually disappear.

Santos grinned. "Amigos, there is a good side to all of this. Now we have horses and saddles."

"What do we do with your sister?" Simon asked with a look of concern.

Rosita took immediate offense, and with hands on her hips, glared icily at Simon. "I will continue on with you. I cannot go back to the village now. There is nothing left for me there."

"Our journey could be very dangerous," Elijah reminded her.

Rosita glared at both Americans. "I would rather face all the demons in hell than those animals when they find out their friends disappeared with me in tow. Besides, give me a gun and I'll do my part. I can handle a rifle as good as any man."

"I'll bet you can at that," Elijah chuckled.

As Elijah and Rosita went to collect the horses, Santos and Simon returned to the cave to gather up the weapons and supplies.

They unbridled and removed the saddles from all but six of the best horses and herded the remaining animals and the three burros back down the trail to a small grassy meadow, and then released them. The chosen mounts were loaded with enough food and supplies to last several days. Simon, Elijah, Santos and Rosita each took a repeating Spencer carbine with plenty of cartridges and three extra rifles as spares. Santos stashed the surplus saddles in the cave and carefully concealed the entrance with brush. The group headed west, hoping to reach the ruins of Coba or Chichen Itza in the next few days. The winding trail broadened and flattened as they descended the mountains into a wide valley.

"This is far enough for one day," Santos announced as they halted next to a small clear stream. "We'll make camp here for the night."

As the sun dipped behind the hills, the evening grew chilly and they gathered around the small fire to cook supper and keep warm. Santos was in an apprehensive mood as he stood looking out over the distant horizon. "Amigos, the thing that worries me now is the fact that we are now moving into hostile Indian country. This is the land of the Tuloupi Indians and they hate outsiders, especially trespassers on their land. I have also heard the Tuloupis are cannibals. We are going to be in their country for a couple of days so we need to be very watchful. I would hate to see what they might do to Rosita if they caught her."

"What about us?" Elijah quipped.

"With us it would be quicker. They would just stick us over a fire and roast us."

"Now there's a comforting thought," Simon said.

Santos killed two fat rabbits with the small bow and arrow he carried with his kit. They dined on roasted rabbit and hard bread brought from the cave. "Enjoy this hot meal because we eat dried meat and bread for the next two days, plus any berries we happen to find on the trail."

The group arose with the sun. A clear sky indicated it would be a warm and cloudless day as they packed up the supplies and mounted the horses. Elijah was in a jubilant mood. "These saddles sure feel better than those damned jackasses. It has taken me two days to get over the soreness in my butt."

"Be sure and keep your rifles ready," Santos advised, leading the way, "in case we stumble upon Indians. With all the noise we're making, they'll find out we're traveling in their country soon enough."

The small party approached a valley filled with tall green grass, dotted with yellow and red wildflowers. It was comforting to see small stands of tall cottonwoods dispersed throughout the gently rolling hills. Santos was hoping the trees would provide cover from any stray hunting party. They stopped for a quick lunch of deer jerky and bread and let the horses graze on the lush grass. "If you look far down into the valley," Santos explained, "you can see a line of mountains in the distance. Those mountains mark the end of Tuloupi territory and that is where we are going. The valley ahead is the most dangerous part of the journey because this is where they live and hunt."

"Can't we ride around it?" Simon asked.

"Unfortunately no, because the valley is surrounded by sheer cliffs and there's no known route around except far to the north along the coast. That would take us a week."

"Good thing we have these repeating rifles," Elijah said. "They might be the only thing that gets us through this place."

They continued westward without incident or contact with any Indians. Rosita rode next to Simon, intent on gaining his confidence. "Why are you Americans here in Mexico when there is a Civil War being fought in your country? I hear you talk to the other American and you sound like you're on opposite sides of the war."

"That's true," Simon replied. "I was fighting for the United States and Elijah was in the Confederate army. We met at a place called Cockelberry Creek and fought each other briefly. Then we decided to call a truce so we could rest and swap coffee and tobacco. When we first met, we noticed how much we looked alike and when we talked about our ancestors, we found that we have the same great-grandfather who came over to America from the country of Ireland. We didn't want to shoot our own flesh and blood so we decided to come to Mexico and sit out the war. We heard locals in the Cayman Islands tell a story about a large sapphire called The Star of the Sun and decided to try and find it."

"The story is a very old legend," Rosita replied. "They say the Star is not a sapphire but a huge diamond as large as a hen's egg. Legend has it that this diamond is like no other in the world; that it contains a blue fire with very strong powers. I don't know of anyone who has ever seen it. Legend also says he who finds the Star will also find the great treasures of the Toltec empire. The treasure contains chests of precious stones and bars of pure gold."

Simon's eyes widened. "Such a treasure is beyond my comprehension, but who knows what our luck might bring?"

The small party continued down a narrow rocky path toward a heavily wooded copse of trees nestled in the valley below. A clear stream wound through a large meadow, mirroring the mountains in the distance. Protected on all sides by large sheer cliffs, the valley provided a sense of peace and serenity.

Stopping for a short break, Elijah abruptly held up his hand. "Everyone, mount your horses and move back into the trees. I saw movement on that hill to the north. It looked like a party of about six men on horses. I don't know if they saw us."

A small grove of cottonwoods allowed them quick concealment from the approaching hunters. Santos peered through the bushes and saw the horses heading their way. "It's a Tuloupi hunting party and they look like they're following our tracks. They probably suspect strangers are on their land. It's certain that any Indian who spots us will report to their chief who will order his warriors out to search for us. Their chief is a very bad hombre named Zapata. In their language, the name means Killer of his Enemies. It is said that Zapata plucked the beating heart from the chest of an enemy warrior and ate it raw."

"We sure could have used him in the 7th Alabama Cavalry," Elijah said with a laugh.

"We'd better find a good hiding place before they spot us," Santos suggested.

The group quickly rode toward the cliffs bordering the valley. Santos picked up a small trail following the cliff wall and the group moved quickly out of sight. As they rounded a bend, two Indian warriors, casually sitting on their ponies, suddenly confronted them. Their faces and upper torsos were adorned with red and black stripes, indicating they were part of a roving war party. Spotting the intruders, the startled warriors emitted a loud cry, then turned and urged their ponies in the opposite direction. Elijah and Simon each raised a rifle and fired. One Indian pitched from his pony and the other grabbed his shoulder and made a mad dash for the trees. Elijah fired again and the fleeing warrior threw his hands high in the air and tumbled to the ground. The rifle reports were loud and echoed across the valley.

"We're in for it now," Simon shouted. "I'll bet every Indian in the valley heard those shots and will know we're here. Grab the pack horses and let's move... fast!"

They spurred their horses along the path at breakneck speed to get out of Tuloupi territory. Intersecting the original trail again, Santos turned to see two large bands of Indians to their right trying to overtake them.

"Head for those boulders to our left!" Santos cried. "The ones close to the cliffs. We'll have a much better chance from the higher ground than trying to outrun them."

A natural redoubt to their front, surrounded by boulders, would offer some protection, so they moved quickly to get to this cover. Dismounting, Rosita secured the horses while the men grabbed the rifles and extra ammo packed in the baggage. Simon called out to Rosita, "Stay with the horses while we try to hold them off."

She grabbed her rifle. "No, I can shoot as well as you and four rifles are better than three."

The intruders found a concealed spot between the rocks and waited for the savages to arrive. A band of twenty-three warriors halted in front and screamed for their hides. Four rifle shots rang out, followed by four more, dropping six warriors to the ground. Another four shots resounded and three more went down screaming. The rest quickly retreated to nearby cover.

Santos was amazed at the power and accuracy of the new rifles. "We have them confused. They have only seen single shot muskets and these new repeaters make it look like we have more men than they thought."

From the west, another band of Tuloupis pressed their ponies toward the makeshift fortification. Elijah awaited the next onslaught. An arrow flew by his shoulder and struck the rock to his left, followed by another that hit the ground and skidded past his feet. Glancing upward, he saw movement to his right, and then spotted an Indian perched on a small ledge high above them. He had flanked to their left and climbed the cliff to reach the ledge. Elijah took careful aim and fired, hitting the Tuloupi in the abdomen. With a confused look on his contorted face, the Indian pitched forward and sailed to the rocks below.

Peering over the boulders, they faced at least forty more Tuloupi. Standing in front and perched on a large boulder was the great Zapata himself, adorned in all his savage splendor. He sported two large black and white stripes painted across his face and more on his chest and legs. They could have sworn he was a demon from hell.

"Look at that magnificent old bastard," Elijah shouted. "He must be in a hurry to catch his evening meal of roasted loin of white man."

"Are you kidding?" Simon replied. "You're too damn tough to eat. You'd choke the old bastard to death and his tribe would feed what's left of you to his pet wolves."

Elijah shrugged and offered an idea. "I want to try an old trick we used on some hostile Chickasaws over in Arkansas."

From his pack, he retrieved a small mirror. "Luckily the sun is facing us or this won't work."

Taking the mirror, Elijah captured the reflection from the sun and beamed it back to the old chief, catching him directly in his eyes. Zapata, momentarily blinded by the blinding reflection, let out a cry and dropped behind a large boulder.

Santos was impressed with Elijah's trick. "They think we are gods with magic medicine and have captured the sun," he chuckled. "This is a great time to clear out while they're in a state of confusion."

The four quickly mounted and galloped toward the mountains, with the packhorses in tow. It took about ten minutes before the Tuloupis realized what had happened and mounted their own horses in hot pursuit. Elijah noticed the ground was beginning to slope higher and realized they were entering the foothills. With at least forty Indians close behind at full gallop and Zapata leading the way, they pushed their horses to the limits. *Looks like the old bastard is mad as hell to see his dinner get away,* Elijah thought as he spurred his horse further up the hill.

With the packhorses slowing them down, the Indians were gaining fast. Elijah shouted to his companions, "We're going to have to make another stand and fight 'em again!"

The trail began to elevate even higher as they raced further up the mountain. Santos noticed a small stand of pine trees directly above them and pointed, motioning for the group to follow. "Make for that grove where we'll have some cover on the higher ground."

Reaching the tree line, they dismounted and dispersed behind the trunk of a large fallen pine. Fanned out below, the Indians drove toward them fast, screaming for blood.

"Make all of your shots count!" Simon cried.

As the Indians charged, four rifle muzzles exploded, dropping three Tuloupis from their horses. The screaming warriors were easy targets. Rosita spotted a large muscular savage running up the hill directly toward her. She fired. The bullet struck a glancing blow to his shoulder, but on he came, shrieking at the top of his lungs. She fired again, but missed. The Indian was only a few feet away when a bullet struck him in the left eye, dropping him in his tracks. Elijah had noticed her dilemma and fired off a quick shot. Several Indians got close, but never quite made the tree line before screaming bullets took them down. The remaining band pulled back to the rocks and gathered for a final assault. Zapata stood up on a large rock outcropping in full view. The old warrior was convinced he was immune to injury from a white man, as he jumped up and down, yelling encouragement to his warriors.

Elijah, seizing the moment, took a deep breath, aimed and squeezed the trigger. The heavy slug caught Zapata directly in his upper chest and lifted him off the ground, slamming him into the warriors standing behind him. The bullet exited his back and scattered a mist of blood over the warriors. This was too much for the remaining Indians. They were defeated. The Tuloupis lifted their old chief from the ground and retreated back down the hill. The white devils were too powerful with their murderous repeating thundersticks.

"Time to move," Santos shouted.

Gathering the horses, the four rode out of the trees and onto the trail leading to the mountain.

Elijah reloaded his rifle and eased it back into his saddle sheath. Now that the excitement was over, he felt a surge of relief having survived what would have been certain death had they not had the repeaters. "These new Spencers are like having an army with us. Can you imagine what would have happened if we only had single shot muskets? That old chief would have us all sitting in a cooking pot right about now."

"Thank you, Elijah, for shooting that big Indian back there," a very appreciative Rosita said with a wide smile. "I thought the brute was going to kill me."

He nodded. "You are most welcome, little lady."

Everyone seemed to relax a bit as the small group headed westward into the fading sun.

5.

Elijah arose early the next morning and his first thought was that he hoped they had seen the last of the dreaded Tuloupis. He started a small fire and boiled water for coffee. The others stirred as the pleasant aroma filled the air. Santos sat down next to Elijah, filled his cup with the steaming brew, and explained his plan for the day. "Once we cross this last range of mountains we'll go through the hills of the eastern boundary of the Toltec and Maya military and cultural province. We will be entering through part of the great Mayan jungle and may see some smaller ruins as we travel toward the ancient city of Coba. There are three things to worry about in this jungle: first, wild animals and poisonous snakes; second, an occasional bandito; and third, the jungle itself. Here a man and horse can be swallowed up in quicksand and completely disappear. They also say the jungle is full of many evil spirits."

"I don't know about evil spirits," Elijah said, "I do know one thing... I hate snakes."

Rosita laughed. "Well, then maybe it will be my turn to save your life."

Simon cackled as Elijah shot him an irritated look.

The trail across the mountains was relatively easy and, by early afternoon, they found themselves in rugged country surrounded by hills and sheer rock cliffs. Ahead, they noticed the vegetation growing thicker and saw large vines climbing high into the trees. As they approached the edge of a jungle, the musty odor of rotting vegetation permeated the air. In the distance, a high waterfall was barely discernable through the fine sunlit mist that surrounded it. Santos suggested the falls would be a good spot to camp for the night. Baths in the pool below the falls would be just what was badly needed for soothing tired muscles and sweaty bodies. It took three hours to reach the falls, and another several minutes to find the overgrown path that bordered a small stream flowing from the pool at the waterfall's base. Approaching, they noticed an overhanging shelf that protecting what appeared to be a large cavern, well hidden behind the falls. "This will be a good place to camp," Santos concluded. "The cavern looks big enough for all of us. We'll secure the horses below the falls."

After attending to the animals and storing their gear inside the spacious cavern, the three men removed their sweaty clothes and entered the water. Rosita walked further down the bank where she modestly removed her blouse and pants and dove in. They all took their dirty clothes and rinsed away the grime and sweat of three days travel. Elijah glanced around at his surroundings, and then leisurely swam across the pool to the falls. The rays from the sun sliced deep into the crystal water and illuminated the sandy bottom with an iridescent glow. A bright and shiny glitter caught Elijah's eye deep below. He took a deep breath and dove toward the glistening object that lay on the bottom. Grasping a small, heavy stone, he returned to the surface and marveled at the sparkling rock he held. Elijah gasped—he was holding the largest gold nugget he had ever seen. It was at least two inches in diameter. "Simon," he shouted, "look at this!"

"Good grief," his cousin responded, "dammed thing must be at least six to eight ounces. I'll bet there are more like it down there."

Simon dove to the bottom and searched through the pebbles and sand. Elijah and Santos quickly followed, searching near the falls where Elijah found the first nugget. The sandy bottom was rich with small particles of gold and it only took minutes to find more nuggets. Together they discovered twenty-eight impressive gold nuggets, though smaller than the first one Elijah had retrieved. Deciding they had found all the nuggets, they climbed out of the water and rested on the small beach.

The two young Americans heard soft singing and splashing from a cove concealed behind bushes. Their curiosity got the better of them as they quietly paddled over to the source of the singing. There, in all her naked and splendid beauty was Rosita, swimming in the clear crystal water.

They could not help but notice her firm and full rounded breasts, and slim, well-curved hips.

Simon whispered, "Isn't that the most beautiful sight you've ever seen."

It took Elijah a moment to respond as he stood there gaping. "My God, yes," he finally moaned. "I hate to say it, cousin, but I don't think we need for Santos to see us staring at his pretty sister's naked body." He was having a hard time tearing his eyes away from Rosita.

Neither could resist one more glance at the sumptuous female figure splashing in the water. Wild and sensuous visions flowed through their minds and it took some effort to control the unaccustomed stirrings within their loins.

The men spread their wet clothes on tree limbs to dry and returned to the cavern to retrieve dry clothing. Feeling rejuvenated, they were ready to explore more of the cavern surrounding them. Rosita finally returned from the pool and changed into clean, dry clothes while Santos ventured outside to gather firewood for cooking the evening meal. He also took a packet of line and hooks in hopes of catching fish from the river.

Aided by glimmers of daylight filtering through the falls, Elijah searched the cavern, looking for artifacts or any signs of past inhabitance. Near the furthest wall, he stumbled upon some rubble containing small bits of flints and chips. "Simon, come here—take a look at this. Scattered around were scores of old arrow points and two discernable flints that appeared to be in the shape of axe heads. Simon grasped a small pointed granite stone.

"This is a shaping tool used to make flints into arrows and spear points and other tools. Indians used these for thousands of years. I saw drawings of them in an anthropology class at the university. Let's look around for more."

The rear wall was barely illuminated, but enough to allow Simon to notice something unusual about the wall, but he could not quite make out what it was. "Light a torch and let's take a closer look."

Elijah went to fetch one of the torches Santos had prepared. It ignited and he held it close to the wall, noticing a faint uniform pattern of cracks forming a rectangle, approximately four by six feet. The immediate area was covered with a crude coating of veneer. A closer look suggested someone had apparently applied it in an attempt to conceal the joints and blend with the rock. The passage of time had cracked much of the plaster film and small pieces had fallen off to reveal narrow rectangular-shaped blocks set in an irregular pattern. Simon ran his fingers along the joints. "Looks like someone didn't want this section to be found. I'll bet it's a false wall; maybe it conceals a hidden passageway," Simon said, examining it more closely. "Let's chip more of this plaster away."

Elijah left to retrieve a small shovel. When he returned, Simon was bending over a smooth round stone embedded in the floor, with an inscription. The stone appeared to be alabaster, with three distinct glyphs carved into the face. "What do you reckon this means?" Elijah asked.

"Not sure, but it could indicate directions or a warning… or a curse. We ought to let Santos examine them before we break through the wall," Simon asked.

Rosita came over to where the two men were standing and stooped down to examine the carvings. She gasped. "I think these markings were carved by the ancient ones and meant to warn us. Santos might be able to interpret them—I feel they mean something bad."

"What's going on back there?" Santos shouted as he entered the mouth of the cavern. "Anyone ready for dinner? I caught some fish in the river and I'm starving."

Rosita shouted, "Santos, come back here! You need to see these carvings."

Quickly he joined them and gazed down at the three glyphs. "I'm not sure whether the inscriptions were carved by the Maya or the Toltecs, but I think they could refer to something behind that wall. It could be warnings. I'm not sure what the first figure means, but the second looks like an armed warrior or maybe a spirit guard. The third marking could signify a burial site, or even a treasure chamber. Something sinister awaits anyone who violates the passage."

"By 'sinister' do you mean deadly traps?" Elijah asked.

"Yes. The ancients invented some very devious and clever ways to kill a person."

"Nonsense," Simon replied. "It only makes it more enticing. If we leave without even checking it out, we'll always regret it."

"Simon is right," Elijah responded. "Let's chip away some of the stones and see what's behind this wall."

He lifted the shovel and began chipping away at the veneer covering. The plaster was made of a primitive mixture of ground clamshell, sand, and clay and had become brittle over the centuries. Large flakes stripped away easily, revealing the stone blocks covering what appeared to be the outline of a doorway. With some effort, Elijah and Simon lifted several blocks from the wall, revealing a dark void behind it. Simon picked up a small stone and tossed it through the opening, listening as the sound of the projectile striking a hard surface echoed back through the breach. "There's a hollow space behind the wall and I'll bet it's a passage that leads to another cave."

They removed a few more stone blocks until the space was large enough for a person to squeeze through. "Hand me the torch," Simon said to Rosita and thrust the flame through the opening. He could barely detect a narrow passageway leading deeper into the mountain. The torch's flame bristled as if a breeze was pushing it toward them. He held it higher in the air. "See how the flame is blowing toward us," Simon said to the other three. "That means fresh air is flowing through the passage. I reckon there's another opening to the outside somewhere ahead. I suggest before we go into that tunnel, we eat and rest first. Besides, we need to cook those fish while they're still fresh."

The fish Santos caught was a species of bass and promised to be very tasty. Santos built a fire and let it burn down to a smoldering bed of hot coals, then skewered the fish and suspended the sticks over the heat.

"Santos, you did it again. This is delicious," Simon said as he devoured a huge bite of the white flaky meat.

"They are called Musu. The Indians like to smoke and dry the meat and eat them as a type of fish jerky."

"Well, I prefer your way to cook them," Elijah said, swallowing a last bite of the succulent bass.

The group was exhausted after a full day of travel and soon bedded down for the night. They were all quietly snoring within a few minutes.

By the time soft-filtered morning sunlight broke into the cavern, Santos had a small fire burning. The others awoke and while they were sipping coffee, he was giving some instructions on how they should proceed. "Before we go through the opening, we'll need several pine torches and enough food and water to last a couple of days. We will take at least two rifles and your pistols because you never know what we'll find down there. The horses are well secured and have enough water and grass to keep them happy for a day or two."

It only took a few minutes to assemble the gear and make their way back to the rear wall and concealed tunnel behind. Santos lit two torches and handed one to Elijah. In single file, they all squeezed through the narrow opening. The passageway was about five feet high and barely wide enough for one person to pass through. The first thing they noticed was the air. It smelled remarkably fresh, despite being enclosed behind a stone wall for hundreds of years. As they moved forward, the passage began a gradual descent and leveled out when they reached a small landing. They were relieved when the height of the ceiling increased and allowed the taller Americans to stand erect. Immediately beyond the landing was a series of steep steps carved into the stone.

"Looks like Indians used this place frequently at some time in the past," Elijah remarked. "The steps are remarkably uniform and fairly well worn. Maybe they lead to a burial chamber."

Continuing down the steps, the group could sense they were moving deeper into the bowels of the mountain. A little further along, they made a sharp right turn and dropped onto another small landing. Rosita shrieked when the torches cast light on the wall above them. Hanging over a passageway opening was a jade mask staring at them with an evil and foreboding look. A thin gold rope chain dangled from its neck. Rosita crossed herself. "I knew it… that face is warning us to go back and leave this haunted place alone!"

"Come on, Rosita," Simon coaxed, "it's nothing more than a carved face some Indian placed there to decorate the wall. Look at all the gold inlay. I bet that mask would fetch a fancy price from an Indian artifacts collector. Let's leave it be and when we return we'll get the gold chain."

As they crossed the landing, they came to more steps. "Amigos," Santos said, "there is fresh air flowing from below. Watch the torch. See how brightly it burns and how the flame bends and flutters. There has to be another opening somewhere close by. Maybe the ancient ones had a back entrance, allowing them access from both sides of the mountain. They may have used this cavern as a sacred temple or as a safe hideout from enemies. If that were the case, they would have surely built themselves an escape route. They also used caverns like this as burial sites where their spirits were protected from enemies in the afterlife. When we reach the bottom of this passageway we'll have a better idea."

Descending another fifty steps, the path came to a ledge. Elijah and Santos held their torches high and saw a large room with brightly colored rock formations hanging from the ceiling and walls. The ledge was a continuation of the small path descending along the wall to the bottom. Carefully they moved along the ledge until they reached the lower level.

"Listen," Rosita said. "I hear running water."

Moving toward the sound, they saw a small stream flowing from under a sheer wall that dropped into a deep pool at one end of the chamber. The far end of the pool disappeared beneath a rock outcropping. "At least we won't go thirsty," Elijah said with some relief.

As they moved near the pool, bright flashes of yellow danced across the wall. "My God!" exclaimed Simon, "Just look at that!"

Embedded across the wall was a twenty-five-inch-wide vein of solid gold, encased between layers of white quartz. The vein seemed to extend nearly thirty feet across.

"I think we found the mother lode!" Elijah shouted, his excitement exploding.

"There's no telling how deep the vein is," Simon said. "No wonder we found all those gold nuggets beneath the falls. There must be several tons of pure gold in that seam!" His excitement was barely containable.

Like the Americans, the sight of gold made Santos gasp. "This must be one of the mines the Indians used to supply the gold for their temples and all the ornaments they wore."

A small stone altar, in the shape of a half pyramid, fashioned from white marble, rested in the middle of the room. A polished flat slab of similar marble served as the altar top. A brilliant block cube rested on it and measured at least one foot across on all sides, made of pure gold. The light from the torches caused the cube to transform into a golden radiance, splashing dazzling reflections across the walls. "I wonder what that thing weighs," Elijah pondered, as he gazed in awe at the golden object.

He walked to the altar and placed his arms around the block. With all his strength, he tried to lift it, only rotating it a couple of inches.

Santos shouted, "No, Elijah! That's not a good idea, it might be a trap."

His warning came too late. In seconds there was a large scraping and grinding noise deep within the walls and the unmistakable sound of something heavy shifting nearby. Well above the entrance that they had earlier ascended, a large slab of stone dropped from the ceiling and wedged tight into the rock ledge. It completely blocked the narrow stairwell and passageway back to the waterfall.

Santos froze. "We've got big trouble now," he said, looking at Elijah. "By moving that gold block you released the rock slab and blocked our way out. The early priests rigged it so no one would steal it."

Simon looked at Elijah with shock and consternation. "Dammit, why did you have to be so curious? Now you've done it. That block was counter-balanced and the weight transfer of the block was enough to trigger the bloody door."

Elijah sheepishly shrugged and held up his hands, "Sorry, I was just trying to see if I could lift it."

Quickly Santos and Simon hurried up the path where the slab was jammed into wall channels. They frantically tried to move it, but the slab was wedged tight. "Well, I sure hate to say it," Simon speculated, "but we have a big problem unless we can find another way out of here. It's ironic that we have all this gold and none of it can help us."

Everyone exchanged anxious glances. Rosita was terrified.

6.

"We're trapped in this hole and we're going to die like rats," Rosita said as her eyes roved frantically around the room.

"No, little sister," Santos reassured her, "the Indians wouldn't allow themselves to be trapped in here. There has to be another way out. Besides, they had to have an easy way to move the gold to the outside and the passageway we came through is too steep to transport heavy loads of gold."

Elijah looked around the cavern. "Let's split up and inspect the cave. Look for a small opening or a false wall."

They examined every inch of the walls and floor, even moving rocks in an effort to enlarge small crevices, but there were no signs of another exit. "We have to find a way out of here before our torches are used up," Santos warned. "We only have six left."

Simon was standing at a spot near the pool where it disappeared under a huge rock overhang. As he turned, he stumbled and fell over a large object. "Santos, Elijah," he shouted, "over here! I found something."

They rushed to where Simon was sprawled on the ground. He picked himself up and peered at the strange oblong-looking obstacle. It resembled a wooden dish with runners on the bottom and a round hole at one end. Dangling from the hole was a short remnant of decayed hemp that crumpled to dust at the slightest touch. Stacked nearby were three more of the strange objects.

"What do you suppose these were for?" Rosita asked.

Santos examined them closely, then took his torch and held it over the pool where it disappeared into the wall. "Look at this. The torch flame is fluttering away from that rock overhang, which means there has to be air movement blowing toward us."

He pondered the strange objects for a few moments. "I think I know what these things are. They have to be transport sleds. This cavern was also a mine where the Indians got their gold ore. You see the large vein of gold in the wall and remember the nuggets we found in the pool under the waterfall? They had to have an easy way to get the gold out. I think they used these sleds to transport the gold through the water to the outside pool. They would fill the wooden disks with gold ore and sink them in the pool, then tie a rope through the holes and a swimmer would unwind the rope under water. The workers could pull the sleds along the bottom and out through an opening under that wall. The air movement coming from under that overhang proves there must be air pockets and an underwater passage. I'm going into the water and see if I can find a passageway under that wall. If I make it through, I'll grab a coil of rope and swim back to get you. If I don't come back, you'll know I either drowned or couldn't make it back through the current. Either way, it beats staying here and dying of starvation in the dark."

Rosita hugged her brother tightly. "Don't do it, there has to be another way."

The young Mexican took both of her hands. "We've searched this whole cavern and there is just no other way out."

Santos waded into the stream, took several deep breaths and then disappeared under the swirling water. He found swimming with the current relatively easy, but when he reached a distance of about fifty feet, he pushed his hand toward the ceiling and touched solid rock. He kept probing the ceiling and finally found a space above the surface where he was able to push his head up and break through the water into a substantial air pocket. After several deep breaths, Santos dove back into the current. Now bathed in total darkness, he felt his way along the ceiling to avoid crashing blindly into a rock. He noticed a faint glimmer of light ahead and, with all of his strength, he clawed through the water and pushed upward. His hand broke through the surface and he emerged into a small room illuminated by a dim glow of light filtering in from under the water. *I must be near the outside.* As his eyes adjusted to his surroundings, he observed shallow ledges carved into the cavern wall. The sepulcher contained fragments of human skulls, bones, broken shards of pottery and decayed fragments of wood. *Is it possible some of the Toltec priests and nobles were buried here?*

Santos rested for a few moments and returned to the water, swimming in the direction of the light. The tunnel rapidly became brighter as he swam forward. A few more strokes and he broke through the surface and into the pool below the waterfall. He treaded water for a few moments while sucking the sweet tasting air into his starved lungs and then slowly paddled toward the bank. Santos was exhausted and lay on his back, resting for a few minutes before climbing out of the water and moving on to the cavern to retrieve the coil of rope he needed. "I have to make it back," he swore with steadfast determination.

Santos tied the rope to his waist, took several deep breaths, and dove under the falls. The current was manageable and the bottom relatively smooth, consisting of a layer of sand and pebbles. He was able to propel forward by walking along the bottom and pulling himself through the current with his arms. He felt the desperate need for air, but forcefully resisted the temptation to take a breath. When he felt his lungs would burst, he looked up and saw the air bubbles pooling on the surface and with a sudden burst of strength, he propelled his body upward to break into the small burial room. Santos rested and inhaled deep breaths of needed air. Doubts of making it back to the cavern entered his mind, but he shrugged them off and, with sheer willpower, dove back into the water. After what felt like an eternity, he desperately needed to take a breath. With all his strength, he propelled forward until it seemed his lungs would burst. The urge to let go was overwhelming, but Santos kept pushing until he reached the spot where he thought the air pocket was located. He stuck his hand toward the roof, felt the shallow pocket and thrust his head upward until his face broke through. "Madre mia," he gasped, as he gulped in deep breaths. Santos knew the last leg would be the most difficult, so he continued to breathe deeply, trying to build up enough lung capacity to press on.

The current was pushing against him, but despite the struggle, he made steady forward progress. Strange bursts of light flashed before him as he fought losing consciousness and avoided the urge to breathe. The pounding in his head was becoming unbearable. He swam with the weight of the rope dragging him downward. At last, just when he felt he was going to black out, Santos emerged through the wall and broke the surface into the cavern. He floated on his back, taking deep gasps of air. Simon jumped into the pool and grabbed him by the shoulders, pulling Santos to the bank. The young Mexican lay there wheezing and sucking in deep breaths of air.

Rosita rushed over crying. "Oh, Santos, we thought you had drowned."

He opened his eyes and gasped, "I didn't think I would make it through that last stretch. The current nearly got me. Swimming the other way is much easier."

Some of his strength slowly returned and he sat up. "I'm okay. Now let's talk about getting out of here. I'll tie the rope to one of the sleds and Simon and I will take the other end and swim to a small cavern I found halfway through the passage. Rosita, you sit on the sled, and Elijah can hold onto the back to help stabilize it while we pull you through to the cavern. The underwater passage comes out under the waterfall."

The two Americans nodded their understanding, but Rosita was not too sure. Santos tied the rope to the sturdiest sled and continued with his instructions. "There are two stops along the way. The first is an air pocket roughly fifty feet into the tunnel and the second stop an ancient burial room another fifty feet, not far from the waterfall. When we reach the burial room, I'll give three tugs of the rope, and you'll know we've arrived. We'll lash the packs and rifles to the sled and Rosita, you can sit on the sled facing forward. Elijah can hold onto the rear to steady it. When you are ready, give three tugs back and we'll start pulling you through the tunnel. Be sure to hold your breath and watch that you don't get the sled stuck or hit your heads on the ceiling. After about fifty feet, we'll stop pulling and you'll find an air pocket just above you. Stick your heads up into the pocket and take several breaths and when you're ready, give the rope three more tugs and we'll pull you on into the burial room."

"Got it," Elijah said."

"And you, little sister?"

Rosita looked frightened … she was not convinced. "Yes," she whispered.

Santos stretched the rope on the ground and began to pace off fifty feet. He tied a knot at this point to serve as a marker. After giving his sister a hug, he and Simon waded into the pool, took some deep breaths, and dove for the passage, unraveling the rope behind them. With strong strokes, they managed to move swiftly through the underwater entrance and into the tunnel. Santos looked up, tugged on his companion's arm, then pointed and broke into the shallow air pocket. After several deep gulps of air, they ducked underwater and continued swimming until they entered the burial room.

"We're not far from the falls now," Santos remarked between breaths. "The remainder of the passageway is fairly well illuminated. Now let's move over to the shallower water near the edge where we can stand, so we have enough leverage to pull the rope."

They found firm footing, and then Santos gave the rope three tugs, quickly answered by three return tugs from Elijah. Both men pulled the rope and could feel the slack tighten as the heavy weighted sled started to move through the water. Rosita and Elijah took deep breaths then held on tightly as the sled quickly sunk below the surface and glided through the entrance into the passageway. After a few long moments, the forward motion stopped and Elijah and Rosita swam upward into the air pocket. Santos had measured the marker knot accurately. They took several deep gulps of the trapped air, then dropped back to resume their ride.

Elijah gave the rope three sharp tugs and felt it propel forward. Suddenly they jarred to a sudden stop, throwing Rosita off the sled. Her eyes were wild with fear as she looked at Elijah in panic. He grabbed her by the shoulders and placed his hand over her mouth to calm her and prevent a sudden attempt to take a fatal breath. Elijah glanced down at the sled and saw that the right runner had jammed between two rocks. He held her hand tightly and pointed toward the rope. Elijah knew they had no time to dislodge the sled so he began to pull her through the tunnel. Santos had explained that the burial cavern was only a short distance from the air pocket so Elijah pointed upward and motioned for Rosita to grab the rope and pull forward. She turned and gave Elijah a look of desperation and despair—she needed air now or she would lose consciousness. He quickly pressed his mouth to hers and blew air as hard as he could. This expelled all the remaining air from his lungs—they had to move quickly.

The breath from Elijah revived her for the moment. They had to inhale fresh air within seconds or they would both die in this watery grave. Elijah grabbed the rope with one hand

and Rosita's waist with the other, and then pulled upward with all his might. With a final jerk, they miraculously broke through the surface into the burial chamber. Santos and Simon grabbed their arms and pulled them toward the water's edge. It took several moments of gasping and coughing before Rosita and Elijah could breathe normally again.

"My God," Simon asked, "what happened down there?"

"Sled got caught between two rocks. Ran out of air. Didn't have time to pull it loose," Elijah sputtered, still taking deep gasping breaths.

"How far back?" Simon asked.

"Maybe thirty feet."

"We need those packs and rifles." Santos reminded them. "I'll go back and retrieve the sled. When I give the rope a tug, both of you pull the rope with everything you got. Okay?"

Elijah nodded and Santos dove back into the pool and swam the short distance to the sled, using the rope to guide him. With some effort, he released the jammed runner and gave a sharp tug on the rope. The two Americans pulled and, within seconds, the sled reached the burial room. Rosita turned to Elijah and kissed him softly on the cheek. "Thank you for saving my life down there."

A warm feeling surged through his body as he felt her sweet breath touch his cheek.

Santos broke the spell. "Now we know how the Indians pulled the gold out of the mine. They filled the sleds with ore, and then pulled them along the sandy bottom through the tunnel."

"Wonder how many poor souls died in the process?" Elijah commented.

Glancing around the dimly lit room, Rosita remarked, "I see why you called this place the burial room; look at all the bones on those ledges. The Indians must have used this chamber to bury their high priests. It would be almost impossible to find. After we leave, it will probably remain hidden for another thousand years."

"The next part is easy," Santos reassured them. "Just follow the same procedure. The passage will be slightly illuminated because we're near the exit below the waterfall."

He re-coiled the rope and, with Simon following, submerged back into the pool. In a few moments, Elijah felt three tugs and responded with three in return. Once again, the sled plunged underwater and propelled toward the entrance. When the sled entered the deeper water under the falls, it dropped to the bottom like a rock. Elijah and Rosita let go and pushed themselves upward. When they broke the surface, two reassuring faces were waiting to pull them to the bank. Another stout tug of the rope pulled the sled to the surface and onto the sandy bank. They were relieved to find the packs and rifles, waterlogged but undamaged.

Simon was agitated. "Damn, that sled was sure heavy; the wood must be completely waterlogged." Then he noticed the extra baggage. "What the hell is that tied to the bottom?"

Elijah sheepishly untied two the small bags and opened them for Simon to see. They were full of gold nuggets.

"No wonder it felt like we were pulling a horse!" Simon shouted.

"Well, with all that gold lying around the cavern, I figured we needed to bring a few samples along. I couldn't just leave it there."

"Good Lord" Simon retorted, "That gold will add at least fifteen more pounds to our load. Glad we brought along two extra packhorses. Speaking of horses, we'd better check to make sure we still have them."

The group returned to the mouth of the cavern to find the horses and supplies undisturbed. Before eating and getting a good night's rest, they made sure the rifles were dried, cleaned, and loaded before turning in.

In the early morning glow of an approaching sunrise, Elijah awoke abruptly, sensing something was not right. He quickly woke the others. "I think I heard noises outside the cavern. It sounded like something shuffling on the rocks."

Gathering their rifles, the men moved cautiously towards the entrance and confronted an Indian, his face and body painted in wide black and yellow stripes of the Tuloupi. He had a fierce expression on his face as he raised his spear and emitted a shrill scream. The spear flew over Elijah's head, missing him by inches. An ear-splitting rifle report exploded and the Indian toppled backward, clutching his bloodstained chest. Santos had reacted quickly and shot the Indian squarely in the heart. Suddenly, six more screaming Tuloupis appeared from under the falls and through the cavern entrance. More shots rang out as Santos and the others fired. Three warriors quickly crumpled to the ground and the other three hurled over their fallen comrades and lunged for Santos and the two Americans.

Santos quickly dropped to a crouching position, causing the Indian to dive over him and slam heavily onto the rock floor. Simon and another Indian collided and toppled to the ground, punching and kicking with the savagery of two mountain lions. Elijah took a step backward and tripped, causing him to sprawl awkwardly on the ground, while the remaining attacker landed on top of him. Santos drove the rifle butt into his quarry's head, knocking him senseless, and then he ran over to help Simon. The Indian had his knife in hand and had raised his arm to drive it into the American when Santos dove and grabbed the arm just in time. He locked his wrists around the Indian's neck while Simon regained his footing. Simon kicked the Indian in the face, knocking out his front teeth, then grasped a large rock and slammed it into the warrior's head. The sound of crushed bone resounded as the warrior fell.

Meanwhile, the other Indian was getting the best of Elijah. He had him pinned to the ground with a stone axe poised to strike when a shot exploded from the rear of the room. The bullet struck the Indian above the right ear and hurled him over Elijah's prone figure and onto the floor. The axe glanced off the side of the American's head, leaving him with a severe bruise, but luckily, no skin was broken. The men glanced up to see Rosita standing behind them with a smoking rifle in her hand.

Santos nodded to his sister to acknowledge her intervention. "Looks like some of the Tuloupis decided to follow us after all and get revenge for killing Zapata. I'm surprised they would follow us this far into Toltec country though—they're supposed to be superstitious of spirits."

"Looks like that theory doesn't hold up," Simon grunted.

"They sure don't give up easily," Elijah added. "I hope we've seen the last of those devils."

"Let's hope so," Simon agreed. "It's time to get moving. This place is starting to give me the creeps anyway."

Packing their gear, the group quietly led the horses away from the falls and down to the river where they could pick up the trail westward. All four of them felt relief, mixed with anxiety. Maybe the old Mexican seaman was right about the ancient spirits. Perhaps they were angered after all.

7.

Once the four travelers reached the spot where the small stream from the falls joined the river, they picked up the trail that followed the riverbank. The river wound through rough terrain, forcing the party to dismount frequently and lead their horses across unstable or inaccessible sections of the path. As they journeyed further west, the terrain began to flatten out, transforming into gentle rolling hills. While the travel became easier, the vegetation was thick, more like the jungle they had passed through earlier. In the distance, the low coughing sounds of a nearby leopard and the distant cries of a thousand tropical birds broke the silence. Santos was leading the way when he turned to Simon. "We're now entering the land of the Toltecs and should start seeing signs of ruins soon."

Ahead, the path wound through a shallow copse of trees, then disappeared into dense vegetation. Sunlight filtered through the foliage, illuminating patches of ferns and flowers, creating a surreal glow of colors and textures. "This must be the home of the Toltec spirits," Rosita reflected. "It looks like a place where they could live."

The procession stopped in a small clearing for some needed rest and lunch. As they sat chewing on hard biscuits and dried venison, Santos moved over to a small tree and gathered several pieces of yellow fruit hanging from the limbs. With his knife, he sliced into one and passed a slice around to each of his companions. "Try this mango. You can't find anything like it in North America."

"It tastes different... sweet," Elijah said as he swallowed with satisfaction. "Why don't we take some with us?"

"They'll last a few days before spoiling," Rosita added.

Santos appeared to be in deep thought—he then turned to Simon and Elijah with an unusually serious look on his face. "There is something important I want to tell you. Unlike many other Americans I have met, you two appear to have an appreciation for our land and our history. I feel I can trust you, so let me share a story I once heard as a small boy."

He took a seat on a fallen log across from the others and hesitated for a moment to collect his thoughts. "Somewhere hidden in this vast jungle is a...lost city called Xepocotec. I did not tell you about it earlier because it remains hidden and is probably more legend than fact. Legend says the city was built in the third dynasty by an ancient Toltec king named Tialoc. Supposedly, he built it to honor his young and beautiful mistress, Xepocotec. Legend has it that she betrayed the king for another lover and stole much of his treasure of gold and gemstones. Her new lover was a trusted young officer in the king's royal guard. The king exacted revenge by killing everyone in the city, including the lover, whose head was chopped off. When the king caught the young girl hiding in the treasure room, he cut out her heart and ate it... raw."

Rosita looked queasy while Simon and Elijah remained riveted to the story. "Soon after, the king abandoned the city and left the treasure hidden behind, because he thought it was possessed with evil spirits. The city is located deep in the jungle and has never been found. Please understand that this legend has been handed down through many generations and no doubt altered into many versions. I have always doubted the part where the king had everyone in the city executed, and I doubt if the king would have killed his mistress. Another version of the story is that the inhabitants suddenly abandoned the city and were never seen again."

"Do you believe any of the legend?" Simon asked.

"I'm not sure. There is another more recent story of a man who claims to have stumbled on the city fifty or sixty years ago. He was a Mexican adventurer who spent most of his life exploring Toltec and Mayan ruins. Supposedly, he and one of his servants inadvertently discovered the lost city while traveling down a river deep in the jungle. The servant somehow died there, but the Mexican crawled out of the jungle days later, half-starved and nearly insane. Indians who lived in the area found him wandering about, raving about bars of pure gold and chests filled with precious gems. They say he even had a large polished diamond in his pocket, but the stone disappeared when he died and has never been seen again."

"Could this diamond be the Star of the Sun we heard about?" Simon asked with anxious excitement.

"Who knows what stories the Indians could have hatched from this," Santos answered. "I don't think the Star legend is real. The explorer died a short time later, having never revealed the city's location. I heard he died of jungle fever, but others say it was suicide. Some people must have believed the story because several groups of treasure hunters spent years searching in vain for the lost city. None of these expeditions ever found it, and most of the hunters never returned. I believe the city exists and is located somewhere in the jungle, but who knows? I also believe much of the treasure of the Toltec civilization remains there to this day. It would take a miracle to find the city, and still no one has proven that it actually exists."

Elijah excitedly responded, "This Toltec treasure you speak of makes the great Star of the Sun story sound like child's play. Maybe we should try to find the lost city instead of looking for the Star."

"As I said, I really doubt if such a gemstone even existed except in the minds of those adventurous souls who wished it to be true."

"In this lost city," Simon interjected, "if such a treasure actually exists, the gemstones alone would be worth a fortune. You said the man found the city by floating down a river. Do you know the rivers in this region?"

"I know of some, but this area has many rivers flowing deep into unexplored regions of the jungle. The story goes on to say the explorer spoke of a small lake with partial remains of a large stone tower nearby. The structure, if it actually existed, could have been a lookout tower to provide warning to the city's inhabitants of approaching enemies. It would also be a good landmark for finding the city, if it's still even standing."

Elijah jumped in. "This is easy. All we have to do is find a river that flows into a lake with a stone tower nearby within hundreds of miles of jungle. This should be a piece of cake for us. Just think of all the things we've been through over the past few days."

Simon, who had been deep in reflection, was now interested in a deeper evaluation of the legend. "Let's think this thing through like the old king would. If he built this city for his mistress, he would want her fairly close by—especially if he was an oversexed old bastard. Agree?"

There were a few nods and Rosita tried to contain a laugh.

Simon continued, his excitement growing as he spoke, "For him to build her a city and name it after her, she must have been a tigress in bed and drove him crazy for her affections. Now all we have to do is figure out where the old king might have lived and assume he would want her isolated, but easily accessible when he wanted to see her. Do you follow my reasoning so far?"

More nods of approval.

"I think we should also assume he would have used a river for access to his mistress since the story of the Mexican explorer specifically mentions a river and lake. Also, the jungle is mostly impassable."

Elijah encouraged his cousin, "You're leading to something!"

"Santos, what large Toltec or Mayan city was built in this region that might have been the home of the old king?" Simon asked.

Santos thought for a moment. "There are two larger cities where the king could have lived, one the city of Coba and the other, Chichen Itza. Both were cultural and economic centers for the ancient empires."

Elijah's mind was racing. "Which of these cities has a river nearby?"

Santos pondered for a moment. "A small river passes within a few miles west of Chichen Itza, but this would have taken the old king a great deal of time to travel there through the thick jungle. I've heard talk of a small river near Coba, but I have never seen it. There were stories of a canal dug by the Indians to connect the city with this river. If this is true, by now it would be dried up and covered with heavy jungle growth."

"How far apart are these cities?" Simon asked.

"Fifty, maybe sixty miles apart. We're about forty miles from Coba now."

"We may need to look at both," Simon concluded. "Let's try Coba first, since it's much closer. Maybe we can identify his palace from the ruins and perhaps we can find some ancient inscriptions that will give us a clue."

Without hesitation and in full agreement they packed their gear, mounted their horses, and headed toward the ruins of the ancient city of Coba.

The sun was setting as they approached a small stream-fed marsh. Santos led the way with the horses wading through what appeared to be a shallow crossing. The water was a chocolate brown color, indicating runoff from recent rains. As they approached midstream, there was a loud bellowing screech from one of the packhorses as he reared into the air and flipped over into the water. A huge black crocodile attacked the helpless animal, clamping his massive jaws into the horse's hindquarters. The croc, at least ten feet long, began shaking the animal violently.

Meanwhile, another reptile joined the melee and grabbed the horse by his neck. The crocs began tearing flesh from the animal, turning the muddy water to a frothy red. In the confusion, Rosita's horse reared up in fear, throwing her into the stream. Santos and Simon had made it to the other shore and Elijah was behind Rosita when the attack began. She was now up to her waist in water and wading to the shore. From the corner of his eye, Elijah noticed two more crocodiles sliding into the river, heading in her direction. "Rosita, hurry! Get to the bank!" he shouted.

The other two also saw the immediate threat and pulled their rifles from the saddle mounts. They began to fire at the approaching beasts. Elijah spurred his mount forward, grabbed Rosita by her left arm and began dragging her through the water. A heavy slug hit one of the reptiles in the head, causing blood to erupt into the water. The other croc, aroused by the smell of fresh blood, turned on the other stricken animal and tore into his underbelly with a vicious swirl. The bloody scene of four thrashing crocodilian monsters was a sight that horrified the group. "Try and save the packs!" Santos shouted.

The supply packs were torn from the animal's body. One sank while the other barely floated on the surface, fastened to the first pack by a thin leather strap.

Elijah pulled Rosita to the shore and dismounted. Weak from fear and exhaustion, she fell into his arms and held on with all her strength. Elijah held her tightly, relishing the warmth of her body.

"You're safe now," he said. "Let me help your brother retrieve the packs, you hold onto the horses."

She looked into his face with tears in her eyes. "You saved my life again."

"Remember, you saved mine when that Indian attacked me in the cave," Elijah reminded her.

Santos took his rope and tied a loop into one end to make a lasso. He threw the lasso toward the pack, but it fell short. He tried tossing it several more times, but it would not encircle the floating pack—he needed to snare it before it became water logged.

"The rope's too light and won't sink below the pack," Elijah called out. "We need to add some weight."

He rushed over to the bank and picked up two small stones that he fastened to each side of the loop with rawhide strips. "Try throwing the rope over the pack now."

His toss landed just above it, missing by inches and sliding to the side. On the third try, the loop encircled the pack and snagged it. He pulled the loop tight and began hauling the pack slowly toward the bank. The lighter pack was only a few feet from the bank when Elijah waded into the water, grabbed it, and carried it back to the shore, pulling the second submerged pack with it. He opened it and was relieved to find his two bags of gold nuggets still intact.

"Elijah, no wonder the pack was so damn heavy and sank!" Simon chided.

"Yeah. And if I'd known it was that pack I would have dived underwater to get it."

"And get your ass eaten by those crocs?" Simon said, shaking his head. "That damn gold is going to get us all killed yet.

"Don't you worry; I'll take good care of the gold."

"Did we lose anything?"

"We lost one of the spare rifles and some ammo and torches," Santos answered, "but we did save some of the bedrolls and food."

Simon was annoyed. "We'll have to leave the gold behind because our horses are loaded and the remaining packhorse can't carry much more weight."

"Hell no!" shouted Elijah.

"Suit yourself," exclaimed Simon, "but you'll have to carry it."

As they left the scene, the large crocodiles had pulled the decimated remains of the horse under water where they would jamb the carcass under a log or exposed roots for later consumption.

Santos turned to the Americans. "Now you have seen another kind of danger we face. The rivers and marshes are full of these scaly monsters and they are always hungry. They migrated up from the Amazon and now thrive in our rivers."

Simon turned to Santos. "When I was in school I read about man-eating fish that live in the Amazon. Do you have them in these rivers as well?"

Santos nodded. "They are called piranha or 'cannibal fish' and they attack in schools when they sense the smell of blood. I have a friend who lost his father to the piranha. He was hunting along a river in northern Brazil, close to the Amazon. He slipped, cut himself, dripped blood into the water, and was attacked by thousands of the killer fish. My friend said his father had all his flesh striped from his body in seconds."

"What a horrible way to die," Rosita remarked.

"The legend also mentions killer fish were placed in the lake near the lost city. The old king might have dumped them there for protection from outsiders."

For the next hour or so, the group rode silently, lost in their thoughts and the dangers that might lie ahead. Soon they found a suitable place and decided to camp for the night. They were exhausted and sleep came easily to the weary foursome who had almost become dinner for some hungry crocodiles.

The young southerner awoke early the next morning and found Santos missing, his bedroll already rolled up and strapped to his horse. Santos soon came walking into camp with several large birds hanging from a stick. "How about some roasted pigeon for breakfast?"

Elijah had prepared a fire, resulting in a good layer of hot coals, and a pot of coffee simmered. Santos sharpened some skewers, then cleaned and gutted the birds. He pushed the sharpened sticks through the breasts and placed them over the coals to roast. Simon chomped on the delicious pigeon meat and said," Santos, I'd like to hire you as a chef in the new café I might open when we get back to the States."

Santos laughed.

"Don't laugh Santos, I'm serious," Simon stated firmly.

After breakfast, they mounted and followed the trail as it wound through the deep jungle. The smell of rotting vegetation began to dissipate as the party reached higher terrain and drier, cooler air. It wasn't long before they were crossing a large plateau with jagged rocks and boulders protruding through the sandy soil. Simon shouted out as he pointed toward the south. "Let's check out these boulders and see if we can get our bearings."

They left the path, headed to the outcropping, and came to a large opening between the rocks. Having secured the horses, Santos walked over to the edge and peered into the space below. The view was breathtaking and totally unexpected. Confined in the small enclosed valley below, stood a magnificent pyramid and temple surrounded by other stone structures in various stages of decay.

"This must have been an outpost for the city of Coba," Santos suggested. "The pyramid and temple look to be pretty well preserved, although time has taken its toll on the outbuildings. This wall of boulders must have offered the warriors good protection during an attack."

Simon was excited to see his first set of ruins. "Since we're here, we should take a closer look at the buildings, especially the pyramid. No telling what we'll find down there."

There was no disagreement as they secured the horses in a well-hidden ravine and started down the narrow winding trail to the ruins.

8.

The path to the valley floor was steep and narrow. Santos held his sister's hand as they negotiated the loose, rough stones scattered along the path. Reaching the bottom, they ambled across the plaza, admiring the functional design and precision artisanship of the stonework. The same methods of construction were prevalent with the ancient tribes of Central America, including the great Inca builders of Peru. The most impressive feat was their ability to move huge, heavy stone blocks long distances, then lift them into place during the construction of their large pyramids and temples. Advanced for their day, the use of counterbalance weights, tackles, pulleys, and other weight compensating devices were common with the more advanced tribes.

However, the primary resource behind the construction and movement of blocks was the universal application of slave power. This was true in ancient Greece, Rome, Egypt, and other ancient civilizations. The great Indian builders were no different. Thousands of captured enemy warriors were enslaved and used in the building of the great cities of ancient Mexico.

Simon and Elijah stood transfixed as they gazed at the remains of this once beautiful town. It was one of many built by the powerful Toltec and Mayan empires. "I wonder what caused their downfall and disappearance." Elijah remarked.

Simon shook his head. "Just the normal rise and fall of civilizations, I guess—too much greed and self indulgence. C'mon, let's climb up and explore the temple."

"These ruins," Santos explained, "like those of Coba and Chichen Itza, have been explored by others, all searching for treasure and Indian artifacts. They have all been pretty well stripped of anything useful. Secret passages and hidden rooms lie deep within many of the pyramids, but we would have to be very lucky to gain access. The Indians used many clever tricks to conceal the entrances."

"But we've come this far, Santos," Simon pleaded. "Let's take a look anyway."

Santos explained how the ancients were expert at perfecting locks to entrances, blocking passageways and rooms deep within their structures. The secret to their locks was their knowledge of weights and balances to move heavy stones. "If you were to press a small stone inset into a wall," Santos said, "it would trigger sand or pebbles that would drop onto a larger balanced stone, creating a progression of movement of larger stones. When this process is completed, a large slab or panel can slide into a wall or drop from the ceiling to open or close a passageway. These ancient engineers also applied these same techniques to construct hidden traps for unwanted intruders, like us. This explains how the large slab dropped down to block the passageway back in the waterfall cave. When we enter the temples, we have to look for stones, handles, or any protrusions that might trigger an opening in a wall or floor. They will usually blend in with the background. In some cases, the trigger could be a small indention in the stone, or even a small stone within a stone that looks slightly out of place. It takes a sharp eye to spot these devices."

Holding their rifles firmly, they approached the massive steps leading to the pyramid. The recent attack by the Tuloupis taught them to keep their firearms close by and ready for use. Suddenly, Rosita pointed to the top of the plateau. "Look, we're being watched!"

High on the rim above, a lone figure stood motionless, watching them.

"I know of no hostile Indians in this area," Santos said as he gazed at the lonely figure above. "He may just be a harmless hunter who just stumbled on us."

"He's just standing there staring at us," Simon observed. "Maybe he's one of those Tuloupi devils who decided to follow us."

"I don't think so. The Tuloupis fear that evil spirits occupy the ruins and they usually stay away from them. From what I can see of his dress, he looks more Mexican than Indian."

At the blink of an eye, the figure vanished from sight. "He's either a lone hunter or a bandito looking to rob someone. Maybe he has friends with him," Santos said.

Elijah was apprehensive, "We left our horses and packs on top of the plateau. I sure would hate to see them stolen by a band of thieves or we'll be walking without any supplies. Santos, let's climb back and make sure they haven't been discovered."

The path was steep and the loose stones and gravel made the climb back much harder than the trip down. Relentlessly, they pushed their way upward, stopping halfway to catch their breath, and then proceeded on to the top, holding tight to their Spencers. Thankfully, the horses and baggage were still concealed where they had left them. At the boulder where they had spotted the figure, Santos observed, "See those tracks in the dirt. There were two horses here so maybe our observer friend was not alone. I see where they mounted and rode off."

"Maybe they were just hunters," Elijah surmised.

"Don't be naïve, my friend," Santos replied.

They walked back to the opening and descended the steep path to the courtyard. Simon and Rosita were waiting for them near the temple steps. "What did you find up there?"

"Tracks where two mounted horses rode off to the northwest. I don't think we should spend any more time here," Santos suggested. "Let's take a quick look at the temple, and then move our horses to a more secure campsite and on to Coba first thing in the morning."

The group gazed up at the pyramid steps and marveled at the majestic beauty of the temple perched at the summit. Winded, but exhilarated from the steep climb, they reached the top and stood on a small terraced walkway circumventing the entire structure. In front of the entrance sat a large carved block of stone that had a slight, hollow depression along the top. Santos recalled the words of a college history professor who had offered an explanation. "This stone is a sacrificial altar that was used by the priests for human sacrifice to their gods. They would lay their victims across the slab and drive ceremonial knives into their chests, then pull out their beating hearts, offering them up to the gods."

"How disgusting," Rosita gasped. "How could they do these things to their own people?"

Santos nodded sadly, "Many of the victims were enemy warriors, but some of those sacrificed were their own young women. A person's life was not worth too much to the early inhabitants of this land. They believed their sun god required human sacrifices in return for a good harvest, strong fertility, and prosperity for the empire."

In single file, they walked through the entrance and found themselves in a large room. Santos stood in the center and carefully looked at the surrounding walls. "Let's spread out and see if we can find anything that might trigger an opening into an inner chamber. Look for anything out of place or unusual."

Each of them carefully examined every square inch and found nothing that might lead to a secret passageway. Santos was becoming apprehensive. "I'm worried about the man who was watching us from the cliff," he said to the others. "It's best we leave here now and find a secure place to camp for the night. We'll be in Coba late tomorrow evening and from there we can look for the canal, and hopefully a river, that leads to the lost city of Xepocotec."

Eastern Outskirts of Mexico City

Major Juan Cordova was a small, slender man who sported a pointed moustache and sneaky, rodent-like eyes. Cordova was in command of the local military police district that oversaw the vast territories east of Mexico City, extending all the way to the Atlantic Ocean. For the past sixteen years, he had worked his way up to a post as commandant. He was the absolute law in the east and loved the power that it gave him. He used it ruthlessly. Both Indians and Mexicans who lived within his district were deathly afraid of Major Cordova.

Within his police district, and located far to the east, were the great unexplored lands of the Yucatan. Cordova was extremely ambitious and understood that the key to real power was money, a commodity he was severely lacking. If anyone needed a special favor, the major always expected a cash token of appreciation. If the amount did not meet his expectations, he was more than willing to convince clients to raise the stakes. He was certainly not one to trifle with, a fact not currently known to the American visitor who was standing outside his office.

Sergeant Perimez knocked on the major's door and waited patiently for the major to respond, then sheepishly opened the door and announced, "Sir, there is a gringo in the front room who insists on seeing you."

"What the hell does he want?" Cordova grumbled.

"Sir, I don't know, but he did say he has an interesting offer for you that may involve lots of money."

"Then show him in, Sergeant," Cordova said with a sarcastic smile and his interest aroused.

Harry Swartz was a heavy-set man in his mid-forties. Slightly balding and supporting an ample belly from years of beer drinking and fine cuisine, Swartz entered the room and stuck out his sweaty hand. Cordova limply returned the handshake.

"Major Cordova, my name is Harry Swartz and I come from New York City in the United States. Our Civil War has made it very difficult to travel here, but I managed to pay the right people to arrange transportation to come here and meet with you."

"I see," said Cordova, smelling the prospects of easy money. "What can I do for you, Mr. Swartz?"

"Have you ever heard of the lost city of Xepocotec, located in the Yucatan?"

Cordova was somewhat surprised. "Everyone has heard the legend of this lost city, but what is your interest here?"

Swartz tugged at his sweaty collar. "I am a collector and dealer of rare north and central American Indian artifacts. I specialize in items that are early empire, such as Toltec, Mayan, Aztec, and Inca. I have heard this lost city may contain many of these artifacts and gold items and gems, which could make us both a great deal of money. You have quite a reputation for getting things done and I know you would be an excellent partner to help me locate the hidden treasures, especially since you probably know that area very well. For your help, I am prepared to reward you handsomely."

The major noticed the fat American was sweating nervously. "The city is only a legend that has been passed down by the Indians for generations. How do you know it actually exists and how do you expect to find it if it does?" Cordova asked, his tone skeptical, his look almost mocking.

"I have done considerable and expensive research about the city. I know that an explorer once discovered it and described treasures of indescribable wealth. I also know of two American cavalry officers, strangely from opposite sides of our Civil War, who recently deserted their posts and stole a large army payroll to go in search of the lost city. My informants tell me they are in the Yucatan now, actually trying to locate the city. I have a man following them and he overheard them discussing the lost city just a few days ago at some minor ruins near Coba. It's possible they may even know the location of this Xepocotec."

Cordova's interest was piqued. He walked over to the window and clasped his hands behind his back. He thought about the exciting possibility of keeping the treasures of the lost city and disposing of Swartz and his party deep in the jungle. He could buy land, retire from this stinking police job, and be a very rich and respected man. "Mr. Swartz," he replied, "your proposal has my interest. What would you have me do to help you?"

"I need for you to provide men for our protection, including several Indian guides who can track down the two American soldiers I mentioned. We could also use your men to help us find and transport the treasure out of the jungle."

"When do we leave?" asked Cordova.

"My three associates and I will meet you the day after tomorrow here at your office. You will need to get your soldiers together and provide horses and most of your own supplies and equipment. I will supply our own mounts and some of the food and camp supplies."

The major readily agreed to the deal whereupon Swartz turned and left the office, mounted his horse, and promptly left for Mexico City.

"Sergeant Perimez," Cordova shouted, "come here quickly, we have some work to do!"

Juan Perimez, a bachelor and twenty-four year career soldier, idolized Cordova. He patronized the major and made sure he knew about anything suspicious in his command. Cordova rewarded this loyalty by making certain Perimez had an adequate supply of whores and tequila. Cordova smiled at his sergeant. "I want you to round up fifteen of our best men and have them equipped for an inspection tour of the Yucatan with enough food and supplies to last for at least thirty days. Send your best Indian interpreter immediately into central Yucatan and hire two of the very best guides you can find. Have them meet us in the town of Vasquez in five days. Make sure they are familiar with Coba and the surrounding jungle. I will explain more about the trip when we are underway."

Perimez saluted his boss and quickly left the office. Cordova still sat there, smiling and toying with his moustache.

9.

The morning's sunrise promised a hot and sticky day. Trees and scrub on one side and a sizeable limestone outcropping on the other sheltered the group's campsite. A clear spring trickled from beneath the boulders. Everyone, even the horses, enjoyed the cold, refreshing water.

"I don't think anyone saw us come in here but we can't be sure," Simon said, still troubled by the feeling of being followed. "That Mexican, Indian, or whoever he was, might have found us by accident, but I have a feeling there is more to this than we know."

"Let's eat quickly and head for Coba before the sun gets too high," Santos hastily suggested.

After a breakfast of cold corn tortillas, mango slices, and coffee, the group mounted and headed west toward Coba. Hidden in the trees nearby, the Mexican that Harry Swartz had hired, watched them file onto the path and resume their journey. When they were out of sight, he and his Indian companion climbed on their own mounts and followed, careful to stay far enough back to avoid being spotted.

"How much further to Coba?" Simon shouted to Santos, who rode in the front.

"About twenty miles. We should reach the ruins around dark. Soon, we will come to a fork and the trail to the left will take us to Coba. The right fork continues on to the northwest and would eventually end up in Mexico City. There are several villages along the way, inhabited mostly by Indians. To the south is nothing but unexplored jungle from here to Coba and beyond to the sea." The next three miles were uneventful as the party reached the fork and turned left toward the Coba ruins.

Not far behind, the Mexican, a man named Javez, turned to his Indian companion. "Tomas, I want you to ride to the village of Vasquez and contact a man named Rico Zara. You will find him in the local cantina. Tell him to contact Harry Swartz and instruct him that two Americans and a Mexican man and woman are traveling to Coba and will arrive there by evening. When you have given the message to Zara, meet me in Coba. Also, tell him to let Swartz know we will wait for him there. He should be on his way to Vasquez with some soldiers by now. Tell Zara to wait and accompany them to Coba. Do you understand all of this?"

With a brief nod, the young Indian took off for Vasquez at a brisk pace. Javez had met Harry Swartz in a bar in Mexico City and, after consuming a bottle of tequila at Swartz's expense, they struck up a unique friendship and consummated a business arrangement. Javez, an accomplished thief known for his clandestine dealings in smuggling artifacts, weapons, and almost anything involving a profit, agreed to travel to the Yucatan, pick up the Americans' trail, and follow them. Among the Indians and Mexican locals in the area, Javez had established an effective communication network of runners and informants. Swartz agreed to pay him a handsome sum for his services.

The ancient city of Coba appeared before the group of hopeful treasure hunters as they emerged from the dense jungle and crossed into the high plains country. The panorama was breathtaking, with a view of ancient structures stretched out in the distance. Santos explained, "Coba was once a Toltec and later a Mayan capital and one of their largest cultural, trading and religious centers in the empire. The city contains several temples dedicated to certain gods. The largest was the sun temple followed by the temple of the moon and so on. Even though many have explored these ruins, I still believe many secrets remain hidden here since the days of the Toltecs. The city is large and would take years to explore it thoroughly. The Indians consider the ruins a sacred place. They don't come here often."

"What happened to all the people?" Rosita asked. "How could a whole civilization disappear?"

"No one really knows. The Toltecs developed their civilization somewhere around the tenth century. They were a warlike tribe and referred to as the Great Builders. Many of these ancient cities were built by the Toltecs, but later occupied by the Mayan empire around the thirteenth century. The Mayans eventually absorbed the Toltecs into their own civilization. The Aztecs, and what remained of the Mayans, were the tribes living here when the Spanish General Cortez landed in Mexico. He and his conquistadors killed all the Indians they could. One of his most brutal lieutenants, Francisco Pizarro, killed and raped entire towns in search of gold. Later, he practically wiped out the Inca civilization in Peru. The Aztec, Maya and Incas were very advanced civilizations with huge armies, but unable to survive the Spanish guns and the deadly European germs spread by the invaders."

"Do you think there is any treasure hidden here in Coba?" Elijah asked.

"Perhaps the largest treasure of all lies in the lost city of Xepocotec."

"We can spend some time in Coba, but I think we would be better off looking for the lost city."

"I agree with Santos," Simon concurred. "We can always come back some other time and explore the temples here."

Santos nodded. "I say we find a sheltered place in the ruins that'll offer us protection from bad weather or stalkers that may be on our trail."

It did not take long to find a suitable hut on the outskirts of Coba, crumbling but serviceable. A small part of the roof was, miraculously, still in place.

Elijah stood up with his rifle. "Earlier, I heard sounds of wild pigs at the edge of the jungle. I'll try to bag us some fresh pork to roast for dinner."

He turned and disappeared into the fading light.

Javez moved silently through the underbrush, trying to maneuver within earshot of the group huddled around the fire. It was only two days ago he overheard one of the Americans talking about the lost city of Xepocotec. Could this lost city really exist? He wondered. He remembered stories from his father and grandfather about its hidden treasures. If he could overhear the gringos reveal the location, he would find the city for Mr. Swartz who might even give him a portion of the treasure. Javez knew Swartz was on his way to Coba with some Mexican authorities, but had no idea the officer accompanying him was Major Cordova. He knew of Cordova and his position as Mexican military officer in charge of the eastern territories, and was aware of the major's reputation, but had never actually met him. Had Javez known Cordova was coming, he would have warned Swartz of the danger he and his associates were facing.

Slowly, Javez inched his way through the underbrush, crouching low to get close enough to hear what the Americans were saying—he knew enough English to understand their conversation. Something was different. He only saw three figures sitting by the fire, yesterday he had seen four. As he shifted to get a better view, something cold pressed hard against his neck. Elijah pushed his boot against the Mexican's back and shoved him hard to the ground. "Make one move, Mexican, and I'll scatter your brains all over the ground. Get up and move slowly over to the fire."

Javez arose and Elijah grabbed the back of his collar and pressed the muzzle of his Spencer hard into his spine. The captive's first impulse was to run, but the American held him tightly by the collar, and would certainly shoot him if necessary. The group was startled as Elijah walked into the camp with Javez stumbling in front. "I found one of those wild pigs I told you about, but not the kind you eat. He was lurking in the bushes trying to hear what you were saying. I thought I saw him following us yesterday and expected this rat might sneak up on us."

Santos gave Javez a hard stare. "He's the same one who was watching us yesterday. His clothes are the same."

Santos demanded, "Who are you and why are you following us?"

Javez nervously shuffled his feet and gazed at the ground. "I was lost and just trying to follow you to the nearest village."

"He's lying," Santos said to the others. "I know some tricks that will make him talk. In the morning we'll get the rope and carry him to the top of the pyramid, meanwhile I'll tie him to the tree for the night."

"What's your name?" Elijah shouted in English.

"My name is Javez and I am only a poor farmer from the town of Vasquez."

"Well, we know he speaks and understands English," Simon said.

"Don't lie to us, Javez. Why you are following us?" Elijah persisted.

The Mexican just glared at them. Santos jerked Javez to his feet and, securing both his arms, they shoved him to the closest tree and bound him tightly to the trunk.

The next morning Santos arose to find the prisoner staring at him with a look of hate and despair. The men had taken turns checking on him throughout the night. Now it was time for some answers. With Elijah and Simon holding his arms, Javez, kicking and tugging, was dragged to the base of the pyramid and up the long flight of steps to the narrow terrace surrounding the temple. Protruding above the stone altar was a large stone-carved snakehead and slender serpent's body jutting out over a pool below. Santos faced Javez somberly. "If you'll look below the snake head, you'll see a recess in the pyramid wall that drops over a hundred feet into the pool. That's where the remains of human sacrifices were once tossed."

Javez was terrified.

Santos took his rope and tossed one end over the serpent's body and, with the Americans holding his feet, tied the other end securely around the captive's ankles. "Now ease him over the side," Santos instructed, "and we'll let him hang upside down for a few minutes. This will loosen his tongue!"

Santos removed a small can from his pocket and rubbed some black sticky resin on a section of the rope and the same substance on the end of a long stick. He touched a match to the end of the torch and watched it burst into flame. The panicky Mexican, dangling perilously above the pool, glared at the flame. Santos was losing his patience. "Now, tell us why you were following us."

The Mexican squirmed and twisted, but said nothing. Santos took the torch, ignited the black resin and shouted to the thrashing figure, "Javez, you have about two minutes before the rope burns through and you plunge into the pool below. All you have to do is tell why you are following us and I'll pull you back and you'll live to see tomorrow."

The Mexican now started screaming and rambling. "I won't tell you American pigs anything. You'll never find the treasure of Xepocotec. It belongs to my friend and me. You'll die here before you find the treasure."

"For the last time, who sent you here?" Santos demanded.

"Go to hell!" screamed the Mexican.

"Don't be a fool, tell us the truth, you only have a few seconds left," shouted Santos.

Looking up at the flames eating through the rope, the Mexican completely lost his nerve and screamed. "Okay, I'll tell you. A group of Mexican soldiers and Amer…"

He never finished the sentence. At that instant, the fire burned through the rope and with arms flailing, he plunged to his watery grave.

Elijah stared down into the void. "Crazy bastard could have saved himself. Now we know why he was following us. Sounds like a party of Mexican soldiers and some Americans are hot on our tail. They're probably searching for the lost city, too, and think we know where it is."

Vasquez, Mexico

Tomas reached the little town of Vasquez and asked several locals the whereabouts of the man called Rico Zara. A shopkeeper told him to check the local saloon. "Zara spends most of his time there."

The young Indian went to the saloon and entered the double doors into an interior smelling of sweat, cheap liquor, and cigar smoke. He awkwardly approached the bar and asked the fleshy bartender where he could find Zara. With a look of disgust, he shouted at Tomas, "Indians aren't allowed in here! Get the hell out, now!"

"I have a message from Javez," Tomas quietly replied. "Mr. Zara is expecting me."

The barkeeper hesitated, and then pointed over to a corner table. "He's the ugly bastard with his back to the wall. The one in the green shirt."

Tomas casually walked over to the table where a dark skinned man was sitting by himself. "Mr. Zara?"

"Yeah, that's me. Whatcha' want, Indian?"

"Javez sent me with a message for you and Mr. Swartz."

Rico Zara was a suspicious looking character with long black hair and a heavy drooping moustache. His pock-marked face and cold eyes gave his face a perpetually fierce look. Zara had ventured into some illegal smuggling operations with Javez and had access to an ample supply of messenger runners.

"Let's go outside," Zara said, "so we can talk more privately."

As they walked into the street, Tomas explained, "Javez told me to tell you to contact a man named Harry Swartz and tell him the Americans have gone to Coba. I am to return and meet him there. He also said you will guide Swartz and the soldiers to Coba where we'll wait for you."

"Okay," Zara replied. "They have to pass through Vasquez so I'll lead them on to Coba. I expect them to arrive day after tomorrow. How will we find you?"

"Don't worry, I'll find you."

Zara dismissed the young messenger and returned to the saloon. Tomas, glad to be finished with the intimidating Mexican, mounted his pony and hastily made his way back to the trail to Coba. He felt a bit more comfortable with the town of Vasquez behind him. Had Zara known of his real identity, there would be big trouble.

East of Mexico City

Harry Swartz, unaccustomed to the heat, was sweating profusely and was most uncomfortable as he bounced along the rough trail on his mount. Major Cordova enjoyed watching the fat, balding American squirming in his saddle. As planned, Swartz and his three accomplices met Cordova at his station and they all left in the early hours of morning. Swartz's three companions were also uncomfortable, but uncomplaining.

Swartz's American associates were more concerned with the discovery of ancient artifacts than the monetary value of the actual treasure itself. Their focus was the historic and scientific value of the antiquities they hoped to find. Robert Drake was an anthropologist from Harvard University with a Ph.D. in the subject. He specialized in early Indian studies. Austin Cain, a noted archeologist who hailed from New York University, was a Ph.D specializing in early Indian cultures, specifically those in Mexico and Central America. Both men were promised a considerable sum of money and perhaps a small percentage of the treasure itself to accompany Swartz. Their primary purpose was to set up an excavation plan and catalog historic artifacts found with the treasure. The third accomplice was Juan Zapata, who worked for the Mexican government. He specialized in Indian artifacts for the Mexico City Museum. It was his duty to make sure his government received their required share of seventy-five percent of any native artifacts found. Being a loyal Mexican nationalist, he strongly believed anything found in Mexico belonged to the Mexican government. He was also not above taking a small portion of gold for himself, which he felt would be an appropriate compensation for trekking through a stinking jungle with these Americans. Zapata certainly did not intend to allow any Mexican treasure to be carted off to America. He felt he could rely on Major Cordova and his soldiers to help him preserve all of the treasure for Mexico. Unfortunately, he did not know the major very well.

Swartz, on the other hand, did not intend to allow any of the treasure to fall into the Mexican government's hands, or anyone else's except the twenty percent share he had offered Cordova to do the dirty work for him. He was confident he could arrange a tragic accident for Zapata at the right time. Like Cordova, Swartz was a greedy, ruthless man who would stop at nothing to enhance his personal wealth.

10.

The next morning, Santos killed a small pig that had wandered near their encampment. The pleasant aroma of fresh roasted pork sizzling over hot coals awoke the others who soon joined Santos for breakfast.

"I'm worried about what Javez told us," Santos confided. "Our pursuers probably know we are in Coba…"

Simon agreed. "More reason to keep moving. You said there was a river near Coba, but so far, we haven't seen any river. We need to think what old King Tialoc would have done to protect his mistress from unwanted suitors. I think it's safe to assume he'd want to be close to her or very accessible to where she lived. He would also want her protected day and night , most likely guarded by his priests and a special security detachment living in a chamber inside the temple."

Elijah added, "He'd also want to be able to get to her quickly, and the fastest route would be by boat or raft. Unless the river flowed close by, the Indians probably built a connecting canal near his palace. I think we should look for either a small tributary or a man-made canal leading to the river."

Simon asked Santos, "Do you know where the king's palace might have been located?"

"I would guess in the southwest part of the city facing the rising sun and at a point closest to the river. If we can find it, we should be able to locate the canal or river. His palace would probably be in an elaborate building located on top of a pyramid. We should also search the outer perimeter and see if we can find a dock or pier large enough to tie up the king's boats."

Elijah and Rosita moved across the plaza to the west while Santos and Simon searched toward the southeast. Their plan was to work their way toward the city's perimeter and converge toward the center of the arc. They examined every building—several structures looked like they might have been suited for a king, but were eliminated under closer examination. Elijah turned to Rosita, "We need to move further out of the city toward the jungle."

Santos and Simon were searching the southern perimeter when they heard Elijah shouting in the distance. They moved toward the sound of his voice and saw him and Rosita standing on top of a large terrace. They were waving and pointing at something toward the southwest. Standing like a majestic sentinel overlooking the city stood the most magnificent pyramid, stretching toward the clouds. Surely, this must be the king's palace, Santos concluded. They hurried across the open plaza and through several streets until they stood at the base. Each of the four travelers felt a rush of exhilaration as they gazed at the ascending stone steps leading up to a magnificent edifice occupying the summit. "My God!" Elijah exclaimed, "Have you ever seen anything like that?"

The climb was steep and strenuous and required several rest stops before they finally made it to the top. Before them lay a stunning panoramic view of the city and the endless jungle stretching beyond. Looking toward the southwest, the group could see a large terraced field, ending with a boundary of dense jungle foliage. The most notable features were two parallel rows of stone columns marking the outline and remains of a sunken paved road. Simon gazed at the columns. "It looks like they follow the road and that road must have been mighty important to someone who saw fit to define it with stone columns. Let's take a closer look."

Descending the long flight of steps, they made their way to the line of columns.

The pillars were smooth and fashioned of granite. "Examine each column and look for any signs of an inscription or marking that might give us a clue to a river," Simon suggested. Twelve sets of the crumbling pillars, amply spaced, marked the boundary of the roadway, but none revealed any significant markings.

"Wonder where it goes?" Elijah questioned. "Looks like the road just disappears into the jungle."

They followed the old track until it stopped abruptly at a wide stone terrace bordering a circular dry lagoon about six to eight feet deep. Time and weather had reduced the surrounding retaining walls to crumbling stone, but it was evident the blocks had once reinforced the entire circular enclosure. With the water long gone, the depression was now only a bed of soil and overgrown weeds and vines. The walls extended at right angles then continued around the enclosure and disappeared into the dense underbrush. Santos smiled at the two Americans. "I am certain this is the beginning of our canal. This area looks like the wharf where the king's boats would tie up. Now all we have to do is follow the old canal bed until it runs into a river."

"So our theory was right after all," Simon said, grinning with satisfaction.

The excitement was infectious as the group returned to their camp to gather the supplies they would need. The horses would be left behind and the extra equipment hidden somewhere in the ruins. A well-concealed spot was located that once could have served as a multi-dwelling site. From small saplings, Santos hastily constructed a wooden enclosure around a grassy terrace and nearby spring, then herded the horses inside the makeshift structure. With everything secured, the travelers headed back to the stone wharf.

Although the ancient canal bed was not easy to distinguish, except for the wide depression in the ground, it was easy enough to visualize the channel being flooded to accommodate a royal barge. On both sides of the canal was ample evidence of the crumbling stone retaining walls that had once held the canal in place. The trek through the thick undergrowth was not easy and the foursome had to use their machetes to hack through vines and dense foliage. Then, after what seemed like an eternity, the canal bed suddenly widened. The walls ended and overgrown banks replaced them, fanning out in right angles to the canal. "This had to be the spot where the canal once emptied into the river," Santos said.

"But where is the river?" Rosita asked.

The old riverbed was completely obstructed by dense vines, roots and foliage. Perplexed, the group stood there looking for answers when suddenly it dawned on Santos.

"The canal fed its way into the river at this spot, but after seven or eight centuries, the river has undoubtedly changed its flow and direction. This is the original bed where the king would have entered the river from the canal on his way to the lost city. I think if we follow this dry riverbed, we should hit the course of the new river."

The Outskirts of Coba

Tomas cautiously returned to Coba in search of his Mexican companion, Javez. He dismounted, climbed a large Banyan tree and perched on a limb looking out over the great ruins. He saw no sign of any movement, so he entered the city, looking for his friend. He found hoof prints and boot tracks, but no sign of life. As he crept through the city, he had a strange feeling he was being watched by evil spirits, and broke into a nervous sweat. He came to a great pyramid within the center of the city and saw tracks where men had dragged something to the base of the steps. Cautiously, he climbed the steps to the summit and walked around the narrow stone terrace. He passed the altar and looked down at the sunken pool far below, then glanced up and saw the outstretched snake sculpture protruding from the wall. He bent over, picked up a small piece of blackened rope and sniffed it, but he did not understand the meaning.

Descending the steps, the young Indian moved further into the ruins, following the boot tracks and crushed grass. Suddenly he stopped, certain he heard the high-pitched neigh of a horse. He moved in the direction of the sound and found tracks leading toward a group of crumbling buildings. Behind the ruins, he found the small corral filled with horses grazing on patches of grass and weeds. He recognized the sorrel belonging to Javez—his companion had to be somewhere nearby. He crept further into the city. Then, the footprints split and went off in different directions. He could only make out four sets of prints, two in each direction, and tried to remember how many people were in the American group.

Reaching the point where they split up, Tomas followed the two sets of faint prints that led toward the southeast. As the prints reached the stone walkways and terraces, they would disappear and he would have to search carefully to pick them up again. He finally came to the huge pyramid at the very edge of the city and thought this must surely be the home of the ancient spirits. His courage wavered, but he continued his search for more tracks. On the far side of the pyramid, he noticed tracks leading in the direction of the rows of crumbling columns.

The footprints disappeared as he reached the stones of the sunken road. Tomas hesitated, kneeled down to examine the worn paving blocks, and then stayed on the path until it abruptly ended in front of a crumbling wall surrounding the depression from the ancient canal. Looking into the depression, he picked up the tracks again. They headed straight into the heavy undergrowth and the jungle beyond.

The Village of Vasquez

To the north, Swartz, Cordova, and the rest of their party arrived in the village of Vasquez. Their first stop was the local saloon where they would have tequila or a beer and prepare for the trip to Coba. Rico Zara had greeted the group on the outskirts of town and escorted them into the bar after getting their baggage moved to the small and dilapidated hotel.

Swartz took one look at the accommodations and gasped, "I have to sleep in this place? What a stinking dump."

Although the accommodations were not up to his usual standards, it was the only hotel in town and was a little better than sleeping in the street.

Zara advised Cordova and Swartz of the current situation. "Javez sent word that the Americans and their guides are in Coba. He is there now spying on the Americans and trying to learn what they know about the location of the lost city. We're to meet him in Coba."

With a scowl, Cordova glared at Zara. "Can we trust this Javez?"

"I've worked with Javez for years. He has always been reliable. He won't double-cross us."

Cordova grunted and grabbed a bottle of tequila and took a long gulp. *We'll see about that. Just another body I'll have to dispose of.*

Swartz, who had been relatively silent up to now, offered a suggestion. "I think we should leave early in the morning, go straight to Coba and find the Americans. I'm sure the good major knows a few ways to make these thieves talk when we catch them."

With an ice-cold look in his eyes, Cordova calmly nodded. "I know plenty of ways to make these American pigs talk. This is my specialty. They will be begging to tell us the location of the lost city and, once I get the information, their bodies will be neatly disposed of and lost forever in the jungle."

Early the next morning, Swartz, Zara, Cordova, and the others secured their gear and headed for Coba. Reaching the outskirts of town, one of Cordova's soldiers abruptly turned his horse around and headed back toward Cordova who was riding at the rear of the column.

"Major," the soldier cried out, "you didn't tell us we were going to the ruins to look for a lost city. The spirits of our ancestors haunt the ruins and I cannot go there. Coba is an evil place and we will never return alive. I wish to resign and return to Vasquez."

Cordova screamed at him, "You damn coward, no one deserts my command! Get back in line, you worthless pig!"

The sweating soldier refused to turn his mount around. The major calmly pulled his revolver from his holster and aimed it between the soldier's eyes. With no hesitation, the major pulled the trigger. With a loud report, the .40 caliber slug punched a neat hole through his forehead, causing the back of his skull to explode. The heavy impact lifted the man out of his saddle and slammed him into the underbrush along the side of the path. Cordova commanded Sergeant Perimez to retrieve the man's weapons and horse. Although terrified, the column moved out, leaving the body beside the roadside where it fell.

Swartz now knew he had picked a cold-blooded killer as a partner and he could not be trusted. He also understood as soon as they found the lost city, his life and the life of his colleagues would be in great danger. He would have to figure out a way to eliminate the major, but first he would have to find some way to frighten his men off, if that were possible. He knew Cordova's soldiers were superstitious and deathly afraid of the major. Given the right opportunity, some might welcome the chance to desert. Swartz worried it would take all of his resources and cunning to outsmart the major and his men. He would have to talk to his two associates and devise a plan. Meanwhile, he needed to remain calm and get along with the major—the treasure and his life depended on it.

South of Coba, Santos, Rosita, and the two Americans slowly made their way along the old riverbed, hacking vines and thick underbrush. They seemed to be making very little progress when Santos finally spoke up. "Be on the lookout for a very deadly pit viper called the bushmaster. One bite will give you about thirty seconds before you die a horrible death. It is a copper-colored snake with black stripes. You notice all the bamboo stalks along the old riverbed. That's where the bushmaster lives and breeds so be sure and look down before you take a step."

They had hiked a little over a mile when the old riverbed started bending to the right, revealing nothing but heavy vegetation, vines, roots and bamboo stalks. Their progress was slow and tiring, but they kept moving slowly forward. Suddenly Santos held up his arm and shouted, "Stop! Don't move! In front of you!"

Elijah looked down to see the five-foot bushmaster coiled and ready to strike. He froze, terrified to move a muscle. All his senses told him to run, but he knew one slight movement could be the end of him. Santos cocked his arm and tossed his machete with all his might. The side of the blade hit the snake and knocked it back about three feet out of its coiled position. Both Americans raised their rifles and fired at the same time. One bullet struck the snake in the side and the other delivered the mortal wound to the base of the head. The snake thrashed about for a few seconds, and then finally lay still. Elijah stood frozen to the spot. "My God," he gasped, with a feeble smile directed toward Santos, "I didn't even see the damn thing! That was too close for comfort. I hate snakes!"

They continued forward for another two hundred yards when Simon stopped them. "Do you hear that?" he shouted.

"No...what?" Elijah answered.

"The sound of running water."

They cut their way through more underbrush until they came to a small clearing and walked out on the bank of a narrow, dull-brown colored river. Santo grinned at the Americans. "Well, amigos, I think this could be the river we've been looking for...and the way to the lost city."

11.

The river was nearly sixty feet wide and flowed with a relatively mild current. Through the passing centuries, the path of the river had moved farther to the south from where it originally flowed when old King Tialoc ruled the province. Santos considered the options. If the river has shifted this far from its earlier location, was it possible that it also moved away from the lost city of Xepocotec?

They would just have to follow the river and find out the hard way.

"How are we going to travel down the river without a boat?" Rosita questioned her brother.

"We'll build a raft out of bamboo stalks. We cut the larger stalks and fasten them together with some of my rope and sections of vines and another layer for our deck. The bamboo stalks are hollow—they make a light and sturdy raft."

"Santos, you're a genius," Simon said.

Santos nodded and laughed. "Of course. Now take your machetes and cut about twenty of the largest stalks you can find, about twelve feet and we can pile the logs here. Rosita and I will cut vines and strips of cypress then, I will show you how to lash the bamboo together. Remember to watch out for the snakes!"

Elijah and Simon walked over to the nearest bamboo thicket and began hacking at the largest stalks. Some were huge, measuring at least eight inches in diameter. Santos and Rosita selected several strong and flexible vines and began peeling and splicing them together as well as a few cypress saplings for the smaller lashings. For added strength, Santos used rope to bind the platforms together. The work was slow and difficult—thicker stalks were lashed together side-by-side and formed the base of the raft. The remaining bamboo was cut into ten-foot lengths and for added strength, fastened together crosswise to the base to form the deck section. With both layers assembled, the positioning and fastening of the sections, with a combination of rope and braided cypress strips, did not take long to complete. The raft appeared strong enough and could easily carry four adults and supplies. Next, Elijah cut four bamboo poles long enough to reach the river bottom. The poles would propel and guide the raft through any rough water. The final knots were completed and the raft was ready to push into the river. Simon stood back, admiring their handiwork. "Not bad. She looks like a seaworthy enough craft. Let's name her the Xepocotec, after the Indian maiden we're chasing."

"How romantic," Elijah chuckled sarcastically.

The large hollow bamboo logs kept the raft floating high on the surface. They loaded the gear in the center then Santos helped Rosita aboard, followed by the Americans. Santos took one of the bamboo poles and pushed the raft from the shore.

"The big question is which way do we go?" Elijah wondered. "We need to think like the king and what he would have done if he wanted to see his mistress."

"Sounds reasonable," Simon acknowledged.

"If I were the king I would head downstream," Elijah continued. "The old man would want to see his mistress quickly, not spend a lot of time paddling the boat upstream against the current. He would save that task for the trip back home."

"Sounds logical," Simon concurred. "Santos, do you agree?"

"Yes, let's go downstream."

The raft maneuvered easily as it picked up the downstream current. Santos stood at the front and watched the overgrown banks pass slowly by. "I have some concern about the change in the river," he said. "We saw how much it changed its course over the years and now it might bypass the lost city. If this is the case, we may never find it. Remember, the legend mentioned a large stone tower standing at the entrance. If we can just find that tower, we'll find our city."

"What if the old tower was undermined by the river current and covered up with jungle?" Elijah asked.

"Then we have a problem," Santos concluded. "We'll have to look for the remains which may be just a pile of rocks. The city was likely no more than a day or two from Coba. However, within that span is five or six hundred square miles of jungle."

The conversation ceased as everyone pondered the situation. Simon was thinking out loud when he murmured, "The lake..."

"What did you say?" Elijah asked.

"I said the lost lake. The key is the lake the old Mexican explorer was raving about. Over a long period, a moving river will alter its course several times, changing its banks and direction. A slow circulating lake is a different matter. A lake doesn't move very much. It's possible this river still flows into the same lake with the stone tower, but just from a different direction. I'll bet if we just stay on this river, it'll take us to the lake or close to it."

"And if we find the lake, we find the watch tower and entrance to the city. Right?"

"That's the idea."

Along the riverbanks, they could hear loud and distinct animal and bird sounds. The jungle was alive with noise. High in the trees a group of spider monkeys chattered and chased each other recklessly through the canopy. Exotic birds seemed to be everywhere. Rosita spotted a toucan and then saw a pair of rainbow-colored macaws soaring across the sky with their long tails fluttering behind. Also high in the sky, they could see the unmistakable V formations of early migrating geese and ducks returning south—they had used this flyway for thousands of seasons.

The raft rounded a bend and came to a large sandbar jutting from the bank. Lying in the warmth of the sun were five large crocodiles, slightly smaller than the huge black caimans they had encountered earlier. Two of the big reptiles sensed the movement of the raft, popped their eyes open and silently slid off the bar into the river. The men gently lifted the poles from the water allowing the raft to float by the bar with scarcely a ripple. Santos reached into a small bag and removed a piece of pig jerky. He heaved it away to the far bank. The splash stopped the forward motion of the reptiles, as they altered their course and headed for the new disturbance. One of the crocs attacked the jerky with a violent crash and began to roll around, with his mighty tail thrashing and stirring up a torrent of frothy water. The second croc quickly drifted toward the first one and found he was too late for his portion of dinner. The raft moved on around the bend and safely away from the hungry reptiles. Rosita heaved a very audible sigh of relief.

The sun was sinking fast and Santos thought it best to stop. "It will be dark soon and we need to find a spot to make camp. We also need to check the lashings on the raft—we don't want it to start unraveling in the middle of the river."

Farther downstream, they found a high and level place to set up camp for the night. After a light meal of pig jerky boiled with a combination of tasteless jungle greens that Santos had gathered, the group sat lazily around the fire contemplating their next move.

"We now know that we're being followed," Simon said. "That Mexican likely has an accomplice who told our pursuers where we're headed. I think it's safe to assume that they know we went to Coba. They're probably there now and I'm sure they would have found the horses. If they recognized the sorrel belonging to Javez, they might think he's still following us or that we're holding him captive. Maybe they found his body floating in the pool. In any case, you can bet they are turning Coba upside down to find us."

Elijah added, "I agree with everything you've said, Simon. They know we're looking for the lost city, but the question is, do you think they know we were looking for this river?"

Santos added his logic. "If I were trying to find someone in the jungle, I'd hire the best scouts in the Yucatan. A good scout would find the canal bed and discover our tracks. He would follow them through the dry riverbed to this river. We have to assume that the Americans, or whoever they are, heard the same story about the lake and the stone tower. For all we know, they could be building rafts as we speak."

"Then we better hurry," Elijah interjected. "We need to find Xepocotec as fast as possible. Darned good thing we have the Spencer rifles. I have a hunch they're going to come in handy real soon."

Outskirts of Coba

A few miles to the north, Swartz, Cordova, and their band were approaching the outskirts of Coba. Cordova shouted at Rico Zara, "Where is this Javez friend of yours?"

"We didn't have a particular spot to meet him," Zara countered. "We'll just have to wait until he finds us. We need him."

Cordova screamed back, "This is ridiculous! We don't have time to wait until this idiot finds us. For all we know the Americans have found the lost city while we're sitting on our behinds waiting for some peasant who may have already joined them."

"Javez would not do that," Zara responded.

"We shall see," spat Cordova.

Cordova called for Sergeant Perimez. "Sergeant, divide the men into four search parties and find that Mexican or traces of the Americans. I want some answers now or, by God, I'll have some heads!"

The sergeant saluted and left to gather the men. With each group assigned a different section of the city, they quickly dispersed. Swartz and his three associates took the center of the city and started searching the buildings and temples close by. It did not take long for one group to discover the corral and horses. Rico Zara quickly identified the sorrel as the one belonging to Javez. Cordova was getting impatient. "Where are the Americans?" he shouted.

"Our two guides are trying to pick up their tracks now," Perimez answered. "They're the best trackers in this area so they should find something soon."

No sooner had the sergeant finished his sentence, one of the Indian scouts trotted up, pointed to a large pyramid in the distance and mumbled something in his native language. Another scout who spoke several native dialects was the designated interpreter for the group.

"He found several boot tracks near the pyramid. He wants us to come."

They hurried to the pyramid and found the Indian scout kneeling and pointing to the ground. He had located several sets of boot tracks leading to the steps of the pyramid. "The guide says the tracks show that one man was dragged between two others and forced up the steps of the pyramid."

Cordova started the long climb up the steps with the others close behind. Halfway to the summit Swartz had to stop to catch his breath. He thought he might pass out. At the summit, Cordova and the others searched through the small building and found nothing. They looked around the structure and peered over the edge to the pool far below. The major spotted a small round object floating on the surface of the pool and shouted to his sergeant, "I want a man to go down there and retrieve that thing in the water."

Perimez turned to one of the soldiers and shouted instructions. The soldier dashed down the steps as fast as he could, Perimez following him. The soldier reached the pool, removed his clothes and swam to the object. He quickly retrieved it and returned to the shore where he handed it to the sergeant who painfully climbed back up the steps and handed it to the major. The object was a cheap straw brim hat, the kind worn by Mexican farmers and peasants. Inside the band were the initials JS. Cordova looked at the inscription, then squarely at Rico Zara. "Now we know where your Mexican friend went—to the bottom of this pool."

Along the Xepocotec River

The sturdy raft continued its journey down river, floating within a few feet of a large mangrove thicket. The exposed roots extended well above the waterline giving an illusion the trees were slowly creeping along the shore. As the raft passed under the limbs, Simon unconsciously reached up to grab a long green vine hanging limply from a branch. Santos saw the movement and lunged forward, knocking Simon over the edge into the water. The vine fell from the limb and began thrashing and rolling about. Santos sprang like a leopard. He grabbed his machete and swung the blade, cutting the slithering "vine" neatly in two. The upper part kept thrashing and striking at the air. It lashed out at a supply pack and buried its short fangs into canvas. Santos took another swing of his blade and the viper's head flew from the body and fell off into the water. Elijah helped Simon, shaken and soaked, back onto the raft. "What the hell was that all about?" Simon asked.

"You nearly grabbed one of the most deadly tree vipers in the world, a poisonous parrot snake. One bite from him would have killed you very quickly. Simon, you have to watch what you reach for in this jungle. It could be the last thing you ever do."

Elijah could not refrain from remarking. "Looks like you hate the slimy bastards as much as I do."

Simon just glared at him.

Santos explained, "The parrot snake lives in trees and its green color makes them almost impossible to see in the leaves. They are just as deadly as the bushmaster. Another snake to avoid is the fer-de-lance, also a member of the pit viper family. I must warn you again to watch what you touch and where you step."

A much shaken Simon said, "Yes, sir," and added, "Thanks for saving my life."

"Ningun problema," Santos replied. "I'm just glad I saw it in time."

Elijah turned to Santos, "I wonder how far we've gone? Don't you think we should have found the lake by now? We must have traveled about fifteen, twenty miles…"

"The old king wouldn't have built the city too far from his home in Coba," Santos reminded them.

Simon suddenly remarked, "I think I know where the lake is." He pointed toward the southeast. "Over there…"

"How do you know?" Elijah retorted.

"Because It's getting late in the day and I saw flocks of geese and ducks dropping down in that direction. They prefer calmer water, so they must be flying into a lake."

Around the next curve, they came to a section where the river split into two channels. Simon considered the options. "Let's take the right fork. That seems to head in the direction where I saw the birds go down."

With poles in hand, they maneuvered the raft into the right fork, continued to drift southeast, and noticed the slope of the land starting to descend lightly. This caused a discernable increase in the current's speed. They could see churning water ahead and saw large rocks rising above the surface. Santos shouted, "Get the poles ready to repel us from the rocks. This raft could break up if we hit one broadside."

They were fast approaching a large dull-gray boulder. Elijah and Santos braced for the impact then pushed off with their poles while Rosita propelled against another rock on the opposite side. The small craft made a complete turn and miraculously slid by the boulder, avoiding the anticipated collision. Barely grazing another rock, the vessel rotated again and shot through a chute of rolling water and finally into a calmer section. The worst was over and the raft came through unscathed. The shaken occupants sat back in relief, catching their breath. They had entered a small sheltered lake.

12.

The lake was placid and reflected a burst of orange and lavender hues from the setting sun. In the fading light, Santos saw a heavy layer of roots and ferns bordering dark overgrown banks, making it increasingly difficult to obtain bearings on their position. He gazed at the shoreline and rejected the idea of finding a safe campsite on the shore. "I think the safest place to sleep tonight is on the raft. We can move it near the shore and tie up to a tree. Our dinner will be jerky again and a couple of the mangos we have in the packs."

Elijah grumbled to himself, "I'd give anything for some fried chicken."

They lowered the poles into the water and found it too deep to reach the bottom. Santos pulled his shovel from his pack and dipped it into the water as a paddle. It was slow moving, but the raft finally drifted to the bank. They made the raft as comfortable as possible, and after some shifting and grumbling, finally drifted off into an unnerving sleep. Jungle noises in the night were loud and constant. The shrieks of jungle cats on their nightly hunts filled the air along with the cries from monkeys and owls. Occasionally, they would detect a splash from a hungry crocodile sliding into the water searching for a meal of fish or small animals that were drinking along the banks. There was always anxiety that a snake might crawl onto the raft or that a croc would try to overturn it.

Morning came quickly as Elijah stood up and stretched. Every muscle seemed to be aching. "Do you suppose this is the lake the old Mexican described?"

"It sure fits the description of the story," Santos replied. "If we find the stone watchtower, we'll know we are in the right lake."

They were quick to realize the raft was immobile in the deeper water, thus it was evident that the first order of business was to construct some paddles. Thick bamboo groves lined the bank, and along with the dense vegetation, much of the shoreline was impassable. Luckily, a few hundred yards further, Santos spotted an area where the foliage was thinner and they were able to maneuver the raft over to the spot and fasten it to a nearby fallen tree trunk.

Santos handed Rosita a rifle and told her to stay with the raft while he and Elijah went to gather some bamboo.

Elijah picked up his Spencer and machete and followed him into the thicket. Rosita felt the sudden urge to relieve herself. She stepped onto shore and found a small clearing nearby surrounded by dense vegetation. There was no way she could have recognized anything unusual about the low depression in the ground covered with leaves and debris. Suddenly, Rosita was sinking up to her knees in mud and water. She tried to pull her feet out, but each attempt made her sink deeper. She had walked into quicksand, and with muck up to her thighs, she was sinking deeper—the suction held her tight. In panic, Rosita let out a piercing scream that went ringing through the jungle.

Simon was closest to the raft, gathering vines, when he heard Rosita's cries. He hurried through the vegetation as Santos and Elijah dropped the stalks and ran back to the raft. Rosita was not far from the raft and easy to find. Simon broke through the bushes and managed to avoid the quicksand by grabbing a limb. Seconds later, Santos and Elijah burst through the bushes, but the southerner's momentum carried him to the edge of the bog and up to his knees in the sticky sand. A few feet away Rosita thrashed about, having now sunk to her waist. Santos grabbed Elijah's outstretched arms and pulled him back toward the bushes. The quicksand released him and he was able to step onto solid ground.

Rosita was out of reach, sobbing and screaming. Santos shouted, "Rosita, calm down and don't move! It just makes it worse. We'll get you out. Just don't move!"

The sound of her brother's voice stopped her screams for the moment. "I'm going to cut a sapling for you to hold onto while we pull you out. Just don't move your feet."

Rosita nodded and quieted down, although she had now sunk to her chest. Santos grabbed his machete and began to hack at a small sapling near the edge of the clearing. He left a few trimmed branches she could use for handgrips. The pole reached Rosita with room to spare. "Grab the pole and use the branches as grips," he ordered. "Hold on tight and don't wiggle your feet."

The quicksand had now reached her armpits. Rosita's tired arms grabbed hold of the sturdy limbs. "Hurry!" she cried desperately.

Santos and Simon pulled slowly on the sapling while Rosita hung on for dear life. They could not move her. Elijah latched on and together the men pulled with all their might, sensing some forward motion. The girl thought her limbs were being pulled apart, but she held on tightly. The quicksand had now reached Rosita's shoulders. The rough wood cut into her hands, and through sheer effort, she willed herself to hang on. They continued pulling and Rosita felt the suction slowly easing and the sticky sand relinquishing its deadly hold. There was more movement forward as her body eased toward the bank. Finally, the ooze released her and the men pulled her out. She grabbed her brother and held him tightly as the tears streaked her mud-covered face. Elijah could not help but notice the outline of her beautiful profile even though covered with a thick layer of mud. Santos led his sister back onto the raft. She began washing the mud off by holding onto the side of the raft and splashing herself with the warm lake water. Simon stayed with Rosita while Santos and Elijah went back to the bamboo grove to gather the stalks.

The bamboo was thick, but easy to cut with the machetes. Four stalks were trimmed, split, and the sections lashed together to resemble makeshift paddles. Though crude, they worked quite well, allowing the small raft to maneuver in the deeper water with greater mobility.

As the raft slowly drifted along the bank, Simon turned to Santos. "I'm impressed that you know so much about this area and the ancient tribes of Mexico."

"I think I mentioned to you earlier in the cave, where we picked up the Spencer rifles, I studied history while in college in New Orleans. I had a special interest in early native cultures. I wanted to learn all I could about the history of my ancestors. Now, can I ask you a question?"

Simon nodded.

"You and your friend fought on different sides of your war yet you are here together looking for the lost city. Isn't that somewhat strange?"

Simon smiled. "The fact is we are of the same blood. Elijah is a distant cousin. We met on a battlefield and decided we didn't want to fight each other so we left together and traveled to the Cayman Islands and then to Mexico. I suppose our armies would call it desertion, but the war was almost over anyway. We've talked about going back if we can come up with a convincing story. We hope our armies have given us up for dead or missing-in-action and we pray the war will be over when we return. I guess we could change identities if we have to. It depends on whether we find the lost city and treasure." Simon's voice was tinged with pessimism. They had already had too many near-death experiences—how long could their luck hold out.

"Don't worry," Santos assured him, "your secret is safe with me. Somewhere along this bank, we just might find the remains of a stone tower. If the tower has fallen, it will be covered with jungle growth and hard to spot. I believe the Mexican explorer told the Indians the tower was sitting at the end of a small finger of land jutting out into the lake. This would have given the sentries a better view of the approaches from both sides of the lake. We need to find that finger of land, although it may have eroded away by now."

As they continued to paddle slowly around the edge of the lake until they saw a small protrusion of land. They hacked their way about a hundred feet inland, but did not find any traces of stone blocks or the remains of any structure. Back aboard the raft, they continued paddling along the shoreline, eventually approaching a small creek emptying out of the jungle into the lake. Suddenly, the silence was shattered with the loud flutter and splashing of flapping wings from frightened blue-winged teals. They arose from the water in flight and took to the sky right over their heads. Rosita cried out as the sudden noise of beating wings made them duck with startled reflexes. Elijah shouted, "Wow, this place is getting us all spooked!"

Simon grinned. "Those ducks came up from that creek bed and I think I saw something else up there. Let's go check it out."

As they approached the mouth of the creek, they noticed square, gray objects protruding from the shallows. Santos stepped into the water and sloshed a few steps toward the bank. Half buried in the creek bottom were four smooth-shaped square stones with their corners protruding above the waterline. Santos ran his fingers along the smooth sides. "These are man-made. They could be stones from the tower!"

The men fanned out along the shore hoping to find more evidence of a tower. Soon other similar stones appeared. Near the creek, they came to a pile of large crumbling blocks scattered around a base of larger foundation stones. Simon and Santos nodded at each other. They had found the remains of the watchtower.

"Now, let's think where the city would have been," Simon said. "If the king came here by boat, he must have had a convenient place to dock closer to the city. He would either have anchored it along the lakeshore or taken it up a canal that connects the city to the lake."

Elijah surmised, "If they placed this watchtower here to keep an eye out for enemies, wouldn't that mean the city would have been further inland from the lake? The canal idea sounds more feasible. The question is where is it?

"We have to assume it's probably dried up and overgrown like the one at Coba," Santos reminded him.

Rosita, silent up to now, carefully scrutinized their surroundings. "If they built a canal from the lake to the city, wouldn't they have wanted it to flow by this watchtower so they would know who was floating up to the city? Surely, there were enough enemies around."

The three men looked at Rosita with stunned expressions as the answer hit them at the same time. "Of course, it has to be the creek. The creek bed must be an old canal," Simon shouted excitedly.

They pulled the raft well up into the stream and covered it with branches. Gathering all of their equipment, they began the slow trek up the shallow streambed. Santos warned, "Watch for snakes and crocodiles. This looks like a perfect place for them."

After wading for about thirty feet, Elijah pointed to the right bank. "Over there! I see some stacked blocks."

Some of the blocks were stacked five and six feet tall. Elijah used his machete to hack away some of the vegetation revealing the unmistakable remains of a retaining wall that had once held the canal in place. Much of the original wall was crumbling away, replaced by eroded dirt and jungle growth.

"The entrance to the lost city should be at the end of this creek," Santos suggested. "Let's be careful and keep our rifles ready—no telling what we'll find ahead."

The Ruins of Coba

Far to the north in Coba, Cordova and Swartz were frantically searching through the ruins looking for signs of the Americans. They had found the horses, so they knew they could not be too far away. The major was becoming more frustrated and agitated as the search continued. He screamed at Sergeant Perimez, "What's wrong with those worthless Indian scouts you hired? If they can't track any better than this then get rid of them."

Swartz overheard Cordova's ranting and raving and decided the major was crazy, and it became more urgent that he figure a way to get rid of him.

Approaching from across the plaza, two of Cordova's soldiers escorted a young Indian toward him and Swartz. They stopped in front of the major and one spoke. "Sir, we found this Indian boy on top of a pyramid hiding in a small room in the temple. He says his name is Tomas and a companion of the man called Javez."

The major looked scornfully at Tomas. "Where is your friend and why were you hiding from us?"

Tomas hesitated, then regained his courage and replied, "I am looking for Javez myself. I was supposed to meet him here in Coba. He came here to keep an eye on the Americans while I went to Vasquez to find Mr. Zara and tell him to meet us here."

"Why were you hiding, boy?" spat out the major.

"I thought you were the Americans returning. I hid in the temple so I could follow them."

"Where did the Americans go?" Swartz asked.

"I followed their tracks to the edge of the ruins where they disappeared into the jungle."

The major looked at his sergeant then turned back to the lad. "Take us there and I might spare your life."

Perimez sent three soldiers out to round up the rest of the party. The major was satisfied Tomas was telling the truth when Rico Zara identified him as the Indian who had brought him the message from Javez. Within minutes, Tomas was guiding them through the ruins toward the magnificent pyramid of the former Toltec king. When they reached the outskirts of the city, Professor Drake turned to Swartz, "This temple is a fine example of pre-Mayan construction. We need to explore it and look for hidden passages."

Swartz was about to agree with Drake when Cordova shouted to Tomas, "Take us to the tracks that go into the jungle!"

Tomas led them around the base of the pyramid to the sunken road with its decaying columns and along the road until it ended at the stone wharf. The first thing noticeable were footprints in the sand that trailed off into the dense jungle. Cordova hid his excitement as he turned to his sergeant. "Prepare our men for a trek into the jungle for a few days. The Americans are now within our grasp."

13.

Washington, D.C., September 1864

Secretary of War Edwin Stanton sat in his office, deep in thought as he looked out the window at the falling rain. He was sipping a cup of faintly warm coffee. His mood was as dreary as the weather. The war was still dragging on and there seemed to be no end to the infernal madness. The huge casualty reports kept piling in and the Union losses in Virginia were staggering. Stanton worried that General Grant was a madman. He kept shoving men into the front lines.

A knock on the door interrupted his thoughts as a young aide entered. "Sir, there is a General Caleb Kirby here to see you. He says it's quite urgent."

"Show the general in, Lieutenant." *More casualty figures,* he thought.

Brigadier General Kirby stood erect as he saluted Stanton, and then he spoke. "Sir, I am with the First Michigan Cavalry. I hate to disturb you, sir, but I have something that I feel is quite urgent to the war effort."

"Yes, General, please have a seat. Would you like a cup of coffee?" Stanton asked.

"No, sir, I think I drank at least two gallons of coffee on the train." Kirby paused to take a deep breath. "Mr. Secretary," Kirby began, "do you recall a report about a Captain Simon Murphy from the First Michigan Cavalry, who disappeared early this year with a large Union payroll of gold coins?"

Stanton's tired look brightened a bit. "I do remember the incident because of the loss of a large gold payroll and the unusual name of the place where he encountered some Confederate Cavalry. Blackberry Creek was it, over in west Tennessee?"

"That's right, sir, except the correct name was Cockelberry Creek. The report stated the captain was thought to have been captured or killed, although his body was never found."

Stanton gazed out the window. "What's so important about this incident to bring you here?"

"Sir, we have information that leads us to believe he is still alive and in Mexico, accompanied by a deserted Confederate officer, looking for a treasure of indescribable wealth."

This last remark got Stanton's attention fast. "General, are you telling me Captain Murphy deserted his command with an army payroll and disappeared into Mexico with a Confederate officer?"

"Yes, sir. As bizarre as that sounds, it seems to be the case."

"I'm curious, General, how were you able to obtain such information?"

"Well, Mr. Secretary, as you may know, with the war coming to a conclusion, several high ranking Confederate officers have escaped into Mexico and other South American countries to avoid being captured. We have spies at key entry points who keep us informed. Recently, two Americans were seen landing at a small fishing village called Puerto

Muerta on the east coast of Yucatan. Our young Indian friend has been following them for the past several days. He was able to identify one as our Captain Murphy and the other a Confederate officer named Elijah Walker. There is an old legend that speaks of an ancient lost Toltec city that supposedly contains a hidden treasure of gold and jewels that could far surpass all the wealth in our U.S. Treasury. The report also says the two men may have identified the location of the city."

Stanton was skeptical as he tried to absorb this startling information.

"And there is more, sir. The army has an agent assigned to keep an eye on a particular New York-based Indian artifacts dealer named Harry Swartz. It seems Mr. Swartz also deals in arms smuggling and we suspect he has been smuggling U.S. Army Springfield rifles to the Confederates in Virginia. Over week ago, Swartz suddenly left New York for Mexico City where he is reportedly tailing the two Americans who are looking for Xepocotec, the lost city."

"Very interesting Colonel," Stanton remarked, "I've heard of this man, Swartz."

Kirby continued. "Two American scientists and a Mexican major named Cordova, with a complement of soldiers, accompany Swartz. Our intelligence says they are currently pursuing Murphy and Walker somewhere in the Yucatan Peninsula. This Cordova character has quite a ruthless reputation. Another problem is that the story has been leaked to the public. Murphy and Walker have now become quite the folk heroes, especially in the South. The Confederate government in Richmond thinks they are trying to find the treasure for the Confederacy to enable them to purchase arms from England and France and continue the war. Of course, if this were true, which I somehow doubt, it would make Murphy a despicable traitor. I personally think they are looking for the treasure only for themselves."

Secretary Stanton thought for a moment, and then said, "Quite an interesting situation indeed. What do you suggest we do, General?"

"Sir, I think we should send a party of special agents down there to locate them and direct us to this lost city. There is probably enough gold and precious gems in this treasure cache to fund the entire war effort."

Stanton stood up and smiled. "General, I believe you have something here. Let's go talk to the President."

President Lincoln was in a rare jovial mood when Secretary Stanton and General Kirby entered his office. After the introductions were concluded, the President offered Kirby a seat. "General, I wish to commend you and the rest of our western Army for your fine work. You now control the Mississippi River and the Port of New Orleans. The South, in the western theater, is cut off from their capital in Richmond. We might just be able to finish this big mess if we can bring Bobby Lee to bear in Virginia. For the first time, we now have General Grant running the Army of the Potomac. A general, I might add, who is not afraid to take the fight to General Lee. But I know you didn't come here to talk military strategy, so tell me what's on your mind."

General Kirby carefully explained the situation to the President and offered a possible solution. "Sir, if we send some highly skilled agents down to Mexico to coordinate with Murphy, we should be able to secure a vast amount of treasure that would essentially pay for our entire war debt.

This wealth would also pay for much of the expense necessary for rebuilding the devastated South. Politically, it will certainly look good to your voters, both in the North and eventually in the South. We could also capture this weapons smuggler, Harry Swartz, and put him out of commission for good."

President Lincoln was thoughtful for a moment. Stanton seemed quite nervous. "General Kirby, do you actually believe such a city and treasure exists?" Lincoln asked.

"Sir, we have reliable information that Murphy was overheard talking about the treasure and the general whereabouts of the lost city. There was also a report of a Mexican adventurer who actually visited the city many years ago, but died a madman when he returned from the jungle. No one to this day knows its exact location. Yes, Mr. President, I think the city and its treasures actually exist somewhere down there in the jungle, and I suspect Murphy is on to it."

The President went over to the window in deep contemplation, carefully stroking his beard. "What will the Mexican government say about our taking treasure from their soil? I know I would never allow the Mexican government to take a lost treasure from our land."

"Mr. President, I would not be too concerned about any reaction from the Mexican government. After all, it was less than eighteen years ago we fought Mexico over Texas and annexed the entire southwest, including California, from them. Many of our present officers, and Confederate officers as well, fought in that war. Besides, the lost city of Xepocotec remains a legend, a myth, and nobody, including the Mexican government, even believes it exists. Our sources tell us Murphy and Walker somehow found the information about its actual location and are on the way there now. They were last reported heading for the ancient ruins of Coba in central Yucatan. The lost city would be somewhere in the dense jungle of the Yucatan that remains largely unexplored to this day. Chances are, our party could land on the east coast and travel west to the Coba ruins and never be noticed by anyone."

The President turned to his Secretary of War and asked, "Mr. Stanton, who do we have at our disposal in the midst of this war, someone who could manage such an undertaking?"

"Mr. President, we do have the perfect man highly suited to organize this expedition. You know him well. He's our head of Secret Service, Allan Pinkerton. He also has some excellent agents who speak Spanish and have some familiarity with the area."

President Lincoln looked down at the two men standing before him. "Gentlemen, Allan Pinkerton is a good choice. He saved me from an assassination plot in Baltimore. I owe a great deal to him for his faithful services to our country and to me personally. Mr. Stanton, I will suggest you contact Pinkerton and set this affair in motion. For you, General Kirby, I would like you to accompany the party to Mexico and act as my personal representative to make certain this wild venture is a success. I know we can rely on you to keep me and the secretary informed of your progress."

Abraham Lincoln then reached into a cupboard beneath his credenza and pulled out three small cordials and a bottle of 1813 French Voliere brandy. He poured each a generous portion and raised his glass in a toast. "Gentlemen, let's drink to newfound wealth for our nation and a quick end to this accursed war."

"To success and the end of this war. Hear, Hear!"

The President hesitated for a moment, then raised his glass and drained it. "By the way, General, if our Captain Murphy is cooperative and helps us to achieve our mission and secure the treasure, you are to escort him home as a hero and offer him a five percent share of the treasure. You can also bring along his accomplice, Captain Walker, and we just might forgive his choice of armies and reward him as well. General Kirby, one more thought, if you please. If our good captain has trouble believing our benevolence in light of his traitorous actions, tell him he has the solemn word of his President."

Allan Pinkerton sat with one of his chief agents reviewing maps of the Carolinas. They had been discussing the undercover work of a secret agent planted within the state government of North Carolina. An aide knocked on the door and announced the arrival of the Secretary of War and a General Kirby. Pinkerton dismissed the agent and aide and stood up to greet his unexpected guests. After brief introductions, Stanton and Kirby provided Pinkerton with a full summary of the Murphy-Walker affair and asked him to recommend a team for the expedition.

"A very interesting proposition, gentlemen," Pinkerton responded, after a brief moment to absorb the wild story he had just been told. "I do have an agent who would be perfect for the mission. How many agents would you need?"

Kirby answered, "I believe we need four of your agents, plus me. The President has assigned me to lead the party as his personal representative."

"I see," Pinkerton responded. "The agent I have in mind is Nathan Dorn, a very capable man who speaks fluent Spanish. Nat is currently with our army down in northern Virginia, but I can get him back to Washington quickly. I also have a second agent in mind, but first I want to ask Nat his recommendations for the other two. General, if you'll meet me in my office Friday morning, I'll have the group assembled for briefing."

"Thank you, Mr. Pinkerton, your help is most appreciated."

As the Secretary of War and General Kirby prepared to depart, Stanton turned to Kirby and asked, "General, is there anything else I can do to help you with this mission?"

"Well, yes, Mr. Secretary, there is one more thing. Could you contact the Secretary of the Navy and arrange for a fast frigate to transport us down to the east coast of the Yucatan?"

Kirby had a couple of days to kill in Washington before Pinkerton could recall Agent Dorn and the others from northern Virginia. Despite the war raging close in nearby Virginia, Washington was a busy and vibrant city, full of good cafes and pretty girls—and it was great to be away from the war itself. While his units had fought well against a very tenacious Confederate Army of the Mississippi, the outcome was inevitable with the constant flow of new troops and war materials flowing in from the north. With the loss of the Mississippi River, the Confederacy was split in half and most of the key areas in Mississippi, Louisiana and Alabama were under Union control. It was just a matter of time before the overwhelming industrial strength of the North would end this war.

With General Grant in full command of the Army of the Potomac, the Confederates would now be confronting a very different and determined commander. Lee may have had his chance to conclude the war at Gettysburg, but the Union victory and Confederate retreat from northern soil had completely altered the course of the war.

General Caleb Kirby was sick of war and actually looked forward to the adventure into Mexico.

Kirby took most of his meals at the old Burlington House where he resided while in Washington. The house boasted of their long-time cook, Mrs. Louise Parker, who could spread a meal as good, if not better, than most of the chefs in Washington. Her roast beef with potato dumplings and apple pie were well known throughout the district. General Kirby could not justify dining in the fancy restaurants when he had Mrs. Parker to feed him.

At eight o'clock on Friday morning, Kirby was waiting in the anteroom of Allan Pinkerton's office. An aide met and ushered him into the office where Pinkerton and four men gathered around a small rectangular table. They were studying a map of Mexico and the Yucatan Peninsula. Pinkerton stood up to greet the general and introduced him to the others. Kirby and Agent Nathan Dorn sized each other up and seemed to hit it off well enough. Dorn then introduced the other three agents and briefly outlined their special talents and background. Agents Cunningham, Morris, and Stephens had all experienced war service and were well qualified for this dangerous undertaking. Agent Morris asked, "General, how much opposition can we expect from this Mexican officer and the smuggler, Swartz?"

Kirby nodded. "Swartz is traveling with three associates. Two of them are scientists and the other a representative of the Mexican government. There is also a small contingency of about fifteen to twenty Mexican soldiers commanded by a Major Cordova. The major is reported to be a corrupt, ruthless, and greedy bastard who would sell his mother for ten pesos. We suspect his troops have great fear of him and will probably escape if given the opportunity. I think he'll be our biggest problem."

"How about Captain Murphy and his accomplice?" Agent Cunningham asked. "Would they be willing to join us or resist us as another party of hunters after the treasure?"

"We'll have to cross that bridge when we come to it." Kirby paused thoughtfully. "By offering Captain Murphy a pardon and a hero's welcome home, I'm hoping he'll join forces with us. After all, the President has authorized me to award them enough of the treasure to provide them with a life of comfort. Also, if they happen to have the stolen military payroll hidden somewhere, they are welcome to keep it without any strings attached, after a brief court of inquiry, of course. We have no idea what happened to it and I doubt if they'll tell us anyway. It won't even be an issue unless we have to bring them back for trial and prosecute them for desertion and theft. As you can see, they will have a great deal of incentive to join us. Our government's primary interest is the treasure cache to help pay for this expensive war."

"I have concerns about his Confederate friend," Dorn responded. "Won't he consider us an enemy and put up resistance?"

"The war is almost over and I imagine his Confederate associate will be more than happy to take an oath of allegiance to the United States and come back as a productive and wealthy citizen. Again, we'll just have to wait and see."

Allan Pinkerton interrupted, "Secretary Stanton was kind enough to contact the Navy who has supplied a frigate waiting to transport your party to the Yucatan. It's called Talisman and carries a crew of twenty-one sailors and eight medium cannons. The captain's name is Herman Potter, who has at least twenty years of sea duty under his belt. The good secretary has also seen fit to secure the weapons and supplies you'll need, including everything on the list General Kirby gave him. Everything will be on board when you depart from the Potomac River wharf."

"Thank you, Mr. Pinkerton," Kirby said.

"By the way," Pinkerton added, "each of you will be armed with a new rifle made by the Spencer Repeating Rifle Company of Boston. This new rifle shoots a .52 caliber bullet housed in a copper casing, the most powerful cartridge issued to our army so far. We've been experimenting with it and believe the new design will revolutionize the weapons industry. The army will be purchasing over ten thousand of these rifles over the next few weeks. The western cavalry units have reported most satisfactory results so far. I was informed, however, that a few weeks ago a band of Apaches stole some of the rifles from our armory at Fort Defiance in the Arizona Territories."

"I sure hope they don't find their way to the Mexican army," Kirby speculated.

"I doubt if the Apaches would let the Mexicans have them without one hell of a fight," Pinkerton responded. These weapons should give you better than even odds against any hostiles you might encounter, including Cordova's Mexican soldiers, who still use single-shot muskets. You're to guard these rifles carefully because we cannot afford to have them fall into the hands of Confederate arms designers, although at this late stage of the war I doubt if it would do them any good." Pinkerton's agents all nodded their agreement. Then he turned to Kirby.

"There's a lot at stake with this mission, General. Should any misfortune happen to you, God forbid, Agent Dorn will be second in command. We have a friendly guide in the small coastal village of Tulum. He'll guide you to the ruins of Coba and from there help you locate the lost city. His name is Juan Sanchez. He should be able to pick up the tracks from Murphy's group and those of Cordova. As soon as he delivers you to your destination, his job is finished. Our sources have also requisitioned another agent, whom I believe you may be aware of, who will contact you somewhere near the town of Vasquez enroute to the Coba ruins."

As the group exited Pinkerton's office, General Kirby heard him say, "Gentlemen, good luck to you and Godspeed."

14.

Standing at the edge of the retainer wall, Cordova glared at the tracks in the old canal bed. Tomas entered the basin and kneeled to get a closer look. "Are these the tracks of the Americans?" he asked.

Tomas stood up. "Two sets look like boot tracks from the Americans and the others are those of a man and woman, probably the Mexicans. They lead into the jungle. Over there."

"You will lead us through the jungle and follow these tracks until we find the Americans," Cordova demanded. "You had better not lead us on a wild chase or it'll be your last."

Tomas nodded and continued to examine the old canal bed. Cordova turned to Swartz. "We're going into the jungle to follow the Americans. You and your three associates can either stay here or go with us, but I warn you, you must keep up or I'll leave you in the jungle to fend for yourselves."

"We'll keep up, Major. I have no intention of staying behind and missing the lost city."

The boot tracks and broken underbrush were easy to follow as the party made their way slowly along the canal bed. The crumbling stone retaining walls provided good definition of the old canal, abruptly ending in an overgrown and wide depression. Tomas stopped, looking in different directions. He tried to act irresolute in order to deceive the major into believing how difficult the trail was to detect. He knew Cordova would probably shoot him when he found the Americans and his services were no longer needed. His plan was to delay Cordova and his men until he could slip away and make his escape. He also wanted to give the Americans more time to find the city. Tomas would have to pick the right time to melt away into the jungle. He thought about his friend, Javez, at the bottom of the deep pool, knowing the Americans probably threw him into the pool when he refused to talk. The major had told him about finding his floating hat, confirming his suspicions. In any event, Tomas would have to pick the right moment to save his own skin.

The young Indian examined the faint tracks and could tell they headed off in a southerly direction. "The tracks lead that way," he said, pointing to the northwest, the opposite direction. "This looks like an old riverbed so the river must have changed course. If we follow this bed north it should take us to a river."

The major was satisfied with Tomas's assessment, so they continued to hack their way through vines and dense underbrush and not question him. Tomas did not know how long his deception would hold up and hoped the Indian guide, Sastula, would notice and support the deception. He saw fear in the older Indian's eyes and knew he wanted to evade Cordova as much as he did. The second guide had disappeared somewhere in the ruins of Coba and apparently had come to the same conclusion of their eventual fate.

Sastula came from a small tribe of Indians on the northern coast. His native language was very similar to that of Tomas. Getting Sastula aside for a moment, Tomas was able to converse with him, "Your friend has disappeared. Do you know what happened to him?"

"Yes, he left this place to go home. I would have joined him, but the soldiers were watching me too closely and I couldn't get away."

"You know they'll try to kill us when we find the lost city," Tomas confided, "so I'm going to try to slip away like your friend when I get the right moment. Why don't you join me and we'll leave together?"

Sastula nodded his agreement and added, "I noticed what you are doing. You are leading them north. I saw the tracks lead to the south. I'll cover you until we get a chance to escape."

Following Tomas, the line of men continued the slow pace along the old riverbed for the next two hours when at last they heard the sounds of flowing water in the distance. They walked out of the jungle and onto the banks of a small muddy river. Little did the major know that Tomas and Sastula had led the party four miles upstream from where the Americans had entered the water. "The trail ends here, but where are the Americans?" Cordova demanded.

"They probably built a raft and headed down river," Tomas replied as he glanced downstream.

"Sergeant Perimez," Cordova summoned, "detail some of the men to cut logs and build some rafts. We'll need about five or six to transport all our men and equipment down river."

"Sir," said Perimez, "I've seen several large bamboo thickets along the way. The bamboo will be much lighter and easier to work with. It should make sturdy rafts."

"So be it," Cordova agreed.

Perimez assigned six of the soldiers to cut the larger bamboo stalks while he ordered the others to gather strong vines and construct the rafts. The men went into a nearby bamboo thicket with their machetes and began hacking away. Suddenly, there was a bloodcurdling scream. One of the soldiers ran out of the thicket frantically holding his forearm. "I was bitten by a snake, help me, somebody please help me!"

He fell to the ground as the deadly venom spread throughout his body. His eyes were wide with fear; sweat spread over his forehead. Another soldier yelled, "It's a bushmaster! I saw two of them in the thicket."

The bitten man went into convulsions and his body thrashed and jerked violently. Suddenly, he lay perfectly still with unseeing eyes wide open. He was dead within four minutes. Most of the men gathered around the dead soldier and stared at his lifeless body. Tomas and Sastula used this opportunity to melt into the background then turned and disappeared back along the dry riverbed. Swartz had noticed their movements and saw them slip away, but said nothing as he considered, at least I'll have two less bodies to worry about.

The two Indians backtracked quickly along the path, and then took a slightly overgrown trail that tracked to the north and slightly west of Coba. As they silently slipped through the heavy undergrowth, they were careful not to leave any signs of their passage, however, it was doubtful anyone in the major's party would be able to track them through the heavy vegetation. After the confusion subsided, the major called for Tomas, but there was no response. "Where's that damn Indian—the younger one?" he shouted.

The sergeant replied, "Sir, all three of our guides seem to be missing. It looks like they've disappeared into the jungle and deserted us."

Their disappearance created a furor, making the other soldiers uneasy. The major was outraged and immediately dispatched Corporal Juan Diaz and two soldiers to backtrack and search for the missing Indians. As Diaz and the men were leaving, they could hear the major shouting, "When you find them, you have my orders to shoot the young one on sight, but bring the older one back to me alive!"

Corporal Diaz and the two soldiers quickly departed while some of the men were returning to the thicket and the task of cutting bamboo stalks. Diaz backtracked over the dry riverbed and reached the old retaining walls of the ancient canal. It was impossible to pick up any new tracks because of all the disturbances of foliage and sand from their previous passage. There were no signs of the missing Indians – they failed to notice the overgrown side path the Indians had taken to the north. As far as the three Mexicans were concerned, the jungle swallowed them up. Diaz looked at his two disgruntled companions. "I don't know why we're in this godforsaken place anyway. Let's get back to civilization while we can."

The smaller man, Gomez, agreed. "Our horses are still in Coba. We could ride away and disappear into the countryside. Besides, those Indians were smart because they knew their lives were worth nothing to the major once he found the lost city."

"And neither are we," Diaz said. He turned to the other two men. "Do you really think the major will let us live so he can share the treasure with us? Maybe the sergeant and the Americans will get a share, but not us. Our lives won't be worth a single peso when he finds the treasure. I say we go back to Coba, get our horses and then get the hell out of here before we all die."

Aboard the Frigate *Talisman*

Far to the north off the coast of South Carolina, Caleb Kirby looked over the starboard rail of the frigate Talisman. He was hypnotized by the vast ocean extending far to the horizon. Dorn joined him at the railing. "She sure is beautiful and peaceful, huh, General? Don't let her looks fool you because this ocean can be a real nasty bitch when she wants to."

"Yes, I know. I've been on a couple of voyages when the weather was pretty bad and I thought I'd never see land again."

At that moment, two dolphins broke through the water directly beneath them, frolicking under the bow for several passes. They glided through the translucent water as if flying effortlessly through air.

"Looks like bottlenose dolphins," Dorn observed. "See how their strong tail flukes propel them through the water? Magnificent creatures, aren't they?"

"Sure are," Kirby agreed, watching the dolphins disappear under the waves.

"Looking at the ocean really makes me appreciate being away from the stinking war. Every man should be able to live like those dolphins, free and joyful."

Kirby turned to Dorn. "Nat, what was your role in the war? I know you were assigned to Hooker and Grant's staff in the Army of the Potomac for awhile."

"Well, I was pretty well devoted to undercover work, trying to identify spies and personnel in our army who sold information to the Confederates. I was also a contact for some of our own agents in Virginia and the Carolinas. We spent a lot of time trying to track down deserters who ran away from a fight or just pulled up stakes and went home. You'd be surprised how many men would just walk away from it and go back home for a spring planting or for a hundred other reasons."

"I know, I've been involved in a few courts-martial for desertion," Kirby replied. "I've seen a few men hanged for it. Soldiers have varying levels of courage and tolerance during war. Some will walk right into musket and cannon fire without flinching, others will turn and run like rabbits at the first sound of a gun's discharge."

Dorn gazed out over the ocean. "General, what do you think awaits us in Mexico? You have to admit this is quite a wild quest we're undertaking."

General Kirby shrugged. "I agree, but I do know the story about Captain Murphy and the Confederate officer, Captain Walker, is true, at least the part about looking for the lost city. We also think they disappeared from the battlefield together with a Union gold shipment. Murphy was one of my officers in the First Michigan Cavalry in Tennessee. He had an excellent record until he disappeared. He was carrying the gold coins when he engaged a Confederate cavalry unit at some godforsaken creek over in west Tennessee. For some reason, Murphy and Walker stopped fighting and established a truce. Soon, they started acting like old friends, gave their troopers a furlough and told them all to go home. It was the most bizarre thing I've ever heard of. Several of Murphy's troopers actually came back and reported to their division headquarters, and that's how we heard about it. One of our soldiers said there was an uncanny physical resemblance between Murphy and Walker, as if they were brothers. Maybe they are brothers. We dispatched several units to look for them, but they had long disappeared with the gold. You can see why we want Murphy back to answer some questions."

The general hesitated a moment to collect his thoughts. "The story about the lost treasure somehow leaked out. Some northern newspapers circulated the story. All of a sudden, Murphy and Walker are folk heroes. The bottom line is, if they join with us and if the government gets the treasure, they'll be welcomed home as heroes. However, if they don't find any treasure or treat us as adversaries, they'll come home as deserters and thieves. In the latter case, they would probably be tried and imprisoned or hanged. How do you like that for interesting choices?"

Before Dorn could respond, Captain Potter, who was making his rounds, walked by the two men. "Good afternoon, gentlemen, I hope you're enjoying the voyage. We expect to have pleasant weather all the way down. I should have you off the east coast of Yucatan sometime day after tomorrow. You'll be dropped off at a small fishing village called Tulum."

"That's great, Captain," Kirby responded. "The trip has been most enjoyable. Thanks for all your help."

Captain Potter nodded, took a big puff on his unlit pipe, and turned to continue his rounds.

"What're our plans when we reach Tulum?" Dorn asked when Potter was out of earshot.

"A Mexican agent has been hired to provide us with five horses. He'll take us to the ruins of Coba and help us pick up Murphy's trail. From Coba, our guide will help us find the lost city and then we're on our own. We have two problems: The first is Murphy and his party, but the biggest threat is Harry Swartz and this Major Cordova and his men. I certainly hope the new Spencer repeaters live up to their billing and can help us take care of the second problem."

In Search of the Lost City

The small creek wound slowly under the low hanging branches as Santos, Rosita, and the two Americans waded carefully through the shallow water. They held their rifles at the ready as the thought of snakes and crocodiles remained uppermost in their minds. The party walked single file with Santos leading the way. He noticed there were no large exposed rocks or boulders in the creek bed, just silt, sand, and gravel. Trudging through the wet sand and mud was slow going, but they ventured on, anticipating this track would lead them to a wharf or some sort of docking wall. At one point, Rosita abruptly sat down and the men joined her. They were resting on the side of a bank when Rosita shouted, "Look over there—behind the bushes!"

They gazed at a decaying stone column sitting on top of what remained of the crumbling retaining wall. Hurrying to the structure, they saw the face of a carved jade mask embedded in the column. Elijah reached up and touched the carving. "This mask is a replica of the one we saw in the cave at the waterfall. Do you suppose this image was carved by the same people?"

Santos traced his fingers gently over the sinister face. "This is a symbol of King Tialoc's empire and it also may have marked tribal boundaries. This would tie together the gold mine, Coba, and Xepocotec. I'm sure this column marks the gateway to the city!" Santos said almost triumphantly.

With renewed energy, the group began walking faster. Simon commented, "Can you imagine how happy the old king must have been sitting in his royal barge when he passed this column and saw the jade mask staring down at him? He knew he was getting close to his lover." Elijah and Santos chuckled and Rosita looked a bit embarrassed.

The creek bed widened and the stone retaining walls became more pronounced as they moved inland. There was little doubt now that this was the old canal leading from the river to the city's wharf. They reached the end of the canal, abruptly stopping at a seven-foot high stone retaining wall. In remarkably good shape, ten stone steps ascended to the top. The group had finally reached the docks where the royal boats and barges once floated. Still, there were no buildings or signs of any city in sight. "Have you noticed the resemblance between this dock and the one in Coba?" Simon speculated. "You have to wonder if the same architects and builders constructed both. The lost city can't be too far from here because I can't imagine the old king walking too far to see his mistress, and besides, this wall had to be put here for a reason."

"Are you kidding? I'll bet the old geezer had his slaves carry him all the way from the boat to her bed chamber,"

Elijah quipped. "They probably even stripped his clothes off and dropped him into her bed."

They ascended the steps and reached a small terrace, partially concealed by vines and weeds.

"Let's cut through this brush and see if we can pick up a path or road of some kind," Santos suggested. "I have a strong feeling the city is close by."

The group moved into the thick foliage, and with some help from machetes, they entered a small clearing where the underbrush began to thin and the ground rose steeply. Santos knelt to the ground and started scraping the soft sandy dirt aside with his knife. Quickly, the blade struck stone. Santos scraped more soil away, revealing a layer of smooth paving stones arranged in an organized pattern. This had to be the main corridor leading from the canal to the city. A little further, the pathway abruptly transformed into a steep flight of steps extending to the summit. It was a strenuous climb, but they finally reached the top where, to their complete awe and astonishment, they gazed down upon the lost city of Xepocotec, with all of her mysteries and spectacular beauty. While Santos and Rosita stood silent, enthralled and speechless by the panoramic beauty of the scene, their American companions could hardly believe the magnificent vista that lay before them. Elijah finally broke the silence, "Well, I'll be damned! Would you just look at that?"

Simon, his eyes wide, added, "Yeah, just look at that!"

The city of Xepocotec sat remarkably intact in the cone of the valley, ingeniously arranged and constructed in a large circular pattern. From the hilltop, there was a huge vista of buildings, plazas, and streets, overshadowed by a very large pyramid rising majestically in the center of a larger plaza.

It reminded Simon of a wagon wheel with the pyramid and central plaza as the hub and the streets extending out as the spokes. Rosita gasped in awe and spontaneously unleashed her emotions. She hugged her brother and then flung herself into the arms of Simon and Elijah. They all embraced one another in a spontaneous display of exhilaration and the thrill of discovery. Elijah was not certain which provided him the most enjoyment—the sight of the lost city or the unexpected sensation of a warm hug from Rosita. In any event, Simon soon broke the spell. He was grinning from ear to ear, as he shouted, "Let's go down there and find the lost treasure of an empire!"

15.

Captain Potter maneuvered the Talisman into an easterly crosswind toward the small fishing village of Tulum. "General, you and your men need to get your gear together and on deck. The ship can only stay briefly so we can hold the high tide back out to sea. My men will have to take you in with a rowboat because of the shallow water."

Kirby acknowledged the captain then went over to Dorn, the other agents, and repeated Captain Potter's orders.

Kirby followed Dorn to their quarters and began packing his gear for departure. He placed his bedroll and kit into a small duffel bag then took his new Spencer repeater rifle and loaded it with seven rounds. He wondered how much he would put it to use. Kirby couldn't help but remember his conversation with Secretary Stanton. The secretary had said, "If only our troops had these repeaters earlier, the war would have been over by now. On the other hand, if the Confederates had these rifles, the war might have ended at Gettysburg and President Jefferson Davis and General Lee would have been dining in fancy Washington restaurants."

Kirby went back onto the main deck as the anchor dropped about a quarter mile offshore. Deckhands lowered the small rowboat into the water and two seamen descended the rope ladder and affixed the oars in place. Kirby approached Captain Potter, warmly grasping his calloused hand. "Captain, I want to thank you for the safe and swift journey here."

"My pleasure, General," he replied. "I wish you and your men a successful and safe journey, wherever it may take you."

The tiny fishing village of Tulum was nestled in a small bay surrounded by groves of palm trees. The azure blue water and the pristine white beach, framed by swaying palms, was a postcard picture of a tropical paradise. However, as they neared the beach, the features took on a more realistic appearance, allowing the Americans to distinguish the worn and weathered shacks of a modest Mexican fishing village. Incoming waves moved the dinghy quickly and it soon came to a halt in the blinding white sand.

The beach was deserted except for a few overturned fishing boats and an old wreck weathering in disrepair. Several small children emerged from doorways and playfully ran down to greet the visitors. When it was apparent these strangers meant no harm, other locals appeared in the doorways and wandered out into the dirt streets. Several yards up the beach an old man was laying his nets out to dry on a sun bleached wooden frame. He stopped his chores, smiled, and walked up to the general and spoke in Spanish. Kirby turned to Dorn. "Nat, you'll have to interpret for me."

Turning to the old villager, Dorn spoke a few words, and then said to Kirby. "His name is Pedro and says we must be the Americans they've been expecting. We're most welcome to their village."

Kirby shook his head. *I can't believe this. What happened to our top-secret expedition? Does the whole damn country know we're here?*

The agent and the villager exchanged a few more words then Dorn turned back to Kirby. "The old man is some kind of a town official. He says a man named Juan Sanchez is here to meet us with horses. He is camped on the edge of town and they've sent word to him. He should be along shortly. Meanwhile, the old man wants us to follow him to our quarters then on to the cantina for a fiesta the townspeople have prepared for us. We're their guests of honor."

The general hesitated for a moment and then relented. "Dorn, tell him we would be most honored to be their guests. We can leave first thing in the morning."

The old man escorted them to a small, weather-beaten, but clean hacienda, where bunks were already set up and an adjoining room attached to store their equipment for the night.

The citizens of Tulum were simple folks who devoted their lives to fishing and planting to survive in this harsh land. A visit by a group of Americans was certainly sufficient justification to hold a celebration. Many of the younger people had never even seen an American. At the cantina, smiling, friendly townsfolk greeted the agents with steaming bowls of fresh baked red snapper, sea bass, crabs, lobsters and shrimp served with sweet yams, baked corn, and an assortment of fresh mangos, pineapple, and papayas. Corn-flour tortillas and jugs of a local brewed beer were placed along the long table. A cheerful-heavyset woman handed each American a plate and motioned them over to the table to serve themselves.

The crowd was in a festive mood. As the meal began, musicians appeared with vihuelas and bongos and loud music filled the room. While the townspeople danced and sang, the Americans ate their fill of the simple delicious food, remembering the bland and tasteless diet they had endured on the ship the past few days. A black-haired young beauty named Carolita became especially energetic after a few sips of the local brew. A Mexican hat-dance began and the crowd screamed and pointed to the young girl, enticing her to perform the fast-paced dance. She jumped to her feet and twirled around the center of the room, her hips and torso rotating with the beat. Her feet and shapely legs carried her around the floor as if she were floating on air. Someone tossed a Mexican sombrero into the center and she approached it with feet and hips flying. As the music grew louder, the crowd started clapping and singing. Carolita whirled around the hat with ease, her pace accelerating as the music increased in tempo. Kirby and Dorn watched in amazed appreciation as the dancer gyrated and contorted around the hat. Finally, the lively song ended as the girl bowed and exited the room. The ragtag Mariachi band then struck up a new tune and three Mexican men began lustily singing a medley of lively native folk songs.

As Kirby and Dorn sat eating and enjoying the whole affair, a slightly built man approached them. "My name is Juan Sanchez, your guide. I have the horses and supplies your government requested. If you wish, we can depart for Coba tomorrow. Meanwhile, please enjoy the festivities and I'll come and fetch you in the morning."

Kirby thanked the Mexican and acknowledged they would be ready for an early morning departure.

The festivities lasted until well after midnight, slowly winding down when the late revelers started staggering off to their homes. The old man led the Americans back to the hacienda where they were more than ready to hit the bunks. Kirby thanked him and placed ten American gold double eagles into his hands. The Mexican gasped when he saw more money than he had seen in his entire life. Kirby smiled and said, "Pedro, please accept this money and buy some useful things for your people and your village." The old man nodded vigorously as Dorn interpreted Kirby's words.

Sanchez met them outside the hacienda early the next morning where six horses were waiting in a holding corral. The mounts had been fed, saddled, and were ready to go. "Amigos," Sanchez said to Kirby and the men, "I hope you had a good time and some rest last night because we have a hard ride ahead. I hope to get you to Coba in four days if possible."

Kirby turned to the Mexican guide. "Juan, why will it take us four days?"

"We're going to take a northwesterly route to give wide berth to a certain area near the mountains—the land of the Tuloupi Indian tribe. They are known to be cannibals and very hostile to outsiders. It will cost us some extra time, but I can assure you it's best to avoid those Indians."

Kirby and the agents acknowledged approval by their silence. They secured their gear to the saddles and, when all was ready, the group mounted up and headed out in single file. The mid-morning sun was well up in the east.

A River Bank near Coba

Major Cordova was having difficulty getting a river worthy raft constructed that would stay together. The first raft had only one platform layer and quickly fell apart when placed in the water. The second raft consisted of two separate platforms and seemed adequate. To test it, four men and their equipment boarded and pushed it into the river. The platforms had been stacked on top of one another, but when exposed to the water, the bindings expanded and the raft began to unravel. In a matter of minutes, the raft fell apart, causing the occupants to fall into the river, grasping bamboo logs to stay afloat. One of the soldiers struggled for a moment, and then silently slipped below the ripples, pulled down by the weight of his clothes and gear. A nearby ten-foot crocodile surged along the water's surface toward the thrashing soldier. When it reached the partially submerged figure, the reptile's attack exploded in a gush of muddy water. The croc seized the body in his massive jaws and disappeared below the surface. "Where the hell is he?" Cordova screamed.

Rico Zara was standing next to the major. "The croc will hold him under until he drowns then wedge the body under some mangrove roots. He'll come back later to eat him. I'm afraid he's gone."

One man swam back to the near bank and the other two continued to hang onto the bamboo stalks, finally paddling to the far side of the river.

Cordova was ranting and raving when Drake interrupted. "Major, the problem with the rafts is simple. It's the way you are stacking the platforms. Instead of placing them in the same parallel direction, you need to criss-cross the two layers." He used his fingers to demonstrate. "This way you have the forces of both platforms stabilizing each other. And tie a knot each time you wrap the binding around each stalk, and do it with both sections."

"Why didn't you tell us that before?" shouted the major, his face turning beet red.

"Well, Major, you never asked."

Swartz had to bite his tongue to keep from laughing aloud.

Cordova turned to Perimez. "Sergeant, please see to it that the rafts are properly constructed. We have already lost one man in the river and don't need to lose any more. By the way, Sergeant, have you seen Corporal Diaz and the other two men I sent to find the Indians?"

"No, sir, I have not seen nor heard from any of them. I would have thought they'd be back by now."

"If we finish the rafts before they return, we'll have to go on without them. Leave a note and tell them to look for us downstream. We'll make an extra raft and leave it for them. Those useless Indians probably gave them the slip anyway."

With the help of Drake and Cain, the first raft was finally completed. Four men reluctantly boarded the vessel, propelled into the current, and were greatly relieved when the raft held together and appeared to be safe. Sergeant Perimez pushed it to the far shore to pick up the two stranded men from the earlier spill. The major was satisfied and ordered his men to finish four more like it. In the process of cutting bamboo, work parties discovered two more bushmaster snakes, but with the stroke of machetes, they were dispatched before anyone was bitten. Although the discovery of the snakes slowed the construction progress, the men continued working until dark when the major instructed them to clear the area for a campsite.

In the middle of the night, Drake and Swartz awoke to the sound of distant thunder. A major storm was moving in their direction. Drake shook Swartz, waking him from a deep sleep. "Harry, there's a bad storm coming toward us and we're camped in the worst place possible in this old river bottom. I think we can expect a flash flood is probably heading our way. We've got to get to higher ground immediately."

Cain and Zapata awoke and gathered their equipment as quickly as possible. Swartz shouted at the major who was putting on his boots. "Major, we have to move north to the high ground we saw back on the trail. We need to move quickly."

The major screamed at his sergeant and the camp became a swarm of frantic activity. The thunder and lightning was terrifying. Fierce winds and torrential rain followed. The soldiers and the Americans ran and stumbled in the semi-darkness, attempting to put as much distance as possible between them and the river. Swartz shouted, "The higher ground should be just to the north of us. Look for any opening or path branching off to the north."

Swartz and the scientists were running as fast as they could with Cordova and his men close behind. The water began to rise, first into shallow puddles, then slowly increasing into a flowing stream. Swartz screamed again between his gasping and panting, "To the left, go to the left…"

Through the flashes of lightning, they stumbled upon the narrow opening in the heavy undergrowth. The rain had turned the path into slippery mud as the men tried to reach higher ground. Over the howl of the wind and rumble of thunder, the roar of the oncoming flood could be heard in the near distance. Cordova saw Swartz veer to the left and prodded his men to follow. Most of the group had started the climb up the embankment when a six-foot wall of water came roaring around a bend, bearing down on them like a freight train. The cascading surge of water carried two men away like insects, but thanks to their quick reactions, another two were lucky enough to grab small tree trunks, holding on for dear life. A few of the lagging soldiers were caught in the rising water, but able to wade through to the higher terrain. Cordova and all but two of his men survived the surge and fell gasping and sputtering to the ground. As the water slowly receded, there was no trace of the two lost soldiers.

Swartz found Cordova shaken, but coherent and very much in charge. The major and his sergeant were busy taking inventory of men and equipment and were dismayed to discover that there were only eight soldiers remaining. The rest were either dead or missing. The loss of the men, rafts, and key equipment did not bother the major as much as the loss of time. This would push them back two days. He wondered if all of this trouble was fate or just bad luck. In any event, they had come this far so he ordered his disgruntled men to find a suitable spot to bed down and tomorrow morning they would move back to the river and start all over again.

Swartz could not remember when he had been more miserable. He was wet, cold, and hungry. God, what I would give for a hot fire and a bottle of brandy. He found a spot next to a small sapodilla tree and rolled into his wet blanket as best he could. He was so exhausted he finally drifted into a restless sleep.

16.

Santos led the way down the steep overgrown path to the city. Xepocotec had been constructed inside a large round bowl, once the ancient fiery cone of an extinct volcano. The sides were elevated nearly one hundred feet from the floor to the top of the hill and the guarded depression provided the city excellent protection from violent storms and defense against potential invaders. It was no wonder the city had remained undiscovered for over eight hundred years.

At strategic locations around the rim stood a series of crumbling watchtowers that once housed sentries who kept a constant vigil for possible intruders. The city spread around a large circular plaza where most of the festivals, religious ceremonies, and social activities took place. The marketplace and trading stalls were located on one side of the plaza with larger buildings that once housed religious and governmental functions on the other. Most of the outer city was comprised of one and two-story stone dwellings built to house the general populace. At the far end of the plaza stood a great pyramid overlooking the city and a majestic temple occupied the summit. Stone paved streets extended from the plaza outward like spokes of a giant wheel and a series of smaller streets circled the city, intersecting and connecting all the main thoroughfares into a huge concentric pattern. It was a sophisticated design, taking full advantage of the geographic features of the circular valley.

Large vines, roots, and a variety of tropical undergrowth now overran many of the buildings, but despite the varying amounts of deterioration, the structures, roads, and terrace walls remained in remarkably good shape. Over eight centuries in the wet, hostile climate had taken its toll on much of the crumbling stonework. As the four intruders explored the rows of outbuildings, they entered the large central courtyard and plaza commanding the center of town. Vegetation and vines covered much of the courtyard as well, but surrounding it was a well-designed plaza with numerous intersecting walkways.

It was easy to visualize the early inhabitants attending their markets, festivals, and sporting events in this place. Much like Coba, skillful stonecutters and masons had fashioned and intricately fitted the thick paving stones in elaborate patterns that formed the roads and plazas. This skill was also evident in the elaborate stone and plasterwork used to construct the buildings, terraces, steps, and other magnificent structures.

The one-story villas consisted of two to three rooms while others were two stories high with four to six rooms, indicating they were apartments that housed larger family units. These early inhabitants recognized the need to maximize the limited spaces for living quarters.

At this moment, Santos had more compelling things on his mind. He reminded the others of the Mexican spy, Javez, and his words of warning. "There might be some very bad characters on our tail, and we have to assume they know we were heading to Coba," Santos said. "When they get there it will be easy to find our horses and pick up our trail in the canal bed. Once they find the river, they will see where we chopped down the bamboo stalks to build a raft. I hate to say it, but we left an easy path for them to follow."

"I agree," Simon replied. "Let's prepare an escape plan before we get ourselves trapped in this bowl."

"Before we explore the city, we should prepare some surprises for our unwanted guests," Santos suggested. "We can at least try to slow them down."

He thought for a few moments, trying to remember stories he had heard from his grandfather about tactics his Aztec ancestors had used on the Spanish Conquistadors.

"Let's backtrack the route from the lake and start from there. We can begin with the canal bed and work our way back to the lost city with a few traps to slow down any followers."

Simon turned to Rosita. "Why don't you stay here with the equipment and we'll be back as soon as we lay some traps."

"You expect me to stay in this scary place all by myself?" Rosita protested. "You can forget that, Mr. Murphy." Her icy glare was convincing enough and Simon and Elijah knew she meant it and nodded. They really could not blame her.

Stashing the gear in a nearby building, each grabbed a machete and rifle, and retraced their steps back to the lake and canal entrance. Santos searched around the banks for a suitable place to conceal the first trap. "The first thing we do is use the lake. I saw an animal skeleton lying near the bank so it's possible piranha still inhabit the lake. Maybe we can use the devilfish as weapons against them. We'll start by cutting some long lengths of heavy vine."

The nearby trees supported an abundance of coral vine and gathering an ample supply did not appear too difficult for Simon and Elijah who volunteered for the assignment. Santos collected a few stones from the fallen watchtower and laid them under two large logwood trees. With rope and muscle power, they managed to lift the stones and position them on two cantilevered platforms Santos had constructed and placed in branches about midway up the tree trunks. The vines were gathered and stacked near the canal entrance. Santos instructed them how to braid and splice the strands to form a long section of cable. Rosita pitched in with her braiding skills and soon a strong cable was finished. They fastened it to one elevated platform and stretched it to the other platform, positioned high in the tree at the opposite side of the canal entrance. There was enough slack in the cable to sink just under the water's surface and out of sight. The heavy stones, delicately counterbalanced on the platforms, would release with the slightest contact and cause the cable to eject out of the water with great force.

A short distance along the canal bed, Santos found a narrow spot lined with strong tree saplings. He gathered thin bamboo stalks from a nearby grove, instructing the group how to sharpen the bamboo slivers into thin daggers and attach them to a sturdy frame to make a lethal impaling board. He then attached the device to a tree sapling and bowed it to ensure the correct tension. The idea was, when released, the assembly would spring forward with deadly force and propel into the chest of an unsuspecting victim.

Another trap was assembled with heavy stones counterbalanced on overhead branches. The object was to drop the stones by triggering a concealed tripwire, causing a noose to ensnare the ankle of any poor soul who happened to step below. Finished and satisfied with their handiwork, the four returned to the lost city. Elijah grinned at Simon. "It's a damn good thing Santos is not on the side of the bad guys."

The Americans could not stand the suspense any longer and decided it was time to explore the buildings. They began with a row of structures that appeared to be former living quarters or villas. Santos and Rosita had gone off to find a suitable site to set up camp. Simon approached the first villa, cleared vines from a doorway, and entered a small alcove that led into a larger room. Although the roof had long since decayed, the dwelling was well preserved and looked as it did over eight hundred years before. Accumulations of dust and debris were all that remained of any wood or cellulous material and the rooms were bare except for bits of broken stone, clay shards, and discarded arrow and spear points. These objects were scattered in such a way that indicated the inhabitants abandoned the premises hastily.

Other buildings and rooms were much the same and all seemed to substantiate the theory of a hasty retreat. There were no logical answers to explain why the citizens of Xepocotec would abandon their city. Where did they go? Any attack on the city by Chichimec or Mayan invaders would most likely have come from the canal, since the rest of the area around the city was nothing but swamp and jungle. Their warriors should have been able to repel an attacking army for days. Had the invaders overrun the city, it would have been sacked and burned, yet there was no sign of charred or smashed evidence left behind. Perhaps there had been a secret pathway leading from the city through the jungle, but evacuating the entire city from a single restricted route would have taken too long. If invaders had breached the summit, they would have poured into the city and either captured or killed off the populace.

They theorized all the possibilities. One thing for certain, there had to be a consistent food source available. Eight hundred years ago, the land around them was likely higher in elevation, allowing citizens sufficient dry land to plant crops. It would have also allowed the inhabitants dryer ground in which to escape in any emergency. There were so many unanswered questions and the mysteries kept mounting.

Santos and Rosita found a substantial stone building to set up camp. Nearby, Rosita discovered a small spring flowing from an underground aquifer that once flowed through a stone aqueduct used to supply the town with their water. The four walked across the courtyard to a magnificent building occupying the far side of the plaza. It was most unusual because it did not have the box-like style of Toltec architecture. It was more like neo-Grecian with four large columns and a massive rounded roof design. This style was highly out of place here and defied all logic since the Toltec civilization developed well after the Greek or Roman empires had fallen.

Elijah offered his thoughts, "Was it possible a European visitor or an explorer from the Mediterranean region might have visited this place long before the first known exploration of the American continent? A visitor from medieval Italy or Greece could have taught these Indians about early Mediterranean architecture and construction methods."

Simon injected, "Remember the Greek and Roman Empires existed at least a thousand years before this city was built and, if a later European had visited this site during the construction, surely some kind of record would have been made."

The silence revealed no one could provide an answer or offer any further comments. In any event, the building was a marvel and further contributed to the many other accumulating unanswered questions. Elijah and Simon could barely contain their emotions and let it be known they were most anxious to explore this mysterious building. Santos gave them another warning, "We have to be careful inside these buildings. I am sure they hold many hidden traps. Examine each object carefully before touching it!"

They approached the steps of the building and studied the huge columns supporting the roof. The stone carvings above the columns were replicas of important Toltec gods, Quetzalcoatl, Tezcaltlipoca, Tl-loc, CentZotl, Itzpap-loti, and the sun god, Tonatiuh. Passing through the main entrance, they entered a large alcove that led into an assembly room. Around the room were fading plaster murals depicting different phases of Toltec life. Some were missing small chunks of plaster and most had cracks and fissures, but all were quite discernible.

The wall paintings represented a treasure of Toltec history with enough intrigue to keep a team of archeologists busy for years. Ancient artists had applied the frescos with colored plasters embedded throughout the layers, enabling them to withstand the erosion of time. There were eight murals spaced around the hall, each representing a different scene of Toltec life. Several depicted the warlike nature of the

Toltecs by displaying human sacrifices, vivid battle scenes, and violent death. Some were surreal examples of basic life functions such as birth, planting corn, harvesting, cooking, sporting events, and the everyday activities of a typical Indian marketplace. The murals were a virtual history book.

Remnants of stone benches remained along the walls, indicating a social and military order where citizens would gather for meetings and assemblies. Even the mild tempered Santos showed his excitement, "We'll spread out and look for levers or buttons that might unlock a hidden door or passage. Look for something unusual, not the obvious."

Each started on the inside walls, examining every square inch of space. They found nothing. Next, they searched the floor for signs of a lever or any type of release device. Still nothing. They moved to the smaller rooms adjoining the main hall and inspected the walls, looking for the slightest abnormality. Santos suspected he might have overlooked something important in the main assembly hall so he returned and stood in the center of the room, staring at the murals. The first mural was an exotic scene of copulation followed by the birth of a baby boy. The second was pastoral, showing neatly terraced hills with Indians cultivating corn and yams. The seventh mural was a battle scene with Toltecs chasing defeated enemy warriors through a field of broken corn stalks. A small red setting sun burned in the background, highlighting the end of the day's battle. As retreating Indians fled across the fields toward the sunset, some were on their knees pleading for the sun god Tonatiuh to save them from advancing enemy warriors. The eighth mural was one of human sacrifice with a lifeless maiden lying naked on a stone altar while a priest held her beating heart in the air. The rest of the group had returned to the assembly hall to find Santos deep in thought, studying the scenes. Simon broke the silence, "If there's an opening in these walls, it would have been used as an escape route, right?"

"Probably," Elijah replied.

"With this in mind, let's think about the retreating Indians and see if we can find some clue within that mural."

They walked back to the battle scene fresco and examined each feature closely. The artist had provided excellent detail, including vivid expressions of horror on the faces of the doomed warriors. Carefully, starting at the bottom and moving upward, they slid their fingers along the plaster face, tracing every inch of the painted surface. Simon had to stand on three stone blocks in order to reach the top of the mural. He worked his way up to where the late evening sun was setting behind dark and distant hills. His fingers moved slowly over the circular shape of the sun and then hesitated. Something was different. He traced his fingers over the sun again and noticed a very slight projection on the surface. He pushed on the circle, but nothing happened. He pushed harder and felt the circle depress slightly. Suddenly, there was a series of progressive rumbling sounds erupting from deep within the walls. Slowly, a four-foot wide stone panel slid back into a recess, exposing an opening. It led into a narrow passageway. The group was speechless as they peered into the black void that lay before them.

Earlier, Santos had prepared several torches. He pulled two from his pack and handed one to Simon. "This passage has not been opened for eight hundred years. There's no telling what we might find in there. I suggest two of us stay out here to protect our backs in case the door closes and we become trapped. The door will open from the mural again. Elijah, why don't you stay here with Rosita while Simon and I take a look inside. If anyone shows up, you can escape into the passageway and seal the door for protection."

Elijah reluctantly agreed, and he and Rosita moved toward the front of the hall to find a good observation point. Santos lit a torch and he and Simon cautiously entered the small opening leading to a narrow passage that was high enough for easier walking. Within a few yards, they noticed the passage began to descend. They advanced a short ways and encountered steps carved into the rock that dropped deep into the structure. The steps were polished and worn. At the bottom, they entered a room so large that its depth extended beyond the light of the torch. Simon lit another torch and then moved toward the far wall. With a start, he came upon stacks of spears, bronze axes, and bows and arrows piled up along the wall. The wood shafts were brittle and shattered into small pieces at the slightest touch. They had discovered a large weapons cache. Santos saw several mummified corpses lying in neat rows. Covering each mummy was a hardened leather shield and spear, indicating they were fallen warriors of importance entombed here by the high priests. The mummies, relatively preserved, had strands of long black hair still in place. Hardened by the passage of time, the mummified skin revealed contorted and sightless faces although ears, lips, and noses were recognizable.

They passed through the room and found the exit to a narrow passage continuing into the darkness. As Santos and Simon moved along the corridor, they came upon smaller rooms, two located on either side. Each room was empty except for one containing several large clay urns. There were remains of torches stacked nearby and wrapped in crumbling oilcloth. The urns contained a dark unidentifiable substance with a rank odor. Santos dipped a small stick into the sticky gel then touched it with his torch. It ignited immediately, emitting a bright flame. Holding the torch high, Santos said, "This was a storage room used to make torches. A few of these extras will come in handy."

He dipped a few more sticks into the heavy resin and they continued along the passageway.

In the spacious hall above, Elijah scrutinized the plaza, looking for signs of any movement. He was concentrating on the plaza when, from behind, he heard a slight rustle. He turned to see Rosita kneeling beside him. The scent from her face and hair stirred feelings deep within him that had been dormant for a very long time. In a contrived effort to see better, Rosita gently brushed up against Elijah, resting her arm against his shoulder. She turned and looked at him with penetrating eyes and an inviting smile. Elijah gently held her face in his hands and lightly kissed her lips. She responded by placing her hands around his neck and returning the kiss a bit more forcefully. "I'm glad you did that Elijah," she said.

"I am too," he responded. "You are a very beautiful woman."

He pulled her tightly to his body, allowing his dormant passions to erupt. The mood was quickly interrupted by a loud shrieking noise near the window. Elijah released Rosita, moved quickly to the opening, and then peered out and laughed. Two colorful blue and gold macaws were chattering noisily at one another in a nearby tree. "Well, I guess they must be telling us to pay attention to our lookout duties," he said.

Rosita smiled and gently touched his arm as she turned and walked back to her assigned position overlooking the plaza. There was no denying that a special connection had been made between them.

17.

Kirby and his agents followed Sanchez as they circumvented the land of the dreaded Tuloupis and finally arrived in the rolling scrub country of north Yucatan. The riding was easy enough despite the oppressive heat and humidity. They camped the previous night near the small village of Valladolid and, rising early, the party resumed the journey, avoiding several small ranches and villages. The festival in Tulum had been great fun, but they no longer had time for leisure activities. Kirby wanted to avoid any more contact with the locals who would no doubt become curious about American strangers roaming their countryside. Additionally, they did not want any word of their presence to pass to the American smuggler, Swartz, and his deranged accomplice, Major Cordova. Surprise was their best ally.

They were making excellent time. Sanchez assured them they would pass through the town of Vasquez sometime the next day, placing them within a short day's travel to Coba. Dorn rode up beside Kirby. "General, how're we going to find the two American deserters once we arrive in Coba?"

"The way I figure it," Kirby replied, "Swartz and his Mexican army companions have already arrived at Coba. Between Murphy, Swartz, and the Mexicans, either they are having a shootout or they left a trail from Coba that a blind man could follow. I'm hoping Swartz and the Mexicans can lead us to them. We'll just have to trust our instincts and good judgment."

"And when we do find them what should our next move be?"

"We've got to convince Murphy and Walker it's in their best interest to join with us. I suspect the Mexicans will be giving them a hard time, so maybe we can gain their trust if we help Murphy neutralize the major and his soldiers."

Dorn was concerned and shrugged his shoulders. "The way I see it, General, this won't be a cake walk. I just hope these new rifles are as good as they said they are. I'm sure we're gonna' need em."

He fell back in line, keeping the rest of his thoughts to himself.

The Jungle near Coba

Cordova was trying to recover from the flash flood. The body of one of his drowned soldiers was found suspended in the branches of a large tree, spread-eagled upside down, like an inverted scarecrow. The major instructed his sergeant to detail two men to climb the tree and bring him down. He did this out of disgust, rather than as a form of respect. To Cordova, the man looked spooky hanging in the tree. The soldier had been carrying a large pack of ammunition and food and his pack had been lost, causing the major to throw another fit of anger. "Clumsy bastard should have held on to his pack," he mumbled.

With their supplies almost exhausted, they had to rely on shooting a wild boar or jungle fowl for food. The major had been in tough spots before. He knew that once he found the treasure, he would get rid of all these "idiots" with him, but right now, he still needed them. His immediate concern was to return to the river and build the rafts as quickly as possible. The good news was that the loss of two more men meant that they would only need four rafts instead of five.

After gathering the remaining supplies, the men retraced their way along the ancient riverbed and back to the river. Cordova immediately ordered them to gather more bamboo and vines for rafts. Unfortunately, the first raft they built earlier and the supply of bamboo logs had been washed away. They had to start all over. This time, with the help of Drake and Cain, the work progressed smoothly and they constructed a river-worthy raft that would carry four men and supplies. After a few angry shouts from Cordova, four soldiers reluctantly climbed aboard, launching it into the river to test it with a full load. While Swartz and the Mexican emissary, Zapata, sat on a log and watched, Drake and Cain constructed the remaining three rafts. It took nearly two days to complete the job because the enthusiasm of the Mexican soldiers was somewhere between low and non-existent. The delay made Cordova even more irritable as he darted around shouted obscenities to the men in an effort to speed things up. Finally, four rafts were ready to launch. Drake directed the crews to cut sixteen bamboo push poles. Sergeant Perimez was about to board when he turned to the major. "Sir, what about the additional raft we were going to leave for Corporal Diaz and the other two soldiers?"

"We have lost too much time already," Cordova snapped. "Leave a note and instruct them to build their own raft and meet us down river. The cowards probably deserted anyway."

The Town of Vasquez

Several miles to the north, General Kirby and his agents approached the small town of Vasquez. It would have been preferable to bypass the town, but their pack mule had gone lame and they needed to replace it. Sanchez thought he might trade or purchase a mule in the village. They found a dismal looking cantina and decided to inquire about Cordova and Swartz. Sanchez went off on his own to search for more food stores and a fresh mule while the general and the other four agents walked into the saloon. The place was deserted except for the obese barkeeper fast asleep at a rear corner table. The only other patrons were three disheveled-looking Mexican soldiers. Ignoring the snoring barkeeper, Dorn walked behind the bar and retrieved four bottles of beer from a wooden water barrel. Kirby approached the soldiers and asked, "Do any of you hombres speak English?"

They all shook their heads. "Dorn, come over here and see if you can talk to these misfits."

Dorn took a big swig, then approached the table and asked them their names.

The soldier, who appeared to be their leader replied, "I'm Corporal Juan Diaz and this is Gomez and Roberto."

"Do any of you happen to know a Major Cordova or an American named Harry Swartz?"

"Si, Señor, we do. We are on a mission for Major Cordova now. He sent us to Mexico City to pick up more supplies and more men."

"Where are they now?"

"We left them in the jungle below Coba. They were preparing to float down the river that flows through the jungle, south of the city."

"What are they doing in the jungle below Coba?"

"They're chasing some thieves that are trying to rob things from our Indian ruins."

Dorn continued to press. "We're trying to catch up with Cordova and Swartz; how will we find them?"

"You can find their trail behind the great Coba pyramid. When we left them, they were walking in the old dry riverbed. You should be able to catch up with them somewhere on the river."

"Where were they going?" asked Dorn.

Diaz shrugged. "The jungle is haunted with evil spirits. We're not sure exactly where they were going."

"You're lying, Corporal Diaz. If you were on a mission for the major, you would have been given a designated spot to meet them with the supplies. You're deserters, aren't you?"

This question brought a look of doubt and fear to the faces of the three soldiers. Gomez panicked and suddenly pulled a pistol from beneath the table, aimed it, and pulled the trigger. The bullet struck Agent Morris squarely in the chest. He gasped as he fell heavily back over a table and was dead as he hit the floor. The Mexican screamed, "We'll never go back to that hellhole! You can't make us go back there. The major will kill us all!"

General Kirby drew his Navy Colt and shot Gomez above his left ear. He dropped like a rock and rolled to the floor with a thud. Roberto was making a slight motion for his belt as Dorn shot him between the eyes. Before Diaz could react, the agents had their rifles pointed at his head. Kirby grabbed him by his shirt and slammed him to the table shouting, "You Mexican bastard, we don't care if you cowards run away or not! All we want is some good information or we'll scatter your brains all over this saloon."

Dorn repeated the question in Spanish and Diaz screamed, "Don't shoot me, Americanos. I will tell you what you want to know."

"Explain to us exactly where Cordova and Swartz went into the jungle and what direction did they take?" With a terrified look on his face, Diaz shouted, "Behind the big pyramid of Coba is an old stone dock that leads to an abandoned canal. We followed tracks up the canal bed until we came to a dried up riverbed. We turned to the northwest and walked until we came to a small river and stopped there to make rafts. Two of our Indian guides deserted and the major sent us back along our route to find them. We saw no signs of the Indians, so we decided to disappear and leave the accursed jungle. This is as far as we got."

"When you get to the river, which way does it flow?"

"Southeast."

"What is the major looking for on this river?"

"The lost city of Xepocotec and the treasure buried there."

Kirby thought for a moment, and then filed the thought away for now. He wondered why they did not turn south and end up down river instead of having to float the extra distance.

"How many men are with Cordova and Swartz?"

"Between fourteen and sixteen, counting the three Americans."

Kirby released Diaz and turned to his agents. "We need to get to Coba quickly and find that trail to the river."

Kirby shouted at the shaking Diaz, "You best get the hell out of here now before we drag you with us and let the major deal with you. I might even shoot you myself, you cowardly bastard." Kirby had a strong dislike for deserters and cowards.

It took no interpretation for Diaz to understand Kirby's meaning. Diaz bolted from the door, running, and stumbled down the street.

The Americans left the bar carrying Morris' body. They found Sanchez standing near the horses with a fresh pack mule loaded with supplies. Sanchez looked at the dead agent and nodded his understanding. "I know of a good place to bury him outside of town."

They placed Morris over his saddle, mounted the horses, and quietly moved out of Vasquez, watched by a few wary peasants in the street. Kirby turned to Sanchez, "Where did you find the fresh mule?"

"It took a little bargaining but I managed to convince the stable owner it would be much easier to deal with me than the four of you."

They stopped near a grove of trees and gave Morris a proper burial on a small hill overlooking a stream. Dorn thought Morris would have been pleased with the setting and location for his grave. They bowed their heads as the general repeated the Lord's Prayer and said a few well-rehearsed words about courage and duty. The sudden loss of Agent Morris was a sobering event. Everyone was silent as the men mounted up and headed to Coba.

In the Lost City

Deep within the passageway, below the ancient Toltec building, Santos lit another torch and continued the exploration. After leaving the rooms containing the urns, they encountered nothing but solid block walls. Santos moved cautiously, observing everything along the walls and floor. Suddenly he stopped and held up his hand. His right foot was barely touching the floor. He eased it back, kneeled down, and ran his fingers lightly along the floor tiles. Satisfied with what he saw, he looked up at Simon and smiled. "Watch this!"

Taking his Spencer, he touched the floor with the tip of the barrel. A large slab of stone silently pivoted open, revealing a huge void of blackness below. Santos tossed one of the burning torches into the dark pit and watched it drop until the flame turned to a mere pinprick of light before disappearing. Simon was impressed. "How on earth did you know when to stop?"

"You remember I told you to be aware of any irregularity. I noticed a hairline crack in the floor and my instincts told me to stop. This city lies within the cone of a prehistoric volcano. The dark hole you see below is an old lava well that drops hundreds of feet. It's very possible there are more traps like this, so we'd better be careful."

Santos felt along the wall and found a small release button to reset and lock the slab. He pressed the button and it silently pivoted back into place. He pressed it a second time and heard a locking bar activate.

"The old priests knew how to press this button and deactivate this trap before walking past. If you look closely on the wall, you can see a small carving of a feathered serpent. The priests knew where to look for the trigger before going any further. Most of the traps most likely have similar devices. The carving of the feathered serpent marks the location of the traps and the trigger that activates them. Anytime you see anything like this, stop and check for a trap."

Despite the cool temperature within the underground passage, Simon felt beads of sweat break out on his forehead. What kind of people were these Toltecs who would build this type of trap?

They walked over the stone slab and continued through the passage, passing two more large rooms. One was empty, but to their amazement, the other was filled with weapons stored in neat stacks. There were spears, metal battle-axes, bows and arrows, shields, and some vests that appeared to be body armor. "Now this is strange," Simon commented. "Wonder why they would put a weapons cache so far back in the passage. The Indians would need quick access out of here in case of an emergency. There must be another opening close by."

"There has to be another exit," Santos agreed.

As they sifted through the weapons, something unusual caught Simon's eye. He walked over to the assortment of weapons and held up a bronze shield with the figure of a feathered serpent hammered into the metal. He also picked up a metal sword sheathed in a badly decomposed copper trimmed leather scabbard. This find puzzled him. "Santos, look at this!"

Santos picked up one of the shields and studied it carefully. "These were definitely not made by Indians."

"No, they're not Indian," Simon agreed. "They look more like Roman or Greek. If the Indians didn't make them, they must have been brought over from one of the ancient empires. This might explain why this building has a Mediterranean appearance. Look at this metal helmet; it looks the same as those worn by a Roman soldier."

Simon picked up one of the short swords and hefted it in his hands. "I believe this is a Roman Gladius-style battle sword. It looks like the Indians requisitioned all this stuff from a Roman Legion. It just doesn't make any sense." He chuckled, and added, "A team of archeologists would have a field day here."

The two men continued a short distance along the passageway until it dead-ended abruptly to a blank stone wall. Santos stared intensely at the wall. "There has to be an opening to the outside to allow them to escape or provide quick entry to the weapons cache. Let's search along the wall for another button or latch."

They retraced their steps back along the passage, starting at the obstruction. Both examined the floors and walls all the way back to the two rooms. They found nothing that was unusual. Santos traced his fingers lightly across every stone and joint, but again found nothing suspect. As he again approached the dead-end wall, he noticed something suspicious on the right side of the floor. It was a small square protrusion in the stone, inconspicuous to the naked eye. He kneeled down and lightly brushed the wall right above the bulge. Dust and debris dislodged, revealing a small carving of the feathered serpent. He shouted, "Amigo, come here, I found it."

Simon rushed to his side and examined the carving. "It sure looks like another release button."

Santos pressed the bulge in the stone—nothing moved. He pressed harder, but still it did not budge. He stood up, placed his foot over the stone and pushed with all his strength until the stone depressed into the floor. They heard a rumbling sound deep in the walls that became progressively louder as counterbalances began to move and shift. A panel wide enough for a man to pass through began to move slowly, grinding back into a recess that opened to the outside. They stepped through the exit and found themselves in the late afternoon air about two hundred feet from the assembly building. The passage was a clever, well-designed avenue of escape. It was also a convenient place to store weapons and other supplies. Santos looked around to get his bearings. "We'd better get back to the assembly building. Elijah and Rosita are probably bored to death sitting there while we've been exploring."

The sun was setting as they walked back through the front entrance. Elijah was the first to see them and he looked like he had just seen a ghost. "How the devil did you get here without coming back through the entrance?"

"The passage led deep underground and allowed us to exit through another building just south of here," Santos replied.

Rosita could not stand the suspense. "What did you find down there?"

"The passage was apparently built as an escape route. We found a few rooms full of spears and axes, also a room where mummies were stacked. They were remains of warriors and probably a few priests."

"The big find were some unusual looking weapons that could not have been made by the Indians," Simon added. "We found swords, shields, and helmets that seemed to be Roman or Greek origin. They really complicate the mystery of this place. Other than that, the rest of the rooms were empty. There's no treasure stored there, if that's what you're wondering."

Elijah was perplexed. "That's ridiculous. How could Roman swords get in the hands of the Indians when Rome is halfway around the world? I thought the Roman Empire fell almost a thousand years before the Indians who lived here.

"I thought so, too," Simon said. "Guess that's just another mystery about this place we can add to all the rest."

"The treasure is most likely buried beneath the larger pyramid," Santos suggested. "We'll explore it tomorrow morning."

Elijah, looking as innocent as possible, said, "Rosita and I have been watching the courtyard and haven't seen a thing. Maybe our pursuers are having trouble finding the place. Let's hope the bastards stay lost, at least until we're out of here."

He glanced out of the window and added, "When they do show up, I sure would like to be there to watch them run into the traps we set." The other three exchanged glances and nodded.

18.

Cordova was standing in the second raft with Swartz, a young corporal named Campalo, and a private whose name he could not remember. He had no idea they had launched the rafts five miles upstream from where Santos, Rosita, and the two Americans had entered the river. He never suspected the young guide, Tomas, had led them five miles in the wrong direction. Had he known this he would have shot him on the spot. Cordova was also unaware of the pending rapids two miles ahead. While the first set of the rapids were relatively easygoing, the last set and twelve-foot waterfall just beyond was the real killer. The river narrowed into a perilous chute leading over the falls and the water in the chute was too deep for a push pole and too strong for a paddle. Once in the chute it was impossible to avoid the deadly falls and the large boulders looming below, waiting to smash a flimsy bamboo raft into splinters. To avoid this mishap, Cordova and his men would have to go around the falls, if they managed to reach the banks in time.

Approximately a mile from the rapids, the major and his men sensed the current increasing in speed and strength.

Another sign was the turbulence of the water surface as they rounded a bend and edged closer. Downriver, they could see whitecaps and the sounds of churning water. Drake, who was on the first raft shouted, "Rapids ahead! Tie down the supplies and hold on!"

Cordova glared at Drake as if to say, I give the commands, you idiot.

Drake's raft drifted into the closest set of rapids and somehow bucked its way through the protruding rocks without mishap. The others also followed with no problems. The second set of rapids was more commanding, but all the rafts navigated safely through. The third and final set of rapids was the most challenging. The current became more turbulent and the many large boulders protruding from the surface were the major threat. Cordova shouted, "Use the poles and push away from the rocks. Don't hit the rocks, the rafts will break apart!"

The first raft swirled around a large boulder and made a complete three-hundred-sixty degree turn. Cordova's raft sideswiped a boulder, and then spun back into the current. Even though Cain's raft avoided the larger boulders, one of the poles wedged between two submerged rocks and bent like a fresh sapling. The pole cracked and the top half shot forward, slamming into the backsides of one of the soldiers and catapulting him into the air like a missile. He disappeared into the churning current.

With all the distraction, they were late to notice the current narrowing toward the center of the river, forming a large trough spilling into the deadly falls. Those on the first and second rafts pushed with all their strength to avoid the chute and reach the safety of the bank. The third raft was succumbing to the powerful current and sliding toward the chute. Drake saw the threat, grabbed a rope from his pack and threw it to Cain who was struggling at the rear. He caught the rope and looped it over the ends of the lower frame then held on and prayed aloud. Drake and two soldiers pulled while Cain and a soldier pushed hard on the poles, somehow miraculously guiding the raft to the shore. A handful of soldiers jumped into the water and pulled the three rafts onto the bank.

They watched helplessly as the last raft entered the foaming eight-foot-wide chute. Rico Zara and a soldier were pushing the poles with all their might while Zapata sat whimpering and screaming for help. In one last effort, Drake tossed the rope to Zara, who, by some stroke of fortune, caught the end and jumped overboard. The soldier saw Zara abandon the raft and immediately dove after him, grabbing his ankle. The men standing near the shore held the rope and pulled slowly, dragging Zara and the soldier against the strong current. Zara thought his arms would pull out of their sockets, but managed to hold on with the soldier trailing behind, both men coughing and gasping for air. Drake, Cain, and the others grabbed Zara and the soldier and helped them to the bank.

Meanwhile, Zapata was still holding on to the helpless raft as it swept through the chute. The Mexican emissary gave the group one last horrified look as the raft balanced briefly at the precipice, then propelled over the falls. The last sound they heard was that of Zapata expelling the last scream of his life. Both he and the raft hit the boulders below with a force that shattered his body and smashed the bamboo logs to bits.

Major Cordova was visibly shaken. Most of the soldiers were superstitious enough to believe bad luck had overwhelmed them and was a result of angering the ancient spirits. Had it not been for the fact that Cordova would execute them without hesitation, they would have bolted many miles ago. The major took a physical count. They had lost Zapata, who was no loss to the major, and one raft with food, rifles, some clothing and blankets, but relieved to learn he still had ten men and three rafts accounted for. While the exhausted soldiers rested, Drake and Cain inspected each remaining raft and repaired or replaced loose bindings. "We'll have to man-handle each raft around the falls," Drake suggested, "but first, we can carry our packs and supplies and then return for the rafts."

Cordova repeated the command and each man picked up a load and started the trek around the falls. The ground dropped sharply, leveling out below the falls. They found a spot on the bank to store the gear, and then returned for the rafts. Without the weight of supplies, the bamboo rafts were manageable and easily lifted by four men. When everything was finally deposited on a sandy and level spot below the falls, the men dropped to the bank, completely exhausted. Even the major had had enough for one day.

Swartz, Drake, and Cain huddled by the campfire, discussing the current situation in soft whispers. Swartz was the most outspoken. "I'm afraid we took on more than we bargained for when we joined up with Cordova. You can bet he'll try to eliminate us when we find the treasure. The only one who might help us is Rico Zara, but we can't be certain of him."

The two Americans agreed.

"There are eleven of them left, including the major and sergeant. The soldiers are scared to death. Most of them will probably desert when they have the chance."

"Won't we need them when we confront the Americans?" Cain asked.

Swartz thought for a moment. "Maybe we can strike a bargain with the Americans, at least until we can move the treasure."

The Outskirts of Coba

Sanchez, Kirby, and the agents were now on the outskirts of Coba. The sun was setting fast so they made camp close to the spot that Santos had chosen on their first night. Early next morning, Sanchez announced, "Amigos, I found the trail where the soldiers departed the city into the jungle. The tracks were easy to follow. The trail leads around the large pyramid at the southwest edge of the city and disappears into a dried up stream bed that leads into the jungle. We should be able to follow the trail easily from there."

"Juan, you've done well," General Kirby said nodding his appreciation. "Now let's try some of that breakfast you've been cooking and then let's go find the lost city."

After eating roasted chukka, guava fruit, and flatbread, they were on the move again. Sanchez led them through the ruins until they came to the pyramid and just beyond, the sunken road stretching toward the jungle and the stone pier. Reaching the pier, Kirby and his agents looked down from the wall to see the overgrown canal bed leading into the jungle. There were plenty of tracks and the well-beaten trail was easy to follow, especially with the debris dropped on the ground by Cordova's careless soldiers. The abandoned track led them to the spot where the canal ended at the dry riverbed. Sanchez examined the ground carefully. "It appears the larger group went northwest, but I also see a few tracks from a second group, probably the Americans, traveling the opposite way. I can't figure out why they would split, but I think the southeast route will lead us to the river and to the Americans much quicker." He turned to Dorn. "I believe you mentioned the deserter said the river flowed south."

"That's what he told us in the saloon," Dorn replied.

"He was probably telling the truth because most of the rivers in this area flow to the south or southeast. The southeast route will save us a lot of time and several miles of river travel."

Kirby traced the tracks leading to the north for a few feet then turned and walked back to the tracks leading to the south. "Sure makes you wonder why the two groups went in opposite directions. Maybe someone was trying to steer the Mexicans away from Murphy. I agree with Sanchez. We should follow the trail southeast."

The Great Pyramid

In the lost city, Santos, Rosita, Simon, and Elijah approached the great pyramid rising in the foreground. It resembled the one in Coba, but the temple on top was slightly smaller, with more elaborate carvings and stonework. The large plaza surrounding the pyramid was paved with tightly set stone tiles. They could not help but marvel at the neatly designed plaza with the market at one end and the elaborate buildings at the other. Commanding the plaza from the south was the great pyramid with its majestic temple dominating the summit.

Santos and Simon explored the west base of the pyramid while Elijah and Rosita worked their way around in the opposite direction. They were looking for a possible hidden opening into the base, but found the stones were set too tight and nothing suspect that might be a doorway. Converging at the front, they started the climb up the long flight of steps leading to the temple. Reaching the top, they looked out over a magnificent view of the ancient city, surrounded by steep walls that once contained the fiery magma of an ancient volcano now covered with dense vegetation.

"We know we're being followed," Santos remarked as he turned to his companions. "There has to be a passageway located somewhere in this temple. I know it. Maybe a maze of passages beneath the pyramid and we have to find the main corridor before anyone else does. I pray the traps we set will delay them long enough for us to find a way in. I'm sure the Toltec treasure is buried deep inside this pyramid."

At the entrance to the temple was the customary altar with a well-worn slab that once held the victims sacrificed to pacify the gods. They passed through a column-lined portico and then into a large room with several smaller rooms branching off. The temple was a simple design. The smaller rooms were no doubt the private chambers for the high priests and the larger room was most likely used for religious ceremonies to honor the Toltec deities. All of the rooms were bare except for scattered stone debris, crumbling pieces of stone benches and tables. They spread out and began searching through the large room. Simon was again amazed at the quality of construction. The blocks appeared so precise and fit so tightly together that the joints were hardly noticeable.

On one long wall the figure of Quetzalcoatl, the feathered serpent, was intricately carved into a single slab of stone. Santos examined every inch of the carving, hoping to discover a trigger release, but to no avail. They examined the floors and walls and found nothing. The group split up and examined the adjoining rooms, diligently inspecting each block of stone. Still they failed to uncover any secrets. Soon the men became frustrated and worked increasingly faster, as each knew time was running out. Toward the rear of the temple, Rosita wandered into a slightly larger room with the faded remnants of delicate painted murals. This had to be the private chambers of the princess Xepocotec, a room befitting the famed mistress of the eastern Toltec empire. On the wall facing her, it stood out like a shining beacon. Rosita shouted, "Santos, in here!"

Her voice echoed through the halls and all three men ran toward the room that Rosita was standing in. When they entered, a large jade mask embedded within the polished granite slab loomed before them. It was the familiar face they had all seen before in the waterfall cave and on the stone column located at the entrance of the old canal bed. Immediately, Santos knew that mask held the riddles of the pyramid and the key to a lost treasure deep within those cold thick walls. If only that sinister face could talk and reveal its secrets from the distant past.

19.

Cordova and his three rafts floated downriver without encountering any further problems. The major was still unaware that the Americans had entered the river at a spot well below the waterfall. At sunset, the rafts came to the spot where the river forked to the east and southeast. Cordova shouted to the flotilla, "Pull to shore and we'll make camp there. I'll decide which of those forks to take in the morning."

They pulled the rafts to shore and found a location relatively free from dense vegetation.

One of the soldiers had seen a wild pig rooting in the bushes nearby and headed with his musket in hand into the underbrush to find it. A short time later, after hearing the report of one loud musket shot, the soldier emerged from the jungle dragging the carcass of a wild boar. The young corporal was the hero of the hour. The carcass was gutted, cleaned, and slowly roasted it over a bed of coals.

Swartz was sitting on a log devouring a piece of loin when Cordova called him, Drake, and Cain to his campfire, offering them a cup of coffee. The Americans were not used to any generosity from Cordova and, although suspicious, accepted it graciously. Cordova demanded input as to what direction to take. "We have to decide what fork of the river the Americans took to the lost city. If we pick the wrong one, it will cost us valuable time and the chance to get our hands on the treasure. Anyone have any ideas or suggestions?"

"If I remember the legend correctly," Drake offered, "access to the lost city starts at a lake, so we need to focus our attention and find a lake. It's probable that only one of the forks will feed into the lake, and the other eventually empties into the sea. My guess would be the right fork has direct access to a lake, just a hunch mind you..."

Cain offered his opinion. "Look at it this way, the right fork appears to have a faster flow so I say that's the main channel and the one that feeds our mystery lake."

Swartz added, "Hell, it's simple. We have a fifty percent chance of being right. I like their idea of the right fork. I vote we go right."

"So be it," Cordova agreed.

At dawn, the rafts were loaded, pushed into the river, and captured by the current flowing into the south fork. They passed by the large sandbar and saw three menacing crocodiles sunning themselves, but luckily, the rafts did not register a signal for food because the crocs continued to lie there, lethargically blinking their eyes. No one spoke or made a sound as the rafts drifted slowly past the ugly reptiles. As the river began its slow bend to a more southerly direction, Drake noticed something unusual protruding from the sand. He shouted to Cordova, "Major, I want to check out something over on the shore, to the right side where that white rock is sticking out of the sand."

Steady hands pushed the poles into the river bottom and the rafts slowly approached the shore to allow Drake to jump and land in shallow water. He sloshed over to where the top of a square block protruded from the sand. "This stone block was definitely made by humans," he shouted to Cain who was wading toward him.

Cain agreed it was a manmade building block similar to the ones in Coba. "Wonder why this would be lying here?"

Cordova had a petulant look on his face, reflecting his annoyance over another delay. He confronted Cain and demanded to know why the sudden stop. "Major, this is a building block similar to those used in Coba. There may be some ruins nearby giving us a clue to the lost city. We need to search inland a few hundred feet to see if there are more like this one."

The major, satisfied with Cain's answer, detailed four men to search through the underbrush and report any findings. The search did not take long as they heard an eager shout not far from the bank. The group rushed toward the commotion, finding Drake and one of the soldiers poking through the ruins of a small structure whose upper half had long ago caved in. Medium-sized rectangular shaped stone blocks were scattered through the underbrush. "What do we have here?" Cordova shouted as he approached Drake.

"It looks like the remnants of an old watchtower and this stone carving is a rough figure of the Toltec god Quetzalcoatl."

"I thought the watchtower was supposed to be at the edge of a lake," Cordova said.

"That's what the legend claims. I imagine this is a different tower placed here as an early warning post. Over the years, the change in the course of the river may have left this structure further away from the riverbank. In any event, it confirms we're on the right track to Xepocotec," Drake explained.

It was late in the afternoon when Drake noticed an increase in the current's speed. As the men looked ahead, they saw boulders looming downriver. "Watch out for the rocks; use your poles to push around them, and be alert for another waterfall," Cordova yelled. After the tragic mishap at the upper falls, the major wanted to take no chances.

Bracing themselves, the men pushed the poles against the rocks and were able to propel the rafts around them into the faster current. In an instant, the rafts slipped through the chute and safely into the calm water of a lake. "Enough of this!" he grumbled to himself.

Glancing over at Swartz, all he could think of was, I hate rafts, crocodiles, and fat Americans.

The three rafts quietly bobbed in the placid water as Cordova shouted to Swartz, "Got any suggestions where we go from here?"

Swartz turned to Drake and Cain, "Well, you two are the scientists, what should we be looking for now?"

Cain hesitated for a moment, and then answered, "According to the legend, we should be looking for an old stone watchtower on the edge of the lake. This is the key to locating the city. It will be similar to the ruins Mr. Drake found upstream."

Drake added, "If you'll remember, from Coba we followed an old dried up canal that led into the overgrown riverbed that eventually led us to the river, even though I'm sure we went far out of our way by going north. I feel certain if we had turned left, or taken the southern route, we would've saved several miles, a couple of days, and avoided the waterfall."

"I knew I should have shot that damn Indian when I had the chance," Cordova bellowed. "That bastard meant to mislead us so we'd have to go through the rapids and pass through the falls."

Drake ignored the interruption and was about to continue when Cordova looked hard at him and shouted, "I understand now why we were led further north up the river. The Indian was hoping the waterfall would stop us or slow us down. The early Indians could not have floated a barge past the waterfall and rapids if they had used the northern access as we did."

Drake nodded slowly. "That's right, Major, I'm positive the southern route of the old dry riverbed would have bypassed the waterfall and rapids completely. The Indians never would have seen a waterfall. I suspect the old riverbed we walked on was a split in the river that flowed by the king's canal and rejoined the main river a few miles downstream, and that branch of the river just dried up. While banks of rivers erode over time, lakes are stationary and not subjected to fast erosion like moving rivers. Eight hundred years is not much time in geological terms so I would say we have the right lake. All we have to do is find a stone watchtower and a manmade canal. If the city is nearby, there must be an old canal or dry bed leading to it. Let's float around the shoreline until we spot the ruins or find what's left of a canal."

This sounded reasonable to Cordova so he ordered the rafts to split up and examine different sections of the lakeshore.

Because of the lake's depth, the men were having trouble maneuvering around the deeper water. Drake suggested they construct paddles from large stalks of bamboo that grew along the river. He showed them how to split the stalks and fashion a paddle from the cuttings. Soon each raft had paddles and could propel around the lake with speed and ease as they looked for signs of stone ruins or an entrance to an old canal.

On the Banks of the River

To the north, Kirby and the agents finally encountered the river where Santos and the American officers had launched their raft.

"That bamboo grove," Sanchez shouted, looking to his right. "You can see where they cut stalks to make a raft."

"Well, gentlemen, let's get busy," Kirby instructed. "We'll make a raft large enough to carry the five of us and our packs."

"Watch out for snakes," Sanchez warned. "Bushmasters like these thick bamboo groves."

Cunningham and Stephens went into the thicket to cut the logs while the rest gathered pieces of vine to bind them together. Dorn was in charge of the construction since he seemed to have some experience and knowledge of boating and river navigation. He even constructed a crude rudder from bamboo and fastened it to the stern section. The agent also had enough foresight to construct four bamboo paddles that he knew would come in handy in the deeper water.

"General," Dorn asked again, "how do we intend to find the lost city and how do we go about finding Murphy and Walker?"

"Well, we know one thing for sure, wherever they went, they had to travel downstream so we'll just float along until we find them or they find us."

The five men climbed aboard and the raft drifted into the current. Kirby reminded them, "Keep your eyes peeled for both the Murphy and Swartz groups and any old ruins that might give us a clue where we might be going."

The day was pleasant enough and the cool breeze kept the mosquitoes and other insects at bay. Kirby thought of his home back in Michigan and the young Sarah he had left behind. How he longed to be there now, holding her in his arms. She was his hometown sweetheart and was waiting nervously for him to return from the war. The war could be over by now and if he didn't contact her or return home soon, she would think he was dead. Sarah would be shocked if she knew he was floating down some godforsaken river in Mexico, chasing deserters through the jungle and hunting for lost treasure. Life was full of strange twists and turns, and he was caught up in a dandy.

20.

The jade mask was clearly a symbol of power to the former inhabitants of the sacred city. Standing in front of the mask, Santos, Rosita, and the two Americans had the eerie feeling they were looking at a sinister guardian who was able to unlock the mysteries of the Toltec empire. They somehow knew this mask held the key to the hidden wealth of the ancient civilization. This was also the private chambers of Princess Xepocotec and they were invading her inner sanctum—the room where the old king found solitude and enjoyed exotic pleasures. They could almost feel the presence of the princess. Rosita thought if she turned around quickly, the princess would be standing right behind them.

Santos moved closer to the mask, tracing its outline with a light touch of his fingers. He gently pressed each individual tile, expecting any minute to hear the deep rumbling sounds of heavy stones moving. All was still. "Press the eyes," Simon suggested.

Santos pressed each tile that composed the figure's black pupils, but still no sound and nothing moved. It was so obvious, but no one but Rosita saw it. "Push the yellow and red tiles, those on the forehead."

Santos pressed the yellow tile, no response; then the red tile and still nothing. "Try pressing them both at the same time," Rosita said.

Santos shrugged and pressed both tiles. To the amazement of all four, the tiles recessed into the wall, resulting in a low grinding sound from deep within the great structure. They could feel the tremors vibrating through the floor as heavy objects were moving. Suddenly, a large stone slab in front moved and slowly rose upward into a concealed recess in the ceiling. With their mouths wide open, Elijah could only think of one thing to say, "Well, I'll be damned!"

"Looks like the opening to another passageway, thanks to Rosita," Santos commented. "They probably moved the treasure through here and to the lower chambers of the pyramid. We'll need more torches and enough food and water for at least three days. We can't leave anything behind because, when our pursuers catch up, we've got to make it as difficult as possible for them to find us. We can't leave any traces of our presence."

Santos and Elijah went to prepare more torches while Rosita and Simon took the water bags back to the spring on the far side of the plaza. Their preparations took two hours. "While we're at it," Santos remarked, "I need to cut a six-foot walking stick to carry along, which may come in handy." He did not have to explain any further.

Rosita and Elijah came back to the pyramid entrance to find Santos already exploring the passageway. He had just located a small release lever embedded in the wall. The telltale symbol was the feathered serpent, Quetzalcoatl, carved in the stone and slightly above the device. They lit two torches and passed through the door in single file. Once in the passage, Santos depressed the lever and heard the deep rumbling noise return, allowing the heavy slab to descend from the ceiling and fall neatly back into place. They were now committed.

On Lake Xepocotec

Back on the lake, the Cordova party drifted slowly along the banks, searching for blocks of stone lying along the shoreline. The raft occupied by Corporal Campalo and three other soldiers drifted close to the entrance of a small creek trickling into the lake. Campalo spotted the sparse remains of the decaying retaining walls disappearing into the jungle. He shouted to the major, "I've found something! Over here, Major!"

The remaining rafts rushed toward Campalo who had turned his raft to the shore and began paddling toward the creek. The unsuspecting raft passed over the concealed vine that snagged one of the forward logs. The sudden tension released two large stones from the trees and propelled the heavy cable high into the air. The raft flew nearly five feet out of the water, propelling the occupants in all directions. The force of the sudden thrust caused the bamboo platforms to unravel. Campalo and another soldier quickly recovered and swam for shore, but the other two floundered, thrashing the water in panic. Neither could swim. One of the soldiers punctured his arm on a bamboo sliver, causing a thin cloud of blood to envelope him.

Deep within the lake, the nerve sensors of hundreds of red-bellied piranhas detected a food source and swarmed toward the blood scent. Reaching the stricken men, the piranhas convulsed into a silver mass of darting and streaking bullets. From all directions, the cannibal fish hit the two floundering men in a sudden wave, attacking every part of their bodies. Thousands of razor-like teeth shredded clothes like paper, then bit into flesh and ripped out small chunks of skin and tissue. The two men screamed as they beat at their bodies, churning up the bloodstained froth around them. Cordova, Swartz, and the others stared at the gruesome spectacle in horror. They could do nothing but cower and watch. Campalo and the other soldier made it to shallow water and waded toward the creek bed. His companion screamed and slapped at his feet as he struggled behind Campalo. The corporal grabbed him by the shoulders and dragged him to the bank, beating the two piranhas hanging from his legs. Finally releasing their grip, the voracious fish instinctively continued to jump and bite into thin air as if their quarry was still within their grasp.

The terrified men pushed the rafts to the shore and scrambled to higher ground. It was all over in minutes. Someone threw a rope around one of the unfortunate corpses and dragged it to the bank. There was nothing left of him, only a few shreds of clothing and a stripped skeleton. Cordova took one look at the unfortunate soldier then turned and retched. He screamed at the top of his lungs, "You American bastards set this trap! You'll pay a thousand times over. I'll rip your hearts out and stuff them down your stinking throats, then feed your corpses to the devilfish!"

It took several minutes for Cordova to calm down. Drake came over to him and Swartz, "If it's any consolation, I think we've found the gateway to the lost city. To the left you can see some of the stonework of the watchtower and, if you look along both sides of the creek bed, you can see what remains of the walls that protected the canal. I'll bet that trap was set in the past day or so. It's a safe bet that the Americans are in the city right now."

In a calm voice, the major turned to his sergeant. "I want to meet up with those American pigs as soon as possible!"

With a young private leading the way, the group moved up the old canal in single file. They advanced a few hundred paces when the lead soldier held up his hand. "Major, take a look at this!"

Cordova, Swartz, and the two scientists rushed to the front and found the private pointing to a stone column. Embedded in the stone was the familiar jade mask carving with menacing eyes staring down at them. The soldiers drew back in fear. Cordova thought that shaming them would overcome their apprehension, "You cowards are scared of a simple piece of carved stone?"

He pulled out his pistol and aimed it at the mask. The bullet struck the right eye, knocking out several tiles and a large chunk of stone. "You see, it's only a stone carving. You men are acting like a bunch of shriveling old women. Now, get a move on. Private Diego, you will continue to lead the way."

The superstitious soldiers were terrified as they trudged along the creek bed—after all, the spirits of their ancestors lived in the lost city and did not want to be disturbed.

As they continued walking, Diego's foot hit the concealed tripwire, releasing the stout sapling. The device sprang forward, thrusting its deadly frame of sharpened bamboo daggers into his chest and forcing the spikes through his torso. His eyes bulged and his mouth opened wide as he let out a muffled cry. Cordova calmly looked at the dead Diego hanging from the frame and, shaking his head, he turned to his sergeant, "Please remove the body from the stakes and bury him. The rest of you get a move on. I want those damn Americans."

Cordova selected another young soldier to replace Diego as point man. He reluctantly took the lead, carefully scanning the vegetation as he slowly inched forward. The unsuspecting party looked cautiously left and right, expecting something dreadful to fly out of the bushes. However, that something was cleverly concealed with leaves and mud. The soldier failed to see the small braided loop hidden beneath his feet. He stepped into the loop, releasing a small retaining hook. The chain reaction was explosive. A heavy vine released the tension on the stone weights balanced high in the tree limbs. They hurled to the ground, allowing the loop to ensnare the victim's ankle. The soldier was jerked upward with a sudden and immense force that instantly snapped his spine—he was dead before he reached the treetops.

"Move on and stay away from the center of the streambed!" Cordova screamed, leaving the corpse dangling high above.

The men ran as fast as they could. Somehow, they managed to miss the remaining spring trap and finally came to the stone retaining wall that defined the old wharf. Drake saw the narrow pathway leading through the foliage and followed it until he came to the stone steps leading to the top of the hill. Though exhausted and demoralized, the men somehow clawed and pushed their way to the summit and fell to the ground, panting and wheezing as they gazed out over the lost city of Xepocotec.

Swartz lay on the ground, trying to catch his breath. He was not used to this much physical exertion and thought he was going to die right there. Cordova stood over him like a vulture ready to attack his prey, shaking his head in disgust. "Sergeant Perimez," he shouted, "come over here and help this Americano off the ground. He looks like he may just roll over and die here like a fat pig."

Several snickers erupted in the background as the sergeant walked over to Swartz. After a few pulls and tugs, Swartz regained his feet and stood there, red faced and panting.

"You okay, Harry?" a voice boomed out as Drake and Cain walked up behind him.

"Dammit, I'm fine," he sputtered loudly.

"Hey, you were right about the city," Drake said in a weak attempt to take Swartz's mind off the major. "Just look out over that valley. I can even see the pyramid and the temple perched on top. I'll bet the treasure is hidden somewhere under the pyramid."

"Probably is," Swartz grumbled, as the group assembled and began to hike down the path leading to the valley floor.

A very humiliated and agitated American antiques smuggler was in no mood to carry on any conversation with Drake or anyone else. All Swartz could think of was his growing hatred for Cordova and the score he would eventually settle with this Mexican swine.

21.

Without incident, Kirby, Sanchez, and the agents encountered the spot where the river split and forked in two directions – one to the east and another fork turning gently to a southeasterly direction. Like the other men who preceded them, they had to make a decision. Dorn forced the issue. "The right fork, let's take the right fork."

"Why the right fork?" Kirby asked.

"I saw a flight of ducks heading in that direction and geese and ducks prefer the still waters of a lake instead of fast moving rivers. Also, the right fork current looks more like the natural flow of the river."

"Sounds logical to me," Kirby agreed.

The raft drifted into the south fork where it picked up the stronger current. Kirby and Dorn used the time for some much-needed sleep while Cunningham and Sanchez kept the raft drifting in the center of the river. It floated by the large sandbar where two large crocs lay motionless, absorbing the warmth of the afternoon sun. One croc opened his eyes and silently slid into the water toward the raft. Cunningham shouted, "Oh shit, the bastard is heading our way!"

Kirby and Dorn awoke, startled to see the ripples of the croc gliding their way.

"Grab the paddles," Kirby barked. "Paddle with all you've got."

The raft responded sluggishly but surged ahead. Kirby grabbed for his pack and groped for a slab of pork jerky. The croc was closing fast, leaving a large wake behind him. They could tell he was at least twelve feet. Kirby threw the meat into the water. There was a slight hesitation then the croc dove for the jerky and carried it to the bottom. The men on the raft exhaled a collective sigh of relief.

They continued drifting peacefully for another two hours. Then the raft gained speed as they entered the swifter and choppier current. As they approached the first set of rapids, the riders braced themselves in anticipation of slamming into an exposed boulder. Cunningham repelled the raft away from the first boulder with his pole, allowing it to swerve around the rock and drift into the second set of rapids. The raft bucked its way through, brushed another boulder, then careened around it and picked up the current into the chute. The force of the fast current propelled them into the lake below.

"Well, we got through that mess," Kirby announced with relief. "All we have to do now is find the entrance to the city and our friends Murphy and Walker. Be sure to keep a sharp eye out for Swartz and his Mexicans. We sure don't need any sudden surprises."

In The Lost City

In the city of Xepocotec, Cordova, Swartz, and the others separated and began a search of each of the larger buildings. They found numerous tracks in the dust, none of them directing their attention to any specific location. Most led to the circular plaza and fanned out to many of the nearby buildings, indicating the Americans had conducted a similar investigation of the surroundings. One larger building intrigued the two scientists, reminding them of similar structures from the Greek Classic or Imperial Roman period. One might conclude it displayed a combination of architectural features from both cultures. It was the first Indian-constructed building they had seen with arches and large fluted columns.

"This just isn't possible," Drake speculated. "This city is located in the new world, not Europe, nor in the Mediterranean. The first exposure this ancient Indian culture would have had with Europeans was when the Spanish Conquistadors came to the Americas much later."

Swartz, Drake, and Cain examined the bold stone carvings above the columns. "Those carvings," Drake explained, "are of Toltec gods, but the building design is Greek or Roman Classic. It should not even be here." He shook his head in confused amazement.

They reached the entrance and found themselves in a large alcove leading into the assembly room. The men stood in awe when they saw the large plaster murals and no one was more astonished than Drake. "Do you realize we've just found a pictorial description of the Toltec civilization? It represents the way they lived nearly a thousand years ago. What an amazing discovery this is!"

Bending down to touch a stone tabletop, the normally shy and reserved Cain said, "This great room must have been where meetings and religious ceremonies were held. It could also have been a museum to house their artifacts. This has to be one of the greatest archeological finds of the nineteenth century."

Drake added, "We need to sketch each mural and search this building for other artifacts. We could spend years studying these paintings and architecture. I know this is hard to believe, but we've discovered a structure that's over eight hundred years old with a strong Mediterranean archectural influence. This building would not look out of place in the middle of ancient Athens or Rome. My conclusion is that pre-Mexican Indian cultures must have had contact with ancient Greeks or Romans about eight or nine centuries ago."

Cain was intrigued with Drake's observations and shook his head in disbelief.

"But we know that's impossible," Drake concluded with finality, "because the earliest advanced Indian cultures, like the Toltecs, Mayas, Aztecs, and Incas developed over a thousand years ago. This theory would place a visitation well after the decline of the Greek and Roman empires. Besides, how could the Greeks or Romans have traveled across the Atlantic Ocean to Central America? They didn't have ocean-going ships, at least for that type of journey. It could take us years to unravel this mystery!"

Swartz confronted the scientists with a look of concern. "Gentlemen, I really hate to break up your dissertation on Indian cultures, but we have a treasure to find and need your help."

Drake was irritated at Swartz's lack of respect for these magnificent findings. "Harry, do you have any idea what we have here? This building and these murals are worth much more than any treasure you may or may not find here."

"I hate to say this, Mr. Drake," Swartz said, his voice dripping sarcasm, "but Major Cordova has two things on his mind, the treasure first, and killing the Americans. We happen to be included in his second objective because if we don't find the treasure, we'll end up very dead."

"And if we do find the treasure?"

"Then we're most likely dead men as well," Swartz retorted, "unless we can find a way to eliminate Cordova and his men first."

"What about the Americans?" Cain interjected.

Swartz was exasperated. "We don't even know where they are. They may be down in a cavern right under our feet looking for the treasure. If we find them, we might be better off throwing our lot with them than with Cordova."

"Speaking of caverns," Drake surmised, "I'll bet there's a secret passage somewhere under this building. I expect the Toltecs would have constructed a hidden escape route. They were known to be very innovative, as well as warlike. They would have stored weapons along an escape route. We should look in this hall for a hidden release device that opens to a way out."

The three began a careful search of the floors and walls of the great hall. Cordova and Perimez walked in and saw Swartz and the scientists probing along the walls.

"What in hell's name are you fools doing?" Cordova shouted.

"Looking for a hidden door to a passageway," Drake said with annoyance.

"Do you think the treasure is hidden under this building?"

"The Toltecs possessed great wealth. It's possible they dispersed the treasure or part of it under this building."

"What do we look for?" Cordova asked, suddenly showing interest.

"A mechanism that will activate a hidden opening. It will be inconspicuous, blending in with the features on the wall or floor. It could be a tiny bump in the surface. Look for anything you can depress, turn, or pull."

Cordova turned to his sergeant, "Get the men in here to help us."

Perimez left and soon returned with his five remaining soldiers, who then spent over an hour examining each stone, but found nothing that might open a door. Drake stood back and stared at the murals, wondering if somewhere hidden within the scenes was a trigger. He started with the scene showing a priest sacrificing a maiden on the altar. He then moved on to the ones of cooking, planting, and harvesting, just as Santos had done. Then Drake got to the last mural depicting the battle scene, showing Mayan warriors retreating toward the sunset. He stopped and stared at the scene. Something in this fresco was curious. The Indians depicted in this wall painting were running towards the setting sun. He traced his fingers lightly over the surface. Then it hit him. "Cain, bring me something to stand on."

Cordova ordered one of his men to get on the floor on all fours so Drake could stand on his back but Drake refused and accepted the small stone bench Cain and Swartz pushed over to the spot. Drake was able to reach up and trace his fingers over the different figures. The tiny cracks around the outline of the red setting sun caught his eye. He pushed lightly and nothing happened. He pushed harder and immediately sensed vibrations and heard rumblings inside the walls. Slowly, the large stone panel slid up into the ceiling, revealing a dark passageway. "I just knew it!" he shouted excitedly.

Cordova could not contain his excitement as he ran to the opening and peered into the dark void. "Sergeant," he cried, "bring us some torches."

Drake reminded them, "These passages may be filled with traps so all of us should not go in there. Half of our party should remain outside to guard the entrance and keep an eye out for the Americans."

"Agreed," Cordova replied. "Sergeant, stay here with three men and Mr. Cain while we check out the passage."

Cain objected, not wanting to miss a new discovery.

Swartz turned to Cain, "Stay here with the sergeant. Drake and I will accompany the major. If we find anything, we'll send someone back for you."

Cain nodded with a look of obvious disappointment.

Torches in hand, the men followed Cordova through the narrow opening. Drake found the reset stone and pressed it. He tensed when he heard the deep rumbling sounds resume and the heavy stone slab sliding back into place. No turning back now, he thought. The claustrophobic effect of the narrow dark tunnel made Cordova and the two soldiers uneasy until Drake explained, "The door can easily be reopened by depressing the reset button on the floor."

They followed the same passageway explored earlier by Santos and Simon, and finally came to the spacious room filled with weapons. Drake and Swartz each picked up the remains of a spear and ax and carefully examined them. "Harry," Drake said curiously, "Do you know what this ax head is made of?"

"It looks like bronze to me," he answered.

"I think you're right. How the devil did the Indians possibly know how to make bronze?"

Swartz could not answer, shaking his head sideways, indicating no.

They were particularly excited when they discovered the mummified warriors lying against the wall.

Drake gasped in awe. "They must have been soldiers who performed courageous deeds to warrant mummification. You also have to wonder how the Indians learned the art of mummification. It was started by the Egyptians and later performed by the Aztecs in a more primitive way."

"Those stinking mummies are no concern to me," Cordova interrupted loudly. "We're here to find the gold and other treasure that's supposed to be hidden in this damn city. If there's no gold here, let's move on."

Drake shrugged disgustingly at Swartz and walked out of the room.

They continued along the passageway until they found the four smaller rooms. Hopes soared when they found the clay containers, but quickly dissipated upon finding them only full of hardened pitch and dust, probably decomposed food. Thoroughly disgusted, Cordova motioned his two soldiers to move along. "Some damned treasure," he mumbled.

As Swartz and Drake trudged behind, Cordova ordered the two soldiers to take the lead. He did not want to be in the front in the event of a sudden mishap.

It happened so fast no one could react. Without warning, the lead soldier stepped on the release stone that triggered the floor slab to pivot downward. He instantly plummeted to his death, screaming all the way down into the huge void. The second soldier's momentum pushed him over the edge and he reacted by turning and grabbing onto Cordova's ankle. The hapless man was dragging Cordova with him. Drake reacted instinctively and grasped Cordova's left arm. The major reached for his revolver and aimed it at the soldier's head. The deafening shot resounded through the confined space. The slug entered the soldier's forehead and, releasing his grip, his body hurled to the depths below. Drake immediately realized his mistake—he could have solved all their problems by simply letting the major slide into the abyss. He knew he would regret this mistake. Ironically, Cordova's ranks had now thinned down to only four men, making the situation somewhat more tolerable. Swartz glared at Drake as if to say, why didn't you just let go of the bastard.

Badly shaken but uninjured, the major pulled himself back from the opening and lay on the floor, panting. Drake lit another torch and tossed the spent one into the opening. "This hole is probably an old lava tube left over from the extinct volcano. No telling how deep it is."

Cordova was much too stunned from the ordeal to speak as Drake crawled over to the stone release and pressed the reset button. The slab retracted. He pressed it a second time and heard the locking bolt jam into place. Then he and the others continued down the passage until they found the two remaining rooms. There was no treasure to be seen anywhere, and, in their haste, they failed to notice the Roman-like swords and shields stacked against the far wall. They continued along the passageway until they reached what appeared to be an impenetrable wall blocking further passage. Cordova, still shaken from the previous ordeal, became even more nervous and claustrophobic. "This was an escape tunnel,"

Drake suggested, "so there has to be an access door located somewhere in the wall."

Both he and Swartz dropped on all fours and began searching for a release trigger. Cordova tried to help, but was still reeling from his ordeal in the passage. Earlier, Santos had brushed away most of the dust from the feathered serpent carving so Drake was able to spot it right away. He pressed the stone release with his foot and a stone slab began to retract. Quickly they passed through the opening and found themselves outside in the fresh air.

22.

Santos led Elijah, Simon, and Rosita through the passage to well-worn steps that penetrated deep into the great pyramid. They descended to a small landing where the tunnel took a sharp right turn. Above them, embedded in the stone, was a jade mask similar to the one they had seen in the room above. The light from the torches illuminated the little green, red and yellow inlaid tiles, creating a supernatural look. Its menacing stare glared down on the group as if it was trying to speak. Santos motioned for the group to stop, "I have a feeling this mask is a warning," he cautioned.

Santos felt something sinister and deadly was lurking around the corner. He grasped the walking stick and gently pushed one end against the first step, then gently pressed his foot and it felt to be solid. He pressed the pole against the second step and felt slight movement. A loud, high-pitched whining sound suddenly filled the confined space as Santos jumped back and slammed into Elijah, forcing both to tumble onto the landing. Suddenly, a large razor sharp circular blade launched from the wall and sliced through the air with incredible speed. It propelled waist high across the passage and disappeared into a narrow horizontal recess in the opposite wall. In an instant, the blade re-cocked, sprung loose, recoiled back across the corridor, and returned to its original resting place.

"Madre mia," Rosita gasped, "what was that horrible thing?"

"That, my sister, was a trap meant to sever a person's body in half and it re-cocks itself after each pass. If I put my weight on the step now, the blade would spring back again. I believe as long as the step is depressed, it might hold until I release the pressure, then it will snap back into the original recess." He kneeled low and pressed the stick against the step, holding steady pressure on the step. The blade again exploded from the wall, across the passageway and held into its recess on the far side. "It should stay as long as I hold the stick down."

"How do we get past the infernal thing?" Simon asked.

"Well, we can't crawl under it because it's too low and we sure can't jump over it until we know how many steps set off the contraption," Elijah concluded.

Santos pondered the two recesses in the walls. "I'll test the steps below the second one."

He lay flat on the landing and pushed down on the third step. The blade shot out once more and completed its violent cycle. Then he extended the pole and pressed on the fourth step and it held solid. "Two triggering steps—the second and third."

Reaching as far as he could, Santos pressed the pole against the fifth step and it felt solid. "Shouldn't be a problem jumping over just two steps."

Elijah offered a suggestion. "Why don't I hold the pole and keep pressure on the second step while you three walk over, and then one of you can grab the pole. I'll follow by jumping over the second and third to the fourth step. You'll have to catch me so I don't break my neck."

"Sounds good," Santos agreed, "but just to be safe, keep a steady pressure on the step. One slip will cause one of us to lose the bottom half of our body."

"We sure can't sit here all day," Elijah grumbled as he pressed the pole tightly to the second step and flinched as the blade shot across the corridor to the far recess. "You three go ahead and cross over while I hold the pole."

"Be sure and hold that damn thing down tight!" Simon shouted.

"Yeah, boss man."

Santos and Rosita followed Simon and made it safely across. Simon shouted at Elijah, "Now, it's your turn. Can you jump over the two steps?"

"Easy!"

"Wait a minute," Santos shouted. "Release the pressure on the pole and jump back!"

The high shrill noise returned as the blade shot from its recess, across the passage and returned to its slot.

"Now what?" a startled Elijah yelled, realizing he almost made a big mistake by jumping too early.

"Throw me the pole and I'll depress the third step, so you can walk down like we did."

Elijah tossed the staff to Santos and leaped, landing three steps down and nearly losing his balance. The two men below caught him.

"Why didn't you just walk down?" Simon asked.

"Cause I don't trust the damn thing."

Rosita, who had been speechless throughout the whole affair, gasped, "That horrible thing was designed by the devil."

Santos nodded and examined the thin recess in the wall. "That was the first trap. I'm sure we'll see some more. If the Toltec treasures were stored in this pyramid, they would have protected it from intruders and robbers. It was the old king's sacred pledge to keep the treasure safe for use in the afterlife." He paused thoughtfully, "Let's rest for a few minutes then move on."

Rosita turned to her brother. "I wonder if those bad people chasing us have found the city yet."

"We left a trail a blind man could follow, so my guess is they're probably searching through the ruins right now."

"Who do you think is following us?" Rosita persisted.

"The U.S. military is a good bet," Simon replied. "But not if there's a stinking war still going on."

"I know my side wouldn't send anyone down here," Elijah added. "Besides they don't know we're alive."

Santos said, "Well, it's certain someone knows we're here, so we'd better watch our backs. I'm sure whoever is looking for us thinks we'll lead them to the treasure."

They soon came to another landing where the steps turned to the left. Santos glanced up and pointed to a carving of another jade mask set into the header stone. Carefully, he stepped around the corner, putting a slight pressure on the first step. Nothing happened. Maybe a false alarm, he thought.

As he put weight on the second step, large wall panels suddenly sprang open on each side of the passage. From one side, a thick wall of sand exploded across the stairwell. The force caught Santos on the leg and spun him sharply around, hurling him down the steps to land hard on his shoulder. The sudden rush also brushed Elijah across his chest, throwing him backward into Rosita, knocking both down to the landing. Luckily, they missed the full force of the blast designed to hurl them through the opposite wall opening and into the dark pit below. In moments, the sand subsided and the two wall panels closed. They had miraculously escaped another clever trap. Although shaken, Santos, who kept rubbing his sore shoulder, was not seriously hurt.

"Don't step on the second or third step," he shouted.

In turn, the three jumped over the two steps and landed safely on the fourth where Santos was waiting for them. Rosita landed heavily and briefly lost her footing and pitched forward. Instantly, Elijah grabbed her waist and pulled her close to him, preventing what could have been a nasty fall. The warmth of her body brought an instant rush to Elijah. She looked up into his eyes and smiled as he helped her regain her balance.

A few more steps brought the four of them into another corridor where an opening led into a passageway. There were two rooms on each side, filled with large clay urns and smaller pots lined in neat rows. Santos chuckled, "At least we won't run out of torch fuel."

The other room was full of neatly stacked weapons, body armor, and once brightly colored shields now faded with age. They found nothing resembling gold, jewels, or precious artifacts.

Returning to the corridor, Elijah glanced at his torch then at Santos, "Have you noticed how the torch flames flutter? It's surprising the air is so fresh in here. You wouldn't expect it inside a deep underground chamber like this."

"That's one of the reasons these pyramids and underground passages are so amazing," Santos replied. "The builders constructed hidden air ducts, allowing for ventilation inside the chambers and tunnels. Here they probably used natural vents and airflows from the volcanic cones to circulate fresh air."

The next two rooms contained the mummified bodies of Toltec priests and chieftains, still adorned in remnants of their once fine robes. Rosita stood over one of the mummies and examined the clothing. "Why are the bodies so well preserved?"

"When they were mummified," Santos explained, "all the fluids were drained and their bodies filled with dry, warm sand. The sand and the dry air have preserved them for a thousand years."

Elijah motioned the group over to a large gilded sarcophagus on an elevated stone slab. It was most certainly occupied by a person of royalty. The cover was composed of a thin layer of hand-hammered gold mosaic and decorated with an intricately gilded carving of the sun god. They each grasped a corner of the cover, and with some difficulty, carefully removed it. The four intruders stared in awe at the mummified body of a young woman adorned in woven gold and silver wrappings. She had a solid gold bracelet around her bony wrist and a delicate gold chain around her neck. Six intricate gold rings with huge rubies and diamonds remained on her skeleton fingers. At the end of the gold chain was a diamond pendant of at least twenty carats that sparkled in the torchlight like a beacon. "This must be Princess Xepocotec," Santos whispered, a tone of reverence in his voice. The group was mesmerized as they gazed at her sightless shrunken face.

Rosita quietly said, "She still looks so noble. I wonder how she died."

"As the story goes, she was caught in bed with her lover and the king tore her heart out and ate it," Santos replied. "And there's another story that says she poisoned herself. Who knows?"

Simon offered his thoughts. "The fact that she was buried in this ornate sarcophagus adorned with gold and jewels tells me she was revered as royalty. I doubt if the king harmed her in any way."

"I agree," Elijah said. "If nothing else, the old king's sexual urges would have kept her alive."

Life in this ancient culture was harsh and cruel for the commoners, but luxurious for those privileged few who had status and wealth. Such was the life of this once beautiful woman who happened to catch the fancy of an old king. Carefully, they replaced the lid over the sarcophagus, then slipped from the room and continued along the corridor in search of the treasure chamber.

The next two rooms looked promising—they were filled with stone carvings and statues of Toltec gods in various poses. The god Quetzalcoatl was reflected in stone relief on many of the wall mounts and portrayed in various poses, highlighting the importance of this god of Toltec mythology. Some of the carvings and statues represented deities of the sky, sea, land, harvest, family, and war. Many of the empire's great artworks were stored in these rooms, representing a vast treasure of archeological significance. Stacked at one end of a room were several tiled jade masks similar to those they had seen in the stairwell and the princess's bedchamber. The masks were symbolic as protectors and a source of strength for the Toltecs.

Neither Elijah nor Simon possessed the scientific knowledge to appreciate fully the value of the relics. "What a shame we don't have a team of archeologists with us who could help us understand their meaning," Elijah said. "I'm sure they'd be of great value to a museum or university."

Santos nodded and added, "These priceless artifacts tell the story of a lost civilization that was once a powerful empire, then somehow disappeared forever."

"I'll bet if the outside world knew about this place, it would be flooded with every archeologist in the world," Simon added.

"Yeah," Elijah interjected, "and every thief in the world would try to beat them to it. They would plunder and loot the city in a matter of days."

Leaving the rooms behind, they continued through the narrow passage and reached a point where they heard the distinct sound of bubbling water. It was coming from a small fountain that protruded from the wall with a small basin fused into the supporting panel. A narrow stream of fresh cool water trickled out and gathered into the shallow basin. The water entered through a hole located on one side of the fountain and emptied through a small opening on the other. The edifice appeared to be made of alabaster, with unfamiliar jade carvings embedded into the sides. Above the basin was a jade mask that stared menacingly back at them, daring the intruders to uncover its secrets. Santos tasted the water and declared it fit to drink, urging each person to drink up and refill his and her canteens.

Just beyond the fountain, they came to a large stone slab blocking the passageway. At first, they thought they had reached a dead-end, but on closer examination, they realized it was a large sealed doorway leading beyond the thick wall. Santos remarked, "It's solid stone—it has to open. I suspect the room beyond could be one of the treasure chambers." He turned to his sister and Elijah, "You two search the floor and Simon and I will check the walls."

They were unable to find any triggering device. Even Santos was perplexed. "This door would require some very complex counterbalances to move it. I'm sure the triggering process starts with something simple that becomes progressively stronger as heavier weights are applied." A further search of the floor and walls turned up nothing.

Rosita thought for a minute and glanced back at the wall fountain. "Santos, what kind of forces would start the opening process?"

"It wouldn't take much—something like small pebbles or even sand could get it started. Maybe even the force of air pressure."

"How about water pressure?"

"Yes, even"…Santos stopped suddenly, and then glanced at the fountain. "Of course, it has to be the water!"

The four surrounded the fountain and studied it carefully. Santos looked at the jade mask above the basin. He reached up and pressed the small yellow tile on the forehead. The tile held firm.

"Try the red one," Rosita suggested.

Santos depressed the small red tile; still no movement.

"Push both of them together, like you did upstairs."

Santos pressed both tiles and a small panel opened in the rear of the basin, diverting the flow of water into the new opening. The four walked back to the granite door and waited for something to happen. Finally, the familiar vibrating sounds rumbled from beneath and the big stone slab slowly rose upward and disappeared into a large concealed recess hidden in the ceiling. Santos turned to Rosita, "Little sister, you are wonderful!" He grabbed and held her in a tight hug. Elijah smiled at Rosita and simply said, "Brilliant…brilliant."

The open doorway revealed a cavern so large they could not see the opposite wall. Elijah was the first to step through the opening onto a large slab of stone. Immediately, the near edge dropped downward and his reflexive jump hurled him high into the air. With a 90-degree turn, the slab's opposite edge pivoted upward and momentarily remained vertical, revealing a black void below.

23.

Sanchez, spotting the rafts abandoned next to the creek, turned to Kirby, "General, it looks like they walked up that old creek bed."

"Good! We'll follow their tracks. Keep your eyes open in case they left someone behind to guard the rear. We don't need to walk into an ambush."

Paddling over to the bank, Sanchez was quick to notice the decayed stone retaining walls. "This creek bed is all that's left of an old canal—it must have been the main route from the lake to the city."

They carefully followed the bed and passed the stone column with the jade mask. Sanchez motioned for the men to halt, then leaned over and picked up an empty shell casing. They could see where Cordova's bullet had struck the mask, shattering part of the eye cavity. Just ahead, they spotted the deadly spike platform still covered with the dark stain of recent blood.

"Some unfortunate soul had an unexpected surprise ending," Dorn observed. "Well, at least he must have died quickly, based on the number of spikes that impaled him."

A little further along, Sanchez held his hand up a second time and pointed. High above in the treetops was a dead man dangling by his ankle and swaying in the breeze. Cunningham pulled a knife from his pocket and cut the heavy vine. The corpse fell to the ground in front of him. "Poor bastard! I'll bet Murphy's guide set that trap."

"Pretty clever," Dorn remarked. "I wonder if there are any more traps the Mexicans missed."

Kirby shook his head, "No way to know, but we'd better watch our step from here on."

Stephens led the way up the creek bed. As they walked, he glanced down and instinctively flung himself to the side, barely missing the foot snare that sprang from the leaves and high into the air. "Damn, that was too close!" he gasped. The others nodded agreement and were convinced to be more observant and watch closer where they stepped.

Soon they came to the stone wharf and crumbling steps. From there the route to the summit was well marked by crushed vegetation from recent footprints. With rifles cocked, they climbed the steps to the top. When they finally reached the summit, they stared over the edge to see the city of Xepocotec. The view was awe-inspiring, far beyond anything they had envisioned.

"My God," Dorn gasped, "would you look at that. The legend is true after all!"

"I sure hope the part about the Toltec treasure is true or this trip will have been a complete waste of time," Kirby added.

"The city looks like it was built inside the cone of an ancient volcano," Stephens remarked. "See, everything is laid out in cylindrical patterns."

Sanchez gazed for a moment at the incredible sight and turned to Kirby, "General, I have safely delivered you to the lost city. Now I must return to my home and family on the coast. If you will kindly pay me the balance of my commission, I will be on my way."

Kirby took the Mexican's hand, warmly replying, "Yes, you've successfully completed your mission to lead us here. All of us, including the United States government, want to thank you."

Reaching into his pack, he pulled out a sleeve of ten American gold double eagles and handed them to Sanchez. "May you journey in peace and safety. How will you travel back up river?"

"I won't return the way we came. I would never be able to get a raft upstream so I'll take one downstream and work my way back to the coast by the river. From there, I can get back to Tulum."

Suddenly, a voice close behind spoke out, "I would like to go with you, amigo!"

With rifles raised, they turned to see a lone Mexican soldier standing close by, his white uniform torn and tattered; his hands were outstretched, empty and imploring.

"Who are you?" Sanchez asked.

"My name is Corporal Campalo and I want to leave this dreadful place."

"Who else is with you?"

"My commander is Major Cordova, a man who will see us all killed."

"And who else?"

"There is an American named Swartz and two American scientists, Drake and Cain. Also, a sergeant named Perimez and five soldiers, counting me. The other ten soldiers have either deserted or died traveling here. Please take me with you. I can help manage one of the rafts."

"Why are you here in this place anyway?" Dorn asked gravely suspicious.

"The major told us we are following American thieves who came here to steal valuable things from our ancestors."

Dorn looked at Kirby and whispered, "I'll bet he thinks Murphy and Walker are here to steal artifacts. He probably has no idea about the real treasure."

Sanchez looked the corporal over before answering. "Okay, I'll take you with me, but no tricks or I will feed you to the devilfish."

Campalo was deeply relieved, "Thank you, amigo, I will be of great assistance to you."

Sanchez shook hands with Kirby and Dorn and went back down the hill with his new companion in tow. The two Americans were sorry to see him go.

Deep inside the Pyramid

Elijah had walked into a preset trap designed to pivot the balanced floor slab when exposed to the slightest weight. It revealed an opening that dropped into a black void. Within a split second, he had dropped back to the slab and was sliding toward the opening. A message shot to his brain telling him to rotate his body and with a thrust of his legs, Elijah pushed off, rotating in mid-air. With every ounce of strength, he lunged for the edge. By some miracle, he caught the rim and slowed his fall. Simon grasped one wrist and Santos the other, and the two men pulled Elijah out of the void before the slab could pivot back. The young southerner lay on his back for a few moments, gasping for breath. He looked up at Simon and Santos with a sheepish grin, "Thanks for being so quick. You saved my life!"

"No problem, cousin," Simon chuckled, "Besides, we need you to help carry the treasure out of here."

Elijah grunted, "I should have known there was some other reason for saving my hide."

"Here's your rifle," Santos said handing Elijah his weapon. "You tossed it backwards when you were in mid-air. I should have known the Toltecs would set a trap at the entrance to this room. Now we need to find the reset and locking lever."

The small trigger button was visible just inside the door opening. Santos reached around and pushed it. The slab quietly pivoted back into place. Another push released the locking bar and jammed it securely under the slab. Cautiously, they walked single file and safely across. Santos pushed the button again, retracting the locking bar and resetting the trap. "I trust this deterrent will make it unpleasant for whoever is following us."

The chamber was enormous with huge blocks lining the walls and floors. Elijah wondered aloud, "How did the Toltecs cut these blocks so exact and move them into place?"

As always, Santos had an answer. "Most likely, the Toltecs recognized the value of diamond dust as a cutting abrasive and used it to shape the stone."

Simon thought about this for a moment. "While I was at the university, we had a weird professor who had a theory about visitors from outer space applying advanced techniques to build the great pyramids of Egypt. Maybe that's how these pyramids were constructed."

Elijah chuckled, "Are you saying that some guy from the moon might have helped build these pyramids?"

Simon replied, "Who knows who might have helped the Indians. My grandfather once told me that hundreds of slaves cut the stones and moved them by rolling them over tree trunks. As the slabs moved forward, they would take the rear logs and shift them to the front. The whole process took a very long time and cost many lives. They probably used a heavy block and tackle rig to lift the stones in place. I suspect they also built a series of ramps to move the real heavy ones. Those so-called primitive Indians knew a lot more about the principles of moving extremely heavy weights and large objects than we could ever imagine, and seems to me some mighty intelligent folks had to teach em' all that stuff."

With the light from the torches illuminating the room, they saw more murals on the walls. Some depicted the construction of the pyramid, temple, and surrounding city; others showed emissaries delivering gold and other treasures to the temple. This convinced the foursome that they must be close to the treasure chamber. The last scene was perplexing. It represented a large hoard of Indians—men, women, and children crossing what appeared to be a large earthen dike surrounded by jungle and water. Like the fresco in the assembly building, the hoard was moving toward a setting sun in the far horizon. Simon studied the murals carefully. "It looks like the citizens evacuated the city and moved west."

Elijah asked the logical question. "If they had to suddenly evacuate, how would they have known to paint this last mural?"

"Maybe the Toltec leaders had a premonition and planned well in advance for an evacuation," Simon replied. "The painting suggests a secret escape route somewhere within the city. Maybe this passage leads to it."

"Perhaps they were under attack from a hostile army," Rosita suggested.

Santos added, "Or maybe they had to evacuate because of a volcano eruption."

"But we didn't see any hardened lava deposits anywhere," Elijah reminded them. "Something happened here that forced them to leave, and apparently they never returned."

On one side of the room was a large stone altar and fragments of stone benches indicating priests used the room for religious ceremonies. Behind the altar was the familiar jade mask resolutely embedded into the wall. Santos walked over to the mask, lightly touched it, and turned to the others. "I wonder what'll happen if I press the center forehead tile on this one."

Reaching up, he pressed the red tile. As before, they heard grinding and rumbling sounds coming from below. As they backed away from the altar, a large floor slab rotated into a wall recess and the altar began to tilt, shifting forward through the floor and revealing a flight of steps. The steps led to another passageway leading further down into the pyramid.

"I'll bet the treasure is somewhere down those steps!" Simon shouted. "I can almost smell it."

Santos walked over to the top step and started down. "We'll go single file and I'll lead the way. Stay alert!"

The others re-checked the torches and moved through the opening and onto the stairway, consisting of about thirty steps. They arrived at another landing that led through a small doorway and into a narrow corridor. Moving carefully, they arrived at another large opening, revealing total darkness beyond. Santos raised his torch and carefully probed the floor to see if there was another trap. He took a cautious step forward. It held his full weight. They walked into a large chamber and immediately caught the sight of brilliant sparkles and flashes of multicolored lights dancing in the distance. As they moved closer, the light reflections became brighter. Holding the torches high in the air, it hit them like a firestorm. Stacked before their very eyes, lay the great treasures and wealth of the Toltec empire.

The magnificence of what glared back at them was beyond comprehension. There were rows of solid gold ingots along one wall, stacked over eight feet high. Many of the ingots were large, but most were finger-sized bars, probably used as a form of currency. Along another wall were alabaster-carved crates filled with precious gems of every size, color, and description. The lights from the torches generated bright-colored refraction bursts from the diamonds, rubies, emeralds, sapphires, and other gems they could not identify. As they approached the stones, the light intensified into a dazzling explosion of dancing colors that spread across the walls and ceiling. Stacked high along another wall were ornamental and religious articles, statues, and artifacts made of gold and silver inlay. Many were adorned with large precious stones of different colors. This treasure was far grander than they could ever have dreamed. The early rulers had counted on these treasures to provide for their comforts in the afterlife. It would appear the Toltec ghosts had to get by with less modest means as the treasure remained untouched and in its original, undisturbed state for centuries. Aside from the gold and silver objects, there were intricate carvings of jade and alabaster. In large stone chests lay an assortment of jewelry and trinkets that would keep archeologists busy for years. Several of the most intriguing objects were the statues of different deities chiseled from large translucent quartz crystals. The torchlight filtering through these statues brought them to life, sparkling like bright, dancing stars.

Santos walked over to the gold stacks and lifted one of the larger ingots, "This bar must weigh at least twenty-five pounds!"

Then he picked up two of the smaller ingots and hefted them several times. Rosita stuck her hand into a chest and grabbed a handful of large cut stones. The flaming red rubies were intriguing, but the bright green glow of the emeralds was equally fascinating. She was especially enthralled by the brilliant inner fires exploding from the large diamonds. Looking at Elijah, Rosita held up handful of the fiery gemstones. "Any of these could rival the Star of the Sun you mentioned a few days ago."

Santos chuckled, "The Star is nothing but a legend and I still don't believe such a thing exists."

"It doesn't matter," Elijah responded grinning. "Some of these stones could make us rich beyond our wildest dreams!"

Simon brought them back to reality. "You realize it'll take an army to move this stuff out of here and back to the coast. What are we going to do with all this treasure? Remember what that Mexican spy told us in Coba. We know we're being followed."

"I almost forgot about them," Elijah conceded. "Do you think they'll find the entrance to the passageway?"

"It's only a matter of time. I'll bet they're in the temple right now looking for our tracks in the dust."

Santos replaced the ingots on the stack, "Once they find the jade mask, they will surely figure how to open the hidden door."

"Do you suppose there might be a back entrance out of here?" Elijah asked, glancing around the room.

"Yes. I imagine the Indians made sure they could escape if need be. The passage probably continues from the large room upstairs. All we have to do is find it."

"I have a suggestion," Simon offered, as he stared at the fortune lying before him. "It's pretty clear we have no way to move this treasure by ourselves. I think we should take a few small ingots and some of the finer gemstones with us. We can load up our backpacks and carry enough to make us wealthy for life. When we get back to America, we can mount an expedition and return for the rest of it and take it out the same way it probably got here—by barge."

Elijah said, "That sounds okay, but I think we need to consider our pursuers first by identifying the threat and dealing with it now!"

Leaving the cache of gold and jewels behind, they backtracked up the stairwell and into the large chamber above. Santos was careful to close the stairs to the treasure room and reset the altar in its original place. Carefully, they relocked and tested the pivoting slab to make sure it was secure, and then returned to the passageway, pausing long enough at the fountain for a quick drink and canteen refill. Approaching the stairwell, Santos was quick to remind them about the two traps located on the steps. When they reached the first landing, it was apparent they would have to jump across the two release steps to avoid triggering the sand chute. With all his agility and strength, Santos leaped the two steps then used the walking stick to pull the remaining three to safety. The deadly swinging blade trap would activate much quicker and they had two more release steps to negotiate. They stopped at the fifth step and Elijah said, "Those two steps might be tougher to jump over from our downhill position. Somehow, they look steeper than the ones below."

Santos thought for a moment. "The ancients would have had a way to lock the blade so they could pass over it freely. There has to be a locking device somewhere…" He stopped in mid-sentence. "Do you hear that?"

They could hear the familiar rumbling sounds transferring through the walls and toward the princess's chambers. "We've got company," Elijah announced.

Their pursuers had discovered the mask release and were now opening the hidden entrance to the passageway. Soon they would be filing through and would be upon them at any moment.

24.

The Americans only had one way to go and that was back to the treasure chamber.

Retreating down the stairs, Santos and the others could hear voices resonated from above—the pursuers had entered the passage and were coming down the first flight of steps. He felt some comfort knowing the deadly blade trap was armed and ready for its next unfortunate victim. They quickly bypassed the sand trap and retreated past the fountain to the large room above the treasure vault. Santos closed the massive door by pressing the control button twice. He looked at the others, "Let's hope the traps and this door will delay them long enough for us to get out of here. All we have to do is figure out how to activate the locking device to the door."

Santos knew how to open and close the pivoting slab by pressing the control button on the wall twice, but the problem was how to lock the massive door from the room. He pondered the situation and said, "Since this particular opening leads into the room above the treasure vault, I think the Toltecs would have designed a locking device to secure the door and treasure chamber below. If the door is activated by changing the flow of water in the wall fountain, how can they lock and unlock the door from inside the chamber?"

Santos stood near the slab door, looking along the base of the wall where it joined the floor. "Simon, Elijah, come over here. Help me figure this out. If the priests used this passage as an escape route, they would want to ensure no one could get through the door. That means they would want to lock it, right?

The Americans agreed.

"So how do we lock it?"

"How about reversing the unlocking process?" Simon suggested.

"But how?" Elijah asked.

"Reverse the flow of water back to the fountain. That's how we opened it."

"I haven't seen any fountains on this side of the door."

"Neither have I," Elijah concurred.

Rosita had been examining the bits of broken shards lying about. "What if the Indians stored water down here for that purpose?"

"How could they do that?" her brother asked.

"Well, they could have stored water in those broken clay urns scattered against that wall."

"Okay," Simon continued, "what if they did store water down here—how would they reverse the flow of water?"

Elijah walked over to the stone door and inched along the wall. He stopped, knelt down and rubbed his fingers along the floor, pushing aside years of accumulated dust and debris. He motioned the others to the spot where he was kneeling. "Take a look at this!"

Carved into the stone floor was a small depression that channeled into a two-inch hole in the wall. He speculated, "Wonder why the Indians would put a drain in this spot? What was here to drain?"

Elijah pulled out his canteen. He poured some of the water into the little basin and watched it quickly flow through the hole. There was only silence, nothing happened. He looked at Simon, "Hand me your canteen."

He poured the contents through the hole and watched. The silence was deafening.

Rosita frowned, "Nothing is happening."

"Give it time to work," Elijah replied, his confidence wavering.

It took several tense moments but they finally heard the familiar noise from under the floor, followed by something solid slammed into the door. "By God," Simon shouted, "you did it!"

Santos grinned at Elijah. "You must have created a backflow of water pressure that activated the locking bar. The door is now secure."

"Do you suppose there's a way to release the lock from the other side?" Elijah asked.

"Probably, but by the time they figure it out I hope we'll be long gone. The lock might only hold them back a little while, so I think it's time we find an escape route."

"Y'know, I've noticed the trigger devices for all these secret doors and traps don't follow a pattern," Elijah observed. "They seem to be random."

"What do you mean?" Simon asked.

"Santos pressed the button near the door to lock the pivoting floor slab, yet we had to pour water through that hole to reverse the flow and lock the door. It took two completely different processes to lock the two. Wonder why the Indians made these blasted devices so complicated?"

"So intruders like us couldn't figure them out and get in here to rob the place," Simon replied. I'll bet only the priests and a few select chiefs and warriors knew how these things worked."

In the Pyramid Temple

Cordova and the three Americans were elated when Drake found the carved jade mask located in Princess Xepocotec's bedchamber. Drake pressed the tiles on the forehead, opening the stone slab and revealing the passageway. Rico Zara stepped through the opening, "Major, with your permission, I'll lead the way."

"Suit yourself," Cordova replied without hesitation.

He turned to his sergeant, "Do we have enough torches, food, and water?"

"We each have five torches so we'll only burn three at a time. We also have rations for two days and our canteens are full," Perimez announced.

"Good. You and two men will stay here and guard our backs in case the Americans sneak around us. If we find anything, I'll send someone for you. Raul and Jose will accompany me, Swartz, Zara, and the scientists."

The men entered the passageway with Rico Zara leading them. When they came to the top of the long flight of steps, Drake and Cain paused several times to inspect the magnificent stonework. Both scientists believed this archeological find would ensure their admission to any prestigious archeological or historical society in America or

Europe. Their ultimate dream would soon come true and honors and fame would quickly follow. It was far more important to them than the phenomenal monetary value represented by a massive treasure, if a treasure even existed.

Cordova said with impatience, "You two are holding everyone up with all this talk of stone blocks and steps. Quit chattering and keep up. We're not on a sightseeing trip."

Cain, normally a quiet, timid man, retorted loudly, "That's precisely why we are here, Major Cordova. The historical significance of these structures is just as important as any damn treasure you may find to satisfy your greed."

Cordova glared at Cain with cold black eyes, "You two slackers get to the back of the line so you won't hold us up. If we leave you, don't expect us to come back and get you."

Cordova motioned to Rico Zara to keep moving. The major was not used to insolence, especially from an American weakling like Cain. He held his temper in check, knowing he would deal with the scientists later and when convenient.

Rico Zara cautiously led them down the long flight of steps. Drake brought up the rear, delaying their progress to examine various features along the way. Swartz, who had said nothing during the exchange, was in front of them and kept his anger to himself. He whispered to the two scientists, "Will you both please keep up? I need your help with Cordova, especially if we find the treasure. I promise you will have plenty of time to conduct your research later."

He was sure the two soldiers would not be a problem and he was betting they would desert at the first opportunity. He also felt Rico Zara would be equally glad to see the last of the major and join them, although, like Cordova, it seemed

Zara's only interest was to find the treasure and get rich in the process.

They continued further down into the pyramid. At the landing, Rico Zara paused to let the others catch up. Cordova pushed him aside and shoved one of the soldiers, Jose, to the front. Jose reluctantly walked past the landing and on to the first step, then the second. Instantly, a loud screeching noise sounded through the chamber as the large circular blade exploded from its recess and whirled across the passageway. The cutting edge hit Jose at his navel, slicing through his mid-section, leaving only part of his spine and fragments of skin and muscle. His eyes bulged in shock as parts of his stomach and intestines spilled out against the walls and steps. When the blade sprung back into its recess, it completed the job by severing the hapless soldier in half. Jose's remains toppled down a few steps before coming to rest in two piles of bloody gore. Cordova and Rico Zara witnessed the carnage and vomited over the steps, retreating to avoid the ghastly sight of the mangled torso. Rico Zara crossed himself several times as Cordova tried to compose himself and remain in command.

By the time Swartz and the two scientists reached the landing, the incident was over but they could see the horrifying results of what had happened. Cordova turned to Swartz, "How do we get past that bloody thing? It came out of the wall when Jose stepped on the second step."

"What thing?" Swartz asked.

"That ghastly blade that cut the poor bastard in half."

Drake looked at the wall and then the steps. "I see the opening where it comes out of the wall. It must be spring loaded and activated by pressure applied to one or more of the steps. Before we cross over, we have to test the steps to see how the thing works. I'll use one of the muskets."

From the landing, Drake pressed the end of a barrel to the first step and it held fast. Pressure on the second step released the blade from the wall and pressure on the third step repeated the same vicious cycle. Reaching as far as he could, he pressed against the fourth step – it held. He then tried pressing again on the second step, maintaining the pressure. The blade made its first pass across, and then held up in the recess on the opposite side.

"Now I think I know how it works," Drake announced. "The second and third steps activate the blade and if I hold the pressure to the release step, it will stop after the first pass. As soon as I release it, the blade returns to its nesting place. A very ingenious and bloody device, I might add."

"How do we get around it?" Cordova asked in desperate frustration.

"I'll apply pressure to the step and keep it there after the blade makes its first cycle. If it holds, we can walk past, I think."

"And if it doesn't?" Cordova snapped.

Drake replied, "Then another one of us will end up in two pieces."

Cordova sighed hopelessly. "The trick is the last man," Drake continued. "He can jump over the first and second step—that should be no problem, providing the men below catch him to steady his landing."

Leaning away from the steps, Drake picked up the fallen man's rifle and pressed the muzzle firmly against the second step. The whining noise returned as the blade swung across the corridor back into the opposite recess. Drake held the rifle butt very low so it would not interfere with the blade.

Swartz was still unsure. He took a second rifle and tested the blade by pushing on each step, but the blade held fast just as Drake had suggested. Satisfied, Swartz followed the others and quickly moved across the two steps, leaving Drake maintaining pressure with the rifle. When the others were safely across, he jerked the musket away allowing the blade to complete its deadly cycle back into its homing niche. He tossed the musket to Swartz and jumped over the two release steps. "What a god awful death machine!" he gasped. "The devil himself thought this one up."

The group quietly filed past the two bloody clumps that once had been Jose. Cordova could not believe his bad fortune. He had started out with Sergeant Perimez and fifteen men and now he was down to the sergeant and three men. With most of his men gone, he would only be able to remove a small portion of the treasure. The thought of having to keep the Americans alive to carry treasure, by force if need be, was repugnant.

Soon they reached the second landing and Rico Zara stopped and motioned for Drake to move forward. "Here is another landing," Zara said. "There might be another trap here."

Drake carefully inspected the walls and floor. Nothing was visible. He took Jose's rifle and motioned everyone back as he pressed the barrel tip against the top step. Nothing happened. Drake motioned Zara to continue. Zara stepped on the first then the second step. The stone panels instantly opened on both sides and the crushing wall of sand shot across the corridor and through the large opening to their left. Zara's instinct told him to move quickly. He leaped two steps forward and Raul, the other soldier next in line, felt the brush of sand that narrowly missed sweeping him away. He fell backward against Cordova and Drake, nearly knocking them down. Within moments, the flow subsided and the panels closed allowing the group to jump safely over the two steps.

Drake observed, "That's what's so damn tricky about these stinking traps. You never know how much pressure it takes to set them off."

Swartz turned to Drake. "I wonder where the sand went as it passed through the hole in the wall."

"When the sand subsided, I could see nothing but empty black space." It probably empties into an old lava tube. There's no telling how deep it is."

Cain, a self-proclaimed geologist with a Ph.D. in archeology, spoke up. "The city was built in the cone of an ancient volcano. A volcano is honeycombed with lava vents starting deep within the earth's crust. When the volcano was active, probably a million years ago, the molten lava came to the surface through these vents and tubes. When the volcano became dormant, the lava receded, leaving hollow tubes that can drop hundreds of feet below the surface. That void you saw was an ancient lava tube. Had anyone been sucked through the opening, their body would have dropped a mile or so down into molten lava."

Drake added, "Well, at least they'd be dead even before they hit the lava."

"Damn comforting thought," Swartz grumbled.

They made it safely to the bottom where the corridor widened considerably and led them to the first two rooms containing the clay pots and urns. Drake and Cain carefully assessed the contents and were ecstatic when they discovered the weapons cache. Cordova was anxiously prodding everyone back to the passageway. "We don't have time to examine every piece of junk we see," he yelled. Drake and Cain were furious.

In the next two rooms, they found the gold-leaf sarcophagus. This was the first sign of gold and caused a stir of excitement, especially from Cordova. "Lift the lid off!" he shrieked.

With a man grasping each corner, they removed the cover to reveal the mummified remains of the princess Xepocotec. The first thing the major noticed was the solid gold necklace around her shriveled neck. He grabbed the necklace and jerked it upward with such force that the skeletal head flew off the body, smashing against the wall into an atomized fog of dust. Immediately they heard rumbling and grinding sounds inside the passageway. Swartz and the major rushed to the corridor in time to see a large stone slab dropping from the ceiling, completely sealing the passageway from where they had come. Swartz screamed at the top of his lungs, "You bloody fool! When you grabbed that necklace, you released the trigger to a hidden door. You've blocked our only way back to the temple! Damn you, you greedy bastard!"

Normally, the tempestuous major would have immediately shot Swartz on the spot, but fortunately for Swartz, the major was too stunned to think of it.

25.

Kirby, Dorn, Cunningham, and Stephens followed the narrow paved road into the lost city and found plenty of evidence of Cordova's presence. The Mexicans had been careless, dropping bits of trash and equipment along the way, having no idea the American agents were following them. The agents fanned out and searched several of the smaller outbuildings, then went to the center of the city. They joined up at the assembly building on the far side of the plaza. While Stephens separated at the square to inspect the large pyramid, Kirby, Dorn, and Cunningham cautiously made their way to the unusual looking assembly building. The general and two agents immediately spotted tracks in the dust near the wall, but not before stopping long enough to marvel at the large murals. "General, there are quite a few footprints around that back wall," Dorn said. "Looks like the whole group might have camped in here."

Stephens entered the room. "I saw a Mexican soldier on top of the pyramid smoking a cigar and, while he was standing there, another soldier stuck his head out and motioned him to come inside. I think they may be guarding something because a third soldier was patrolling the far side."

"You probably saw Cordova's rear guard," Kirby noted. "I'll bet the rest of them are inside searching for Murphy's group."

Cautiously, they circled the pyramid. Dorn whispered instructions to Stephens. "See if you can get up those steps without them spotting you. We'll approach from the other side and try to divert their attention."

Stephens nodded and approached the rear flight of steps, crouching as low as possible. The others moved around to watch the front entrance for signs of movement. Halfway up the steps, a rifle report sounded and a bullet struck just in front of Stephens, ricocheting off the stone and barely grazing his left shoulder. He quickly backed down. Hearing the shot, Kirby, Dorn, and Cunningham circled back to the south side and fired their Spencers—several shots entered the two open windows. The Mexican soldier backed away and ran to get his sergeant as bullets pelted the walls around him. He and Perimez nearly collided as he rounded the corner of the hallway.

"Sergeant," he cried, "we have some gringos firing at us! They keep shooting without reloading. Never seen rifles like that."

With pistol in hand, Perimez glanced out the open window and saw four men crouched at the base of the pyramid. He fired three wild shots, then quickly ducked behind a wall as a fusillade of bullets answered back, peppering the wall behind him. "Madre mia," he shouted, "what kind of weapons are those?"

The sergeant backed away from the window and went to the passageway entrance. The two soldiers were waiting with terrified expressions. "Sergeant, who are those gringos?" one asked. "I don't think they are the same American thieves we've been following."

"We are looking for two Americanos and a Mexican man and woman," Perimez answered. "All these men are gringos. Maybe they are searching for the other Americanos. Those rifles…I have never seen weapons like that before. We don't stand a chance against them. They fire many shots without reloading. We have to find the major."

The two soldiers reluctantly followed Perimez through the bedroom opening into the passageway. "How do we close the door?" one of the soldiers shouted.

"How should I know?" the sergeant yelled back. "Forget the door. Just follow the tunnel until we find Major Cordova."

The sergeant lit two of their eight torches and led the way. They came to the long flight of steps and followed them down into the pyramid. When they reached the first landing, Perimez hesitated and peered around the corner. He could barely make out the two sodden piles lying on the stairs below them. He looked again, holding the torch in front as far as he could reach. He recognized the bloody head and upper torso of Jose. The two soldiers behind him were trying to peer around the corner, but Perimez was blocking their view. "I saw Jose below and his body has been cut in half. There's a trap around the corner so we can't go any further until we find out what it is."

"Sergeant, why don't we just get the hell out of here?" one soldier pleaded.

"We can't go back now—the Americanos are probably following us. We must go on or we'll be captured or killed!"

Perimez took one of the rifles and poked on the first step. When nothing happened, he pushed on the second step. Suddenly the high-pitched noise screamed out as he stepped back just in time to avoid the blade propelling from the wall. "My God!" he gasped. "What the devil was that?"

He pressed the rifle to the step again and backed away as the singing blade repeated the cycle. "It must be the weight on the step that causes that thing to fly out of the wall."

He pressed the step again to see the blade spring across once more. He pushed the barrel harder. Now the pressure kept the contraption recessed into the opposite wall. Perimez motioned both soldiers over the steps. Safely on the other side, he instructed one of the soldiers, to grab the rifle butt and hold the muzzle so he could safely step across. "That bloody thing belongs to the devil!" Perimez swore.

The three stopped just long enough to glance at the mutilated body of Jose, and then continued downward. All three were shaking.

Kirby and his agents carefully worked their way up the pyramid steps into the temple. It only took moments for Cunningham to discover the bedchamber of Princess Xepocotec and the door to the passageway still wide open. Kirby peered through the opening into the darkness, "Looks like our Mexican friends escaped through this passage in a hell of a hurry. They didn't even bother to close the door. Dorn, light some torches and we'll follow them."

Dorn and Cunningham prepared the torches while Kirby looked at Stephen's grazed arm. "It's nothing but a scratch, General."

"I know, but out here in the jungle a scratch can become a deadly infection."

Kirby took some sulfur powder from his medical kit and sprinkled it over the area, wrapping it with a strip of white linen.

Dorn lit the torches and passed one to Cunningham. "Let's make sure we take full canteens because there's no telling how long we'll be down in this hole."

"Canteens are full, General," Stephens announced as they cautiously passed through the opening.

Perimez and his two soldiers hurried down the steps. Without pausing, the lead soldier rounded the landing and proceeded down the steps. When he placed his weight on the second step, the panels on either side of the corridor sprung open and the wall of sand exploded directly into the soldier's body. In an instant, he was gone. The only sound they heard was the rushing sand flowing across the passage. As the sand subsided, Perimez looked through the open panel and saw nothing but endless black space. The two panels closed, allowing Perimez and the remaining soldier to jump over the two steps and avoid the same fate. The sergeant was distraught. With only one soldier left, Perimez worried that Major Cordova might shoot him before he could finish explaining what had happened.

Kirby and his group reached the first landing and hesitated. Dorn thought he saw something on the steps below. He held his torch high. It illuminated a sickening sight, "General, I think we have a problem. Looks like a severed body down there. I think we have a trap just ahead and the steps probably trigger it."

He pressed the barrel of his rifle on the first step and nothing happened, then the second one and the whirling noise erupted. Dorn and Kirby reacted quickly and fell backwards as the blade exploded from the wall, slicing empty air and returning into its recess. "My God!" Dorn shouted. "That damn thing could cut through a man like a stalk of wheat!"

"Push it down again and let it cycle back, then keep the pressure on the step to see if it holds."

Dorn maintained pressure on the second step—the blade held fast. The three agents jumped over the two deadly steps as Kirby took the rifle and held the barrel firmly against the step, allowing Dorn to cross.

Kirby turned to Dorn, "Look above the first step and tell me what you see."

"Another one of those spooky looking jade masks, except much smaller."

"Right! The builders probably placed them there to warn the local priests and citizens. Keep a sharp lookout for any other masks embedded in the walls. If you see one, warn us so we can find the bloody trap before it finds us."

Above the Treasure Vault

Santos, Elijah, Simon, and Rosita carefully searched every inch of wall in the room above the treasure vault, looking for a possible passage to the outside. Their probing turned up nothing. "There has to be a way out of here," Santos said.

"The Indians would not have put themselves in a situation where they could be trapped like rats."

Although they felt secure knowing the giant door was locked, they knew it was only a matter of time before one of their pursuers would figure out how to unlock it. If they did not find a way out quickly, they would surely die from either a bullet or starvation. After a third search along the walls, they found nothing resembling a trigger to open a door. Rosita was the first to offer a simple assessment, "If there's no other opening in this room except the one to the treasure vault, then perhaps the escape route starts from the treasure room and not this one."

"Yeah, it has to be the treasure room," Elijah concurred. "There's nothing here."

The four retreated to the altar and Santos reached for the jade mask. The stone table shifted forward then pivoted backwards and disappeared into the floor, revealing the steps to the chamber below. They filed down and quietly moved back to the treasure vault. The reflections from the torches and refractions from the multicolored gemstones and crystal carvings once again displayed a thousand dazzling flashes across the room. The walls and ceilings exploded with multicolored fireworks. Simon had to break his hypnotic stare at the treasure so he could concentrate. "Let's search for a key."

They carefully probed each stone, joint and the floor slabs intersecting the walls, to no avail. "Do you suppose they hid the door behind the stacks of gold bars?" Elijah speculated.

"That doesn't make sense," Santos said. If they needed a quick escape, it would have taken them too long to move and restack the bars."

"Look over against that far wall," Elijah shouted, pointing past some crystal statues. Several shards and bits of clay urns were lying about. "Water jugs, the same size jugs as we saw upstairs. This probably means the door is activated with water, just like the one upstairs. Look for a small basin with a hole in the wall."

They concentrated their search along the floor where it and the wall intersected. The hole they were looking for was covered with eight centuries of dust and debris. Rosita's keen eyes finally located the small depression behind several containers of gold jewelry and ornaments. Carefully, she brushed the dust away.

Santos looked at Elijah. "How much water do we have left? I have about a half canteen. You and Simon used your water to close the door upstairs."

Rosita hefted her canteen and replied, "I have about three quarters left."

Elijah said, "If this doesn't work, we may be trapped in here and die of thirst, unless those guys upstairs get to us first. Make every drop count."

Santos took both canteens, knelt, and poured the water into the small drainage basin, careful not to spill a drop. The group silently watched the little reservoir empty as the water disappeared through the small hole in the wall.

"Nothing is happening," Rosita gasped in desperation.

"It's like the one upstairs, we have to give it enough time," her brother reassured her.

The four waited in desperate agitation. Simon finally erupted, "Well, dammit-to-hell, like she says, the bloody thing doesn't work."

"Yes it does…listen!" Santos hissed.

The familiar scraping noise of moving stone sounded below, growing progressively louder, as a large panel door in the far wall slowly opened up and disappeared into a cavity in the ceiling.

26.

Sergeant Perimez and the remaining soldier ran until they came to the first group of rooms. They only glanced at the weapons and art objects but did not stop to investigate; they had far more urgent concerns. They rushed through the corridor and bumped into the blank wall Cordova had thoughtlessly triggered when he jerked the gold necklace from the mummy's head. Perimez gasped. "We're trapped here, no way out!"

They became frantic when they heard the Americans approaching from the second landing. Perimez's first impulse was to hole up in one of the rooms and fight it out, but he remembered those repeating rifles and quickly changed his mind.

Kirby and the agents reached the bottom of the steps and Dorn cupped his hands and shouted in Spanish, "Amigos, we mean you no harm! Throw down your guns and come out!"

There was dead silence and Dorn shouted again, "Throw your weapons out in the hallway where we can see them. We won't harm you. You have my word."

Perimez hesitated for a moment then yelled back, "Don't shoot, amigos. We're coming out."

Both he and the soldier slid the muskets and his pistol into the corridor and walked out with their hands high in the air.

"Where's the second soldier?" Dorn asked, his Spencer pointed at Perimez.

"He was swept away back on the steps by a trap. There are only the two of us."

"Where's Major Cordova and the American, Swartz?" Dorn pressed.

"They're somewhere on the other side of the wall. We were just trying to rejoin them."

Kirby looked at Dorn. "Tell them they have three choices. One, we can shoot them on the spot. Two, we can tie them up and leave them here to rot. Or three, we can let them go if they promise to leave the city now and never return."

Dorn interpreted the general's choices. Sergeant Perimez answered without hesitation. "This city is an evil place. There is only death here. If you release us, we will leave now and return to Mexico City where we belong." The other soldier next to Perimez nodded emphatically.

"So be it," said Kirby. "You're free to go, but if we see you here again, we'll lock you down in this pyramid and you'll die like rats."

"Gracias, amigos, you will not see us again." Perimez paused. "Sir, may we have our weapons back. We might need them in the jungle."

"I'll only give you the pistol," Kirby offered as he unloaded and handed the gun and bullets back to the sergeant.

The Mexicans hurried back to the stairs and began the long climb to the top. They were able to bypass the sand trap easily and continued up toward the complicated circular blade trap. Approaching the first landing, Perimez realized he had no rifle to hold against the step. He glanced at the landing and motioned to his soldier. "Run fast and leap over the second two steps and you'll miss the blade."

The soldier hesitated in terror. "I can't jump that far!"

"Yes, you can. I told you you'll miss the blade and we can both cross over."

The soldier stood frozen to the spot. Perimez shoved him aside and jumped for the steps. Misjudging the distance, his left foot brushed against the second step. The blade sprung from its cover and flew across the corridor as Perimez safely hit the first step and tumbled onto the landing above. Pablo then followed his sergeant up the steps.

Perimez screamed. "Stop! Not yet, you fool!"

Pablo was not quick enough. The blade recoiled and sliced him through the lower back, severing his spine. His lifeless body pitched down the steps to rest beside the two piles of mangled flesh that had once been his comrade. Perimez was horrified. He turned and ran up the steps with the little remaining strength he had left. He knew he would never see his major again. He also knew he had to return to the river and try to make his way to the coast on one of the rafts. He had never felt so alone in all of his life.

Kirby and the agents pondered the large slab blocking the corridor. "I wonder what triggered the door to shut," Dorn queried. "The sergeant told us Cordova and the others are on the other side."

"It must've been activated by accident," Kirby surmised. "They had no idea we were behind them, only the sergeant knew."

"What should we do now, General?" Cunningham asked as he poked around the blocking slab.

Dorn spoke before the general could answer. "General, before we came on this wild excursion, Mr. Pinkerton sent me to the Washington Museum for a briefing on Central American Indian architecture and archeology. We studied Toltec, Inca, and Mayan buildings and pyramids. One of the instructors told us about traps inside a pyramid." Dorn described the mechanics of the small weights and balances that moved larger objects. "The force that moves them could be the weight of stones, sand, water or even air pressure. I'll bet this stone slab can be moved if we can just find the release mechanism. We need to search the walls and floor."

The four Americans crawled on the floor, probing every crack and irregularity they could find. They found nothing except a small square hole positioned halfway up the wall. The hole intrigued Dorn. He knew it was too small for ventilation.

Dorn returned to the rooms and searched through the debris and shards, and examined the walls scanning along the surfaces. He finally spotted a small unobtrusive square peg protruding about a half inch from the head of a tiny winged serpent carving in the wall. With some difficulty, he extracted the peg from the wall and immediately heard a distinct thud deep within the floor, but still nothing happened. He raced back into the corridor. Excitedly, he said to Kirby, "I may have started the unlocking sequence by removing this peg from the wall. If I insert it into the hole on this side, it might complete it."

"Let's try it."

Kirby and the other two agents looked on, fascinated but skeptical. Dorn inserted the peg and heard something click. A faint rumbling noise resonated deep within the walls, and after a few long moments, the huge slab moved upward and disappeared into the ceiling.

"Congratulations, Mr. Dorn, for that fine piece of detective work." Kirby said.

Dorn nodded his acknowledgement. "Now, let's move on," the general added.

Major Cordova, Swartz, and the others reached the water fountain. The basin was bubbling with clear water. "How convenient the Indians put a water fountain here," Swartz remarked.

"I don't think that was their only purpose," Drake said.

"What do you mean?"

"Just a hunch, but this fountain probably has more than one use, besides drinking."

A few yards further, they encountered another blank wall blocking the passageway. Cordova rubbed his aching head and turned to Drake. "What now, Mr. Drake? You seem to be the expert. How do we open it?"

Drake studied the dead-end, searching for a release device on the walls and floor. He found nothing. Cain walked over to the fountain and noticed the small jade mask above it. He called to Drake, "Do you think this fountain has something to do with opening the door?"

Drake stared at the flowing water, "Of course! It has to be the water flow. Nothing builds up pressure and force better than water."

He instinctively placed his hands on the jade mask, pushed on the center tiles and watched them depress an inch into the stone. Still nothing happened.

"Maybe If I push again, it might change the flow of water."

He pushed the two tiles a second time and the water reversed direction into a new drain hole that had opened on the opposite side of the basin. The first distinct reverberation was the sound of the locking beam extracting from the wall. The rumbling became progressively louder as it turned into a deep grinding noise. The stone slab slowly rose and disappeared into the ceiling.

Cordova shouted excitedly, "Now I know we're near the treasure!"

Swartz felt the exhilaration and shouted, "It's got to be close!"

The excitement was contagious as Rico Zara, Cordova, and a soldier raced for the opening. "Hold it!" Drake screamed, but his cry went unheeded.

His warning was too late. With Cordova lagging behind, Rico Zara stepped on the slab, his weight causing it to drop and rotate downward. In that split second, the soldier slammed into Zara's rear, pushing him forward and reversing the slab's pivot rotation. The slab tilted forward, allowing Zara enough momentum to lunge and grab the forward edge of the floor. The lower edge of the slab shot upward and knocked Cordova to the floor, with his arms extending over the opening. He looked down and saw nothing but blackness. As the slab rotated, the soldier slid off the stone and fell screaming into the black void. Zara held on to the top edge as the slab revolved to an upright position then rotated downward until it slammed tight over the opening. The panel severed his hands at the wrists and released him into the dark depths below. His body careened off a large boulder, shattering his skull, and his severed hands remained clinging to the threshold. Cordova jerked his right arm away, but was too slow moving his left arm. The rotating slab caught his last two fingers and severed them at the knuckles. He rolled over, howling and holding his injured left hand with his right. The remaining soldier rushed over and tied a handkerchief around the stumps in an effort to stop the bleeding.

"I hate this stinking place!" Cordova shrieked, grimacing in pain. "I'm going to kill every one of those American bastards! I'll cut their hearts out!"

While Cordova was screaming, Drake was trying to figure out how to lock the pivoting slab. For lack of a better solution, he went back to the jade mask above the fountain and pressed the red tile twice. The locking beam shoved into place. He took one of the rifles and applied pressure to the edge, satisfied that the slab held firm. He then tested it with his foot and it still held tight. "I think it's locked," he cried.

Drake held his breath and walked across. It held his weight. He turned to Swartz and the others. "You can come across now."

Entering the large chamber, Drake and Cain noticed the altar to one side, but their attention focused on the twelve murals evenly spaced across the walls. The scenes depicting the construction phases of the city and pyramid were astounding enough, but the two murals illustrating the Toltec treasures were the most exciting. Cordova had calmed down a bit as he stood holding his injured hand. He gazed at the murals depicting the Indian envoys transporting hoards of gold and jewels into the temple. "I knew it," he shouted. "The treasure is here and we're close to it! All we have to do is find another opening to the treasure vaults."

"I hope you're right, Major," Swartz said ominously.

In the treasure room below, Santos, Elijah, Simon, and Rosita entered the new opening and found themselves in a natural cavern. Santos discovered the release button on the inside wall and successfully closed the massive door behind them. The cavern was formed of sheer black basalt and it was so huge that the light from the torches only illuminated the immediate area around them. "Where do you suppose we are now?" Elijah asked.

"I would say we're in one of the lava cones," Santos said. "Look at the path. I'll bet this tunnel was the escape route from the city. It should lead us to the outside."

Simon picked up a large stone and heaved it over the side. They never heard the stone strike bottom. "This cavern must drop down a mile or so," Santos suggested.

What the devil have we gotten ourselves into now? Elijah wondered.

"Be sure and stay close to the wall and watch the path in case a rock slide knocked some of it loose," Santos warned.

As they walked, they soon heard the noise of splashing water ahead. Around a small bend, they encountered a waterfall that spilled from an opening in the rock far above. The water cascaded into the black void. Over centuries, the water had eroded the path to no more than two feet. Crossing this slippery section of rock would be treacherous.

"I'll cross first," Santos volunteered. "I'm going to fasten my rope to the wall and pass it over to you to attach on this side. We'll use it as a safety line and handrail."

"Be careful," Rosita shouted.

"Don't worry, you know I'm part mountain goat," he answered with a grin.

"How are you going to attach the rope to a solid rock wall?" Elijah shouted.

The young Mexican reached into his pack, searched for a moment, then pulled out two small climbing bolts with threads on one end and a ring on the other. "I never go anywhere without these."

"What are they for?" Rosita asked.

"They screw into the cracks of rock surfaces and the ring is used to attach a rope. Can't climb a rock wall without them."

Simon took one of the bolts and examined it carefully, "Why don't you attach the rope on this side first and use it as a safety harness when you cross over?"

"I need both hands to pass through the falls," Santos explained.

Handing his rifle and backpack to Simon, he placed the rope over his shoulder and carefully stepped onto the narrow strip of rock. He groped for a handhold and found a small crack in the wall. Inch by inch he moved forward. The tumbling water was cold and the rock ledge under him was slick as glass. Halfway under the falls he began slipping and grabbed the wall frantically in search of a handhold. The others held their breath. At the last second, Santos jammed his fingers into a crack, held on with all his strength, and managed to stabilize his feet and pull forward to hug the rock wall. He inched another three feet to the left and felt his foot touch dry rock. He was safely across. He stood a few moments catching his breath then shouted to Simon, "Find a crack in the rock and screw the bolt in tight. I'll do the same here and throw you one end of the rope under the falls."

Simon found a small fracture and twisted it tight. "Okay, throw it to me!" he yelled.

Santos called back, "After Rosita and Elijah come across unscrew the bolt and tie the rope around your waist and I'll keep it attached as a safety line. You can cross over like I did."

Simon screwed the bolt into the crack and tied the rope securely to the ring, then tugged on the rope to test it. It was secure. Using the rope as a handrail and safety line, Rosita and Elijah made it across the narrow shelf with relative ease. Simon removed the bolt and placed it in his pocket, then tied the rope around his waist and stepped on to the narrow ledge. Slowly he inched across, holding on to each fracture and handhold he could find.

When Simon reached the halfway point, he felt his feet slipping. He frantically grasped for a secure handhold and only felt smooth rock. He slid backwards over the ledge and tumbled into space. His body jerked upward when he reached the end of the slack. The bolt Santos had attached held as Simon swung back and forth. "Are you okay?" Elijah shouted at his suspended cousin.

After a brief hesitation he shouted, "I think I'm still alive if that's what you mean."

"Hang on. We'll pull you up!"

"Hurry…this damn rope is cutting me in half."

Santos and Elijah pulled with all their strength. Simon was able to rotate his body and place his two feet on the wall, and in effect rappel his way up and provide leverage with his legs. They finally hauled him back over the ledge. He lay there gasping for breath as Santos untied the rope, extracted the bolt from the rock and said, "Now you see why I carry these bolts with me?"

After a few minutes, Simon had recovered enough to stand on shaky legs. Elijah lit two new torches and the group continued along the winding path. They could feel the temperature rising. A faint glow reflected from the walls as they rounded a bend. Santos stopped to gaze into the crevice below. "Look over the ledge," he shouted. "Careful! Not too close!"

Far below, they saw a bright winding orange ribbon. "You are looking at a river of molten lava flowing its way through a lava tube. It's probably been here for thousands of years."

"Is it dangerous?" asked Rosita.

"Not as long as it keeps moving. If it stops flowing, the pressure builds and that's when the flow rises up the tube and eventually blows out the top. The good news is we wouldn't suffer long because we'd be vaporized in seconds."

"I hope it keeps flowing peacefully, at least for a few more days," Elijah remarked.

They left the river of lava behind, hoping the ancient path would lead them out of this mountain of death.

27.

Cordova had finally stopped the bleeding. He and one soldier were all that remained of the original Mexican army unit; the others had either deserted or died. Swartz recognized this could be his last chance to dispose of the major, but the big question was how to pull it off. With the loss of most of the soldiers, his hopes of hauling off large amounts of treasure were gone. He figured he and the two American scientists could fill their packs with enough to allow him a life of comfort for a long time. Neither Drake nor Cain carried a weapon and the 1851 Navy Colt revolver Swartz had buried in his pack was so worn he was not even sure it would fire. He had always depended on others for protection. There was still a possibility they could catch Cordova off-guard and push him into one of the traps when the opportunity arose. Just be patient, Swartz kept telling himself, the right time would come soon.

For now, his main concerns were finding the treasure and staying alive. Drake seemed to have more knowledge about the pyramid than anyone else in the group and he needed the professor to find a way out of this room and into the treasure vault. "Mr. Drake," Swartz shouted, "we need to find the opening to another passage."

"I know, I know," Drake answered. "I'm working on it."

The men searched for nearly an hour and came up empty. It was Cain who finally noticed the small jade mask above the altar, wondering how they could have overlooked it for so long. He placed his hands on the mask and pressed the small tile on the forehead. The rumbling noise began and the altar pivoted through the floor, revealing steps leading to the chamber below. The group gathered around the opening and peered into the dark cavity. Drake took the lead as they descended in single file with Swartz bringing up the rear behind Cain, the remaining soldier, and Cordova. Swartz was able to retrieve his old Colt from his pack without anyone seeing what he was doing. He loaded the pistol and stuck it in his belt, concealing it under his shirt. They reached the bottom and followed the narrow corridor.

The light from the torches illuminated the dazzling brilliance before them, generating an explosion of colors that danced across the walls and ceilings. They had finally reached the treasure chamber. Like the Americans, the radiance of the color confusion hypnotized them. The stacks of gold mesmerized Cordova, while Swartz groped greedily for the precious gemstones. The art treasures and ancient artifacts attracted both scientists, but one particular item caught Drake's eye. He leaned over and picked up what appeared to be a Roman style helmet encrusted with gold and silver inlay, the top plume having long since decayed. He was dumbfounded. This did not make any sense. It was as baffling as the great assembly building they visited earlier with its Mediterranean design. Drake thought these early

Indians must have had contact with Roman and perhaps Greek emissaries from half a world away, but the timeline kept killing the theory. Both he and Cain could not think of any reasonable explanation.

The carved crystal statues of the Toltec deities were fascinating as well, the most notable being the large statue of the winged serpent, Quetzalcoatl. Near the back wall, they found a stack of Roman type shields embellished with the feathered serpent. Next to the shields lay several Roman Gladius-like swords, further compounding the mystery. The two scientists were exuberant as they considered the Roman influence on an Indian tribe existing in another time and worlds apart. Impossible? They were determined to find the answers.

Swartz was sifting through gemstones when he noticed the small water basin near the floor. It still had signs of moisture left from Santos's canteen. Swartz motioned for Drake to examine his discovery. "It looks like our American friends also found this," Swartz concluded.

Drake poured water from his canteen into the receptacle and watched with fascination as the water drained through the small opening. Within moments, they heard the familiar grinding vibrations through the floor and a heavy panel lifted from the far wall, leading into another dark cavern. Cordova stuck several of the small gold ingots into his pockets and turned to see the wall panel open. He stood up and let his curiosity push him toward the opening. Suddenly, a loud voice boomed from the far end of the room, "Freeze! Throw your hands in the air! Do it now and no one gets hurt!"

Rifle poised, Dorn repeated the command in Spanish and approached the major, as Kirby and the other two agents followed close behind. Swartz, Cordova, and the scientists turned to see Kirby and the agents with four intimidating rifles pointing at them. They quickly put their hands up. The brief diversion, caused by the radiance of the vast treasure around them, allowed Cordova and his remaining soldier to leap for the opening and disappear into the darkness before anyone could react. The torchlight spilling from the chamber illuminated the path enough to allow Cordova to inch along the wall and down the narrow rock path before he would dare light the torch he carried in his belt. By the time Dorn reached the doorway, the two Mexicans had disappeared into the darkness. The biggest obstacle for Cordova was crossing the eroded path under the waterfall. He sent his soldier across to see if it was passable. It took him a few minutes of hugging the slippery wall but he was able to inch slowly across until his left foot touched solid footing. The soldier lit a fresh torch and nodded for his commander to follow. With his injured hand, the crossing was difficult for Cordova and he nearly lost his footing, but somehow managed to hold on by jamming his good hand into small fissures to maintain his balance. Were it not for his insatiable hatred for the Americans and overwhelming desire to kill them, he might not have made it.

Back in the treasure vault, Swartz looked at the strangers. "Who the devil are you?"

"My name is General Caleb Kirby of the United States Army and my associates here are U.S. federal agents. And you, Mr. Swartz, are under arrest for smuggling illegal arms to the Confederate States of America, among other things that would fill a book."

"You know my name?"

"Yes. We have quite a lengthy dossier on your activities. Smuggling is bad enough, but when you are found aiding and abetting an enemy of the United States during wartime, the charges are more serious. You're wanted on other federal charges as well."

"You can't arrest me!" Swartz replied with a scowl. "We're in Mexico and you have no jurisdiction here."

"Try me," responded Kirby. "These guns say I do."

For another brief instant, Kirby and the agents glanced at the vast treasure stacked throughout the chamber and became distracted long enough to briefly take their eyes off Swartz. He fled through the opening, but unlike Cordova, he had no torch with him. Stephens was close enough to react and jumped through the doorway, slamming into his backside. They both fell to the ground. Stephens grabbed Swartz by the arm, slung him around, and threw a right uppercut to the jaw. The smuggler felt his jawbone crack and front teeth dislodge. He reached into his belt and pulled out the Colt, lifted the weapon and pulled the trigger. The explosion echoed through the chamber like a cannon as the forty-four caliber slug caught Stephens in the chest, penetrating his lung. He knew his wound was fatal and with diminishing strength, hurled his body into Swartz, locking his arms around the fat man with a vise like grip. Swartz fired again, hitting Stephen's heart, killing him instantly. The inertia from the charge carried both men over the ledge. Swartz's last earthly thought was of the diamonds as he fell into the deep volcanic tube and bounced off a protruding rock, smashing his heavy body to pulp.

Kirby and Dorn ran to the opening in time to see the second flash from the gun and the two men career over the edge into darkness. Stephens was gone and there would be no trial and no hangman's noose for the New York smuggler. Dorn was distraught at the loss of his second agent. He always took the loss of his men hard, even though he knew their job was always dangerous.

Turning to Drake and Cain, Kirby asked, "Who are you two?"

"Well, sir," Drake replied, "I'm Dr. Robert Drake, professor of anthropology at Harvard University and this is my associate, Dr. Austin Cain. He's a professor of archeology at New York University. We were commissioned by Harry Swartz to accompany this expedition and document ancient Indian artifacts. We're merely scientists—"

"Good," Kirby interrupted. "Effective immediately you are commissioned by the United States government as the scientific members for this team."

"Fine with me," Drake said.

Cain nodded his firm approval with much relief.

"Tell us about Major Cordova," Kirby asked.

"The man is a lunatic," Drake said. "We realized he was planning to kill us all once we helped him find the treasure. Swartz wanted to eliminate him, but couldn't find the right moment. They were also chasing two other Americans ahead of us somewhere in the cavern. Swartz concluded they were American military officers sent here to steal artifacts and treasure. Cordova and his men were hired by Swartz to stop them. I think their only motive was to follow the Americans so they could steal the treasure for themselves."

"You're partially correct, Mr. Drake. One of the Americans is a captain in the United States Army and the other a captain in the Confederate Army. They're both deserters who traveled here to find the treasure. It's our job to capture them and bring them home."

Turning to Dorn and Cunningham, Drake offered his condolences. "I'm sorry about your agent."

"Yeah, Stephens was a good man," Dorn said sadly.

"In the meantime, gentlemen," Kirby announced, "the treasure will have to wait. Our immediate goal is to find the two Americans, so let's gather our things, light some fresh torches and head into the cavern. Mr. Dorn, please make sure we have plenty of rope. We may need it down in that hole." Turning to Drake and Cain, he asked, "Do either of you know how to handle a rifle?"

"I do," Drake replied.

"Then you take Agent Stephens' rifle. Mr. Dorn here will show you how to operate the weapon. It's a new type repeating rifle made by Spencer. It'll let you shoot seven shots without reloading."

"My goodness, what'll they think of next!" Cain declared.

Checking packs and lighting two new torches, Kirby, the agents, and the newest members of the team entered the dark cavern.

Far ahead of their pursuers, Santos, Elijah, Simon, and Rosita noticed the path was leveling and becoming wider. "Why do I have the strange feeling we're being watched?" Elijah confessed.

"I've had the same sensation," Santos concurred, "ever since we left the section back there with the lava flow. Better stay alert."

They came to a patio carved into the rock face with a doorway leading into a small anteroom. It served as an entrance to a much larger room containing a substantial weapons cache of spears, bows and arrows, and other assorted armaments. Santos picked up what appeared to be a metal Roman style helmet inlaid with gold and silver. There were several metal shields lying about and short swords resembling the traditional Roman battle swords made famous by the emperor Gaius Julius Caesar and the imperial legions of Rome. Simon held up another helmet. "The only thing missing is the imperial eagle pressed into the metal. That would really make them authentic Roman origin."

"Did you notice the feathered serpent design pressed into some of the shields?" Elijah asked.

"I noticed that. The serpent represents the Toltec god, Quetzalcoatl, who was supposed to protect a warrior during battle."

"Yeah, I'll bet," Elijah snickered. "It was the strength of the metal and a strong arm wielding the sword that protected him, not some picture of a snake."

The find was not only remarkable but also extremely perplexing. "But how could a civilization that existed nine hundred years ago possess weapons from another civilization that existed two thousand years ago and were an ocean apart?" Simon pondered aloud.

"That, my dear cousin," Elijah answered, "we'll let the scientists figure out someday."

He picked up one of the Roman swords and ran his fingers along the edges. "This blade is still sharp. I don't see any signs of corrosion or decay. Whoever made this blade sure knew something about forging good steel."

Rosita called the men over to one side of the room where she was holding something unidentifiable in her hand. They stared at the strange looking object. It was a dull silver device, slightly oval, lightweight, with small curved sides. The inside was hollow. There were two small wires protruding from either side that reattached back into the top. It looked like a large seashell shaped to fit over a person's head. Along the top of the hollow device was a thin crack that allowed it to be pulled slightly apart. "What do you suppose this thing is?" she asked.

No one had an answer. Santos rapped on it with a stone. It made a dull hollow sound. Simon tried slipping it over his head but it was too small. "Rosita see if you can put this over your head?"

She lifted the object and tugged until it covered her head. Rosita stood motionless, and then with a horrified look on her face, she suddenly staggered and fell backward. Simon caught her. "Get it off, get it off!" she cried, with arms flailing.

Santos reached over and pulled the object from her head. Rosita blinked a few times and tried to focus. Her vision cleared as she slowly recovered from what appeared to be mild shock.

"What happened?" Simon asked.

"I don't know. My head started spinning and all I could see were strange colored shapes. I've no idea what they were."

"What kind of shapes? What did they look like?"

"I don't really know. They were unusual things… like circles, squares and things I've never seen before. There were many different colors and they moved about."

"We'd better take this thing with us," Simon decided. "Maybe it will prove to be useful. Now, let's see if the passage leads us out of here."

"You American pigs aren't going anywhere!" an unfamiliar, heavily accented voice shouted from the doorway.

They turned to see two Mexican soldiers blocking the door. One was unarmed but the other was holding a U.S. Navy Colt revolver pointed directly at them.

"Who the hell are you?" demanded Simon.

"I am Major Juan Cordova of the Mexican Army."

"Are you with the Americans who have been following us?" Simon asked.

"None of your damned business, gringos."

"What do you want with us, Major?"

"I intend to kill you American pigs. You have cost me the lives of most of my men. I couldn't care less about the men, but you also cost me my two fingers," he shouted, holding up his left hand, displaying the bloody rag protecting the stumps. The Mexican soldier turned furiously to face Cordova. "So you never cared about any of us! All you wanted is that treasure for yourself!"

Cordova turned and shot the soldier between the eyes. As he turned back to face the Americans, Simon threw the strange object with all his might. The major fired and the bullet hit the flying object in midair. Elijah was still holding the Roman sword and hurled the blade end over end into Cordova's mid-section. The blade penetrated his stomach, hitting with such force the point tore through his back. The major cried out, staggered backwards and dropped his pistol. Elijah rushed forward, and grasping the handle of the sword, pushed Cordova toward the doorway. The major's eyes were bulging and a thin stream of blood trickled down the corner of his mouth. He tried to speak but could only murmur gurgling sounds. Grabbing and twisting the handle, Elijah shoved Cordova through the alcove and out across the path to the ledge. A final shove and Cordova tumbled into the deep cavern below. He was dead before he splashed into the river of molten lava. "I commit your soul to hell," Elijah muttered in disgust.

Back in the small chamber, Simon picked up the strange object and looked for a bullet hole. The slug had hit it squarely and bounced off without leaving a scratch. "Whatever this thing is made of, it is stronger than anything I've ever seen before."

The bullet had apparently shattered upon impact because no one could find any fragments. "Can you imagine what we could do with this if we only knew what it was and how to make it? It might be stronger than our toughest metal. I'll take it with us and maybe someone can identify the material when and if we get back home."

He fastened the strange device to his pack while Elijah picked up another Roman sword and strapped it to his pack.

"What about the body of the soldier?" Rosita asked.

"We'll toss it over the cliff and let the lava provide him a proper cremation."

Santos crossed himself, then dragged the body to the edge and rolled it over and into the chasm. They left the room behind and continued following the path, hoping to find an exit soon. They knew the torches would not last much longer.

28.

Kirby, the agents, and scientists moved along the rock pathway, stopping as they approached the waterfall. Dorn, recognizing the climb under the waterfall would be difficult, said, "General, I'll go first. The rest of you can follow. I'm going to tie the rope around my waist and you three hold on and play it out as I cross over because if I fall, I sure as hell hope the three of you can hold on and haul me up. Once I'm on the other side, I'll secure the rope to the wall and one of you pull it tight on this side so the others can use it as a handrail and safety rope. The last man over can do as I did and tie it around his waist. I'll have it anchored in case he falls."

"I'll go last," Kirby volunteered. "Just be careful, Nat."

Dorn fastened the rope around his waist and started across the narrow ledge. With the cold water drenching him, he concentrated on the precarious footing and slippery handholds. When it felt he might lose his footing, he stopped long enough to regain his grip, secure his feet, and move on. He made it through safely. Dorn pulled a small sharp object from his pack and started tapping it into a crack. "What's he doing?" Cain asked.

"He's hammering a metal crampon into the wall so he can attach the rope. You go first, Mr. Drake."

With the far end of the rope firmly anchored and Kirby and Cunningham holding the other end, Drake inched across, using the rope to steady himself. Cain was next and made it across surprisingly easy. Cunningham began to move across. Halfway through the falls, he looked up and took a blast of water in the face, forcing him backward toward the edge. He fell against the taut rope pressing against his back, bounced toward the wall, but was able to regain his balance. The agent made it over and now it was Kirby's turn. The general tied the rope around his waist and started across the narrow ledge, groping the wall for handholds. He was doing fine until he hit a slick spot, slipped and slid backwards. Reaching out for a protruding rock, his fingers grasped a small outcropping and he hung suspended over the edge.

"General, let go and we'll haul you up with the rope," Dorn shouted.

It took all of Kirby's willpower to release his precarious hold. He felt as if he were being sliced in half when the rope abruptly stopped his fall. Luckily, the crampon held tight. It took the strength of Dorn, Cunningham, and Drake to drag Kirby safely back to the ledge. Between gasps, the general stammered, "I put all my faith in you fellows. You didn't disappoint me!"

As they passed through the lava dome, each man peered over the ledge and stared at the bright yellow-orange snake of fire winding its way far below. "This place reminds me of what hell would look like," Cunningham remarked as he peered over the ledge.

"Yeah, and you'll think you are in hell if you fall," Dorn reminded him. Instinctively, each man inched closer to the wall.

In a matter of minutes, they left the ribbon of lava behind and reached the alcove entrance to the weapons cache. Drake was the first to spot the Roman helmets and swords. Like Murphy's reaction before him, he could not conceal his excitement.

"This is unbelievable," Cain shouted. "These weapons are Roman origin. It's just not possible they could be here in Mexico. It doesn't make any sense!" Drake wholeheartedly agreed.

"Look at the figure stamped into this shield," Drake pointed out as he picked up a shield and held it at arm's length. It's not a Roman eagle but the winged serpent, Quetzalcoatl. This has to be Indian origin. There's no way a Roman would have known about the Indian god, Quetzalcoatl."

"Gentlemen," Kirby addressed the two scientists, "I assure you we all want to know more about this place but we need to press on. Perhaps we'll find more answers ahead."

"Perhaps," Drake conceded, as he hefted one of the swords and strapped it to his pack.

As the men left the room, Drake said to Cain, "Did you see the Imperial Roman style helmets? They were inlaid with gold and silver. There has to be a logical explanation how these weapons got here. It would also explain the unusual design of the assembly building—the Mediterranean architecture and those fluted columns are definitely Roman or Greek influence."

Cain was equally intrigued. "We have to come back here."

In the cavern, well ahead of the general, Elijah whispered to Simon as they walked along the stone path, "Why do I keep having this eerie feeling we're being watched?"

"Maybe it's the ancient Toltec spirits looking over us," Simon said, only half joking.

They were now walking uphill. Soon they encountered a series of steps in groupings of twenty or more, confirming they could finally be heading toward the outside. Even the dominating black basalt lining the lava tube gradually changed to limestone, indicating that they were definitely nearing the surface. Soon they came to another large landing with steps leading sharply to the left. Embedded in the wall above the landing was the familiar mask carved into the limestone. Unlike the other masks, it was a plain emblem without any jade tiles. Santos poked the steps with the barrel of his rifle and found them to be solid. He carefully examined the walls and saw no evidence of a trap or other impending danger. Very slowly, they tested each step, anticipating at any moment for a panel to drop or the steps to collapse. Still nothing happened. Santos faced the others and shrugged. He looked perplexed, "This mask is the only one we've seen that doesn't have jade tiles, and it doesn't open a door or activate a trap. I think this one has a different purpose. Any ideas?"

"Maybe, it marks the way out of here," Elijah offered without any basis.

Rosita looked at Elijah hopefully, "I pray you're right. I'm ready to see some sunlight."

They reached the top of a second landing and stood before a large double stone doorway with sculpted handles protruding from each panel. Elijah and Rosita grabbed one handle, Santos and Simon the other. They pulled with all their strength, but neither door would budge. "Damn things are locked down tight," Elijah grumbled. "There has to be a simple way to unlock it. Let's try pulling on the left door first."

They all grabbed the left door handle and tugged. Nothing moved. The right door was also unyielding. Santos walked back down the steps and studied the mask carving. The two cold eyes stared back mockingly, daring him to unlock its mysteries. He gazed back into its piercing eyes and whispered, "What is your secret, you cunning devil?"

Elijah retreated down the steps to find Santos reaching into the pack and pulling out the two rock climbing bolts. He pushed the end of a bolt into one eye socket of the mask. It went in easily. He pushed it in as far as possible and heard a discernable click. Then he pushed the other bolt in the second eye and heard a similar click and the sound of a heavy thudding noise near the doors. He retracted the bolts and ran back up the steps. "Let's try them now!"

This time when they pulled the handles, the heavy doors slowly opened. Cautiously, they stepped inside and pulled the doors back into place to find themselves standing inside a huge limestone cavern. Even with the light of the torches, they could not see any of the surrounding walls. The ceiling was at least fifty feet in height, studded with numerous stalactites.

Simon was the first to notice it. It resembled a gigantic inverted shell. The surface was a dull silver color, covered with centuries of dust and debris. "What the hell is that thing?" Elijah asked, as he walked toward the strange object.

"Beats me," Simon answered. "I've never seen anything like it."

Santos was speechless; Rosita wouldn't even hazard a guess.

They cautiously approached the peculiar discovery. Simon took out his hunting knife and dragged the point back and forth across the surface. To their astonishment, there wasn't even a scratch. "This surface is much harder than the steel on my knife," Simon said in amazement.

Elijah began at one end and paced off the length of the huge object. "My God," he said, "this thing is almost a hundred and fifty feet long." Then he paced off the width. "And nearly a hundred feet wide!"

"It looks higher than a one story building!" Simon surmised as he ran his hand along the glass-like surface.

Rosita stared at the object's shape. "Maybe it's some type of shelter the Indians built from an unknown material."

"No! I think it might be some type of floating vessel that got trapped in here during a flood," Elijah countered.

Simon thought for a few moments. "You're going to think I'm nuts when I say this."

"Well, we already know that, but what's your idea?' Elijah asked.

"How about a flying ship?"

"You mean like some of the flying observation balloons used during the war?"

"No, something that flies much higher," he said, gesturing heavenward.

"Now we know you're nuts," Elijah responded. "That's crazy talk!"

"Remember that college professor I told you about—he had a theory about visits from people from other planets. He believed they used special airships to fly through space. We thought he was crazy, so did the university. They finally fired him."

"Who did he say these people were who visited earth?" Santos asked skeptically.

"I don't know," Simon replied. They might not have been people, but weird-looking creatures who lived on another planet."

"Maybe they were from the moon," Elijah responded with a sarcastic laugh.

Suddenly a small blue light began to pulsate on the unusual device attached to Simon's backpack. Rosita was the first to spot it. She cried out, "What's that?"

Simon dropped his pack and backed away as the mysterious blue light continued to blink. Rosita was frightened. "I think when you got close to that weird thing the light started to blink."

Simon turned to Rosita, "Tell us again what you saw and felt when you put that thing on your head?"

"I saw strange images and then I got really dizzy."

"When you saw the images, did you try to block them out?"

"I guess so. They scared me to death."

"What did they look like?"

"Strange shapes made of lines, dots, and curves; maybe it was like some foreign language—oh, I don't know." Rosita's eyes widened. "Look, it's still blinking."

"I see it," Simon said. "Remember the reaction Rosita had back in the cave when she put this thing on her head? Maybe it's some sort of headpiece used for communicating. Maybe it sends and receives signals, maybe even from this shell here. Do you reckon it's possible the shell is designed to carry people or things from…well…way up there?" he said pointing skyward.

Elijah looked at Simon suspiciously, "I think you're as crazy as that professor you talked about."

Simon ignored the remark, picked up the helmet and placed it on his head. It was too small. He tugged at the sides and it widened enough to fit snugly. His vision adjusted quickly, and then small objects and strange figures began to pass before his eyes. He shut them tight, and then reopened them. The images were still there. Don't fight it! Concentrate! Concentrate! Think of questions and look for some answers.

The figures slowed and the images became more focused. Who are you? Simon thought.

The images stopped flashing. There was complete silence and soon a garbled metallic sound flooded his ears. It was a combination of strange gurgling noises interspersed with unintelligible words. With a look of distress, he tore the piece from his head, dropped it to the ground, and backed away. "My God!" he whispered.

The others were dumbfounded. "You okay?" Elijah asked.

Simon nodded. Regaining his courage and composure, he slipped the headpiece back on. He heard the same garbled sounds although now emitting at a slower rate. Within seconds, the sounds became clearer and a barely discernible metallic voice spoke into the helmet. "You…use…strange words…new to us. You…speak bits…Proto-Indo European and Saxon… derivatives… Latin, Sanskrit… German. We try…assimilate…reconstruct your language…communicate with you. Give us time…we access more…information… our databanks." Then there was silence.

Simon tore the helmet off. His expression was one of sheer disbelief.

Elijah looked at him with concern, "What in the world happened?"

Simon had a wild look in his eye, "The thing is speaking to me, but first it wants time to learn our language."

"What are you talking about?" Santos said, confusion written all over his face.

"I'm telling you the thing actually spoke to me in broken bits of English," Simon retorted.

As the other three stared at him, he carefully picked up the helmet, placed it back on his head and waited. The voice continued, "We now understand most of the language you speak. What do you require of us?"

"Who are you and where do you come from?" Simon asked.

"We are the exploratory ship SREX235 from a galaxy far from your earth. We have been observing your planet for three thousand of your earth years. This ship was stored in this location for repairs eight hundred and ninety-six earth years ago, but was unable to return to our galaxy. The early inhabitants here welcomed our explorers and we honored them with our knowledge. Our explorers are all dead now."

Simon did the math in his head. "This thing was put in here around 869 A.D.," he enlightened his companions. "Who am I talking to?" he asked, turning to the headset.

"I am XTX472. Interpreted in your language we are the databank from this ship. I am still active and will be so as long as our fuel element, Tracx, is active."

Simon's interest was soaring. "I am not sure I understand. Please tell me what Tracx is."

"Tracx is a basic element that emits a strong form of energy. An active Tracx cell lasts for one million of your earth years. You and I are communicating through one of our headsets."

"Earlier, you mentioned the word databank. What is a databank?" Simon questioned.

"It is a storage repository for all the information in both of our galaxies, and others as well. It also stores all the data used to operate this craft. You are actually talking to our computer, a machine that operates the databank."

Simon still did not understand but would try to make his mind imagine into the future.

"How can we open your ship?"

"Just command it."

Simon hesitated for a moment. His three puzzled companions stared at him as he shrugged dubiously. "I command you to open the doors to your flying ship," he said firmly and with as much authority as he could muster.

"In your language we call it a spaceship," the voice corrected.

Everyone held their breath as a soft humming noise transmitted from the giant shell and a panel opened to unfold metal stairs that slowly extended to the ground. Simon removed the helmet, took a deep breath, and looked at his companions, "You won't believe what I'm about to tell you. I'm hearing words and things our world has not yet even considered. I'm talking about words and concepts that are still far into the future. I have been speaking to something called a databank that stores information. The voice told me I was actually talking to some sort of a machine called a computer that operates the storage thing it called a databank. This is a flying ship from outer space that was stranded here almost nine hundred years ago. The space people are all dead now, but the ship and all its machines operate by some space element they call Tracx that stays active for a million years. That's why the thing is still alive."

"How can it be talking to you?" Elijah questioned. "There has to be a live person somewhere inside this thing that speaks to you."

"No, I'm actually talking to some kind of a machine that calls itself a computer. It must be an artificial brain that understands what I'm saying."

"This is crazy," Elijah exclaimed, shaking his head vigorously.

"Look, I am just as dumbfounded as you are. All I can tell you is what the voice is telling me. This databank or computer thing talks just like a human."

"Will the ship still fly?" Santos asked.

"I don't think so. It apparently stopped here for repairs and for some reason they were unable to return to their world, so the space people just got stuck here with the Indians and eventually died out."

"How did you get the ship to open the door?" Rosita asked nervously.

"I gave it a command, just like the voice told me to do."

"I think we should go inside and check it out," Elijah suggested with false bravado.

With mixed feelings of fear and curiosity, Santos crossed himself. "I do not know of such things. Maybe we should not be near this demon shell. If we go inside, it may eat us."

"No, Santos," Simon said trying to be reassuring. "This is a spaceship that carries people through the sky. It sounds friendly enough. I don't think it wants to hurt us. It may even help us get out of here."

Rosita gathered her courage and touched the outer skin of the ship. She jerked her hand back quickly, expecting a shock or something terrible to happen. "It seems harmless…," she slowly conceded. "I wonder what the people were like who flew inside this shell."

"Let's go inside and find out," Simon replied.

29.

Simon took a deep, calming breath then led them up the ladder and through the open hatchway. The inside was illuminated by an iridescent soft green glow that seemed to diminish their fear. They were now entering the inner sanctum of an alien and distant world. The interior was more spacious than anticipated. Once the four were inside, they heard a soft humming noise as the ladder and hatch door automatically retracted back into its recess. The spacious cabin appeared to be a reception area containing several rows of comfortable recliner-type chairs. A set of steps led to the upper compartment, most likely the command center, and a narrow corridor led to the forward section of the ship and another toward the aft. Simon warned his companions, "Let's stick together. Don't wander off on your own."

They all noticed a series of small, round, evenly spaced portholes that had not been visible from the outside. Oddly, when they looked out into the cavern, the strange translucent glass transformed the darkness into a dimly lit display of the cavern. "How can this be?" Rosita marveled. "I don't remember us leaving any lighted torches inside the cavern."

"We didn't," Simon replied. "Somehow, the glass in these windows has a way of illuminating the darkness. Let me put this helmet back on and try to get more information about the ship."

He tugged it over his head, pressed the little button to turn it on, and spoke into the microphone. "Hello! Are you there? Hello, Databank, can you hear me?"

There was a pause, some faint static then the metallic voice answered, "This is the ship's computer databank responding to your call. Our sensors tell us that you and your companions have now entered our ship and are within our reception lounge."

"Yes, that is right. We wish to learn more about you and your ship."

"We will answer your questions as long as they do not breach our safety and security protocols. You may proceed."

Simon looked at his companions with a quizzical look, "Tell me more about the databank. What exactly does it do?"

"It's a storage medium that collects billions of bits of information about this ship and the universe. We also utilize passive modules called computers. These are electronic machines that disseminate, interpret the information, and provide command signals that drive the machines that power the ship."

"I'm afraid you lost me here..."

"The computers are the mechanisms that control the lights, circulate the air, and feed the correct amounts of Tracx fuel into the engines that power the spacecraft. Our computers drive everything on the ship."

"In other words," Simon queried, "you are telling me that your computers think and function like human brains?"

"The intelligence levels of our computers are far more advanced than your human brains."

Thanks for the compliment, Simon thought. They must think we're primitive animals.

He noticed how much the databank's use of the English language had improved. By listening to their conversations and conversing with Simon, the ship's computers had mastered the use of the English language within minutes.

"We would like to explore your ship. Where should we go from here?"

"Proceed to the front through the hallway. You will enter the officer quarters and our laboratories."

They filed into the hallway and moved forward. Each compartment was bathed in the same soft green light. They passed several small rooms on either side of the corridor, all very similar in size and furnishings.

"These must have been the officer quarters," Elijah assumed. Each room had a single bunk alongside an end table; a small desk recessed into a wall. Above each desk was a panel with numerous buttons. The bunks were approximately five feet long. "Guess these folks were pretty short," he added.

In one room, a crumpled silver jumpsuit lay on the bunk. It had two leg and arm sections and the chest area was significantly larger in proportion to the lower section. Simon held the suit up and said, "These space explorers must have had very large upper body cavities. Maybe they had larger chest organs than humans."

"That would mean they had very big hearts and must have been kind and happy people!" Rosita almost giggled.

320 | ALEX WALKER

"I doubt that," Elijah remarked. "It means they were top heavy and probably had big duck feet to keep them from toppling over."

The group chuckled and realized they were all more relaxed now since Simon had communicated with the strange machine. They certainly felt less threatened. When the four reached the second bank of rooms, they discovered a mummified body of one of the former officers lying on a bunk. The head was slightly oversized, with an elongated skull, and there was no sign that it ever had any hair. There were no protruding ears, only small holes high on each side of the skull. The face had once sported a relatively large nose considering the size of the mummy's nasal cavity and the amount of dried cartilage remaining. The empty eye sockets were spaced far apart and high on the skull and the thin mouth cavity was wide in relation to the skull size. Elijah humorously thought that if still living, this alien thing would have been an oddity among humans and would have made a fine sideshow sensation with a traveling circus.

Simon continued with his non-scientific analysis. "Well, he may look odd, but the size of his skull and brain cavity means these space travelers had far superior intelligence than us. The existence of this ship, and the fact they were here on earth, proves they had to be far advanced. Can you imagine what we can learn from the databank on this ship?"

He placed the helmet back on his head. "Databank, how have you managed to keep the air in this ship so fresh and dry?"

"Our Tracx fuel cells have kept the ship active for hundreds of earth years. Our filters continuously circulate the air. The oxygen and hydrogen inverse scrubbers keep the air purified and eliminate excess moisture."

Simon repeated the databank's response to the others.

"Wonder what all that means," Elijah commented.

"It means they have a way to keep the air fresh and circulating throughout the ship indefinitely," Simon explained, then asked the databank, "What happened to all of your original explorers?"

"They died of old age and disease about eight hundred seventy earth years ago. They all lived well over two hundred years."

"My God," gasped Rosita.

Santos added, "I wonder what their secret was?"

"Maybe good living and lots of sex," quipped Elijah.

Simon asked the databank, "Do other planets like earth exist in space?"

"Yes, there are many, but your earth is the only one in your solar system with abundant water and other necessary elements to support a vast variety of life forms."

"How many languages do you understand?"

"We can speak six thousand four hundred fifty-seven different languages and dialects from one hundred thirty-two planets in four galaxies and fourteen solar systems."

"How does our planet earth rank in order of development and evolutionary advancement?"

"Your planet ranks twenty-second. Many planets have primitive life forms in comparison to you humans, but most have no life at all. Twenty-one planets are more advanced than your earth."

Elijah looked at Simon with a quizzical expression, "Where did you learn all that space language and stuff to ask them about evolution and planets?"

"I know it's hard for you to believe, but I did attend the University of Michigan for three years."

"Hell, we never heard of things like that where I come from," Elijah chuckled.

"Cause you were too damned busy plowing cotton fields and chasing your female cousins." Elijah poked Simon in the ribs and countered, "You ought to see some of my cousins."

The next cabin was furnished with six tables, tightly arranged, and banks of storage lockers. They opened a few bins and found the remains of clothing and several more silver-clad jumpsuits. "We must be in one of the laboratories," Elijah suggested, as he gazed at two large tables with beaker-like containers and other strange objects scattered about.

Santos spotted and pointed to sixteen large translucent cylinders, filled with a clear liquid, lined against the walls. To their dismay, eight of the cylinders contained well-preserved naked human bodies, five males and three females. Three appeared to be Caucasian and the others, Indian. One heavy-set male had long blond hair and could easily have been a Norseman or Viking. They were floating, suspended inside the clear liquid, with sightless eyes. When the initial shock wore off, Simon offered his opinion. "They may have used these bodies for dissecting and study or maybe they died of natural causes and were kept here in order to bring them back to life at a future date."

Santos had never considered anything like a spacecraft or live creatures from outside his world could possibly exist. He simply could not grasp the significance of the situation, but suggested they move on and explore the rest of the ship, then quickly get out of here.

The forward sections contained compartments for the crew and a row of square containers lined some of the walls. "Maybe these are the databanks you spoke about," Elijah surmised.

"They sure don't look like anything that could talk back to us," Rosita said.

A steady humming noise in another compartment indicated this was where the Tracx fuel cells and power source were located. They knew better than to touch anything and kept their distance. Passing through a larger room, they came upon a series of low tables, benches, and two work areas. "This was probably the mess hall," Elijah suggested. Stoves or cooking vessels were missing, but along the workspaces, there were a series of metal tubes protruding from the wall panels. Small valves were mounted above each tube.

"What if I turned one of these valves? Do you suppose any food would come out?" Rosita questioned.

"Yeah," Elijah laughed. "You might get some thousand-year-old green goop."

Retracing their steps, they returned to the reception room and approached a narrow stairway leading to the top level. "Let's check out the upper compartments," Simon suggested.

He led the way up the steps and into a large room filled with very complex looking equipment. The walls were lined with panels and odd glasslike cylinders. There were numerous banks of control buttons and levers positioned along the side panels and a labyrinth of unusual looking gadgets unknown to the earth intruders. Most of the control devices had labels with symbols and glyphs, obviously in the original occupant's language. Like the rest of the ship, the control room was illuminated by the soft green light. Lying on a small table, Simon found what appeared to be a logbook bound with a velvet-like cover and filled with soft metallic-like pages. Each page contained rows of symbols and glyphs similar to those on the instrument labels. As he thumbed through the pages, he came to a section of diagrams. He could not believe his eyes.

"Everyone—over here! You have to see this."

Clearly illustrated on several pages, were precise diagrams of classical Roman and ancient Greek buildings and other forms of early Mediterranean-style architecture. There were details of Roman and Greek columns and arches. All four stared at the revealing logbook in astonishment. Simon turned more pages. There were several well-defined sketches of Roman weapons, specifically shields, helmets, and the classic Roman short swords. Some of the diagrams even displayed helmets with the imperial eagle crest pressed into the metal and plumes adorning the crown. Simon looked at the others, "Now we know where those Roman-like weapons came from. Maybe this is what the databank meant when it said they rewarded the Indians by sharing information with them. I guess Roman weapons were the most advanced humans knew about a thousand years ago. I'll ask the databank," he said, placing the helmet back on his head. "Hello, databank, are you there?"

"We are always here."

"Did your explorers supply the Roman weapons to the Toltec Indians?"

"Yes, it was a reward for their hospitability."

"Did they actually come from Rome?"

"The designs came from the Romans, but the weapons were made here. Our explorers taught the Indians how to forge the steel. The swords and spear points are actually stronger than the real Roman weapons."

"What happened to the Indians who lived here? Why did they disappear?"

"That information was not programmed into our databank. We do have our theories although we cannot prove them."

"What do you think happened?"

"We have old records that show our sensors recorded heavy concentrations of sulfurous fumes, hydrogen sulfide, and carbon monoxide within the volcanic cone. We believe the Indians were driven from the city by these gases."

Simon looked at the others with a quizzical shrug. "How did you get the ship into this cavern?"

"This cavern was a temporary storage hangar used to berth the ship. It was flown in here on its own."

"Can this ship fly again?"

"Yes, but the power link and modulator stabilizer element need repair."

"I have no idea what that is."

"They are inside the power module and help drive the Tracx booster system. It is the internal propulsion modulator that nullifies gravity and moves the craft off the ground away from the earth's gravitational pull."

"I am afraid I do not understand. What makes this ship go?"

"Once we are past the gravitational pull of your planet, this ship is powered by energy from our Tracx fuel cells and ion generators."

"How fast can you go?"

"We can reach speeds equal to pure energy transfers, especially within many outer space mediums. We call it Vartz speed. The human mind cannot comprehend these speeds."

Simon looked at Elijah and shrugged his shoulders, "This data thing is using scientific and technical words I don't understand. I have no idea what it's talking about but I think it has something to do with getting the ship back into the air and flying. It sounds like this thing can really move fast."

He returned to his questions, "How can we find some of this Tracx fuel you mentioned?"

"It does not exist on your planet. It only comes from two planets in our own solar system, Aarnon and Terchez Zen."

"You said this place was a storage room. How can we open the cavern door to the outside?"

"There is a lever on the floor near the west wall. When you pull the lever, a large door will open to the outdoors."

Simon took a deep breath and removed the headset. Elijah, Santos, and Rosita looked at him questioningly. "It would be great if we could fly this thing out of here, but it needs repairs with the power mechanism. Some of the information the databank is talking about is just gibberish to me."

"Maybe the voice could help us fix it by talking us through it," Elijah suggested. "Just think, if we could fly this thing back to the plaza, we could load it up with treasure and fly anywhere we wanted. Besides, I'll bet you this thing will fly itself if we just got it up in the air!"

Simon nodded. "Let's ask it. Databank, do you have the parts on board to fix this ship?"

"That's affirmative."

"If you have the parts, why didn't you fix it?"

"Most of our explorers became ill from an unknown earth disease and died. They were getting old and had reached the closing stages of their life span. Our crew had no immunity from your planet's complex microbes and germs and had to be quarantined by our command center. They were instructed not to leave earth and remained here until the last one died."

"How long were the explorers here with the Toltec Indians?" Simon asked.

"Only twelve of your earth years."

"Could we repair the ship if you could talk us through the process?"

"That depends on your level of intelligence."

"If we did repair it, can you fly this ship using our voice commands?"

"Yes, we can receive your voice commands, translate them into a code, and then transmit the code to the computers. The computers will follow the coded instructions and fly the ship."

Simon conveyed this information to the others.

"You see," Elijah replied, "we can fix this thing and fly it back to the States filled with the treasure. We can fly it over a few battlefields then land in Washington and probably stop the war. This will scare the hell out of them—maybe give all the generals something to think about besides running around shooting at each other."

Looking at the others, Simon pondered the situation, "Well, I'll admit it does give us a possible new option, but meanwhile, let's try and open the cavern door and get into some fresh air." The others agreed.

"Databank, please open the door so we can leave the ship," Simon requested.

He stuck the headset back in his pack then descended the steps to the reception room, finding the door open and the ladder extending to the ground.

Santos lit two new torches and they filed out of the ship on to solid ground. He was glad to be out of the creepy thing, alive and in one piece. As the door closed behind them, Elijah looked around the cavern. "Wonder which wall is the west wall?"

"Probably that wall facing the front of the ship." Santos suggested.

Elijah whispered anxiously to Simon, "I still have that feeling we're being watched."

It did not take Santos long to find the lever at the edge of the wall, which he pulled inward. A deep rumbling noise erupted and two huge panels rose, spilling bright sunlight into the cavern. At first sight, they noticed a large earthen dike leading into a swamp. Standing on the dike facing them were several hundred Indians dressed in splendid multi-colored costumes. They were carrying spears, bows, Roman shields, and short swords. As the group turned back to the spaceship, another large group of warriors moved into the cavern from either side and surrounded them.

"I would swear they are either Toltecs or Mayans by their dress," Santos whispered. "As a sign of peace, keep your guns pointing down. We don't want to provoke them."

While Rosita inched closer to the men, Elijah looked at Simon and whispered, "Do you remember the question you asked the machine about the fate of the Toltec Indians? Well, I think we've found our answer!"

30.

The contingent of warriors, adorned in bright-colored feather studded costumes, quickly surrounded Santos, Rosita, and the two Americans. Crowding around the mysterious intruders, they seemed more puzzled than angry. These were the first outsiders the Indians had ever seen, and because they had entered the spaceship and walked out alive, many of the warriors thought they were deities. For hundreds of years the spaceship was considered home to very powerful gods and no Indian would dare go near it, much less attempt to enter the ship. Of course, there was no way they could possibly have known that the only way to gain access was through a simple command sequence using the helmet and microphone.

One of the warriors, standing in front, displayed his rank and command. He looked like a military leader or chieftain and motioned the new arrivals to move forward and follow him to the dike. The four detainees stayed close to one another with Elijah keeping an eye on the rear. They were not sure what to expect and kept their rifles ready, but the Indians maintained their distance and did not show any signs of hostility. It appeared their mood was more of curiosity.

The path leading over the dike led in a westerly direction, fueling Elijah's curiosity of what he had seen in the pyramid. "Have you noticed this view is exactly what we saw on one of the murals?"

"You mean the path leading west toward the sunset?"

"Yes, the scene showing the hoard of Indians walking from the volcano on the embankment?'

"It's remarkable," Simon agreed.

"Santos, what are they saying? Do you understand any of their language?"

"I understand some of it," he answered. "The dialogue sounds like Nahuatl—a universal language in ancient times. Some of it is still recognizable in eastern Mexico if you can wade through all the Spanish influence. The Conquistadors did more than just destroy the tribes of Mexico and Peru; they also decimated the languages."

The dialect became more intense between two important looking Indians.

"Those two are arguing," Santos pointed out. "The one who looks like a chief is defending us. He keeps saying we are spirits and gods from the sun. Somehow, they know we were inside that space shell."

"You see, I told you we were being watched!" Elijah exclaimed. "One of them must have been following us in the tunnel."

"Have you noticed they haven't tried to take our guns or packs?" Rosita said.

"As long as they think we might be gods," Simon said, "they'll probably leave us alone. Must be why the chief is arguing with the older man."

Santos turned toward the two Indians. "The older one could be a high priest. He claims we're enemies sent here to destroy them."

"I like the chief's argument better," Elijah muttered.

Similar to most nineteenth century earthen dams, the bridge was about twenty feet across, nearly fifty feet high, and a true marvel of ancient engineering and workmanship. It must have taken many years and countless lives to construct and stretch the dam through the swamp and jungle. It gave the Indians a clear and secure passage to and from the cavern. As they marched along the road, the Indians kept their distance to the front and rear of these strange visitors. The air was hot and humid. Soon the foursome were soaked with sweat as swarms of mosquitoes buzzed around their heads and arms, seeking their evening meal. For some reason, the mosquitoes did not bother the Indians. Years of adaptation had somehow provided the tribe with a special scent that repelled the ferocious insects.

The dike wound along for about two miles before it turned to a well-worn path terminating on a high plateau. Lying before them was a shallow oval-shaped valley lined with tall trees, exotic flowering plants, and a huge assortment of other flora and fauna. It was a virtual paradise in the midst of a hostile swamp and jungle. As the four outsiders gazed across the beautiful valley, to their astonishment, a small city lay before them, shaped much like Xepocotec, with buildings closely resembling those in the lost city. It was as if the Indians had literally picked up the lost city and moved it to a new location—the only difference being its smaller size. A pyramid stood majestically in the center, with an ornate temple on the summit.

The Indians led the group down to the central thoroughfare lined with small open stalls and stone dwellings. The streets and plaza had filled with inquisitive natives who stared at them with fascination and curiosity. Men, women, and children were dressed in their colorful garb and a group of chieftains stood at the foot of the pyramid awaiting their arrival. Various council members and other dignitaries stood nearby. The mob shifted nervously as if some great heavenly event was about to occur.

"What's going on, Santos?" Simon whispered.

"It looks like we're about to meet all the chiefs of the tribe. Some must think we are space gods and the others are not too sure. Let's try and act like space gods."

How in hell do we do that? Elijah wondered.

With some prodding from their hosts, the intruders were paraded in front of the royal assemblage and motioned to stop. There was silence as the chiefs examined them. One particularly shriveled old priest began making wild gestures to a regal figure who appeared to be the tribal leader. At the same time, the military officer who had escorted them from the cavern stepped forward and started talking to the leader.

"What are they saying?" Simon whispered again to Santos.

"The priest is telling the chief that we are evil intruders who are here in advance of an invasion by enemies from far away. He thinks we should be sacrificed to their god, Quetzalcoatl. The warrior chief is defending us by telling him we have been inside the spacecraft and descendants of early space explorers. He thinks we are here to help them, just as the space explorers helped their ancestors. He's telling him we are space gods and should be treated as such."

"Perhaps we need to give them a sign to show our godlike powers," Elijah suggested. "Watch this!"

"Hold it!" Simon cried, moving his hand out to calm Elijah. "What the hell are you planning to do? You want to get us all killed?"

"Don't worry, cousin, I'm not going to shoot anybody unless they charge us. I'm only going to show them a sign from the sun god."

Elijah raised his arms to the sky and gyrated a bit as if he were summoning the powers from the heavens above. He pointed to the top of the pyramid. A hush came over the crowd as they watched him raise his Spencer, taking careful aim. He squeezed the trigger and the loud shot echoed over the plaza, causing the large crowd to gasp in fear. Some scattered into open doorways lining the plaza. At the top of the temple, a fat pigeon fell from the roof and bounced halfway down the steps. A nearby warrior retrieved the dead fowl and brought it to the dignitaries. One of the chiefs took the pigeon and held it high in the air as he watched the fluid oozing from the gunshot wound. The chief began talking excitedly and pointing to the pigeon, then to the four strangers. Many Indians backed away from the outsiders with alarm and awe.

"What are they saying now, Santos?" Elijah wanted to know.

"The leader is saying we possess godlike powers with our thunder sticks and can hurl lightning bolts into the sky that can strike down living things. He is telling his people we are not to be harmed, but treated as guests, at least for now. We are also to be watched closely. The old priest is still not convinced and not too happy with the decision. I think the old man could be trouble."

Inside the Lava Dome

Kirby, his agents, and the scientists were moving along the narrow pathway and they, too, noticed the sudden incline and subtle changes in the rock formations from basalt to limestone. They arrived at the landing and saw the two massive doors blocking the passage before them. Dorn and Kirby took the handles and pulled with all their strength, but the doors would not budge. "What do you suggest, Mr. Dorn?"

"Well, first we need to look around and find a key to unlock the doors. Examine the walls and floor for a triggering device. We all know what to look for..."

Drake noticed the simple mask carving on the wall and the two dark holes bored into the eye sockets, giving the face a more sinister look. This was puzzling. None of the other masks he had seen had holes like this in the eyes. He also wondered why one hole was slightly larger.

Kirby was equally as curious. "Nat, maybe those eye slots are the key! Look for something that will fit into those holes."

Dorn went into his pack and pulled out the serrated crampon he had used earlier to secure the rope at the falls. He tried to push it into the larger hole, but without success. Unlike the bolts used by Santos, this one was flat and too wide. Drake turned to Cain and said, "Austin, there has to be some kind of instrument nearby that will fit these holes."

After several minutes of thorough searching, Drake said with a sigh of frustration, "Something had to allow the priests and warriors to get through these doors, especially in an emergency. I wonder what Murphy and Walker used to open them."

"What would a priest be carrying that would open those doors?" Kirby asked."

"I don't know what a priest would carry, but a warrior would carry weapons," Dorn added. "You know, like spears, bow and arrows, knives, and axes. And based on what I've seen, some of the Indians could have been carrying a Roman sword and shield."

Drake thought of the weapons room and remembered the sword strapped to his pack. It was a simple Roman Gladius blade with a short round hilt for protection from an enemy sword thrust. The Roman infantry legions had developed it as an effective weapon for fighting in close quarters. He untied the sword from his pack and hefted it. He felt along the handle and the round hilt, and noticed a very inconspicuous tiny button on the underside. He pressed the button and two short slender bars sprang from each side. Dorn hurried to the wall and held the sword up to the mask, turning it to the side. He inserted the shorter bar into the right eye socket. It slid neatly into the hole and he heard a distinct click. He reversed the sword and inserted the other bar into the left socket, then heard the familiar sound of a bolt retracting into a wall recess. He gazed at the sword in his hand. Ingenious, he thought. Quickly, they ran back to the landing and with two men on each handle, they pulled hard and the two massive doors swung open to reveal a huge void of darkness. Kirby looked at Drake with great relief. "Well done, Mr. Drake, well done indeed."

As the group walked into the huge cavern, the meager light from their torches was insufficient to penetrate the darkness. It took a few minutes to get their bearings.

"What in the hell is that thing?" cried Cunningham, pointing to the far left wall. All eyes turned toward the faint image of the huge dull silver-gray colored shell sitting along the wall.

Dorn was astonished, "I've never seen anything like that before."

The group circled the large object, but had no idea what it could be. Drake, who had the most technical knowledge of the group said, "Whatever it is, it's been sitting here awhile."

"Maybe it's a shelter of some kind," Cunningham offered.

"It looks to me like a big clam or turtle shell," Cain countered.

"No," Drake concluded as he walked around the object, carefully observing its features and streamlined shape. "I think it's something far more sinister."

"What then, Mr. Drake?" Kirby prodded.

Drake hesitated, "I'm just not sure...."

"What?" Kirby demanded. "Let's have it."

"It might be a boat, maybe an ironclad...or maybe it's a flying ship..."

"A what?" Dorn said as if he hadn't heard it.

"A flying ship! A ship that flies through the sky."

"Have you been into a rum bottle, Mr. Drake?"

"No, General, I've heard about the possibility of flying ships. All I'm saying is that it appears similar to drawings I once saw of flying ships that were supposed to be from some far off places from our earth. A professor I knew at Harvard believed in stuff like that."

"Robert, your imagination is in full gear today," Cain said.

Dorn interrupted, "Are you saying this thing could be from another place, like the moon?"

Drake shrugged, "Well…I'm not sure, but it sure resembles some drawings I once saw in school. Try scratching the surface and see if you can make a mark," Drake challenged.

Dorn took out his pocketknife and dragged the point hard against the skin. "Well, I'll be damned," whispered Dorn. "Whatever this thing is made of, it's tough as hell."

"If people actually flew in it, do you think there might be a way to get inside?" Cain asked.

"Possibly. Finding a door would be one thing, opening it may be another matter. If this really is a flying ship from another place, it would fly at unimaginable speeds. Any door would have to be so tightly sealed that I doubt we would be able to see any evidence of it on the surface."

"Over here, Dorn," Cunningham called out. He had been exploring around the cavern while the others were inspecting the strange object.

Dorn and Kirby walked over to a wall to see Cunningham standing by a large metal lever protruding from the floor. Kirby said, "Give it a try."

Cunningham pulled the lever and a deep rumbling noise vibrated from the floor. The huge panels slowly raised upward, spilling the late afternoon sunlight through the widening cracks and illuminating the large room. As they looked toward the opening, the earthen dike loomed before them. Drake looked at Cain, "So this is how the Indians left the city! Just like the mural we saw."

Dorn turned to Kirby, "It seems to be the only route available. I'll bet Murphy and Walker are somewhere out there."

"Wonder what happened to the major?" Drake questioned.

"Who knows? Maybe he caught up with Murphy."

"Okay, Mr. Dorn, I think it best we follow the dike," Kirby said firmly.

Drake and Cain were visibly shaken. To them, capturing Murphy and Walker was meaningless compared to the treasure and the research potential the pyramid and this strange vessel represented.

"General, aren't we going to try and explore that shell, or whatever it is? This could be the discovery of the century!" Drake pleaded.

Cain interrupted, "Even in the history of mankind! It would substantiate early cave drawings found in Europe years ago. Some scientists have speculated the drawings are several thousand years old and represent objects from another world. Consider what this discovery could do for humanity. It could propel us out of the horse-and-buggy age."

An exasperated Kirby replied, "Look, I know you two are much more educated than I am, but don't expect me to believe that this thing is really from outer space. It's probably a shelter of some type. Sorry, gentlemen, we have no time for this now. Our first mission is to capture Murphy and Walker and then secure the treasure. I'm sure our government will eventually send a scientific team here to study the lost city and pyramid. In fact, I'd be the first to recommend both of you to head up such a team. Meanwhile, let's follow the dike and see where it takes us."

As they followed Kirby out of the cavern, Drake and Cain shook their heads in frustration and disbelief.

31.

Ten menacing warriors herded Santos, Simon, Elijah, and Rosita to the top of the pyramid, escorting them to a heavily guarded room inside the temple. The sparsely furnished room had two narrow windows overlooking the plaza below. Elijah was annoyed, "I thought after the pigeon display we would have been treated like royalty."

"I think you scared the hell out of them and pissed them off," Simon grumbled as he sat on a small bench trying desperately to make some sense of their situation. The one thing he and the others were reasonably sure of was that these Indians were descendants of the Toltecs, whose ancestors once inhabited the lost city.

Santos said, "I think they're just trying to figure out who we are and what to do with us."

"What do you suppose really happened to force the Toltecs to leave Xepocotec and build this newer city?" Rosita asked.

"We may never know the answer," her brother replied. "My first thought was a volcanic eruption, but there's no evidence of lava deposits or volcanic debris in the streets.

Except for normal decay and erosion, the buildings looked to be in decent shape."

Simon offered his opinion, "Remember, the databank told us their sensors had detected poisonous gasses from the volcano and thought that's what drove them out. It's the most plausible explanation I've heard so far. Maybe the Toltecs built that elaborate tunnel anticipating they would have to evacuate the city someday."

"But if they escaped from Xepocotec, wouldn't they have moved back to their abandoned city once the gasses dissipated?" asked Rosita.

"Maybe the gases never left, but stayed around long enough for them to build this new city, then they never moved back," Elijah offered. "Maybe the tribe experienced a plague, something like the black plague that hit Europe.

"I don't know about that," Simon reasoned. "Remember, this new city is only four or five miles away, much too close to avoid a plague or killer disease of some sort. Remember what the databank told us. I still believe their theory that the volcano spewed poison gases that killed some and drove the rest away."

"It's the best theory I've heard so far," Elijah conceded. "But why would they build this city so close to the old one?"

"Remember, the old city lies inside the cone of the mountain and if the gas theory is true, maybe the gases were contained within the bowl."

"Makes sense to me," Elijah agreed. "They must have spent thousands of hours building the dike. Wonder why it was so important to have access to the cavern and the old city."

"I think I know," Santos offered. "The tribe needed access to the lake for fishing and the river for transportation. The quickest way to the lake was through the lost city. The two cities are surrounded by swamp so they needed a passage that was high and dry."

"What about the space explorers?" Rosita asked.

"I imagine they died long before the city was abandoned," Simon added. "Remember, the databank said it didn't have the fate of the Indians programmed into memory. That means there were no alien explorers left alive to feed the databank the information. The Indians probably still inhabited the old city when the last of the space visitors died."

"But doesn't that data thing accumulate its own information without help from the aliens?" Rosita asked. "I mean like it did when it learned to speak English."

Simon thought for a minute. "You have a good point, but it might have been hard for it to get any new information all sealed up inside that cave."

Elijah paced back and forth in the small room. "We've got to get out of here and get back to civilization. We can always organize another party and come back for the treasure later. With our Spencer rifles, why don't we just blast our way out and back through the lost city to the rafts?"

"Because there are too many warriors," Santos reminded him. "We wouldn't have a chance in a running battle."

"Well, we just can't sit here hoping for a miracle," Elijah groaned.

"What exactly do you propose?" Simon asked.

"We wait until dark and overpower the guards, then go back to the lost city by the same route we came."

"Easier said than done, cousin. The Indians could throw at least a hundred warriors at us at once. Let's say we're expert shots, which we're not, and bring down twenty-eight warriors with the first volleys. How do we stop the remaining seventy-two or so while we're reloading?"

"Okay, you've made your point," Elijah conceded with a sinking feeling in the pit of his stomach.

On The Earthen Bridge

Not far away, Kirby, Dorn, Cunningham, and the two scientists were following the numerous footprints along the well-worn dike path. "What do you two experts think?" Kirby asked.

Drake and Cain examined the prints, and Drake finally said, "The prints were made by moccasins. Looks like a lot of Indians recently passed this way."

"I can see that. What else?" Kirby asked anxiously of Cain.

"You see those heel prints? They came from boots. I'll bet the Indians captured Murphy and his group."

Kirby nodded, "That's the way I see it. Let's follow the dike."

As a precaution, Cunningham was sent ahead to reconnoiter. Fifteen minutes later, he returned and announced the presence of a group of twenty warriors coming their way. "Make for that grove of low bushes on the right side," Kirby instructed quietly. "Get as low as you can. Don't make a sound."

The group moved off the path and down the steep slope. Low-lying bushes and tall weeds allowed limited cover to the Americans, but enough so that the Indians never noticed them. When they had passed, Kirby asked, "Did anyone get a look at them?"

"I had my head too low in the bushes," Dorn answered. "I heard some of their conversation though. Sounded like an ancient Indian dialect, very different than what you'd hear in Mexico today."

"What's that supposed to mean?" Kirby wanted to know. "How do you know anything about ancient Indian languages?"

"You forget, General, before the war I studied early Indian cultures. I was going west before Pinkerton recruited me. That's one reason he selected me for this mission. I would say those Indians are direct descendants of the ancient Toltecs or Mayans who once inhabited the Yucatan. This dike probably leads to a village and our American friends."

Drake, overhearing Dorn's comments, concurred. "The dialect sounded like ancient Nahuatl, spoken by the early tribes of Mexico."

"I'm impressed," Kirby conceded. "Now all of a sudden I have experts in early Indian languages surrounding me. If they happen to capture us, you two can talk our way out of here."

It did not take long for Kirby and the others to reach the end of the path. The view of the valley was far grander than they could have ever imagined. "It looks a lot like the lost city," Cain observed. "Looks like they just picked up the old city and moved it here. There had to be a good reason..."

Kirby did not need, nor did he have time for a historical debate. "We'd better move down the path and find a good hiding place before we're spotted. We need a good vantage point so we can see where they're holding Murphy and Walker."

In single file, they hurried down the narrow path to the outskirts of the city, blending into the lush vegetation that grew along the embankment. The light was beginning to fade as the deep red sun dipped below the horizon. It was nearly dark when they found an abandoned two-room villa on the outskirts of town with a good view of the plaza. It offered excellent access to the stone path leading back to the dike if a quick escape became necessary. Cunningham took first watch.

The first rays of morning sun spilled through the narrow windows of the small room only to find Elijah awake, peering through the window and watching the increasing commotion below. A large crowd of Indians had gathered in the plaza with a group of dissident priests. One of the old priests was gesturing with his hands and speaking excitedly—the same one who had advocated their execution the day before. The crowd murmured and swayed in a deep spiritual trance, then chanted louder and louder. A few more priests jumped to the front, swaying and gyrating, inciting the mob to further frenzy. "They're frightening me," Rosita said, looking out the window.

"They may be starting some type of ceremony," Santos replied.

Simon glanced down at the crowd. "I don't like the looks of this!"

Four tall warriors entered their room and motioned the group to come with them. Surprisingly, the Indians allowed them to carry their backpacks and rifles. One of the warriors escorted them down the pyramid steps, and as they approached the plaza, the crowd became silent. The old priest glared at the outsiders, continuing his feral movements and gyrations. Stripes of crimson and white paint covered his face and body. "He looks like a creature from hell," Elijah said nervously. "What's he saying?"

Santos whispered, "He's telling them we are not gods but enemies of the great Toltec empire. He's trying to convince them we are not from the great shell. He insists we be sacrificed to the great sun god, Tonatiuh."

"Where's the chief who defended us yesterday?" Rosita wanted to know.

"Don't see him around. Maybe the priests got rid of him," her brother answered.

Suddenly, the four husky guards grabbed Rosita by her arms and legs, lifting her high into the air. Santos retrieved her fallen pack and rifle as he helplessly watched the warriors carry her back up the long flight of steps. She let out a shrill scream.

The old priest, accompanied by two younger priests, followed the warriors up the steps. Elijah started to raise his rifle when Simon grasped the barrel and pushed it back toward the ground. "No, not yet, not yet! We'll only harm Rosita. Let's see what they plan to do with her first."

A large stone altar was visible to the right of the temple door. They had missed seeing it the night before. The Indians carried the shrieking girl and placed her face-up on the altar, then ripped her blouse open and exposed her naked flesh. She screamed again as her breasts heaved and strained against the warrior's grip. The old priest brandished a large knife, holding it high for the crowd to see, enticing more chants and screams. The assembled mass roared their approval. Simon shouted, "Those bastards are going to sacrifice her!"

The priest began to chant as he held the blade high in preparation for the downward thrust into Rosita's chest.

Elijah and Simon raised their Spencers, but before they could aim, a rifle shot rang out from the rear of the plaza and the bullet hit the priest in the chest, knocking him backward against the temple wall. He dropped the knife, clutched his blood-soaked chest, and bounced from the wall, stumbling forward over the steps and rolling halfway down before his body came to a stop on a narrow landing. Six more shots cut down the warriors who were restraining Rosita. One slumped over the altar while the others toppled over the steps to the landing below. Another volley hit the two young priests. One took a bullet in the forehead and the other in the stomach. They dropped in a heap around the altar. This allowed Rosita to get up, jump to the ground, and run down the steps as fast as she could. Elijah turned and looked toward the far side of the plaza shouting, "Who in the devil fired those shots? It wasn't one of us!"

"I don't know," Simon barked, "whoever it was, let's head their way before these savages recover from the shock."

Rosita reached the bottom and threw herself into her brother's arms, sobbing, "Thank God for your rifles."

"We didn't fire those shots," Santos shouted. "It was someone else across the plaza."

"Let's get the hell out of here," Simon yelled.

The rifle shots had frightened and distracted the frenzied crowd, who thought lightning bolts had been launched by the gods. Men, women, and children headed for the safety of nearby buildings. In the confusion, the four captives grabbed their packs and rifles and ran across the plaza toward the path leading to the dike. They reached the avenue on the far side and continued the uphill climb. Halfway up, they heard a voice shout in English, "Murphy, over here! Over here to your left!"

Simon glanced over to see a tall figure motioning them toward a small building. The four ran through the open doorway, nearly colliding with one of the men standing in the shadows. There were five armed white men staring at them. Santos and the Americans gasped. "I don't know who you are, but thanks for saving all our lives."

General Kirby smiled slightly. "You can thank Mr. Dorn here for shooting the executioner; he's the marksman of the group."

Elijah recovered enough to ask, "And gentlemen, to whom do we owe the pleasure of this untimely, or maybe I should say timely meeting. You don't know how happy we are to see you."

"You may not be too happy when you know who we are," Kirby replied, as he and Dorn slowly raised their rifles.

Simon looked at the general in disbelief. "I know you from somewhere. You're an American. We've met before…"

"Yes, Captain Murphy, we have. I'm Brigadier General Caleb Kirby, Commanding Officer of the First Michigan, United States Army. I was your commanding officer before you deserted and fled from hostilities in Tennessee, along with an army payroll. We've been following you for a long time. We were sent here by the United States government to arrest you and Captain Walker. Desertion and theft of government property are rather serious crimes."

Simon and Elijah tightly clutched their Spencers and backed toward the door.

"Relax, Captain, we're not going to arrest you. We're actually here to make a deal and see you safely home, perhaps as heroes. Let's all put down the rifles and talk. We don't have much time before those savages figure what's going on."

"How can I trust you, General?"

"Don't worry Captain, you have my word, and under the circumstances, you really have no choice."

"Okay, General. Meet Captain Elijah Walker, formerly of the Confederate States Army, and our guides Santos and his sister Rosita Lopez."

"My pleasure, folks," Kirby responded. "This is special agent Nat Dorn and agent Cunningham of the U.S. Secret Service, and our two scientists, Robert Drake and Austin Cain. Drake here is an anthropologist and Cain an archeologist."

"About Captain Walker here," Simon explained. "He's a relative of mine, a cousin to be exact."

Kirby nodded and smiled, "I can see the close resemblance. You almost look like twins. The war is over by now so I'm prepared to offer him a pardon if he'll take the oath of allegiance to the United States when we return. Besides, we'll need plenty of good men to help us rebuild the south."

Elijah looked at the general and said, "Well, General, in that case I'm most pleased to meet you. I'm sure we can work something out. You say the war is about over?"

"Yes. When we left Washington, General Grant had your General Lee pretty well bottled up at Petersburg, Virginia. With his Army of Northern Virginia running out of supplies and starving, Lee was unable to escape and join up with Johnston in North Carolina. I'm sure the war is over by now and the Confederacy thoroughly broken, and the South once again a part of the United States.

"Well, I'll be damned," Elijah exclaimed, then slowly his look turned despondent. "I sure hate to think of what waits for me at home."

Kirby sighed sympathetically. "I know General Sherman did a thorough job destroying parts of Georgia and the city of Atlanta, but it might not be as bad in Alabama and west Tennessee." He grabbed his pack and headed for the door. "Let's make for the dike before all hell breaks loose."

"Too late," Dorn suddenly shouted. "Here they come!"

Thirty or more bloodthirsty, screaming warriors were charging up the street. Drake and Rosita took up positions at the windows while the rest moved outside, seeking cover behind a low stone wall. Their first volleys killed the first row of seven attackers and the second eliminated six more. One particularly ugly brute somehow escaped the initial onslaught and charged at Kirby, who was firing in another direction and failed to see him fast approaching. The warrior was nearly upon him with his axe raised high when Elijah swung his rifle around and fired. The slug hit the savage under his chin and slammed into his brain, killing him instantly. Kirby, realizing what had just happened, looked at Elijah and shouted, "Thanks, Captain, I owe you one! Let's get the hell out of here...now!"

The other Indians turned and fled back toward the plaza where hordes of screaming warriors were rapidly gathering. The Americans grabbed their packs and scrambled to the earthen embankment. With Dorn leading the way, they jogged along the path leading to the cavern. They had covered over two miles when Dorn turned toward Kirby. "General, looks like the Indians we passed earlier are returning. I think they've spotted us."

"Spread out across the path and hold your fire until I give the order," barked the general.

The band of warriors cautiously approached. They saw the Americans crouched in the pathway and charged, brandishing axes and swords and screeching in their strange language. The first volley caught the front five and stopped them cold, but the others continued the charge. Another six received the full impact of the second volley and toppled over the dike to the swamp below. Still, on they came until they were almost upon the Americans. More close shots brought down another six as the heavy slugs slammed into their bodies while the remaining five engaged the Americans in hand-to-hand combat. Elijah swung at one warrior, catching him on the side of the head with the butt of his rifle, dropping him like a rock. Dorn confronted another warrior, deflecting an axe blow with his rifle barrel. Another Indian charged into Dorn with a force that threw both men over the embankment and into the water. Dorn slipped in the mud and the Indian seized the advantage and lifted his axe high in the air. His arm plunged downward, but Dorn suddenly rolled to his right and caused the axe to deflect a glancing blow off his shoulder and bury deep into the bank. Dorn pulled his knife and brought it upward into the Indian's stomach. His intestines began to spill into the swamp as he made loud guttural noises, thrashing about in his final death throes. Dorn rose and steadied himself on a large rock. Cunningham moved quickly down the hill to Dorn's side, helping him climb back up to the path. It was over. All around them lay nineteen dead and three badly wounded Indians.

"Anybody seriously hurt?" Kirby asked the group.

Cunningham had a minor knife wound to his arm, Dorn a slight gash to his shoulder and several had bumps and bruises. The general, gasping to catch his breath, said, "We're lucky to have these Spencers. Let's keep moving before we have to fight the entire city."

As they hurried along the dike, Kirby glanced over at Elijah, "Thanks again, Captain, for getting that Indian off my back."

"My pleasure, General."

"By the way," Kirby said, turning to Simon, "how did you get those Spencer repeaters? They're supposed to be a top military secret."

"Well, General, our Mexican guide, Santos, got them from a friend of some Mexican bandits. They supposedly stole them from a band of Apaches over in Arizona Territory who had taken them from the U.S. Cavalry stationed there."

Kirby laughed ironically, "So much for our great government security and the top secret weapons. Soon every damn Indian and outlaw in the west will have them."

Dorn held up his hand as they approached the entrance to the cavern. "I saw some movement inside. There may be more Indians waiting to ambush us."

Cautiously, they all approached the opening with rifles poised. A lone Indian emerged from the dark cavern holding his hands out and palms up. He was young and carried a pack on his back similar to those of the group. His clothes were also similar. The general shouted, "Hold your fire! Let's see what he wants, but keep your rifles handy, just in case it's a trick."

352 | ALEX WALKER

The young Indian approached the Americans and spoke in excellent English. "Greetings, Americanos, could you please tell me which one of you is General Kirby?"

Kirby nodded to the Indian.

"Hello, General, my name is Tomas. Your government commissioned me to be your contact in the Yucatan. I am at your service, sir!"

32.

After the initial shock, Kirby realized this young man was their contact arranged by Pinkerton in Washington. "How on earth did you find us here?" he asked.

"I've known about the lost city since I was a boy," Tomas explained. "My grandfather used to tell me many stories about Xepocotec. I am a direct descendant of the Mayas and visited this place two years ago. I knew your American friends would eventually find it."

"I was hoping you'd make contact with us in Coba," Kirby replied.

"I wanted to," Tomas answered. "I had to deliver a message to a man in Vasquez and couldn't get there in time."

"Were you traveling with a Mexican called Javez?"

"Yes, he was following you to Coba. He is also the one who sent me to Vasquez to deliver the message. I was with Major Cordova when they found Javez's hat in the pool in Coba. He was working for an American smuggler named Swartz. The major forced me to join up with his group as a guide to help find the other Americans."

Kirby turned to Dorn and Cunningham. "This young man is the second contact I told you about."

"Mr. Drake told us you had been with Major Cordova's group but you escaped into the jungle."

"Yes. His soldiers captured me in Coba and forced me to guide them until I was able to slip away. The major is mucho loco and would have killed me if I had stayed with him."

"You don't have to worry about the major anymore," Elijah injected. "His ashes are floating in a river of lava."

"And the rest of his party are dead, too," Santos reassured Tomas.

"How did you find us?" Rosita asked.

"I escaped into the jungle with another guide. We traveled north until some Indians told me four Americans and a Mexican guide had passed their village on their way to Coba. I knew it must be you so I doubled back and followed your trail here."

"Did you come through the pyramid passageway?" Simon asked.

"No, I came through another underground tunnel. The entrance is not far from here. The Indians call it the Fire Tunnel. It's the route the Indians sometimes use to get to the lost city, but they seldom go there anymore."

"Why is that?" asked Kirby.

"The passage drops deep below the city. It is very dangerous from the heat and fumes of the molten rock. A river of fire."

"Could we make it through that passage before the Indians get into the city?" Kirby asked.

"I don't think so. The entrance is too far up the mountain. Our best option is to return through the pyramid passage."

"We can't go back there," Kirby said. "The Indians would block us at the other end."

"Maybe we should try the tunnel Tomas used," Dorn suggested. "Our only chance of surviving is to get to the lake and our rafts as soon as possible."

Cunningham shouted from a large rock overlooking the dike, "Whatever we do, we'd better do it fast because there's a large mob of Indians moving along the dike."

"General," Tomas reminded him, "we would never make it to the fire tunnel now. They would catch us before we even got to the entrance."

"Where is the entrance to the fire tunnel? I'm willing to try for it," Dorn shouted.

"I'll go with you," Cunningham added.

"I'll go, too," Cain said. "I can't possibly make it back through the pyramid."

"It's about a half-mile up this path," Tomas advised. The entrance is behind a large boulder, but you really don't have time to make it because the Indians are almost on us."

"We're going to try for the tunnel! Are you coming with us, Tomas?" a determined Dorn shouted as he turned toward the path.

"No, I'll stay with the general."

"Quickly, back into the cavern," Kirby commanded. "We can shut the entrance with the same lever we used to open it. Once inside, we'll try to lock it down. Dorn, come with us; you don't have time to make it to the fire tunnel."

"Sorry, General, I'll take my chances."

Dorn, Cunningham, and Cain scrambled toward the path while Kirby and the remaining five quickly hurried back inside the cavern entrance.

A large horde of Indians rounded the bend and saw the group retreating to the cavern. Bloodcurdling screams and chants were piercing the air as they gathered courage for a charge. The Toltecs wanted revenge—the intruders had killed and wounded too many of their warriors.

"Drake, pull that lever and close the entrance!" Kirby shouted.

Santos and the Americans fired into the mass of screaming Indians and watched the front ranks fall. The onrush of warriors pushed over the bodies in continuing pursuit as Drake pulled hard on the lever and the large slabs began to descend from the ceiling. "Keep firing!" Kirby yelled.

The Spencers spewed their deadly charges into the oncoming mass of black and white painted, half-naked bodies. As fast as they fell, more warriors replaced them. The huge panels fell into place at last, sealing the entrance. They were safe for the moment. Large stone locking bolts on each side of the slab slid into place. The warriors gathered around the blocked entrance, frustrated and enraged. Some Indians had spotted the three men who were dashing toward the fire tunnel and went after them in frenzied pursuit.

Cain was a frail man who had led a sedentary life. His only physical exertion came from occasional field trips and archeological digs. Acknowledged in his field as a renowned teacher at his beloved New York University, he was not accustomed to violence or great physical strain. It was now very difficult for Cain to keep up with Dorn and Cunningham. He ran as fast as he could until he felt his lungs would burst. Within a hundred yards of the large boulder concealing the entrance, he lost his footing and tumbled over the edge, landing in small scrub on the side of the embankment.

Although he heard the Indians fast approaching, he was just too exhausted to move. Dorn heard the commotion and turned to see the Indians stopping to intercept the stricken man. Both agents raised their rifles and fired a volley. One of the savages tumbled down the embankment and another took a bullet in the side and sprawled headlong into the swamp. Watching their companions fall, most of the remaining warriors charged toward Dorn as the others rushed to Cain. The agents fired again, dropping two more.

"What about the scientist?" Cunningham shouted.

"We'll have to leave him," Dorn reluctantly replied. "It's too late to help him anyway. Head for the tunnel. We have to save ourselves."

They turned and ran for the large boulder just ahead, as two Toltecs reached the groaning, shaking Cain and grabbed him by the arms, then up the embankment where other warriors were waiting. Hands lifted the hapless professor high into the air and carried him back down the pathway to the cavern entrance. Cain was terrified. "I can't hurt you! I'm your friend! Please don't harm me!"

He pleaded as if he expected the Indians to understand his English. "I'm an American. I can give you money!"

He was on his knees begging for his life as a muscular warrior raised his Roman-like sword high above Cain. A brief reflection of sunlight burst from the blade as it sliced through the air and Cain's neck, severing his head from his frail body. Another Indian grabbed the head by the hair and flung it into the swamp below. The splash attracted a large crocodile that lunged and grabbed the bloody head in its huge jaws. Several warriors grabbed Cain's torso and heaved it into the pool where it was mauled by two more reptiles. The muddy water became a red-stained froth as Austin Cain disappeared forever.

Dorn and Cunningham reached the boulder and found the narrow entrance. They entered the tunnel where, luckily, they found a supply of torches stored near the opening. Each agent grabbed a handful and quickly moved as far into the tunnel as they could and still see light from the outside. The pursuing Indians reached the entrance. The backlight provided a perfect silhouette of two pursuers entering the entrance as the agents took careful aim and fired, killing both instantly. Two more warriors entered the opening and met the same deadly reception. None of the others dared to stick their heads into the tunnel, at least for now. They lurked outside the entrance, intending to wait until dark. With this respite, Dorn and Cunningham ignited two torches and moved deeper into the tunnel, reinforced by a thread of reassurance, knowing that Tomas had just passed here to get to the cavern. They assumed it would eventually lead to the lost city and from there the route back to the lake where the rafts would carry them safely away. Dorn also knew they would have to allow time to re-enter the pyramid to fill their packs with enough treasure to secure their future.

He noticed, as they moved deeper into the cavern, the limestone walls gradually transformed into dark basalt, confirming they were deep inside the ancient lava tube. Their gradual descent resulted in a steady rise in temperature and this could only mean they were getting very close to molten lava.

Dorn glanced at Cunningham. "This passage doesn't look as bad as the one inside the pyramid. When we reach the surface, we have to go back to the treasure room and fill our packs. From there we can get to the rafts and head for the coast."

Cunningham smiled, "We'll get first choice of the treasure and be gone before anyone else knows it." Then he added, "I don't know about you, but I think it's getting hotter than hell in here."

"Yeah, it is. We must be getting near that lava Tomas was talking about."

The heat intensified and the smell of sulfuric fumes was overpowering. The darkness relented to a dull reddish glow as they moved along. Rounding a small bend, the men could now peer over the edge to see a winding river of yellowish-red molten lava. The sensation of being so close to certain death was enough to keep the two agents moving steadily forward.

The sulfuric fumes became stronger and both men were getting nauseous. "I don't like the looks of this," Dorn remarked. "We've got to get the hell out of here before we pass out. This place is as close to hell as I ever want to get."

They moved quickly, neither man daring to venture too near the rim. Suddenly, something grazed Dorn's head, and ricocheted from the wall into the fire below.

"What the hell was that?" Cunningham shouted.

A second object flew by and hit the wall above Cunningham's head, shattering into several pieces. Dorn kneeled and picked up a small fragment. "An arrowhead! Someone is shooting at us!"

Dorn heard a muffled gasp and turned to see Cunningham against the wall, the shaft of an arrow protruding from his chest. Blood began to stain his shirt. He looked at Dorn and emitted a dull cough, frothy blood collecting at the corners of his mouth. From the corner of his eye, Dorn saw shadowy movements to his left. He aimed the rifle and fired. There was a cry of pain as he saw a figure tumble over the edge and cartwheel into the molten lava. With a brief flash, the body instantaneously vaporized. The agent squeezed off two more shots. He heard another cry and saw a second shadow tumble into the lava river. Dorn yelled to Cunningham, "Some of the bastards are in front of us—maybe I got all of them!" There was no further movement or sound. "Cunningham, we need to get you to the surface. Can you make it?"

He nodded and attempted to take a step, stumbling as Dorn grabbed him. He tried to move him forward but Cunningham's dead weight was dragging Dorn down. "You've got to try and walk. I can't carry you. Can you do it?"

Cunningham's only reply was a soft coughing and gurgling sound.

Dorn realized his companion was choking on his own blood.

The agent slumped to the ground and lay there looking at Dorn with dull glassy eyes. "Cunningham, can you hear me?" Dorn pleaded.

There was no answer. He felt Cunningham's wrist and neck—there was no pulse. The agent was dead. Dorn had always liked Cunningham. He was a loyal employee of the agency and had followed Dorn's orders faithfully. He reached down, grabbed him by the belt and collar and jerked him to a standing position. He pushed his corpse over the precipice and into the molten lava. Then Dorn took the dead agent's rifle, emptied the unused shells, shoved them into his pockets and threw the Spencer into the lava flow. He briefly looked into Cunningham's backpack, retrieved his hunting knife and tossed the pack over the edge. He could not carry the extra weight.

"I guess a proper cremation is in order," a remorseful Dorn mumbled to himself.

33.

Kirby knew the Indians would eventually break through the outside doors, forcing the Americans to either make a stand or leave the cavern through the pyramid tunnel. Santos and Elijah searched the immediate area around the massive doors, trying to determine how to unlock them. Somehow, when they had been previously shut, a secure locking system was activated. Both wondered if they had enough time to find the unlocking mechanism. Kirby, Drake, and Tomas searched the rest of the cavern. Rosita sat by the entrance, listening for noises or sign of any threatening activity.

"There has to be another way back to the tunnel," Santos said with growing anxiety. "The Indians wouldn't allow themselves to be trapped like this."

"You forget they knew where all the locking and unlocking devices were located," Simon said. "The way back through the pyramid was easy for the Toltecs."

Santos was on his knees looking along the base of the wall when Rosita called. Santos and Elijah ran back to the cavern entrance and saw Rosita standing with her ear against the slab. "What is it?" Elijah asked.

"I hear banging noises outside. Listen!"

"What's going on over there?" Kirby shouted.

"It seems our Indian friends are trying to knock a hole through the doors," Santos yelled back.

"Can they actually break through that thick slab?" Rosita asked.

Drake studied the doors for a moment. "They are made from limestone, which is nothing but seashells that were deposited and compressed millions of years ago. It is a softer rock and with the right tools, it can be broken into easily. We'd better find a way to open the passage door soon."

Elijah turned to Simon. "Think there's any hope we can get through those doors into the tunnel?"

Simon scratched his head. "Not unless we find some blasting powder to blow the damn things apart."

"Well," Elijah replied, "there may be another way out of here, I think."

Simon turned toward the far wall. "Are you thinking the same thing I am?"

"Possibly," Elijah answered, "and we both may be as nutty as two squirrels in a barrel of pecans."

Simon opened his pack and retrieved the space helmet. He adjusted it to fit, tugged it over his head and spoke into the microphone. Nothing happened. "I don't see any light."

"Wouldn't it help if you turned it on?" Elijah suggested.

Simon gave his cousin a sarcastic look.

He pressed the small button and a tiny blue light appeared on the inside chin guard. He pulled the helmet over his head and began to speak. Kirby, who was watching the two men, was flabbergasted. "What the devil are you doing? What's that gadget?" Kirby looked angry and confused.

"Hold on, General…"

Simon spoke into the mouthpiece, "Databank, can you hear me?"

The response was instantaneous. "Yes, Commander Murphy, your voice has been recognized by our voice sensing module—welcome back!"

"Who in God's name are you talking to?" Kirby asked, staring at the strange device on Murphy's head.

"Watch this, General," Simon said with a smirk. "Databank, please open the spacecraft door for us."

Immediately, they heard the low whining noise, followed by a panel opening on the side of the ship and steps unfolding to the ground. Simon glanced over to Kirby and smiled, "General, you'll never believe what I am about to show you and Mr. Drake."

"I'm afraid to ask."

Santos, Tomas, and Rosita stood outside the spacecraft and watched the entrance doors for any signs of a breakthrough while the four Americans entered the strange craft through the hatchway. Drake was speechless, and his expression almost comical, as Simon explained in detail their previous visit and the information they had learned from the databank about the early space explorers. Nothing had prepared the professor for what he was about to see. Simon provided them with a brief tour and answered as many of their questions as possible. Even Drake's scientific mind and good sense of reasoning was completely rattled. The existence of this ship and the head device were real, not imagined. When they came to the laboratory, Kirby and Drake could not take their eyes off the bodies suspended in the liquid-filled cylinders.

"These bodies are over eight or nine hundred years old and still well preserved," Simon said with renewed awe.

Viewing the mummified body of the alien explorer was the icing on the cake. Drake could visualize himself standing in front of the prestigious National Explorers Society of London presenting the mummy and other features inside this craft. His name would be forever enshrined as the greatest explorer of all time. Simon described how the ship needed repairs and that the databank had told them all the necessary parts were stored aboard. He told Kirby and Drake that with the proper commands, the databank could instruct them how to repair the ship so it would actually fly. "As a matter of fact," he explained, "with the tunnel door hopelessly locked and the cavern door in the process of being shattered by the Indians, I believe this may be our only option. I think it's time to repair the ship."

It took Kirby and Drake several moments to process what Simon was suggesting, then with the thought of facing the multitude of savages, Kirby relented, "Okay, Captain, we'll assist you, but don't expect too much…"

Simon replaced the headset and spoke clearly, "Databank, we are going to repair this ship and need your help. Can you guide us through the repairs in simple terms we can understand?"

There was a brief pause then the computer-generated voice replied, "We can help you, Commander Murphy. Where do you wish to start?"

"First, we need to know where the problem is, what parts are necessary, and where they are located."

"The necessary parts are in a storage chamber in the rear of the ship. They will repair the power linkage that controls our

Tracx fuel distribution and booster system. You must install a new modulator to the propulsion turbine. The propulsion turbine converts our Tracx fuel element to ion energy, allowing the ship to neutralize your gravity, liftoff from your planet's surface, and hover in the air. Do you understand all of this?"

"No, not a word. You will need to teach me step by step."

Kirby and Drake stared at Murphy with incredulous looks.

The databank continued, "Go to the rear of the ship. The storage chamber is the room with the blue door and red stripe. Most of the rooms in this ship are color coded for easy recognition."

The general kept shaking his head, "I must be totally nuts for going along with this crazy idea. Drake, you and Captain Walker assist Captain Murphy with the repairs. I'll remain outside with the others to keep the Indians at bay—and to pray."

The storage compartment was easy to find. It was a small room, neatly partitioned. Simon and Elijah entered the room and looked around.

Simon spoke into the headset, "Databank, please tell us what we will need."

"Go to the yellow coded section and find a metal container with a large yellow circle on the side and three red triangles in the center. This is the power linkage. In the same section, look for a small metal box with a yellow circle and three red squares in the center. This is the attachment assembly for the power linkage. Go to the last section coded green and look for the large box with a large green triangle and three small blue hexagons on the side. This is the modulator element that will attach to the Tracx booster system."

"How about the tools to work with?"

"You will need only two and they are in a small silver tool container in the cabinet by the door. When you gather all the parts and tools, take them to the Tracx power room in the forward compartment. You can recognize the door with a diagonal yellow stripe across the front panel."

Simon turned to the others and said urgently, "We have our work cut out for us, and not much time to do it."

The parts and tools were easy to locate, but the tools were very strange and would require precise instruction by the databank during assembly and installation. The three men loaded the parts containers onto a large dolly and transferred them to the Tracx power compartment. It took two trips. Simon pulled the handle to open the compartment door, only to find it locked. He spoke into the headset, "Databank, please open the door to the power room so we can replace the parts."

After a brief pause, the voice returned and said, "Sorry, I cannot comply. This room can only be opened by authorized personnel; you do not have an authorized signature."

"Oh, no!" Simon moaned. "How can we fix the damn thing unless we can get into the power room?"

"You are not authorized."

"How can I get authorized?"

"You have to be given the special code."

"What is the code?"

"You are not authorized."

"But you instructed us to carry the parts to this room."

"You are not authorized."

"Well, fellows," he said, turning to his companions, "we're at an impasse here. Any suggestions?"

"Let me try," said Elijah, moving to the door and taking the handset from Simon. "Databank, you are authorized to open this door by command sequence and since I am next in command, I command you to open the door to the power room. Now!"

"I do not recognize your voice signature. Commander Murphy is in command."

Simon was astounded. "Hear that? It said I'm in command."

Elijah had to laugh. "Yeah, because you were the first one to talk to the machine with this headset."

He handed the set back to Simon, who spoke into the small device, "Yes, databank, I am in command and I authorize you to open the door to the power room."

There was a loud click and the door swung open. "Elijah, you'd better jamb that door open so we won't get trapped in here."

Drake looked confused, "How do you suppose the last request got whatever it was to open the door?"

"I think we confused it," Elijah said. "I learned in the army that if you issue enough quick commands, you always end up with total confusion." Simon could not help but chuckle.

The power room housed an array of complicated looking equipment. They spotted the compartment cover with a yellow circle and three red triangles. "This has to be the power linkage component," Simon said.

At the far end of the room, they found the cover with the green triangle and three blue hexagons. "And this must contain the modulator element," he said with relief.

Elijah opened the toolbox to see two peculiar looking objects. Each consisted of a dull metal rod with a raised metallic handle and large button embedded in the handle. One button displayed a symbol interpreted as a positive sign and the other tool had a black button that had to be the negative sign. Simon spoke into the headset, "How do we remove the covers to get started? Also, please explain how these tools work."

The databank responded immediately, "The many parts on this ship are connected by strong positive electro-magnetic charges. You have two tools. The black tool is for negative charges and the red is for positive charges. The only way to loosen a part is to reverse the positive charge to negative. That is what the black electron tool does. To loosen the connection, take the negative charge tool, place the socket tip over the connection stud, and press the black power button on the handle. The negative charge will reverse the positive charge and break the connection. To reconnect the parts, place the red tool to the fastener head, press the red button, and a positive charge will tighten it. Remember, black for loosening and red for tightening. When you replace the parts," the databank continued, "be sure you look carefully at the connections and secure them just like they were when you disconnected them."

"How will we know the parts have been replaced correctly?" Simon asked.

"Our computers will perform a system analysis and confirm the power linkage to each new part. All you have to do is fasten the connections to the correct parts and we will do the rest."

"We'll start with the power linkage," Simon announced to Drake and Elijah, then explained what the databank said. Drake took the negative tool and placed the socket over the connection head. He pressed the black power button and felt a slight vibration pulsate through his hand. The connection was broken. He repeated the procedure with the remaining five connections and the part came loose. They lifted the cover and saw the bizarre looking mechanism the databank referred to as the power linkage. It was loosened using the same negative tool. Elijah lifted the new linkage part from its container, set it in place, and then reconnected it by pressing the red button on the positive tool. The positive tool tightened all the connections. The cover was reinstalled by applying the same positive charges. "This sure beats tightening nuts and bolts with a wrench," Elijah said, duly impressed.

The next step appeared to be more complicated. They would attempt to loosen the Tracx booster cover and replace the modulator element. All connections were similar, including those on the four ion generators. Simon consulted the databank again. The three Americans heard a commotion in the hallway and looked up to see Kirby enter the power room. He paused to catch his breath, "The Indians have broken a small hole in the right door and are trying to widen it with mallets."

Simon responded without looking up, "We've just installed the power linkage. We have to work on the propulsion element that attaches to the booster system, whatever all that means."

"Better hurry up. We'll try to hold them off as long as we can," Kirby said as he left the power room.

Kirby returned to the cavern to see a narrow ray of light coming into the room from a small hole. Santos said with agitation, "General, they have also busted a hole through the other door."

The first hole was now nearly a half-foot wide and getting larger with each blow. Kirby could see the movement on the outside and occasionally a face would appear at the hole. Kirby fired into the opening and heard a sharp cry as the bullet struck flesh. He fired again and heard another shrill cry. He repeated this several more times before the Indians backed away. A few bold warriors shot arrows through the hole, bouncing them off the floor with no effect. Kirby and Santos answered with their rifles but there were just too many Indians. Where one would fall, another took his place. Kirby turned to Rosita and shouted, "Go to the spacecraft and tell Murphy and Walker that we need more ammunition!

Rosita ran into the ship and found Simon, Elijah, and Drake hovered around the machines, "The general says we're running out of ammunition for the rifles."

"Elijah, reach into our packs and hand her some of the spare ammo."

"Tell him we need to install a new part but we're having trouble getting the thing to fit. We'll need at least another hour."

"I don't think we even have thirty minutes," she said desperately to Simon, then hurried back into the cavern with the spare ammunition.

Simon spoke into the headset, "Databank, why does the connection in the large green box not fit? We can't get the ends and the connections to meet. They're about three inches too short."

The voice responded, "Did you try to install the adapter sleeve?"

"What's that?" asked Simon, exasperated.

"It is the connector necessary to span the distance between the modulator intake valve and the Tracx power supply cells you see housed in the large green unit."

"Where is that part?"

"In the storage compartment in the green coded section. Look for a container with a green circle with one red square."

"Elijah, you stay here and watch these things while Drake and I get the part."

When they reached the room, they hurriedly searched for a box with a green circle and red square.

"Dammit, Drake, the box isn't here!" Simon shouted, as he grabbed for the headset. "Databank, there is no container here with a green circle and one red square."

After a brief pause, the voice answered, "Our inventory logs show two of those parts available. Please continue your search."

They rummaged through each container again, but to no avail. "The damn thing doesn't exist," Simon shouted in complete frustration and distress. Drake looked at him in silent horror.

34.

Dorn rushed through the fire tunnel—the heat and fumes were unbearable and his head pounded with splitting pain. He was drenched with sweat and weak from dehydration. He drank all the water in both his and Cunningham's canteen. It took every ounce of his strength to place one foot in front of the other and keep moving. As Dorn trudged forward, he felt a slight breeze on his wet body and thought he was dreaming. His pack and rifle felt like a thousand pounds and he wanted to lie down and rest but knew if he did, he would never get up again. Dorn had developed a sixth sense that comes from facing constant danger and he sensed it now. Far to the rear, on the pathway below him, were flickering lights, dancing off the walls. "My God," he gasped, "those bloody bastards are following me through the tunnel!"

Inside the Spaceship

Simon was at his wits end. In desperation, he spoke into the headset again, as calmly as possible. "Databank, we have looked everywhere for the symbols you suggested but I cannot find them. "

"What are you looking for?" the metallic voice asked.

"The adapter sleeve to attach the modulator element to the Tracx booster cells. Don't you remember? This is what you told me we needed."

"You need an XTP expander collar with the four round connectors."

"I thought you said we needed a connector sleeve."

"If you were connecting the modulator to the ion exhaust system you would need the sleeve, but since you are only connecting the modulator to the booster cells, you need an XTP expander collar. Inventory tells us we have three of those in stock."

"Where are they?" Simon asked, trying to conceal his anger.

"In the blue containers marked with two yellow triangles in the center."

"Databank, why didn't you give me the correct information before we spent all this time looking for the wrong part?"

"You failed to request the correct part," the voice responded.

Drake looked at his companion and whispered, "You better not respond to that last statement or we might never get out of here."

Simon located the right container and he and Drake brought it back to the Tracx power room. It took several more minutes to switch the connector sleeve with the expander collar, tighten down the connections with the positive tool, and reinstall the housing cover. Simon said a little prayer and spoke into the headset, "Databank, we are all connected. You may begin your system analysis now."

"We will immediately begin the test and power sequence, Commander Murphy."

"I'm only a captain in the United States Army," Simon answered.

The electronically generated voice replied, "As the new commander of this ship, you have been promoted to our general command rank."

When Simon relayed this information, Elijah laughed. "How does it feel to be the only person in the world to be promoted by some damn talking machine?"

The equipment began to come to life with all sorts of strange noises, whines and shrill sounds. "This is databank for Commander Murphy."

"Commander Murphy here," Simon responded, with a grin on his face.

"All connections, power links, and equipment checked and verified. Ship is now ready for flight sequence."

Elijah sheepishly asked his new commander, "What did it say?"

"It said we're now ready to take this big monster up in the air and fly. Let's move to the command center. Mr. Drake, will you please call the others in so we can try and get this flying bucket off the ground."

"Aye, aye, sir," he said with a grin and a stiff salute.

"Not necessary, Mr. Drake," Simon chuckled and turned to Elijah. "By the way, I'm appointing you second in command, Captain Walker."

Elijah responded with a formal salute as Simon grinned, enjoying his newly assigned command and authority. The rank of commander sounds pretty neat, he thought.

Drake ran down the steps into the cavern and shouted to Kirby and the others, "We're ready for flight. Commander Murphy wants everyone aboard at once!"

The constant pounding had widened the holes and a few more well placed blows to the first door would make it large enough for a body to slip through any moment now. Rosita was the first to board the ship, followed by Santos and Kirby. No one saw Tomas so it was assumed he had boarded earlier. With everyone now safely on board the ship, Simon spoke into the headset, "Databank, please retract the steps and close the hatch door."

They gathered in the command center. The pale green light gave them all a ghost-like appearance. The command center was equipped with viewing ports for external observation and one port provided an excellent view of the cavern doors with the expanding holes emitting bright streams of sunlight. They saw one Indian finally slip through and into the cavern. Kirby turned to Simon, "If you get this thing to actually fly, how do you plan to get the outside doors open?"

"I'll ask the databank to open the doors," Simon said confidently, then spoke into the headset. "Databank, you may start the motors and lift this spacecraft off the ground, four feet into the air."

"The Tracx turbines are powered up," the voice answered. "The ship is ready to launch."

A light vibration shook through the ship and they could hear a shrill whining noise. The ship's power system began the unimaginable process of defying the earth's gravitational pull. The four landing pods retracted into the hull while the craft hovered exactly four feet off the ground, just as Simon had commanded.

"You may now open the cavern doors."

"We do not have that capability, Commander Murphy. The lever has to be operated manually."

"Oh damn! One of us will have to go outside and pull the lever!"

"Not a good idea!" Drake shouted, looking through a porthole.

Elijah glanced out and agreed. "I can see several Indians inside the cavern and more pouring in behind them."

Kirby thought of the obvious solution. "Does this ship have a cannon or something that can blast the doors open?"

"I'm sure it has some sort of weapon system, but we haven't found it yet."

"Ask that machine," Elijah suggested.

"Databank, does this ship have a weapon that can blast the doors open?" Simon asked.

"Yes, this craft is equipped with two ion generated laser guns that can remove an entire mountain in seconds."

"Where are the controls to these guns?"

"That panel to the right of the central navigation monitor. The one with the red and blue buttons. You can sight a target with the monitor screen or with the visual scopes on each side of the control panel."

Elijah peered out the window and watched as more Indians crawled through the openings, shouting and pointing to the huge spacecraft hovering above the floor. One threw a spear at the craft, merely bouncing off the impenetrable skin.

"Look over by the right door," Elijah shouted.

The slim figure of Tomas silently moved out of the cavern's dark shadows. Remembering to retract the locking bolts, he eased over to the lever and pulled it with all his might, allowing the heavy doors to rise and spill bright sunshine through the widening cracks. Before the screaming savages realized what was happening, Tomas removed his shirt and pants and slipped under the door, blending in with the other warriors. He picked up one of the swords and jumped up and down yelling with the others to make them believe he was one of their own. As the doors opened, the Indians flooded into the cavern. Tomas easily drifted toward the rear of the mob and hurried up the path toward the hidden fire tunnel entrance.

Rosita cried, "We have to stop and pick Tomas up!"

"We can't stop this thing on the side of the mountain," Elijah shouted. "Let him be, he knows what he's doing. He'll be fine."

Simon addressed the headset. "Databank, move the ship forward and out of the cavern."

There was little sensation of motion as the craft moved forward through the cavern doors, out into the open air, knocking down several Indians in its path. Some tried to grab hold of the hull as it moved forward but slid off the ship's smooth glass-like surface like drops of water. Many of them ran back toward the dike as the flying monster floated out of its nesting place, crying and shouting that gods had unleashed this flying creature to destroy them all. As the ship increased altitude, the panicked Indians below began to look like tiny ants scurrying around an anthill.

"Databank, move the ship over the mountain and land in the central plaza of the city of Xepocotec," Simon commanded.

The craft rapidly gained altitude and moved over the crest of the mountain, hovering over the lost city. The four large retractable landing pods extended from the craft as it drifted downward, resting gently in the plaza. There had been no sensation of movement unless they looked out a porthole to see the buildings and trees passing by. Simon had an idea and posed a unique question to the headset. "Databank, is there a way to communicate with you without having to wear this headset?"

"Press the red button twice on the control panel and we will transfer our voice to the internal speaker system. Our communication protocol will remain the same."

Not knowing exactly what the databank meant, Simon removed the helmet and pressed the button as instructed. "Can you hear my voice?" he asked, speaking normally.

The metallic reply came back clearly through hidden speakers located into each wall. "That is affirmative."

The command center was still illuminated by the green light and the group on board experienced feelings of renewed strength and energy. As the strange light bathed their skin, their sore muscles, aches, pains, and other maladies slowly disappeared. They also felt a heightened sense of awareness and confidence in the ship and their companions. Simon spoke to the databank again. "Databank, why are we feeling these strange sensations?"

"The green light is healing your bodies. This light is composed of elements not found on your planet. They are creating a photosynthesis effect within your bodies, regenerating molecules necessary to rejuvenate old cells, build new ones, and slow the aging process. This light emits a substance much like your earth's chlorophyll that transforms radiant energy into a chemical form that enhances cell growth. The process is extremely complex and one your human mind cannot comprehend. A simple explanation would be that our Tracx energy system transfers a chemical substance, much like your hydrogen sulfide, into a form of energy through an oxidation process called chemosynthesis. The energy transforms into the green light. Your human bodies will look and feel years younger by absorbing the light. This is one reason our early explorers were able to live so long compared to you earthlings."

Elijah whispered to Drake, "Do you understand any of that?"

"Not a single word," Drake replied.

"Can you imagine what a business we would have if we could take this green light to a big city like New York and charge folks to pass through it?" Elijah said with exuberance.

"A fountain of youth!" Drake agreed.

"Yeah, and can you imagine the problems we'd create by letting people live to be two hundred years old?" Simon said to his entrepreneurial companions.

Simon moved over to the ion laser guns and examined the aiming device. "How do the guns work?" he asked the databank.

"Push the green button to activate the tracking screen and laser generators. Next, identify the target on the screen and use the small lever to bracket it within the circle. It will lock in immediately. Push the red button and the lasers will emit a light beam with a burst of destructive energy. The beam will destroy anything it strikes. You can control the strength of the beam by rotating the small silver knob to the right or left. Left is weaker. All the way left to zero will merely stun a human. If you turn the knob all the way right, you could destroy a section of your planet. Each click represents a five percent change in the laser power, exponentially increasing or decreasing the strength by ten times. Most targets only require fifteen to twenty-five percent."

Simon pressed the green button and the screen opened as if he were looking through a bright glass window. He rotated the lever to fifteen percent and bracketed a small building at the far end of the plaza. He heard a click as the target acquisition circle locked on to the targeted building. He pressed the red button. Suddenly, a bright light flashed from a hidden port beneath the ship, struck the building, causing the stone structure to vaporize into a small pile of rubble and ash. "My God!" he gasped, "did you see that?"

The databank continued the instruction. "The second silver knob controls the width of the beam. If you turn it to the left, the beam will widen for use on broader targets. The beam narrows as you turn the handle to the right. You can move it all the way right to get a sharp beam that will cut through rock or metal. By holding the red button, you can maintain a steady beam for cutting and slicing through objects. The narrow beam normally requires no more than thirty-five percent strength."

Simon turned the triangular-coded knob to the right and adjusted the strength to thirty-five percent. He aimed at a large stone block at one end of the plaza. The target was locked onto immediately. He pushed the red button and a single narrow finger of light burst across the plaza, slicing the top of the block. By moving the control lever down, the ray sliced through the huge stone like it was a stick of butter.

From one of the left ports, Santos saw movement far to one side of the plaza. He called to the others. "See that figure running and stumbling along the edge of the pyramid."

"It's Dorn!" General Kirby shouted. "Look to his left, there are six Indians chasing him!"

"Now let's see what this gun can do to humans."

Simon brought the laser to bear on the Toltec warriors. Once the circle locked on the Indians, it continued its tracking sequence as long as they stayed in view. He turned the intensity wheel back to fifteen percent strength and the beam width to twenty percent, and then pushed the red button. A bright flash shot from under the craft, illuminating the Indians for a microsecond before completely vaporizing them into nothingness.

"This weapon is incredible!" Elijah shouted. "You only had it set for fifteen percent power and look what it did!"

Simon spoke to the databank. "Please open the hatch and lower the steps."

"Santos, will you and Mr. Drake please retrieve Dorn and bring him to the ship before he collapses."

Kirby was astonished. "We have a weapon here whose power is beyond the imagination of modern man. Whoever controls this ship controls the world. It could destroy armies in a second and nations within minutes!"

"That, gentlemen," Simon reminded them, "is why we can never let this craft fall into the hands of any military command."

"I remind you, Captain Murphy," Kirby said, "even though you are classified as a deserter, you are still an officer of the United States Army and obligated to share any military secrets you find with your government. And I also remind you, Captain, I am still your commanding officer and commander of this mission and this ship."

"Sorry, General, not any more. I am now the official commander of this ship and Captain Walker is my second in command."

"By whose orders?" General Kirby demanded.

"By orders from the databank and the official operating powers of this ship, I have been appointed commander and Captain Walker is my second in command. Both of our voice imprints have been approved and logged by the databank. If I happen to be in a position where I cannot perform that function, he will give commands. This ship will not be used for the propagation of war or conquest over other nations. It will only be used for peaceful purposes throughout the world."

"Very well said, Commander, very well said," Drake shouted as he entered the command center.

Kirby fumed for an instant then thought it better to be silent before continuing to speak. He was in an alien environment and did not understand the inner workings and command structure of the ship. He needed to think this through. After a few moments he sullenly responded, "You know, Captain, I mean Commander Murphy, you are absolutely correct and I apologize. This craft is much too powerful to be used as a weapon of war. We don't know enough about it or even where it originated. There may be others like it in secret places, poised to destroy our world by invaders from other worlds. This craft must be contained in strict secrecy or every rogue nation in the world will be trying to steal it. I will agree this craft should only be used to enforce peace and to protect the United States from invasion by hostile nations."

Dorn was helped up the steps to a waiting bunk in the officer quarters. Santos and Rosita left the room to see if he had sustained any severe wounds. Except for exhaustion and dehydration, Dorn was in decent shape, considering what he had endured.

"Tell us what happened to Cain and Cunningham?" Kirby asked.

"Neither of them made it, sir," he explained. "The Indians got Cain before we reached the tunnel entrance and Cunningham caught an arrow inside the tunnel and fell into the molten lava. The Indians were almost on my back when you saved me."

"Just get some quick rest because we'll need you to help us move the treasure," Kirby said, giving Dorn a few pats on the shoulder.

Back in the command center, Simon, Elijah, and Drake discussed their next plan of action as Kirby returned and took a seat beside Drake. Simon said, "General, I believe you said the United States government would grant us a full pardon and percentage of the treasure if we help you retrieve it and bring it back to Washington. Is that correct, sir?"

"Yes. That was President Lincoln's position and he gave me his solemn promise."

"Elijah and I have decided to help you secure and transport the treasure with a few provisos. Santos and Rosita will be provided enough money to buy a nice farm in western Mexico or any other location of their choice. Secondly, all charges will be dropped against Captain Walker and me. Third, some of the treasure will be used to rebuild the South. Elijah will have his full American citizenship reinstated and finally, this craft will be kept in our possession and used for peaceful purposes."

Kirby hesitated for a moment soaking up these requests then nodded and said, "Agreed! I will ensure our government carries out your wishes. Now, let's go back into that damn pyramid and start loading treasure into the ship!"

35.

The transport of the treasure to the ship produced two major problems. One was the time it would take to neutralize the traps and the other the threat of the Toltecs who would have no trouble finding them anywhere inside the pyramid. Simon thought it best to block the lava tunnel exit first, since it was nearby. Sealing it would be easy enough with a thirty-five percent blast from the laser gun, but Tomas was probably in there now, making his escape. He realized the immediate danger. Pursuing Indians could slip out of the tunnel and into the city before anyone noticed. With Tomas to consider, sealing the exit now was not a viable option. They chose to take their chances and hope the spacecraft itself would frighten their pursuers enough to allow a successful escape.

They briefly pondered whether to retrieve some of the treasure now or travel back to the States and return later with more men as added security. Kirby made the first assessment. "If we go back to Washington empty-handed, everyone, including the President, will be skeptical a treasure even exists. I think we should make one run to the treasure chamber and fill our packs with gemstones and gold ingots—as much as we can carry. This will at least give Washington a sampling of the treasure. They can always send another expedition to the lost city to retrieve the remaining treasure and besides, we might not have another chance to use this flying machine."

"I agree," Simon nodded. "In order to carry the treasure back to the ship, we'll need to neutralize the traps and jamb the doors open so we can make the return trip as fast as possible."

"I may be able to help there," Drake replied, entering the room.

"Me, too," shouted Dorn as he entered the command center.

"Well, we're glad you're back from the dead, Mr. Dorn," Kirby said. "You sure look a lot better than you did thirty minutes ago."

"All that water I drank and a short catnap did the trick, General."

Simon told Rosita to stay with the ship and look out for Tomas should he emerge from the tunnel. "If you see Tomas, tell him how to find to the entrance to the Princess's chamber and follow the passage to the treasure room. Also, tell him we will have neutralized the traps and doors blocking the way. To be safe, retract the steps and close the hatchway by pressing this activation button here. I can open it with my headset when we return to the ship with the treasure. You'll be safe here, I promise."

Rosita reluctantly agreed. She knew the importance of protecting the ship and watching for Tomas, but was scared about being alone in this alien environment. The men took canteens, rifles, and ammunition and headed for the pyramid.

Halfway up the steps, they heard shouting below. Tomas had emerged from the tunnel and crossed into the plaza when Rosita spotted him. He saw the Americans climbing to the summit and shouted for them to wait. "Tomas, you've made it back in one piece!" Kirby shouted as he returned to the plaza to greet him.

"Yes, sir, I was lucky I guess."

"Did any Indians follow you through the tunnel?" Simon asked.

"Not that I know of, but I can't be sure. I didn't see any of them behind me."

"Good, we need you to help carry some of the treasure to the ship. Go to the ship and tell Rosita to give you an empty back pack."

No one looked forward to the return trip through the dangerous pyramid passages. Had it not been for Kirby's insistence, Simon and Elijah would have gladly boarded the spacecraft and left this place. They knew, however, they would be much better off if they returned to Washington with some of the treasure and received pardons from a thankful President and government. The men entered the temple and moved directly to the royal bedchamber. Santos opened the tunnel entrance by pressing the tiles and Drake jammed a broken section of a stone bench into the opening to prevent the door from closing. Elijah found a three-foot granite bar and lifted it to his shoulder. They easily moved through the first segment of the passage, making good progress down the stairway until they reached the landing where the first trap was located. Santos pushed the barrel of his Spencer against the second step and jerked back as the familiar whirling noise echoed through the corridor and the retractable blade shot out of the wall, slicing through empty air. Simon turned to Elijah and said, "Hand me that stone beam."

The beam was three inches wide and three feet long and it appeared to have been a support from a table or bench. Santos pressed the second step once more and watched the blade again spring from its nesting place and into the slot in the far wall while Simon jammed the bar into the homing slot and stepped back. The returning blade slammed into the stone bar with a force that shattered the blade into numerous pieces. With the trap now neutralized, the men continued forward and over the remains of the bodies lying on the steps. The smell was nauseating.

When they approached the second landing, Santos reminded them of the sand trap. The way to avoid the blast of sand was to jump over the first two steps. Each man took his turn and cleared the steps, successfully making it to the bottom and past the two large storage rooms and finally to the room holding the sarcophagus of Princess Xepocotec. Cordova had left the gilded stone cover off the sarcophagus to expose the headless mummy of the princess laying there in her eternal sleep. The six large diamond and ruby rings still encircled her mummified fingers. No one paid any attention as Elijah stopped long enough to remove the rings and place them in his pocket. He noticed that the gold and diamond necklace was missing and assumed it was now with Cordova's ashes in the lava stream.

As they passed the weapons cache and archeological treasures, Drake stuck his head inside and marveled at all the statues and other Toltec carvings. He would rather collect these artifacts than all the precious gems and gold ingots in Mexico. It pained him greatly to bypass these rooms. Kirby, sensing his disappointment, reassured him. "Don't worry, Mr. Drake, you'll soon return for these artifacts with plenty of time to evaluate them in the Washington Museum."

The water fountain was a welcome sight. The familiar jade mask gazed menacingly at Dorn as he pressed the two tiles in its forehead and the heavy door opened into the large chamber above the treasure room. The next obstacle was the pivoting stone threshold at the entrance. It had already cost two lives and two fingers from the hapless major. Santos remembered the stone trigger, leaned around the door, pressed the button twice, and then heard the locking bolt slide into the slab. They re-entered the large chamber and hurried over to the jade mask located above the altar. Santos pressed the red tile and the altar pivoted backward into the floor, exposing the stone staircase leading down to the treasure chamber. The room beyond, filled with thousands of gemstones, shimmered from the color-speckled radiance and glowing colors dancing across the walls and ceilings. As before, the mere sight of the numerous stacks of gold ingots and multitude of other priceless treasures left the group speechless.

Kirby spoke out and broke the spell, "Drake, you and Tomas, start collecting the best specimens of gold and silver jewelry and art pieces. Fill your packs with as much as you can carry. Murphy and Walker, fill your packs with the gems and the biggest diamonds you can find. Santos, Dorn, and I will load our packs half with gold finger ingots and the rest with various gems. We need to return to the ship before the Indians regain their courage."

Each man went about his assigned task with a sense of urgency, filling their packs with gold bracelets and necklaces, huge diamonds, rubies, and emeralds, most of which were finely cut jewels whose facets had been carefully fashioned by ancient gem cutters. As a parting gesture, Drake grasped one of the exquisite crystal statues of Quetzalcoatl and fastened it to his pack. He was certain this piece would please a grateful President Lincoln and First Lady. Finally, when all their packs were overflowing, they helped one another sling the loads over their shoulders and headed for the staircase.

Back in the spaceship, Rosita paced nervously, frequently glancing out the port window at the pyramid. She gasped when she saw a large group of Indians approaching the plaza heading in the direction of the ship. "Madre mia!" she cried.

Rosita had watched Simon fire the laser gun and tried to remember the process. She went over to the weapons display, pressed the green button, and watched as the screen came alive with a clear view of the Indians entering the plaza. Now what do I do?

She placed her hand around the small lever below the screen and rotated it until the circle located and framed the Indians. The circle lit up and a shrill sound filled the room—the target was acquired and locked. She tried to remember what Simon did to fire the laser.

Her thumb hesitated for an instant then she pressed the red button and jumped back as the bright explosion of light shot across the plaza and illuminated the Indians and surrounding buildings. In an instant, the Indians were gone.

Kirby was the last to reach the chamber above the treasure room when he heard a loud grinding sound from the room below. Screams shattered the silence of the cavern as Indians poured into the treasure chamber. As they approached the bottom steps, the torches threw dancing shadows across their painted bodies—they looked like nightmarish creatures from the underworld. As they rushed for the steps, Kirby yelled, "Fire at the bastards!"

Six carbines opened up from the floor above and the forward ranks of warriors were hurled backward into their onrushing comrades. The Americans fired four to five more volleys, leaving a pile of stacked bodies at the base of the steps. The Indians retreated to the treasure room to reorganize. Kirby pulled his group back through the doorway and across the pivoting slab into the passage. Santos reached around the wall and depressed the small lever to unlock the slab while Simon, the first to arrive at the fountain, pressed the red tile twice. The door began grinding into the floor, blocking the passage, but it was only a temporary respite. The Indians, familiar with the tunnel, would know how to open the doors and neutralize the traps. The men fled as fast as their heavy loads would allow, finally reaching the long flight of steps leading to the temple.

The Indians climbed over bodies and clambered up the steps to the chamber above. One of the more knowledgeable warriors pressed the button to open the door, but in his haste, forgot to push it twice to engage the locking bolts into the floor panel. When the door rose from the floor, several warriors rushed for the doorway at once and onto the deceptive floor panel, causing it to pivot downward and hurl three Toltecs into the bottomless cavern. A veteran warrior rushed back to the button and pressed it twice, allowing the floor panel to retract and locking bolts to slide back into their slots. Now they could safely cross the pivotal threshold into the passage beyond.

The Americans reached the spot where the sand trap was located. Santos stood on the fourth step and tossed his pack across the two lethal steps to the landing. With all his strength he leaped, his right foot barely missing the second step, and fell in a heap on top of his pack. Elijah slung his pack up to Santos. The young Mexican held out his rifle and Elijah grabbed the barrel, pulling himself over the two trigger releasing steps. The same procedure was repeated until the last man reached the safety of the landing.

Farther up, they passed by the disabled circular blade, the most deadly of the traps, without incident. The weight of the packs slowed their progress as they forced strained limbs to keep climbing. Shouts from the pursuing Indians could now be heard below. Near the top, they saw light spilling through the opening from the bedchamber, the entrance still jammed open. Tomas yelled and Simon turned to see a torch and two black and white painted faces just below them. He fired and hit the nearest warrior squarely in the forehead. Simon cocked and pulled the trigger again, but the rifle jammed.

The second Indian was upon them in an instant, with two close behind. The Toltec slammed into Simon, knocking him heavily to the ground. The Indian swung his ax, but because his balance had shifted, he was only able to connect with the side of Simon's head with the handle and heel of his hand. A sharp jab of pain shot through Simon's head as a burst of stars flashed before his eyes. Elijah, two steps ahead, turned in time to squeeze off a shot, hitting Simon's attacker and hurling him backwards down the steps. Another charging warrior piled on top of Simon in a scratching and pummeling heap. The attacker raised a long knife and aimed at the American's chest when Elijah rammed the muzzle of his rifle into the Toltec's mouth and pulled the trigger. The slug exploded the back of the Indian's skull. Elijah helped his cousin to his feet and pulled him toward the corridor opening.

The Americans made it out of the passage and through the entrance into the princess's bedchamber. From the top of the steps, Kirby and Santos fired four more shots below while Drake and Dorn pried the stone jamb loose and pushed the small red tile on the mask. Two more piercing screams were heard in the darkness as the door slowly dropped, closing the entryway. The group had only a few precious seconds to grab their packs and rush to the plaza and the safety of the ship.

Rosita was watching from a porthole when she saw her companions emerge from the temple door. She ran to the wall panel and pressed the red button, allowing the hatch to open and ladder to extend silently to the ground. As the Americans reached the lower steps, Indians poured out of the temple and onto the portico. One muscular warrior hurled his spear high in the air and into the plaza below. By chance, it struck Dorn's right thigh and pitched him forward to the plaza floor. Elijah and Kirby grabbed the straps of his heavy pack and dragged him across the ground to the ship. The ladder was only yards away. Santos was first up the steps, followed by Simon, Drake, and Tomas. Kirby reached down, pulled the spear from Dorn's leg, and angrily threw it to the ground. He and Elijah heaved their heavy packs to the others and then maneuvered Dorn up the ladder and through the hatchway.

Several enraged pursuers sprinted toward the ship, attempting to reach the steps. Rosita quickly pressed the button and the ladder began to retract into its recess. One wildly painted warrior leaped for the ladder and caught hold of the last step as it lifted into the air. Elijah took careful aim and put a bullet into the Indian's chest, watching him drop like a stone to the plaza floor. The ladder disappeared into the ship and the hatch closed tight. Rushing to the viewing ports, the survivors anxiously watched the horde of fiery Toltecs pouring into the plaza from all directions.

36.

The new crew gathered in the command center as Simon conferred with Elijah and Kirby about what to do next. The Americans knew that none of the Indian's weapons could penetrate the ship's outer skin and, for now, they were secure inside the spacecraft. A few Indians pounded on the ship with their axes and swords, only to see them shatter against the tough hull. "If we fire that laser we could take them all out," Elijah suggested.

"No," Simon replied, "They can't harm us now, besides they're only following their instincts and trying to protect their city. Enough Toltecs have died at our hands so let them be. They're no longer a threat to us. Is someone attending to Mr. Dorn's leg?"

"Yes, Commander," Drake answered, "I cleaned the wound and bandaged it. He's now resting comfortably in one of the officer's rooms."

"We have to figure out our next move," Simon said, turning to Elijah. "I want to carry the general and the treasure back to Washington, but first we need to learn how to operate this ship."

"How do you propose to accomplish this, Commander?" Kirby inquired.

"We'll make a few test runs to see if the databank and ship's computers follow our voice commands. I want to be completely comfortable that the ship will do what we tell it. We have to learn to control it."

The strange flying machine made Tomas very uncomfortable. "Simon… I mean Commander, I cannot go with you to America. This is my country and I want to stay here. Can you take me to my village of Campeche, about one hundred fifty miles to the north?"

"Of course we can," Simon quickly promised. He turned to Santos and Rosita.

"What about you two? Will you accompany us to America? We owe you more than we can ever repay. I'm sure the good general here can pull a few strings and obtain U.S. citizenship for you both. With your part of the treasure, you'll live very comfortably anywhere in America. You might consider California. They say it's is a great place, similar to western Mexico. We might even be able to take you there in this ship."

Santos smiled gratefully, "Rosita and I have nothing left in Puerto Muerta. We may just take you up on your offer to go to California."

Elijah noticed the smile on Rosita's face as their eyes met and she nodded her approval.

Everyone found a seat, and although nervous and apprehensive, each tried to get as comfortable as possible while the new commander adjusted the helmet and headset. He hesitated for a moment, laid the helmet back down and spoke directly into the wall speaker, remembering the wall speakers had been activated. "Databank, this is Commander Murphy, do you hear me?"

"Yes, Commander."

"We are ready to depart. I instruct you to fly the ship to a town called Campeche, a hundred-fifty miles north. We need to land there to allow one of our passengers to depart. Do you understand?"

"Yes, Commander,"

"Then lift us from the ground and fly there."

"You must specify the altitude and speed of flight," the databank replied. Simon looked confused.

"That means how fast and high we want to take the ship, Commander," Kirby clarified.

"Databank, what height and speed do you suggest?" Simon asked.

"For this short distance, we recommend a height of fifteen thousand feet and a speed of four hundred miles per hour."

"Nothing can travel that fast!" Elijah exclaimed.

"Is it safe to go that fast?" Simon asked the databank.

"I can assure you, Commander, this ship is capable of flying at vartz speeds that equates to velocities far beyond your imagination. At four hundred miles per hour, we will only be traveling at an infinitesimal fraction of our top speed. Please be assured that this is an extremely safe speed."

"How about the height—it's almost three miles up into the sky!"

Rosita and Santos were terrified. Rosita gasped, "Birds can't even do that!"

Drake interceded, "Remember, this ship traveled millions of miles to get here. And it was designed by a civilization far more advanced than we humans are."

"I agree with Mr. Drake," Simon added. "The databank seems to know what it's capable of doing."

Rosita looked out a porthole to see a group of Indians with a large battering ram rapidly approaching the ship. She shouted, "We'd better do something quick!"

Simon gave the final command. The ship emitted soft whining and whirling sounds and effortlessly lifted vertically to a height of fifteen thousand feet. "This is unbelievable. I bet we can see a hundred miles in all directions!" cried an ecstatic Drake. "We're the first humans to ever go up this high, even in a hot air balloon."

The spaceship was surprisingly quiet as it sped through the sky at the unimaginable speed of four hundred miles per hour. The occupants heard a faint humming noise and assumed it was from the machines that powered the ship. Actually, the sound was a form of kinetic energy coming from the small generator that distributed the energizing green light throughout the ship. The travelers were still mesmerized by the view of the ground speeding beneath them, when after only twenty minutes, the craft stopped and began its vertical descent to the ground. The ship extended its four landing pods and gently landed on a grassy knoll at the outskirts of Campeche.

Simon, Elijah, and Kirby accompanied Tomas to the open hatch that awaited his departure from the ship. Surprisingly, a small group of Indians and Mexican peasants stood in the distance, watching the strange apparition with a mixture of fear and fascination.

Kirby faced the young Indian, smiled and shook his hand. "Tomas, you have performed a great service to the United States of America and we'll be forever grateful."

He handed the young man a small leather bag. "There are enough gold coins and ingots in here to provide you and your people with anything you might need. We wish you well. In the near future we may ask you to accompany us on another expedition to recover the rest of the treasure."

"I will be honored to join you again, General." Tomas climbed down, waved to everyone, and was gone.

Simon glanced at Kirby and sensed his rising confidence. "Let's make a few test runs over the Atlantic Ocean then across the country to get the feel of this ship..."

"Fine with me," Kirby said with a nod. "But I do want to get to Washington as soon as possible."

"Databank, please retract the steps, close the hatch, and take us to an altitude of thirty thousand feet."

Elijah asked nervously, "Do you realize you're sending us nearly six miles up in the sky?"

"Nope, but we're sure going to find out what it's like and fast!"

Everyone scurried to a window. Within seconds, the ship reached the requested altitude of thirty thousand feet. "My, God!" Drake shouted, "I can't believe how far we can see. I think I see part of Florida, maybe the Keys!"

Rosita cried out, "No one will ever believe this." She turned to Simon, "We're not going to crash, are we?"

"No. We'll be fine," he assured her. Turning back to the control monitor, he said,

"Databank, fly the ship at our present height at a speed of six hundred miles per hour, one thousand miles due east.

When we travel one thousand miles, stop the ship and hover until I issue further commands."

The spacecraft immediately rotated and accelerated to six hundred miles per hour on a course due east. Since the craft was now much higher in altitude and flying at a much faster speed than before, the viewers could now clearly sense the speed by seeing the ground zoom by beneath them. Within seconds, they were passing over water as the coastline of the Yucatan faded out of sight. Moments later, there was nothing but sparkling water beneath scattered clouds with a vast panorama of the endless ocean stretching out before them. The sensation of speed now became unnoticeable. Rosita excitedly pointed. "Look at those clouds," she shouted.

Billowing cumulus clouds rose well beyond the ship's height. This gave the travelers a sensation of drifting through mounds of fluffy cotton. The lower clouds appeared like massive fields of drifting snow. The sight was so captivating that no one noticed the ship had now stopped and was hovering far above the water. Only when they observed the tall billowing clouds had now become stationary did they realize they were at a complete stop. They were now far over the ocean, nearly six miles high. It had only taken them one hour and forty minutes to travel one thousand nautical miles!

With a look of accomplishment, Simon turned to Elijah and Kirby, "Well, it appears we can successfully command this ship to go anywhere we want. Before we go to Washington, I would like to make a quick trip across the country to the west coast and back."

Santos sat quietly in his seat, nervously gazing at the clouds. Overhearing Simon's plan, he turned to his sister,

"Rosita, I've been thinking. I really don't want to go back to Mexico and I don't want to go to Washington. Do you?"

"Not really," she answered.

"Let's ask Simon to let us off the ship in California. Our cousin, Hernando, lives in San Juan Capistrano. We could start all over there."

Kirby reluctantly agreed to a quick cross-country trip so Simon spoke into the wall speaker. "Databank, head due north for eight hundred miles and then turn due west toward the North American continent. You will continue to fly due west across the entire North American continent until we reach the west coast of North America where we will stop and hover over the coast of California. Let us fly at a new speed of one thousand miles per hour."

"We have no record of a California," replied the databank. "We do have the current continental land mass programmed, but it shows it to be mostly uncharted territory."

Drake quickly realized the databank's dilemma and turned to his commander. "It could not have known about American state names and locations because the ship has been in hibernation for the past eight to nine hundred years and America was only discovered about four hundred years ago. Maybe it picked up some information by listening to the Indians talk, but nothing about geography. You'll have to navigate by physical landmarks, not by boundaries of cities or states."

"I forgot about that," Simon conceded. "Databank, just take us to the west coast of the continent, where the land mass meets the Pacific Ocean and hover there and wait for further instructions."

Kirby reminded Simon of the urgency to return to Washington. He was concerned about the time it would take to travel to California. "Do you realize, General, that at this speed, the flight to the west coast will only take slightly over two and a half hours?"

It took Kirby a moment to absorb this. "I guess you're right!" he said completely awed by Simon's words. "I can't even imagine these phenomenal speeds. It's just so unbelievable!"

Simon was enjoying his new role as commander. "Everyone, just think about it—we are the first explorers to travel across the entire country in just over two hours. Now that's something you can tell your grandkids!"

The spacecraft rotated to the north and began the acceleration for the first leg of the journey. The eight hundred mile dash due north passed quickly, in thirty-six minutes to be exact. Before anyone realized it, the craft was passing over the Outer Banks of North Carolina, moving westward at the astonishing speed of one thousand miles per hour. Although they were nearly five miles high, the identification of the terrain below was very discernable. They traveled over North Carolina's flat eastern seaboard, and within moments, they could see the terrain transform into rolling hills, followed by the gray-bluish Appalachian Mountain chain, and then into the central plateau country of middle Tennessee. "Look, there's the Mississippi River!" Drake shouted. "Look at how wide it is and how it curves back and forth on its way to the Gulf of Mexico! My God, I think I can even see the Gulf of Mexico!"

The terrain flattened as the craft now entered the Missouri territory and then over the grassy plains of the Oklahoma and Nebraska Territories. The travelers were amazed at the way the lush fields and vegetation disappeared as they veered slightly to the south and flew over the rolling prairie land of northern Texas. The green grass plains changed into brown scrub as the craft cruised over the arid mountains of northwestern New Mexico into the dry mesas and jagged peaks of the territories of northern Arizona and southern Utah. Far to the north, they noticed a series of high snow-covered peaks rising high into the sky. "Those must be part of the great Rocky Mountains I've read about," Drake remarked. "The Lewis and Clark expedition had to cross those peaks on their way to the Pacific Ocean."

"My goodness!" shouted Rosita, "Look at that deep canyon winding across the horizon."

"I know about this huge canyon," Kirby was quick to say. "Some of our western cavalry units have actually been there. They referred to it as the Grand Canyon."

"One hell of a ditch!" Elijah wisecracked.

Soon they passed from the dry desert country of western Arizona and soared over greener and fertile fields. Within moments, the ship stopped, hovering over a rocky coastline stretching to the north and south as far as the eye could see. Simon announced, "We're now hovering over the western coast and the Pacific Ocean. Since crossing the coast of North Carolina, we have traveled two thousand six-hundred and forty-two miles in exactly two hours and thirty-eight minutes. Now, you really have something to tell your grandkids!"

"Quite impressive, Commander Murphy, quite impressive!" Kirby acknowledged, totally overwhelmed with the flight. "Now, I think it's time to pay our politician friends in Washington D.C a little visit. I can't wait to see the expression on President Lincoln's face when we land in his backyard and present him with the treasure. I think it will result in a second star on my uniform and who knows, Commander Murphy, what honors await you and your ex-Confederate cousin!"

"Can I speak with you for a moment, Commander?" Santos asked, motioning him aside.

Simon walked with Santos away from the others. "Rosita and I have decided we would like for you to leave us here in California. We have a relative who lives in a small mission town along the coast called San Juan Capistrano. Our cousin will give us shelter and food until we get established."

"Rosita wants to do this?"

"Yes, we have both agreed."

"Santos, you and Rosita have saved our lives many times during our great adventure. We owe you a great deal. If this is what you really want, of course we'll take you there. We'll also provide you with enough treasure to buy land and a house. Now, you will have to help me find this Capistrano by sight since the databank doesn't have any towns around here programmed into its memory."

With a broad smile on his face, Santos said, "I have been there once when I was a child. It's on the coast about fifty or sixty miles south of the City of Angels."

Simon spoke into the headset, "Databank, take the ship down to two thousand feet and travel south along the coast at two hundred miles per hour until we see a small town called Capistrano."

"Yes, Commander," the databank responded through the wall speaker.

The spacecraft effortlessly descended to two thousand feet, flying along the coast. It passed the City of Angels and continued south. Most of the southern coast was empty of towns, with an occasional ranch house dotting the countryside. The sunlit waters of the deep blue-green Pacific were shimmering with radiant sparkles.

"There it is!" Santos cried, pointing to a small cluster of buildings. "I see the old mission. You can land in that field behind it. Please don't land too close to the village though, the ship may frighten the people and we might not be very welcome."

The spacecraft moved silently over the field, slowly settling on its four pods. Simon and Elijah met Santos and Rosita in the assembly room. "Here, Santos," Simon said, holding out a large leather pouch. "This is your part of the treasure. We wish you well in this new and beautiful land."

Rosita wrapped her arms around Simon's neck, kissing him on the cheek. She went over to Elijah and gently embraced him, then kissed him fully on the mouth and whispered into his ear, "Elijah, since our souls have met, why don't you stay here with me? We can build a new life together here in this wonderful land."

"That sounds real tempting Rosita, but I can't stay. I have to return with my cousin to Washington and help rebuild my country. I'm needed there now, especially after the terrible war. Someday I'll return… I promise."

In her heart, Rosita knew Elijah could not stay. She turned, smiled sadly, and walked through the opened hatch, followed by her brother. She turned once more to look back and wave at Elijah.

"I hope they find happiness here," Elijah said to Simon.

"Don't worry, cousin, Santos is a smart young man. I'm sure he and Rosita will do just fine here in California."

Simon noticed tears in Elijah's eyes as they closed the hatch.

37.

Reaching the requested altitude, Simon instructed the databank to travel north six hundred miles and then due east all the way back across the North American continent to the east coast. He was hoping his dead reckoning would place them near the Potomac River and Chesapeake Bay. He calculated the trip would take two and a half hours if they maintained a speed of one thousand miles per hour. His route east would start at the northern coast of California with direct passage over Wyoming and Dakota territories. He hoped to arrive as close as possible to the Virginia coast, thinking Washington D.C. would be easy to find from there. General Kirby had been to Washington many times and Simon was fairly certain he would recognize the city from the air.

The spacecraft followed the magnificent rugged coastlines of California and Oregon, largely untouched land inhabited by Indians and wildlife. The ninety-degree turn that the craft made onto the northern route proved to be even more spectacular when they crossed the Rockies and the Continental Divide. The snow covered Grand Teton peaks rose majestically, the sight of which mesmerized the spaceship observers as they stared in silence. They flew across the vast Dakota Territories, traversed the Black Hills, and were soon over the huge expanses of water known as the mighty Great Lakes. Finally, the ship made its last swing across Ohio and the newly formed state of West Virginia.

In two hours and thirty-six minutes, the craft began to decelerate, indicating it had reached the Atlantic Ocean. The view below revealed a large complex of streets and buildings bordering a long finger-like island. "Where are we, General?" Simon asked, peering out of a forward port window.

Kirby peered out and glanced back at Simon and Elijah, "If I'm not mistaken, I think we're hovering over the city of New York. The narrow island down there must be Long Island. If we follow the coastline south about two hundred more miles, we should reach Washington." It's located a few miles inland at the mouth of the Chesapeake Bay."

Simon gave new commands to the ship, requesting it drop to six thousand feet and change speed to three hundred miles per hour. From their present position, it would take about forty minutes to reach Washington.

While the travelers in the craft watched the land features pass silently beneath them, numerous citizens below saw the spaceship speeding across the skies. It caused a mass panic as hundreds of people on the streets gazed up at the strange object. Speculating that the occupants of the large disk were either Confederate guerillas or creatures from another world, the mayor of New York sent a telegram to the President of the United States advising him that the craft appeared to be heading south along the coast toward Washington.

Having received the telegram, the President summoned Secretary of War Stanton into his office and advised him to prepare the Army for an invasion of the city. General U. S. Grant received urgent orders to pull more troops back into the capital and remobilize the Army of the Potomac for immediate action. Although the army still had active units stationed in and around northern Virginia as occupational troops, and many units still in the immediate area preparing for deactivation from service, Grant knew his orders would never reach the units in time to move them into any defensive position. He nonetheless gave orders to his staff to move any available troops to the White House in hopes that any contingency of military would be present. Priority orders went out to the Third Pennsylvania Infantry Division and the Sixth New York Infantry Corps to move immediately to the Capitol grounds and White House to provide protection to the President and members of Congress. Only a few units were immediately available and hastily took positions around the Capitol and White House grounds.

It was mid-afternoon when the ship reached the Chesapeake Bay and moved slowly up the Potomac River.

The spacecraft slipped quietly along, passing over a small section of Maryland. "I can see old Fort Belvoir to the left overlooking the river," Kirby informed them. "If you look beyond it, you'll see Mount Vernon, the home of George Washington!"

Dorn came into the command center and sat next to a port window. As the ship slowly descended, the men could distinguish the broad panorama of streets, boulevards, and tree-lined avenues. Kirby shouted again, "Look to the left. There's the White House!"

"Where would you like for us to land, General?" Simon asked.

"Let's pick a spot right behind the White House so President Lincoln can have a good view of the ship."

Large groups of top ranking political and military figures nervously gathered on the White House lawn, awaiting the arrival of the strange flying object. Major General John McWhorter walked over to General Grant, saluted and asked for instructions. "Sir, the troops are assembled and we have several Rodman artillery pieces ready to fire upon your command."

"Let's hold tight, General, and see what their intentions are!"

Grant was not interested in provoking another war, especially with an unknown entity possessing machines that could fly through the air. He discounted any Confederate threat—he knew the defeated South did not possess the knowledge or materials to build such a craft. Standing next to him were the President, Secretary of State, William Seward, Secretary of War, Edwin Stanton, and the President's top security agent, Allan Pinkerton. A contingent of congressional representatives was also present and scattered about. Several small units of blue-clad army troops encircled the area with their Springfield rifles loaded, ready to respond to any act of hostility from the sky invader.

Stanton turned to the President, "Sir, what would you have us do?"

"Nothing yet!" the President replied. "So far they haven't fired on us or shown any indication that they mean us any harm. They may be here on a peaceful mission. Tell our troops to hold fast, and for God's sakes, don't provoke them unless they open fire first!"

Hovering a thousand feet above, Simon spoke into the wall speaker, "Databank, you may start the landing procedure and set the ship down on that huge lawn directly below us."

The large crowd drew back as four small hatches opened and the four landing pods retracted from their housing to touch the ground. The spacecraft slowly settled over the pods and came to a complete stop. The space monster had landed.

The President whispered to General Grant. "Hold tight, General. Don't fire unless I give the command!"

A nervous hush came over the crowd as dark thin cracks magically appeared in the hull. A hatch door opened inward and a retractable ladder extended from the ship to the ground. A tall human-like figure appeared at the door, followed by two more figures with similar appearances. They actually look just like humans, the President thought.

"My God!" Secretary Stanton bellowed, pointing to the figure on the steps, "That's General Caleb Kirby!"

"And there's Agent Nat Dorn behind him!" Pinkerton shouted. "He's one of my agents."

"What the hell's going on here?" the President exclaimed.

"We don't know, sir, but I'm sure we're about to find out," a very bewildered Secretary Stanton nervously responded.

Kirby walked down the steps, followed by Dorn and Drake, then Simon and Elijah. Kirby approached Stanton and saluted. "Sir, I'm pleased to report that we have successfully accomplished our mission. May I present Commander Simon Murphy and Captain Elijah Walker, formerly of the Confederate States Army."

"My God, General Kirby, what on earth have you got there?" Stanton asked, pointing to the spacecraft.

"That, sir, is a flying machine. It is not from our planet earth but from another world far away from our solar system. I have a fascinating story to tell you, but first I would like to report to President Lincoln, as he had requested upon my return."

"I'm sorry, General," Stanton responded with remorse. "I regret to tell you that Mr. Lincoln is no longer with us. He was assassinated in April."

Kirby was visibly stunned and saddened. "I'm sorry. I didn't know. He was a great man and the country will sorely miss him."

Stanton grasped Kirby by the arm and escorted him over to a stately looking man of medium build and stature. "General Kirby, may I have the honor of presenting you to the President of the United States, the honorable Andrew Johnson. Will you also please introduce your associates to our new President?"

"It's an honor to meet you, sir! Mr. President. May I present Commander Simon Murphy, formerly of the First Michigan Cavalry, and Captain Elijah Walker, formerly of the Confederate States Army."

Simon saluted and shook the President's hand and Elijah did likewise, adding, "Pleased to meet you, sir!"

"And, sir, this is Dr. Robert Drake, head of the Department of Anthropology at Harvard University."

"General Kirby," the new President spoke after acknowledging the introductions, "even though I did not attend your meeting with our former President, Secretary Stanton and Mr. Pinkerton have fully briefed me on your mission. I am calling a cabinet meeting first thing in the morning and would like for you and your associates to attend. We'll begin with a briefing of your mission, then discuss the unique vessel you have delivered here. Also, can I assume your mission was successful?"

"Yes, sir!" Kirby replied. "We have seven large packs filled with a fortune in gold ingots and precious gems. There's much more to be recovered, but we didn't have the time or resources to return with all of the treasure we found in the jungles of Mexico."

"Very well, General, I'll have Mr. Pinkerton detail an armed guard to transport everything over to our Treasury to be evaluated by Secretary Chase and his people. We look forward to seeing you in the morning and learning more about your mission."

Allan Pinkerton was overjoyed to see his favorite agent, Nathan Dorn. As Pinkerton listened, Dorn described the fate of the other three agents and provided a few highlights of the trip, but promised to be more detailed and specific during his debriefing. Pinkerton looked over Dorn's shoulder, staring at the huge spacecraft sitting on the White House lawn. "For Godsakes, Dorn, please tell me what that monstrosity is?"

"Believe it or not, Mr. Pinkerton, that is a spacecraft from another world. I think you will find the meeting in the morning quite interesting."

That night, Secretary Stanton treated Kirby, Drake, Simon, and Elijah to an exquisite meal at his dining club. It was their first good meal since entering the jungle and they pounced on the food with the appetite of a grizzly bear. Dorn, on the other hand, had dinner elsewhere with Pinkerton and a few friends and associates.

In the course of the dinner conversation, Stanton turned to Simon and Kirby and asked, "Captain Murphy, the general referred to you as commander, which is a naval ranking, instead of your previous army ranking of captain. Would you care to explain?"

Kirby replied, "Mr. Secretary, please allow me. Captain Murphy was the first to communicate with the alien craft and the forces that control the ship registered his voiceprint into their information banks and designated him as the ship's new commander."

Stanton was confused. "General, I don't understand what you're talking about. What are information banks?"

"If you'll permit me, sir," Simon interrupted, "the spacecraft comes from an alien world far away from our own earth. It has been resting dormant in a large cavern in the Yucatan for over eight hundred years. The power source that drives the craft comes from an element called Tracx, which is inexhaustible and will stay active indefinitely, although there is no source for Tracx on our planet. The craft is operated by machines they call computers. They operate from an intelligence source—something they refer to as databanks, sort of like a brain, as we know it. The databank has the ability to communicate with us and we've been able to guide the ship through my voice commands."

"Does this craft have weapons like our cannons or new Spencers?" asked Stanton.

"Yes, it has a weapons system, but their weapons are much more advanced than any of ours. It can fire a beam of light called a laser that can destroy an entire mountain within seconds."

"My, God!" Stanton gasped. "Can you imagine what our armed forces could do with such a weapon? Would you please arrange for a demonstration tomorrow for some of our top military officers, a few cabinet members, and me. The President may also wish to accompany us."

"Yes, sir," replied Simon. "We'll do so after the cabinet meeting in the morning."

"And you, Captain Walker, I understand you were with an Alabama cavalry unit in the Confederate Army?"

"That is correct, sir."

"How did you become associated with our Captain?" Stanton asked.

"As it turns out, sir, we're related on our great grandfather's side. One of his sons was Commander Murphy's grandfather and his daughter was my grandmother. I believe that makes us blood cousins."

"A fascinating coincidence, Captain. You do know the war is over and the south is now part of the United States?"

"No, sir, I wasn't sure, but assumed it might be over by now."

"The President has issued you a personal pardon. All you have to do is take the oath of allegiance to the United States and your citizenship will be restored. Most of your former comrades have already complied."

"Sir, I'll be happy to do so, too."

The next morning at the meeting, in addition to President Johnson and his cabinet members, there were several important military leaders in attendance. Simon and Elijah recognized Generals Grant and Sherman by photos they had seen in newspapers. Pinkerton and Dorn arrived on time. Kirby, Simon, Elijah, Drake, and the others took their seats directly across from Pinkerton and Dorn. The attendees became silent as The President took his seat and stared at the guests through thin wire spectacles.

"General Kirby, I have heard parts of your story from Secretary Stanton and must say that you and your associates have experienced a most extraordinary adventure. Our Secretary of the Treasury, Salmon Chase, assembled a team of appraisers who were up all night evaluating the seven bags of treasure you brought back. I am happy to report that their preliminary estimate is most promising. This added wealth will go far to rebuild and heal our country. It was unfortunate that I did not attend the meeting between you and our departed President Lincoln, but as Vice President, I was not always privy to all of the President's private meetings and arrangements. It was only after the President's passing that I was informed of your mission to find our lost captain here and secure the treasure."

Looking directly at Robert Drake, Johnson continued, "Mr. Drake, we appreciate all you have done to help General Kirby. With congressional approval, I would like to offer you the job as our National Curator of Antiquities and accompany the general on another expedition to the Yucatan to retrieve the balance of the treasure. We also intend to exhibit many of these artifacts in a new national museum we are planning for the city. Upon your acceptance, you will naturally be in charge of this museum, as curator."

Drake's face lit up as he thanked the President profusely. "I'd be most honored to accept this appointment, sir!" Johnson shook Drake's hand and turned.

"Gentlemen, one of General's Kirby's assignments was to arrest both of you for desertion in the face of hostile fire. I believe stealing a federal payroll of gold coins was also on the list of charges. These offences are usually punishable by firing squad. Because of a promise made to General Kirby by Mr. Lincoln, and due to your cooperation and valuable service to our country, these and all charges are to be dropped."

President Johnson paused for a moment. "Mr. Murphy, you are hereby reassigned to the United States Armed Services with the naval rank of commander, consistent with the assigned rank from that weird contraption you brought back. You are to serve as commander of our new machine which will be commissioned into our military arsenal."

"Captain Walker," the President continued as he faced Elijah, "you have two choices. You may accept the rank of major in our Army and serve as Commander Murphy's second in command or you may return to civilian status and go anywhere you please. Due to the importance of this unique craft, we feel it necessary to have both branches of our armed services represented in a command position. This is why your commission is directed to the Army."

"What about our percentage of the treasure?" Elijah asked the President.

Johnson looked puzzled. "What do you mean, sir?"

"General Kirby told us that President Lincoln had promised us five percent of any treasure recovered if we helped the general locate it and bring it back here," Elijah said politely.

"That's true, sir," General Kirby confirmed.

"I'm afraid I know nothing about any financial commitments," the President replied. "You two are getting off scot free. I would think that would be enough reward. Besides, the Army gold shipment you absconded with is yours to keep. That is, if there is anything left of it. Now, gentlemen, I must excuse myself as I have emissaries from France waiting to see me in the east wing." President Johnson stood up and abruptly left the room.

The President's stern remarks and the brevity of the meeting left Simon and Elijah sullen and silent as Kirby explained the details of the Toltec adventure to the Cabinet members and military. Both Simon and Elijah wanted out of there, as far away from politicians and generals as possible. When the meeting finally adjourned, they left the White House and walked toward the Potomac River.

"Dammit, Elijah, we're getting screwed!" Simon exploded angrily. "We were promised a percentage of the treasure and now we get nothing. The fact is I really don't want to command that spaceship for the Navy or Army or anyone else! No nation on earth, including ours, should possess something as powerful as the laser guns on that ship. I am sick and tired of these politicians and generals with their inflated egos. I just want to return to my home in Michigan, settle down, and raise a family. How about you? Are you going to take that major's commission with the Army?"

"No, I don't think so… not if you don't. I was thinking about going back to a small hamlet called Gurleyville—it's in Alabama—one of the prettiest places I've ever seen. I'll buy me some rich farmland down there, meet a pretty girl, and marry her. Then we'll have a bunch of kids to help me do the farming. Simon, that land is so fertile you could stick your finger in the soil and sprout nails."

"Before you and I do anything," Simon reminded him, "we still have to take the brass and some congressmen on a ride in the spacecraft and demonstrate the laser weapon.

Secretary Stanton told me that the Navy has anchored a decommissioned schooner out in the ocean for us to use as a target. They all want to see the laser destroy something. We only have an hour before they show up, so I guess we'd better return to the ship. Remember, you and I are the only two humans on earth that can even open the hatch."

"Why don't we just pack up and leave. We can go somewhere out west and get lost," Elijah suggested. "To hell with the whole bunch of 'em."

"Are you kidding me? You forget we're marked men. If we don't show up for that demonstration, the whole damn union Army will be after us within minutes, and when they catch us, and they will, we'll both be hanged on the spot. Right now, you and I have to take them for a ride and blow up that old ship anchored out there."

38.

It was only a short walk back to the White House where the spacecraft was now under heavy security. Simon chuckled, "Can you imagine what this bunch will do when I command the ship to rise up ten miles and fly around the earth at five thousand miles an hour?"

He would give them a show they would never forget. Based on information from the databank, Simon knew even that speed was slow relative to what it could do in deep space. About the fastest thing anyone had experienced so far on earth was a racehorse or perhaps one of the new B&O Railroad steam engines. Still, the speeds he was contemplating were inconceivable enough, so why push his luck.

At two o'clock, the entourage of politicians and military heavyweights gathered around the cloistered spacecraft. General Kirby was one of the first to arrive. He was all smiles as he worked the crowd, shaking hands and making small talk. He took Simon aside for a moment and apologized, "I'm terribly sorry about what happened at the meeting this morning. President Lincoln specifically told me to offer you five percent for your help. Unfortunately, our new President apparently doesn't see it that way. I'll try to talk to him privately when I get the right opportunity."

The attending members of Johnson's cabinet were Secretaries Seward, Stanton, and Wells. Next, a contingency of congressional representatives came aboard, followed by Generals Grant, Ferrero and Halleck of the Army, Commodore Porter, and Rear Admirals Dahlgren and Wilkes representing the Navy.

The newly appointed President decided he would not attend should there be a mishap, especially since so many other important dignitaries were present. Just as well, Simon thought. He now thoroughly disliked President Johnson.

Simon opened the hatch and helped Kirby direct everyone aboard the strange craft. Most of the men took seats in the reception room. General Kirby, however, invited General Grant, Commodore Porter, and Secretary Wells to the command center located in the cabin above. Elijah stayed on the main floor to answer any questions the visitors might ask.

Kirby made the first announcement, "Gentlemen, we welcome you aboard the spacecraft that we have appropriately named TOLTEC. You have now entered into the realm of a distant and alien world originating millions of miles from our planet earth. All the machines and equipment on this ship were designed and constructed by aliens who traveled here from another planet. Their intelligence and technology levels are centuries ahead of us. All of the materials are composed of advanced elements we have never even heard of and probably don't even exist on earth."

A senator raised his hand, "General, how did you learn all these facts about this craft?"

"Sir, the databank, or information storage banks, told us all about the ship."

"Is this so-called databank a live alien that was left behind?"

"No, sir, the databank is a machine that thinks and talks like a human."

The visitors were at a loss for words, which Simon noted was probably the first time in their lives they were confronted by a situation far beyond their current of levels of understanding and imagination.

Kirby continued, "During this trip, you'll find yourself feeling rejuvenated from the green light you now see illuminating the interior. This light emits a special energy element that rebuilds the cell structures in our bodies and reverses the aging process. We are also told that the alien inhabitants of this ship lived to the unbelievable age of two hundred years. We have no idea how the light actually works, but based on our own experience, it does have a positive effect on the human body. For example, the spear wound on Agent Dorn's leg was almost healed within two days."

These comments generated murmurs and gasps from the group. "Will it help me get rid of this stinking gout?" shouted a senator from the rear, which resulted with sporadic laughter from the others.

"I'd guess that, with enough exposure, it could very well help your condition," Kirby responded. "I'm now going to turn the demonstration over to Commander Murphy who'll guide us through the flight. He's in the command center, so you'll hear his voice through a speaker system."

"Thank you, General Kirby," Simon said as his voice boomed from a wall panel. "First, we'll test the laser beam weapon on a derelict schooner anchored outside of

Chesapeake Bay in the Atlantic. The second phase will be a quick flight completely around our planet Earth!"

The visitors were appalled. Secretary Stanton challenged this preposterous statement. "Commander Murphy, did I hear you say around the world?"

"Yes, sir. You see, the earth is a little over twenty-four thousand miles around and we'll be traveling at five thousand miles per hour and nearly ten miles high. We should be home in time for dinner in about four hours and forty-eight minutes."

"That's incredible, Commander!" Stanton shouted. "It takes me damn near that long to ride out to my cousin's house in Frederick County!"

A few more laughs were scattered around the room. His comments seemed to release the nervous tension, allowing the group to relax a bit.

Simon instructed the ship to proceed to an initial altitude of five thousand feet on a course that followed the Potomac River across the Chesapeake Bay. Anchored fifty miles off the coast was the large three-mast schooner, S.S. BALBOA. The ship had suffered severe damage in the war and was on the list to be scrapped within the next few weeks. Simon took his position and activated the laser-aiming device, carefully scanning the ocean. The automatic imaging scanner acquired the target within seconds. The TOLTEC was twelve miles away when the scanner confirmed the image. Simon set the laser power at thirty percent and pushed the trigger. A burst of light flashed from beneath the craft and sliced into the doomed ship with the speed of a lightning bolt. Within a split second, the schooner vaporized and completely vanished from sight. The only evidence left was an area of disturbed water and clouds of rising steam. For a moment, there was complete silence in the two compartments, then, suddenly, everyone began shouting at the same time. General Grant walked over to Simon and pumped his hand, "Son, that's one hell of a weapon you have there! Now, let's take that ride you promised!"

Simon took his seat and turned again to the built in microphone for the internal speakers. "Gentlemen, we'll be climbing to an altitude of fifty thousand feet. That's about nine and a half miles high. I have instructed TOLTEC to set a course around the earth following the fortieth parallel at a nautical speed of five thousand miles per hour. The flight will take us directly over the Atlantic Ocean, Spain, southern Italy, Turkey and northern China. We plan to cross the Pacific Ocean and re-enter the North American Continent somewhere in northern California. The ship will carry us across the central United States territories and finally back into Washington. The entire trip should take only four hours and forty-eight minutes. In other words, gentlemen, as we used to say in the cavalry, "We'll be making fast tracks and have you home in time for dinner!"

The applause was spontaneous. Simon gave the databank the commands, then took a seat. The sleek craft began the fast climb to fifty thousand feet, turning east for the run around the earth. It took less than fifteen seconds to accelerate to five thousand miles per hour. There were numerous gasps and a few prayers as the visitors crowded around the observation ports. At this height, the curvature of the earth was clearly discernable. The men marveled at the cloud formations rapidly passing below. As they headed across the Atlantic, some commented on the millions of sunlit sparkles dancing over the azure water, noting as they passed over deeper water that the color turned from dark blue to jet-black.

"Gentlemen, if you look directly below us, you can see the coast of Spain and the Mediterranean. Directly in front of us is the Italian boot."

The sight of the earth passing below was breathtaking. One observer shouted, "I think I see Paris!"

Another said, "No, that must be Lisbon. Paris is further north!"

One of the generals shouted, "I think I see Rome up ahead!"

Simon thought it comical to see the visitors trying to impress each other with their geographical knowledge, when, in fact, none had ever been to Europe or knew exactly where they really were. In a few more minutes, it became dark as they entered the opposite side of the earth. Simon announced that they were over eastern China. After passing over the northern tip of Japan, they zoomed over the Pacific Ocean, with most of the visitors quieting down, but their silence spoke volumes. Then Simon announced they were now passing over the coast of California, fully visible in daylight that had returned while over the Pacific. They rushed back to the port windows with more excited comments and questions. They reminded Simon of new school kids attending their first grade class.

Finally, Simon announced that they were approaching Washington D.C. He commanded the craft to descend and land in a vacant field between the Potomac River and the Capitol building. They did not want to disturb the President again. The four pods extended and the ship landed gently. General Grant announced that this amazing trip and safe return called for a drink. Everyone knew the general imbibed far too much, but no one refused the suggestion.

Everyone in Washington was talking about the spacecraft and asking questions about the men who had captured it. The names Murphy and Walker were becoming household names. Several members of the Washington press corps tried to approach the ship to obtain interviews, but Secretary Stanton had assembled troops around the craft to ensure complete security. No one was allowed near the ship without special clearance from the military high command. Even the well-known Civil War photographer, Matthew Brady, was prohibited from taking photos of the strange craft. The famous photographic pioneer was furious.

Simon and Elijah were exhausted and looked forward to a good night's rest and a day of leisure on Saturday. Their hopes were over-ridden when a Presidential aide awakened them at six o'clock in the morning and politely informed both men they were to attend an important high-level meeting at the White House in two hours.

39.

"Gentlemen," President Johnson announced to the assembled military brass, congressional leaders, Simon, and Elijah, "I called this meeting for the purpose of discussing the disposition of our newly acquired airship and determine how we can best utilize it in our national defense program. General Grant and Secretary Wells have informed me that the demonstration yesterday revealed that the ship's weapons are far more powerful and effective than anyone could have anticipated. As such, we have concluded that we now possess a weapon that can protect our nation from any conceivable potential threat."

The President sat down and motioned to Stanton, who continued.

"Thank you, Mr. President. We have assigned our best weapons developers and scientists to study the mysteries of the ship and learn her secrets. Can you imagine the implications if we could utilize the light beam principles to our field artillery or naval cannons? With this firepower, our armed services would become invincible. We could easily control the entire continents of North and South America and eventually harness all worldwide resources and materials.

This would be invaluable to the growth and prosperity of our expanding country."

While the attendees nodded their pleasure and approval, Kirby noticed the shock on the faces of Simon and Elijah. Even he could not believe what he was hearing.

"This is turning very frightening," Simon whispered to Elijah.

President Johnson, noticing Simon's concerned expression, interrupted the secretary. "Gentlemen, I hope you don't construe the secretary's remarks to imply the United States has any plan or desire for world domination or expansion into other countries. He is merely illustrating the scope of the power we now possess here…"

Simon raised his hand.

"Commander Murphy, you wish to make a statement?"

"Yes, Mr. President. It is well beyond our capabilities to comprehend the ultimate power of this spacecraft. We don't even know what makes it fly. It was built by a civilization from an unknown planet located outside our solar system, millions of miles away. If we try to probe into the inner-workings of this craft, we just might unleash unknown substances with dire consequences. I believe this craft has the potential to destroy our world as we know it!"

"Nonsense, Commander," Secretary Seward interrupted. "This is the very reason why we must control this machine. I'm certain we have scientists and other experts available that can learn and control the secrets of the craft. One of the major by-products of the war is our advancement with new machines and other inventions."

"No one will argue with that, Mr. Secretary," Simon continued. "But the technical composition of the TOLTEC is many centuries ahead of us. Our current technology and our knowledge of outer space travel and the physics applied with this craft are extremely primitive compared to those who built it. The outer skin, for example, is composed of a foreign material not available on our planet and the power source, Tracx, only exists on two planets located well outside our galaxy. I believe this machine has the capacity to destroy our entire planet if its full powers are unleashed in an irresponsible manner."

Secretary Wells scowled, "Commander, your statements are noted, but the potential power of this machine is much too significant for us to ignore. If this craft ever fell into the hands of a foreign country, we would be completely at their mercy. We cannot take that chance!"

Kirby asked to be recognized, "Gentlemen, I was with these men when they brought the craft to life after over eight hundred years of hibernation. The ship possesses some type of a mechanical brain called a computer. It has the power to reason and think on its own. I heard it speak as if it actually had a human mind. It even learned our English language in a matter of minutes. It has the unique ability to reason, make independent decisions, and take decisive action if it feels threatened in any way. I am concerned that the intelligence of this craft could turn its power against us and deliver destruction in ways we cannot even imagine. It could well destroy the human race. It's also possible that there are other space machines, like TOLTEC, still in hiding, and could attack us should they feel threatened."

"Thank you for your views," President Johnson said tersely.

General Grant, who had been silent, finally spoke up. "Gentlemen, we've been through four hard years of death and destruction. I saw what the light laser did to that ship and I can well imagine what it could do to one of our cities if its power were unleashed against us. I tend to agree with General Kirby and believe we should heed his concerns. We're dealing with an unknown and immeasurable power."

President Johnson interrupted, "General, I'm surprised at your words of warning. Your reputation on the battlefield does not portray you as a man of such caution, especially having sent thousands of our young men into battle at Cold Harbor and in the Wilderness campaign."

This hit a nerve and Grant responded sharply, "Mr. President, during the war I knew what I was up against, but with that space machine, I don't and you don't!"

"And what would you have us do, General?"

"Sir, I would command the ship to return to its own world."

"Nonsense, General," the President retorted.

The exchange brought gasps and shouts across the room. The President was impatient and irritated with the proceedings, "Gentlemen, it is my opinion that we must control this completely new form of power that is within our grasp. It is my final decision that the space machine be immediately commissioned into our Navy under the direct command of Secretary Wells and Commodore Porter. I am choosing the Navy due to the machine's ability to transcend oceans and fly over continents. Commander Murphy and Captain Walker can make one of two choices. Accept the ranks given to you and remain in the service of your country, or resign your commissions and return to civilian life, with an honorable discharge of course. I expect to receive your decisions within the next twenty-four hours."

The President stared coldly at Simon and Elijah, and then continued, "The craft is to be quarantined in a secure place with a twenty-four hour guard. General Grant, you will establish and coordinate top priority security measures around the ship. Secretary Wells, you will solicit the best scientists and technicians available to begin a research program to learn all we can about the ship's secrets. An initial team of scientists should be assembled and begin investigating the ship by noon tomorrow and I will expect each of you to keep me fully apprised of the progress of the investigation. Thank you for your attendance this morning." Not a sound was heard as the President stood up and left the room.

Kirby looked at Simon and Elijah and could see the anger and frustration on their faces. The general accompanied the two men as they left the White House. "Simon, I wish there was something I could do, but you must understand that my hands are tied. It's clear that all the brass really cares about is the tremendous power this brings to our military. It'll be interesting to see how the Army is going to maneuver around the Navy to try to get control of the ship."

"General, it seems like you're the only person in Washington with enough sense to understand the danger here," Elijah said.

"I think General Grant agrees, but he has to take orders, too."

Simon appreciated Kirby's words. "I'm convinced the ship is a virtual time-bomb with its intelligence and power to destroy. God help us if our military leaders try to control that ship."

"What do you propose?" Kirby asked.

"I think the ship should be destroyed!"

"You may be right, Simon, but I'm afraid it's too late. The Army and Navy have surrounded it with a strong detachment of armed guards. I doubt if you or I could now board the ship without escort. Even though I agree with you, I'm still an officer of the United States Army. I must follow orders like everyone else in the military. My suggestion to both of you is to accept the commissions offered by the President and stay around to command the ship. At least in the capacity of commander, you can retain some control."

Simon and Elijah exchanged glances as Kirby gave them a quick salute, turned, and walked back to the White House.

40.

It was Sunday morning in Washington with overcast skies and a light rain falling. Simon had spent a restless night and had a heavy sense of foreboding. He knew that the President and his military were making a dreadful mistake. The potential worldwide consequences were too frightful to contemplate.

Simon was sitting in the boarding house kitchen sipping hot black coffee when Elijah walked in and poured a cup. He sat down at the table across from Simon. "Those power-hungry fools don't have any idea what they're doing."

"I know, I know!" Simon responded, shaking his head. "By the way," he said, looking at his cousin, "you haven't told me what you're going to do about your new commission."

Elijah took another sip of coffee. "I'm going to turn it down and head back to Alabama and buy me a place in that valley I told you about. Who knows? Maybe I'll go to California and look up Rosita."

Simon eyed Elijah suspiciously, "What's this about you and Rosita anyway? I saw the way she looked at you when she left the ship. Don't tell me something happened between you two."

"I will only tell you that she is one special lady," Elijah replied with a shrug and a laugh. "And what are you going to do, dear cousin?"

"I'll either accept the commission and stay with the ship or go back to Michigan, but I hate to leave the spaceship under their control. At least as the ship's commander, I might be able to keep everything in check and maintain some control. They've watched me give commands through this helmet and if I have to relinquish my command of the ship, I'll have to surrender the helmet and headset…"

"How long do you expect the military to keep you around as commander, especially knowing how you feel about what they want to do with it? Simon, they'll find a replacement to take command as soon as possible. Hell, I'll bet they already have someone lined up to replace both of us."

"You're probably right, but remember, any replacement will have to have his voiceprint approved through the databank and only you and I can do that."

"All it'll take is a Presidential order and we'll have to approve the new voiceprint with the databank. We can't disobey a Presidential order. That would be grounds for prison or execution. You and I are already in enough hot water with the charges they have against us. Hell, they could hang me anytime they want by branding me a Confederate spy!"

Simon hesitated for a moment and then turned to stare out the window. He grabbed the helmet with the headset and shouted, "Elijah, get your coat. You and I are going to the ship!"

The rain had eased and the Sunday afternoon sun was breaking through thinning clouds as the two men left the boarding house for the short walk over to the ship. They left by the back door, slipping past the guards posted at the front who were assigned to watch over them. The ship was sitting in a field about twenty minutes away. A large contingency of armed guards patrolled the area and, as usual, the ever-present newspaper reporters were milling about trying to get as close as possible to the TOLTEC. The press was desperate for a story, any kind of story. The public was hungry for more information and the news media needed to oblige them. This led to exaggerated editorials and columns that added more fuel to the mystery of the strange oddity from beyond the stars.

As Simon and Elijah approached the ship, they could see the muted silver-gray hull against a background of trees and clearing sky. Approaching a small contingent of guards, they revealed identity papers and were immediately recognized and saluted. A young lieutenant said, "Good afternoon, Commander. I assume you and the captain wish to come aboard the spacecraft."

"Yes, Lieutenant, we have more work to do to prepare for another demonstration flight."

"Very well, sir, you may proceed."

Simon walked up to the sleek hull and spoke into the headset. "Databank, please open the hatch."

The door opened and folded back into the hull as the retractable steps extended to the ground. The two men climbed the steps and entered the ship. "Databank, you may close the hatch," he commanded as they headed straight to the command center. Simon was getting agitated, "Dammit, Elijah, we face a major dilemma here. It's not right for any one nation to control a weapon such as this. If I turn control of this ship over to someone else we'd be endangering the entire human race."

"I know, we've been over this a hundred times!" Elijah snapped. "Just calm down...okay? Besides, I have an idea. Ask the databank if this ship has a self-destruct system in place and how to make it operational."

"What's that supposed to mean?"

"Just ask the ship if it has the capability to destroy itself."

Simon spoke into the headset. "Databank, is there a self-destruct system in place and how can you activate it?"

"That is an affirmative, Commander. The self-destruct sequence can only become operational by a direct order from both our commander and vice-commander."

"I am your commander; can I give you the command to self-destruct the ship?"

It answered back, "That is affirmative."

Elijah was looking out of one of the observation ports and suddenly shouted, "I'm afraid we've got big trouble!"

Standing outside the craft were Secretary Stanton, Wells, and several military officers, including General Kirby. They were motioning to the guards to open the hatch, not remembering the guards had no way to do so. "What the hell do they want now?" Simon grumbled. "I guess we'd best open it. You stay here and I'll meet them in the assembly room and see what they want. You take the headset and give the command to open the hatch."

The hatch opened and Stanton, Wells, and their entourage entered the ship. Simon walked over to Stanton and, with some effort, greeted him in a forced pleasant tone of voice, "Good morning, Mr. Secretary, I didn't expect to see you today."

"Commander Murphy," he announced, "I'll come right to the point! We're here by direct order of the President to take possession of the ship and place it under the command of Secretary of the Navy Wells."

Wells nodded his approval, and then faced Simon, "Sorry, Commander, but you're hereby relieved of your command and are so ordered to turn direct command of this ship over to Captain Robert McNabb of the Navy. The President has ordered that you inform the machine's intelligence of the immediate change of command and have it provide the new commander with complete control."

"Sir, I am afraid I can't do that," Simon responded politely.

"What the hell do you mean, you can't do that? You have been given a direct order from the President. I can have you immediately taken outside and shot for disobeying," Wells shouted, his face turning beet red.

"But sir," Simon protested, "you don't understand. I am the appointed Commander of this craft by the ship's operating intelligence and to change command so abruptly would be considered a threat to the ship. This spacecraft is capable of doing things on its own that we have no control over. To make that change now and so suddenly might prove disastrous!"

"We're prepared to take that chance," replied a very agitated secretary. "Also, Commander, it is my duty to inform you that your services and those of Captain Walker are no longer needed by your government. Please be advised that effective immediately, the officer's commission offered to you is rescinded and you are now assigned a civilian status. The President also asked that I thank you again for your assistance in bringing us part of the Toltec treasure and this…uh… spacecraft, as you call it."

As a final gesture, he added more calmly, "Both you and Mr. Walker are now civilians and free to go wherever you please. I have a packet of discharge papers and Presidential letters to help you move freely through our military checkpoints. They'll be especially valuable to you in the South, should you choose to travel there. We'll also provide you with two horses to allow you to travel where you wish."

Elijah appeared from the command center in time to hear what Wells said to Simon. He was still holding the space helmet in his hands when the secretary turned to him and said, "I believe Mr. Murphy has to speak into that helmet to authorize the change of command to Captain McNabb. Please hand him the helmet so he can give that authorization command to whomever or whatever runs this bloody ship."

Elijah looked at Simon, hesitated briefly and handed him the helmet. He could not help but notice his cousin's anger and frustration. Simon reluctantly placed it on his head, but hesitated to give the orders. "You are ordered to give the command now!" Stanton yelled.

The now ex-commander spoke into the helmet, "Databank, this is Commander Murphy speaking. I am relinquishing command of this ship and hereby turn command over to Captain Robert McNabb. You are authorized to recognize Captain McNabb as your new commander and approve his voice-print."

Simon was defeated. He handed McNabb the helmet, whereupon Stanton handed Simon and Elijah four envelopes containing the letters allowing them some degree of official protection and bid them farewell, "Gentlemen, thank you again for your services; you are free to go."

They quietly and reluctantly turned and left the TOLTEC for the last time.

Simon was furious as they walked back to the boarding house. They looked back at the alien craft and noticed several strangers going on board carrying canvas bags and boxes. "Well, I see the so-called scientists are already entering the ship to try and find out what makes her tick," Elijah grumbled.

"Yeah, there's no telling what kind of damage those idiots will cause," Simon shouted angrily. "They will never understand the craft and the internal workings. They'll probably get the databank all pissed off and the ship will go berserk and take off on its own, shooting that laser at every human it sees."

With a second glance over the shoulders, they observed Stanton and Wells leaving the ship, climbing into a buggy that had appeared through a prearranged signal from an aide.

A stop at the boarding house was brief for Simon and Elijah—they only had a few personal belongings to pack. Although there was a feeling of relief as they mounted the horses, compliments of the United States Army, and headed toward the Potomac River, Simon still felt a deep anger and frustration. He shouted, "Dammit, Elijah, we shouldn't have let them bully us to leave the ship! I should have never let them aboard. We should have flown to some remote island in the Pacific where they would never find it! Hell, maybe we should have taken it back to the cavern in Mexico where we found it! I should never have authorized the databank to accept McNabb as the new commander."

"You didn't!" Elijah said, smiling mischievously.

"Those people are not qualified to operate the ship, they know nothing about the damn thing," Simon shouted.

"You didn't authorize it!" Elijah repeated louder.

"What the hell are you talking about?"

"I said you didn't authorize anything. You never actually spoke to the databank!"

With a devilish grin, Elijah reached in his pocket and pulled out several small objects attached to a thin metal-like cord. "When you gave me the helmet in the command center, I removed the headset, and when you went down to meet the group in the assembly room, I stuck it in my pocket before I handed you the helmet. You were talking into a dead helmet. When McNabb tries to give the ship a command, not only will it reject him, the databank won't even hear him because I deactivated the wall speakers. Remember, only you and I have our voiceprints approved and with this headset in our possession, you are still in command."

Simon looked at Elijah, as a smile of understanding slowly appeared. "You are one sly bastard. I can't believe you actually got away with this!"

Simon took the headset and flipped it to the "on" position, then spoke into the small mouthpiece. "Databank, this is Commander Murphy, can you hear me?"

"That's affirmative, Commander," it answered.

"Databank, as your commander, I would like to know if there are similar spaceships from your world still located on our planet."

"That's affirmative, Commander."

Simon looked at Elijah with exasperation and shock. "Can you tell me how many ships are still on Earth?"

"There are two other ships currently on the planet Earth."

"Can you describe them?"

"Yes, Commander, one is a transport ship identical to the one you command and the other a larger battle cruiser."

"Where are they located?"

"The transporter is located in the Andes Mountains and the cruiser is located far to the north in the Arctic ice belt."

"Can you give me more specific locations of the two ships?"

"That's negative, Commander, our banks are not allowed to give out additional secret information without the top Zar-B code keys held by our fleet commander in the command center."

"Where is your command center?"

"Negative, Commander. You are not authorized to receive the information without the code keys."

Simon turned to his cousin in astonishment, "My God, Elijah, you heard that. The fleet commander is either long dead or returned to his own planet several hundred years ago and their command center was probably located on the moon or some planet a million miles away!"

"Databank, did the other transporter ship visit the Incas of Peru like you did the Toltecs?"

"That is affirmative, Commander."

He turned to Elijah, "We can never tell anyone about these other two ships."

"Databank, I have a very important and final command for you."

"We await your instructions, Commander."

"Effective in exactly one hour from now, I command you to close the hatch and fly the ship to an altitude of fifty thousand feet. You will then head due east, exactly four hundred miles, at a speed of two thousand miles per hour. This will place you well over the Atlantic Ocean and over very deep water. When you reach this destination, you are to stop and hover at your assigned altitude of fifty thousand feet. You are then to activate the ship's self-destruct system and destroy the craft over the ocean. Do you understand these commands?"

"Yes, Commander, but to comply with your command requires backup confirmation from our Vice Commander, as well as yourself."

Simon handed Elijah the headset, "Databank, this is Vice Commander Walker. I wish to reconfirm the self-destruct command issued by Commander Murphy."

The databank responded, "We acknowledge the self-destruct command and will start countdown and commence with all commands in fifty-eight minutes."

"Well, that takes care of that!" Simon beamed.

"Not quite! First, we must clear all those people off the ship."

"And how do we do that without implicating ourselves and have the entire United States Army come after us?"

"We don't," Elijah answered, "we let the databank do it for us."

He took the headset and spoke once more. "Databank, this is Vice Commander Walker. Commander Murphy and I would like for you to switch to the wall speakers and make an immediate announcement for everyone currently inside the ship."

"Yes, Vice Commander, what announcement do you want to make?"

"You are to announce over the speakers that everyone must immediately evacuate the ship. Explain that poisonous gas has been detected and that all personnel must evacuate until your system cleans the air and fixes the leak. You are commanded to make the announcement in ten minutes, and when the last man is out, you are to close the hatch and continue your countdown for departure and climb to your assigned altitude. Our previous command for self-destruct still stands."

"We will comply," the databank answered.

Simon could not contain himself. "Brilliant, cousin, brilliant!" he chuckled.

From a distance, Simon and Elijah watched tiny figures begin to pour out of the hatchway. Sixteen men were counted exiting the ship and when all had left, the steps slowly retracted and the hatch closed tight. They recognized Captain McNabb—his appearance assured Simon that the ship was clear of all occupants. "I think it's time for us to get out of here before all hell breaks loose when the ship leaves the ground."

They spurred their horses to a trot and headed for the outskirts of Washington.

"How much time left?" Elijah asked.

Simon glanced at his watch. "Only twenty-four more minutes."

They rode across the Potomac Bridge into Virginia, turning just in time to see a large silver-gray disk rapidly soaring into the sky. Within seconds, the spacecraft became a tiny speck, heading eastward across the Atlantic Ocean. After what seemed like an eternity, they saw a pinpoint flash of bright light high in the eastern sky, followed by a faint thunderclap as the spacecraft exploded and scattered into millions of pieces across the wide expanse of the Atlantic.

Simon took the headset in his hand and looked at it hesitantly. He suspected it could be the key to awakening the other dormant alien craft revealed by the databank. Even though his curiosity told him to hold on to it, his sixth sense told him to let it go. Finally, he stood up in his stirrups and hurled the headset as far as he could into the Potomac River. The small splash was barely visible as it disappeared beneath the ripples and drifted down into the soft Virginia mud.

EPILOGUE

Simon and Elijah had traveled only a few miles into the Virginia countryside when a lone rider caught up with them. It was Kirby. "Hey, you two, I didn't think I would ever find you."

"How in the world did you know where to look for us?" Simon asked.

"The proprietor at the boarding house overheard you say you were planning to take the Arlington Pike Road into Virginia. I've been riding like the devil to catch up with you two."

The lathered and heavily panting horse confirmed this.

"I'm not sure what happened to the spacecraft," Kirby went on, "but all hell has broken loose in Washington. The ship evacuated everyone on board, announcing that poison gas had been detected. It closed the hatch and took off into the sky. A distant flash of light was seen, then a faint boom, but no one is exactly certain what happened. Anyway, Stanton is blaming McNabb for vacating the ship without the helmet and Wells is blaming the scientists for upsetting the databank."

Simon and Elijah exchanged smiles as Kirby continued, "The President is blaming everyone even remotely involved with the ship. He was last seen screaming at Stanton and Wells for relieving the two of you of command, even though it was his idea. He wanted me to bring you back to resume command of the ship, but now that it has disappeared, there's nothing left to command. I guess the President was too upset to realize that. Anyway, I'm glad I caught up with you."

The quizzical look on his face betrayed him, "You two didn't have anything to do with the spacecraft disappearing, did you?"

"Who, us?" answered Simon, all innocence. "General, you know us better than that."

With a chuckle, the general said, "It's a good thing no one but me on board understood enough about the helmet to notice the missing headset. It's also fortunate McNabb left it in the spacecraft before it closed the hatch and took off."

Elijah laughed loudly.

"You didn't tell them, did you?" Simon asked Kirby.

"No, I haven't told anyone. In fact, I fully agreed with you all along. That craft was much too dangerous for any nation to possess. All the generals and admirals were already bickering over what branch of service should control it. The Army brass was furious when the President assigned it to the Navy. They claimed they did most of the fighting to preserve the Union and deserved to have it more than the Navy. It would have ended up with everyone fighting over the damn thing and destroying us all. No, my friends, your little secret is safe with me."

Kirby reached into his saddlebag, "Anyway, the President wanted me to give you this as a token of appreciation. I guess his conscience started bothering him about the treasure and Mr. Lincoln's promise to you."

He handed Simon a small leather pouch.

"By the way, we had a hell of an adventure, didn't we? Maybe you boys will accompany me back to the Yucatan to get the rest of that treasure."

"No thanks, General," Simon chuckled, "we'll pass on that one. I think we've had enough adventure for awhile."

"Well, good luck to you both and if I were you, I'd get as far away as possible before the President changes his mind and sends the whole Union Army after you."

"Thanks for everything, General. It's been a pleasure knowing you. I have a strange feeling we'll meet again," Simon said.

"And I second that," Elijah added.

With a nod of understanding and appreciation, General Kirby turned his horse and spurred him back toward Washington.

Simon opened the small pouch and poured the contents into his hand. He was shocked to see finely cut diamonds and rubies sparkling from the reflected light of the fading sun. There were twenty large diamonds weighing five to seven carats each and twenty large rubies the same size.

"Well, how about that! At least we might have enough here to buy us each that little farm we wanted!"

"How about a big farm instead?" Elijah countered, reaching into his coat pocket.

He pulled out six large gold and jeweled rings.

"My God!" gasped Simon, "where in the hell did they come from?"

"You remember our beautiful princess mummy Xepocotec? She had these rings on her fingers. Well, I figured she didn't need them anymore so I removed them and placed them in my pack for safekeeping. They should bring us a fancy sum in one of the large city auction houses." He handed three of the rings to Simon who accepted them with a look of satisfaction.

"Elijah, you are one sly devil. Maybe our little adventure will pay off after all..."

"But that's not all, dear cousin. Do you remember those two bags of gold nuggets I gathered in the old Indian mine, and then dragged them through the underground river on the sled?"

"Yeah, I thought they would get us all killed. I remember you hid them somewhere in the ruins of Coba," Simon said.

"Actually, I lugged them all the way to the lost city and hid them in the ruins of Xepocotec, then retrieved them when we landed in the spacecraft to get the treasure."

He reached into his saddlebag, pulled out a heavy leather pouch and handed it to Simon. "There should be enough gold nuggets in each bag to buy us a very nice farm."

"Well, I'll be darned. Any more surprises?"

"No more for now. I'll ride with you as far as Front Royal, and then I'm heading south to east Tennessee and Chattanooga. By the way, about this time next year, why don't you plan to meet me somewhere in north Alabama and we'll take a ride over to our oak tree on Cockelberry Hill and dig up our forty thousand in gold coins? We can call it the spoils of war. In fact, I distinctly heard the President say we could keep that gold," Elijah grinned conspiratorially.

"Sounds like a plan to me," Simon agreed. "Besides, by next fall I'll probably have had my fill of a plow and ready to sneak off in search of more lost treasure somewhere."

"Funny you mention it. I've heard that the famous pirate Blackbeard buried some of his treasure on a remote Caribbean island called Jamaica."

Their laughter could be heard echoing through the woods as they rode toward the sunset slowly sinking behind the trees.

ACKNOWLEDGEMENTS

Writing novels, such as *TOLTEC*, takes a great deal of support and encouragement from many people. My first thanks go to my dear wife Diane who had to endure many hours by herself while I typed away and poured my wild fantasies into my computer. Her patience and understanding is greatly appreciated.

I owe a special acknowledgement to my good friend Tom Murphy and his wife Sharron who suggested I take a short parody I wrote about our Civil War ancestors and turn it into an adventure novel.

A special thanks to my daughters Laurie and Shannon who both read my manuscript and offered me helpful suggestions and encouragement along the way.

I wish to thank my friend Don McCall, with his literary experience, who made a preliminary edit of the manuscript and offered several fine suggestions as to the storyline and content.

I have to offer a real special thanks to my incredible literary editor Ann Fisher of **Creative Editing** who professionally edited the manuscript and offered many suggestions in content, composition, grammar, and word usage. I learned so much from her novel writing expertise.

I also extend my sincere appreciation to Leanne Polsue who performed a final proof editing of the novel and helped me correct many pesky grammar and word errors that plague all authors. Her keen eye for word usage and correct grammar was an invaluable help.

Special thanks go to my new friend Bob Babcock, President of Deeds Publishing, who embraced *TOLTEC* and agreed to publish and help me market the novel. I look forward to a fine and productive relationship with Bob, his son Mark, and the other members of his staff.

To my good friend George Scott, book store owner, official book seller for the Atlanta Writer's Club, and Director of the Books for Heroes Charity Foundation, I owe my sincere appreciation for his constant encouragement and overall knowledge of authors, publishers, book readers, and the overall book business in general. George inspired me to keep writing and putting my wildest fantasies to paper. In gratitude, I felt compelled to name one of the characters, a quite colorful and adventurous character I might add, after George, in my next novel—*Cuzco*.

It has been a wild ride to put this adventure together and now, thanks to this incredible group of family, friends, and professionals, the real journey begins.

-Alex Walker

About the Author

William (Alex) Walker was raised in Knoxville, TN and graduated from the University of Tennessee, majoring in Business Administration, Marketing, and Traffic Management. Walker spent eight years in U.S. Army Reserve with an honorable discharge and the rank of captain. He spent a long career with United States Gypsum Co. in various marketing and sales management positions. He is currently retired.

For several years he operated a small company, Executive Fly-Fishing Services, that organized and conducted fly-fishing trips for corporate managers and key customers to various rivers in the western U.S. and Canada.

He wrote several fly-fishing articles published in an international fly-fishing magazine, *Rackelhanen Fly-fishing.*

He wrote the 28 chapter historical documentary *From Our Past* published on the Gurley, Alabama website. www.contactez.net.

He wrote a magazine article titled *The Lost Gold of Keel Mountain* published in the December 2006 *Lost Treasure* Magazine.

He has completed two historical Action /Adventure novels titled *TOLTEC* and *CUZCO*. (Part of a three book series) currently in the possession of Deeds Publishing.

Walker currently lives in Peachtree Corners, GA with his wife and has three children and six grandchildren. His interests are novel writing, photography, fly-fishing, golf, acoustical guitar, and song writing.

COMING IN 2013—THE EXCITING
SEQUEL TO TOLTEC

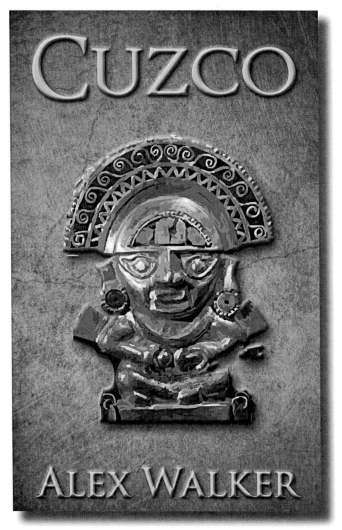